ANIMAL LIFE IN FIELD AND GARDEN

NATIONAL
LIBRARY
OF AUSTRALIA

Animal Life in Field and Garden

by

Jean-Henri Fabre

Contents

CHAPTER I

WHAT UNCLE PAUL PROPOSES TO TALK ABOUT

"IN THESE talks that we shall have together," said Uncle Paul, as he sat with his nephews one evening in May under the big elder tree in the garden, "I propose to designate as 'friends' those forms of animal life that, though not domesticated or cared for by us, nevertheless come to our aid by waging war on insects and various other devouring creatures which would in the end, unless their excessive multiplication were kept in restraint by others besides ourselves, eat up all our crops and lay waste our fields; and it is these ravagers of the farmer's carefully tilled acres that I shall speak of as 'foes.'

"What can man's efforts avail against those voracious hordes, multiplying as they do every year to an extent beyond calculation? Will he have the patience, the skill, the keenness of vision necessary for waging successful warfare on the tiniest species, often the most formidable, when the June-bug, despite its far greater size, baffles all his endeavors? Will he undertake to examine his fields and inspect every lump of soil, every spear of wheat, every separate leaf on his fruit trees? For so prodigious a task the whole human race would be inadequate, even if it united all its efforts to this one end. The devouring hordes would reduce us to starvation, my children, had we not able helpers to work for us, helpers endowed with a patience that nothing can tire, a skill that foils all ruses, a vigilance that nothing escapes. To lie in ambush for the enemy, to track it to its remotest retreats, to hunt it unceasingly, and finally to exterminate it—that is their sole care, their never-ending occupation. Urged on by the pangs of hunger, they are relentless in their pursuit, both for their own sake and on behalf of their progeny. They live on those that live on us; they are the enemies of our enemies.

"Engaged in this work are the martins that just at present are circling over our heads, the bats that fly around our house, the owls that call to one another from the hollow willow trunks in the meadow, the warblers that sing in the grove, the frogs that croak in the ditches, and many more besides, including the toad, which is an object of loathing to most people. Thanks be to God who has given us, to serve as guardians of our daily bread, the owl and the toad, the bat and the viper, the frog and the lizard! All these creatures, wrongfully cursed and shamefully abused by us, and foolishly looked upon with repugnance and hatred, in reality lend us valiant assistance and should take a high place in our esteem. To repair the injustice they have suffered shall be my first duty as we come to each of them in turn. Thanks be to God who, to protect us from that great eater the insect, has given us the swallow and the warbler, the robin redbreast and the nightingale! These, the delight of our eye and ear, creatures of infinite grace—must I again raise my voice in their defense? Alas, yes, for their homes are ravaged by the barbarous nest-hunter.

"It is my purpose now to acquaint you, my children, with these various helpers of man in his labors as tiller of the soil. I will tell you about their ways of living, their habits and their aptitudes, and the services they render us. My object will be attained if I succeed in imparting to you a little of the interest they deserve. I will begin with those that have teeth. But first let us take a glance at the shape and structure of teeth in general; for it is this that determines the kind of food required by the animal."

CHAPTER II

TEETH

"**I**S IT not true," resumed Uncle Paul, "that each kind of work demands its own special tool? The plowman must have the plow, the blacksmith the anvil, the mason the trowel, the weaver the shuttle, the carpenter the plane; and these different tools, all excellent for the work to which they are applied, would be of no use in any other. Could the mason rough-cast his wall with a shuttle? Could the weaver weave his cloth with a trowel? Evidently not. Is it not true, then, that from the tool one may easily guess the kind of work it does?"

"Nothing could be easier, it seems to me," replied Jules. "If I see planes and saws hanging on the wall, I know that I am in a carpenter's shop."

"And I should know," said Emile, "from seeing an anvil, a hammer, and a pair of tongs, that I was in a blacksmith's shop. But if I saw a mortar-board and a trowel, I should look around for the mason."

"Well," Uncle Paul went on, "every creature has its special task in creation's great workshop, where all take part, all work, according to the design of Divine Wisdom. Each species has its mission—I might say its trade to follow—a trade that requires special tools just as does any work done by man. Now, among the innumerable trades of animals there is one that is common to all without exception, the most important trade of all, as without it life itself would be impossible: it is the business of eating.

"But all animals do not take the same kind of food. Some need prey, raw flesh, others fodder; some eat roots, others seeds and fruit. In every instance teeth are the tools used in

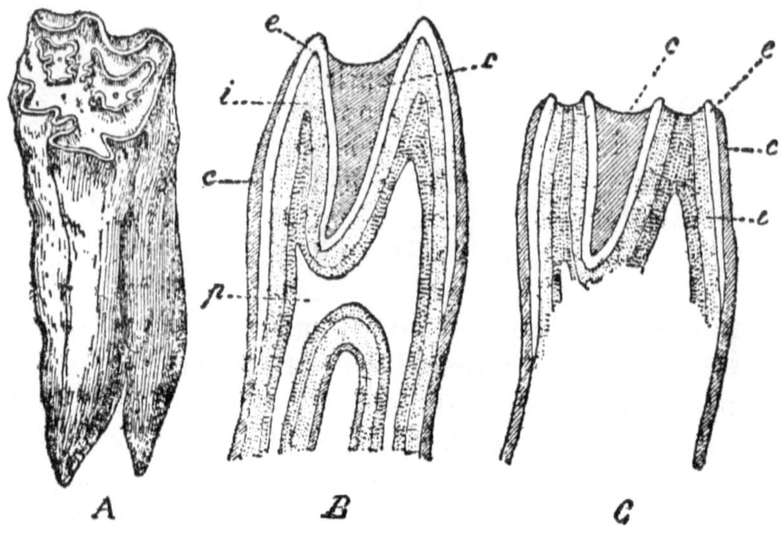

Tooth of a Horse

A, the tooth entire; *B*, cross-section of an unworn tooth; *C*, cross-section of a worn tooth; *e*, enamel; *c*, cement; *i*, ivory; *p*, dental pulp.

the work of eating; so they must have the shape appropriate to the kind of food eaten, whether that be tough or tender, hard or easy to chew. Therefore, just as from his tool the artisan's work may be inferred, so from the shape of its teeth one can usually tell the kind of food eaten by any animal.

"Herbivorous animals are those that live on grass, fodder, hay; and carnivorous animals are those that eat flesh. The horse, the donkey, the ox, and the sheep are herbivorous; the dog, the cat, and the wolf, carnivorous. The food of the herbivorous animal is tough, hard, fibrous, and must be ground for a long time by the teeth in order to be reduced to a paste-like mass suitable for swallowing and, after that, for easy digestion. In this case the teeth in both upper and lower jaw must have broad and almost flat surfaces that will come together and grind the food as millstones grind grain. On the other hand, the flesh eaten by the carnivorous animal is soft, easy to swallow, and easy to digest. All that the animal has to do is to tear it apart and cut it into shreds. So the teeth here must have sharp edges that come together and operate like the blades of a pair of scissors.

"I think I have said enough on that subject. Now, which of you will tell me what kind of food goes with each of the teeth I show you here?"

And Uncle Paul laid before his hearers the two teeth pictured on these pages, with others to follow.

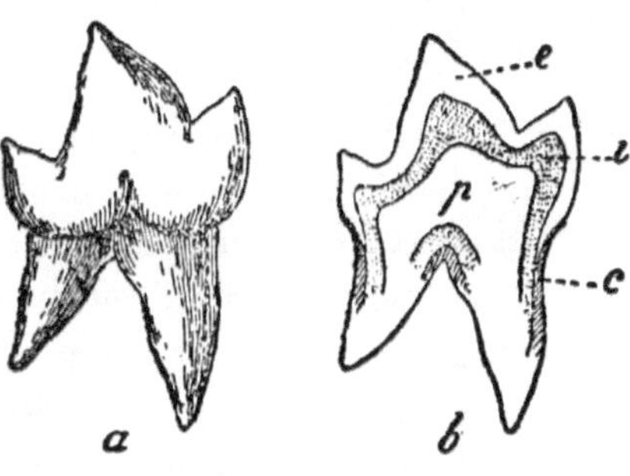

TOOTH OF A WOLF
a, the tooth entire; *b*, cross-section;
e, enamel; *c*, cement; *i*, ivory;
p, dental pulp.

"The first tooth," said Emile, "is flattened and very wide at the top; it must crush and grind by rubbing against a tooth of the same kind in the opposite jaw. So it is the tooth of an animal that eats fodder."

"It is indeed," Uncle Paul replied, "the tooth of an herbivorous animal, a horse."

"The second," continued Emile, "is composed of several broad points with edges almost as sharp as knife blades. It must be meant for cutting flesh."

"Those winding folds that you see in the horse's tooth—what are they for?" asked Jules. "There is nothing like them in the wolf's tooth."

"I was going to tell you about them," his uncle replied. "If the horse's teeth had perfectly smooth surfaces, without any roughness to act as a grater, is it not true that in pressing and rubbing, each against the opposite tooth, they would simply crush the fodder or hay as you would crush it between two smooth stones without changing it into fine powder? Millstones, if they were polished like marble tables, would flatten the grain without making flour of it; they must be rough on the surface in order to seize the wheat during the grinding of the upper stone on the stationary lower one and to make it into powder.

When by long use the surface is worn smooth, the stones are of no service until they are dented again with the hammer. Well, the folds of a horse's teeth may be likened to the roughness of a millstone: they project a little above the general surface of the tooth, making a sort of coarse file that tears to pieces blades of grass or hay when rubbed by the opposite tooth."

"I think I see a danger threatening the herbivorous animal," put in Jules at this point. "Those projecting folds must soon be worn down by rubbing against one another, just the same as the roughness on the millstone. If smooth millstones can't make flour without being roughened again, no more can the herbivorous animal's worn teeth go on grinding."

"That is provided for, admirably provided for, my boy. Everything in the world is arranged so that it can do its work: a wisdom that nothing escapes watches over the smallest details; everything, even to a donkey's jaw, shows this to be so. Listen, and judge for yourselves.

"There are two different substances in a tooth: one very hard, a little like glass and called enamel; the other quicker to wear out, but very difficult to break, and known as ivory. These two substances are combined in different ways, according to the animal's diet. In the horse, the sheep, the ox, the donkey, and many other herbivorous animals the ivory makes up the main part of the tooth, while the harder substance, the enamel, extends in winding sheets throughout the former, projecting a little above its surface in a fold which varies in form in the different kinds of animals. So, then, it is the enamel, a substance as hard as a pebble, that composes the folds in the herbivorous animal's teeth. From the rubbing of the lower teeth against the upper the ivory wears away faster than the enamel, so that the folds of the latter embedded in the mass of the tooth have their cutting edges brought above the general level as fast as required, and thus the grinding surfaces are kept in constant repair. You see how it is: in the donkey's food-mill, for instance, the millstones re-roughen themselves as fast as necessary for the chewing of a thistle; the machinery is self-repairing even while at work."

"What you tell us, Uncle, is wonderful," commented Jules. "I never should have guessed that such an arrangement was necessary for chewing a thistle."

"And only the other day," put in Louis, "I kicked out of my way a jaw-bone that was lying in the road. How gladly should I have looked at it closely if I had known all these things!"

"Ignorance always kicks things aside like that, my boy, but science is interested in everything, knowing that it can always learn something. But let us return to the teeth of the carnivorous animals and examine those of the wolf.

"Here the irregularities of the nutmeg-grater, the parallel ridges of the file, and the roughness of the millstone would be of no use, since the animal's food is to be torn into shreds and not chewed into paste. For the wolf's food cutting blades are needed—sharp scissors which are hard enough not to become blunt. Hence the working edges of the wolf's teeth are not flat like millstones, but shaped rather like pointed chisels. The ivory forms the central body of the tooth, making it tough and strong, while the enamel, harder but more brittle, is spread as a continuous layer over the tooth and furnishes the requisite cutting edges. In like manner a skilful cutler, when he wishes to make an edged tool that will cut well and at the same time withstand violent blows, makes its central mass of iron, a tough material that bears considerable violence without injury, but is not hard enough to furnish a keen cutting edge. He then overlays it, to obtain such an edge, with fine steel, which combines excessive hardness with the fragility of glass. The best that man can contrive in the making of edged tools is met with in perfection in the teeth of carnivorous animals."

"If I understand you, then," said Jules, "ivory, which is not so hard as enamel, but less brittle, forms the interior of the teeth of carnivorous animals, and enamel, which is harder and more brittle, forms the outside layer. Ivory makes the teeth strong; enamel makes them cut."

"Yes, that is it."

"Now, I don't know which is the more wonderful, the donkey's or the wolf's set of teeth."

"Both are wonderful, as both are admirably adapted to the kind of work they have to do."

"What surprises me most," Emile interposed, "is that a lot of things we should never pay any attention to turn out to be very interesting when Uncle Paul explains them to us. I never should have thought that the time would come when I should listen with pleasure to the history of a tooth."

"Since that interests you," said Uncle Paul, "I will continue the subject a little further and will tell you about human teeth, about yours, my boy, so white and so well arranged, and so admirably adapted for biting a slice of bread and butter."

CHAPTER III

THE DIFFERENT SHAPES OF TEETH

"MAN HAS thirty-two teeth, sixteen to each jaw," Uncle Paul continued.

Emile already had his finger in his mouth, passing it from one tooth to another, to count them. His uncle paused until he had finished the count.

"But I have only twenty, all told," declared the boy; "twenty, and not thirty-two."

"The other twelve will come some day, my boy; at present you have the right number of teeth for a child of your age. They do not all come at one time, but one after another. We begin with twenty, and no more. They are called milk teeth, or first teeth. When we are about seven years old they begin to fall out and are replaced by others stronger and set in more firmly. In addition to this second score of teeth there appear later twelve others, bringing the total number up to thirty-two. Those farthest back, in the inmost cavity of the mouth, come late, when we are eighteen or twenty years old, or even older, for which reason they are called wisdom teeth to signify that they appear at an age when the reason is well developed. These thirty-two last teeth constitute the second cutting. I call them last because they are never replaced by any others; if we lose them, that is the end of our teeth; no more will come."

"I have two now that are loose," said Emile.

"They must come out soon to leave room for the new teeth that are to take their place. The others will get loose, too, and the twenty that you have now will be succeeded by twenty others, to which, sooner or later, will be added twelve more which

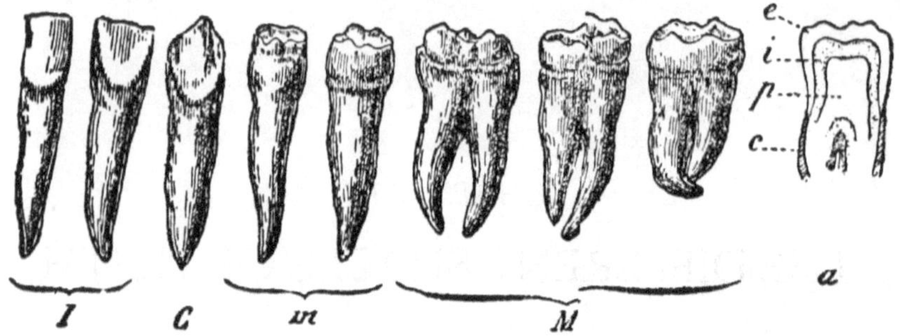

HUMAN TEETH

I, incisors; *C*, canine tooth; *m*, small molars; *M*, large molars;
a, cross-section showing, *e*, enamel; *c*, cement; *i*, ivory; *p*, dental pulp.

come only once. These last occupy the back part of the jaws, three on each side, top and bottom. Thus the final number will be thirty-two.

"These thirty-two teeth are divided into three classes according to their shape and the work they must do. The same names being repeated top and bottom and right and left, I show you merely the eight teeth of half a jaw. In every tooth there are two parts to be distinguished, the crown and the root. The root is the part that is embedded in the jaw-bone like a nail hammered into wood; the crown is the part that comes into view, and it may be likened to the head of a nail. The root holds the tooth in place, fixes it firmly; the crown cuts, tears, and grinds the food.

"In the two front teeth in each half-jaw the crown grows thinner toward the top. The edge is straight and sharp, fitted for cutting food, dividing it into small mouthfuls. Therefore these teeth are called incisors, from the Latin *incidere*, meaning to cut. Their root is a simple pivot. The next tooth is called canine. Its root is a little longer than those of the preceding teeth, and its crown is slightly pointed. The dog, the cat, the wolf, and carnivorous animals in general have this tooth shaped like a powerful fang, which serves to catch and hold prey, but above all acts as a weapon in attack and defense. It is the canine teeth that you see crossing one another, long and pointed, two on each side, when you raise the upper lip of a cat or a dog. Because of these remarkable fangs of carnivorous animals, especially the dog, which in Latin is *canis*, the name canine has been given to the teeth that in man are like them, if not in form and use, at least in the position they occupy.

"The next five teeth are the most useful of all. They are called molars, from the Latin *mola*, a millstone, because they play the part of millstones in grinding the food. For this purpose their crowns are blunt and broad and slightly irregular, not flat like the horse's molars or with sharp cutting edges like the wolf's, because man's food is not composed exclusively of either vegetables or flesh, but of both at the same time. For food as varied as man's, there is need of molars fit for all sorts of service: they must grind like those of the herbivorous animals and cut like those of the carnivorous; in short, they must be like those of both. And, indeed, their wide crowns are suited to vegetable food, and their rather sharp irregularities are adapted to animal food.

"The first two are called little molars or, in more learned language, bicuspids, because they have each two cusps or points. They are the least strong of the five and have only one root each. The two little molars, the canine tooth, and the two incisors (of each half-jaw) are the only teeth that are renewed. Multiply them by four and you will have the twenty teeth of the first cutting, teeth that begin to fall out toward the age of seven and are gradually replaced by others. That is the state of Emile's teeth at present, there being but twenty of them.

"The other three teeth, in each half-jaw, come only once. They are the large molars, of which the very end one is also called the wisdom tooth. As in the act of mastication the large molars have to bear strong pressure, the root is composed of several pivots or prongs reaching down each into a special cavity or socket. This makes them strong and firm, so that they can stand pressure both downward and sideways.

"To sum up, the grown man has thirty-two teeth in all, sixteen to each jaw; namely, four incisors, two canines, and ten

molars. These last
are divided into
four bicuspids or
little molars and
six large molars;
the milk teeth do
not include these
last six."

Here Jules had
a question to ask.
"Ivory and enamel,"
said he, "those two

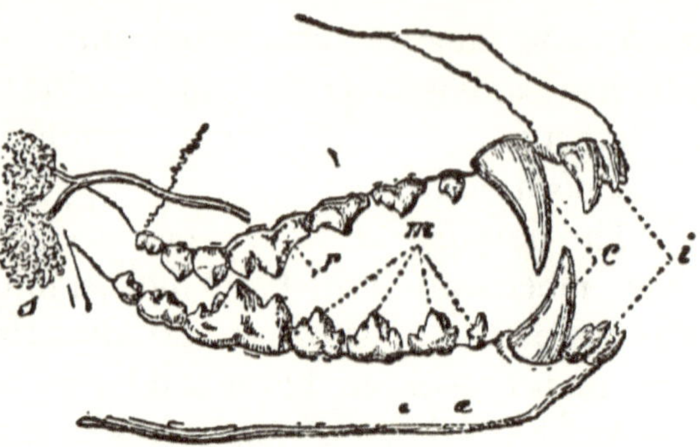

JAWS AND TEETH OF A WOLF
i, incisors; *c*, canine teeth; *m*, small molars;
r, large molars; *s*, salivary glands.

substances of different degrees of hardness that you told us
were arranged in such a wonderful way in horses' and wolves'
teeth—are they in our teeth, too?"

"Yes, they are there. Ivory forms the entire root, which must
serve as a firm support, and it also fills the crown, while enamel
merely covers the outside as a hard protecting layer."

"I am going to get the cat and look at her teeth," said Emile.
"Has she twenty, like me, or has she thirty-two?"

"Neither twenty nor thirty-two, but thirty when full-grown.
Dogs and wolves have forty-two; horses and donkeys forty-four.
In fact, the number varies with different animals as much as
the shape. Perhaps a few words on this subject will not be out
of place.

"First, here is the picture of a wolf's mouth. If one did not
already know, one could easily guess the animal's diet by merely
looking at its teeth. Those deeply indented molars, those strong,
curved canines—surely they call for wild prey and show great
strength. The whole set indicates clearly enough a carnivorous
appetite. At *i* are the incisors, six in number. They are small
and of slight use, for the animal does not cut its prey into little
mouthfuls, but swallows it gluttonously in great strips. At *c* are
the canines, veritable daggers which the bandit plunges into
the sheep's neck. The little molars are at *m*. The large molars

come next. The first, marked *r*, is the strongest, and it is with this that the wolf and the dog crack the hardest bones. Finally, the picture shows the salivary glands; that is, the organs that prepare the saliva and let it ooze into the mouth through the canal *s* as the animal eats. Without dwelling on this point, which would take me too far from my subject, I will merely say that saliva serves to soak the food and make a soft mouthful that

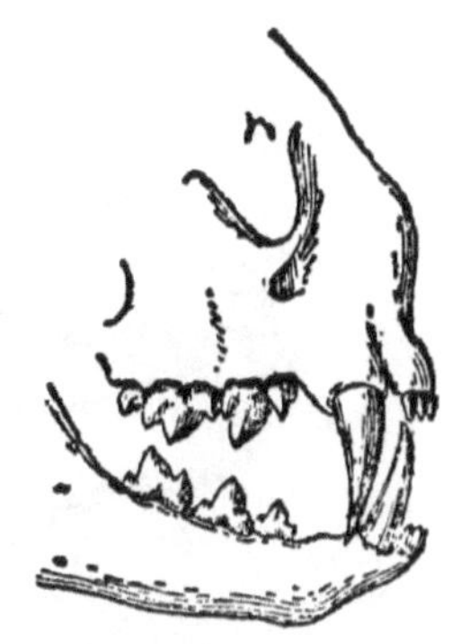

JAWS AND TEETH OF A CAT

can be easily swallowed, and it also plays an important part in the stomach in reducing to a fluid pap the food taken in; that is to say, it helps to digest the food.

"Let us pass on to the cat, another typical flesh-eater. Six small incisors are ranged in the front of the jaw like a row of elegant but useless pearls. They are ornamental rather than useful to the animal. A mouse-hunter needs very long and pointed canines for piercing the prey seized by the claws. In this respect the cat is armed in a very formidable manner. What do you think of it, Louis?"

"I think," he replied, "a rat must be very uncomfortable between those curved canines the picture shows us."

"One day," said Emile, "when I was pulling the cat's mustache, she gave me a bite that felt like the sharp prick of a needle. It was done so quickly I had no time to draw my hand back."

"The cat brought her canines into play and wounded you with one of them as quickly as a steel point could have done.

"Now look at the molars. There are four above, the last one very small, and three below. Their cusps or points are still sharper than the wolf's; so, too, the cat's appetite—like that of its kindred, the tiger, the panther, the jaguar, and others—demands more flesh than that of the wolf and animals like it, such as the fox, the jackal, and especially the dog. Have you ever noticed how disdainful the cat is when you throw her only a piece of

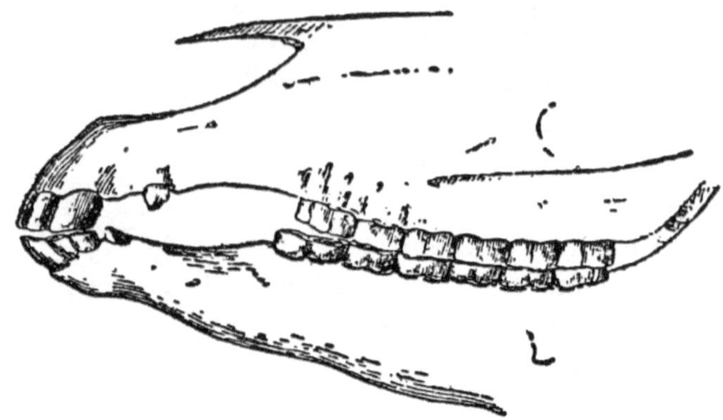

JAWS AND TEETH OF A HORSE

bread? Scarcely has she smelt it when she makes a movement of superb scorn, tail in the air, back raised, and looks at you as if to say: 'Are you making fun of me? I want something else.' Or, if very hungry, she reluctantly bites the bread, chews it awkwardly, and swallows it with distaste. The dog, on the contrary, our good Azor for example, catches the bread joyfully in his mouth without letting it touch the ground, and if he finds any fault with the piece it is for being too small. You call the cat a glutton. I take her part and maintain that it is not the vice of gluttony she shows, but that her teeth must have meat. What could you expect her pointed canines and keen-edged molars to do with a crust of bread? They demand, above all, a prey that bleeds, a quivering bit of flesh.

"What a difference between the teeth of the hunter and those of the peaceful chewer of grass! Let us examine this picture of a horse's head. Here the incisors, six in number, are powerful; they seize the forage and cut it, a mouthful at a time. The canines, of no use here, show only as little knobs on the jaw-bone. Next beyond comes a long vacant space called the bar; that is where the bit is held in the horse's mouth. Back of the bar you see the real grinding mechanism, composed of twelve pairs of strong molars with square, flat crowns furnished with slightly projecting folds whose use-

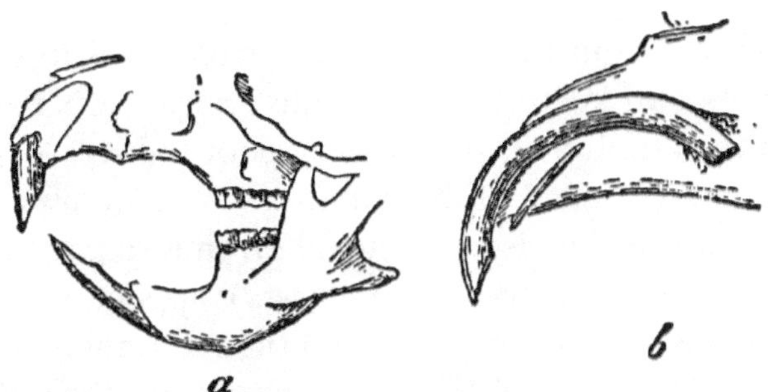

JAWS AND TEETH OF A RODENT
a, hamster's jaws and teeth; *b*, upper incisor of a rabbit.

fulness I have already pointed out to you. If I am not much mistaken, here we have a mill capable of grinding tough straw and fibrous hay.

"Finally, here is a rabbit's head. Each jaw is furnished with two enormous incisors set deep into the bone, bent backward above, and ending each in a sharp-edged crown. What are such incisors as those made for?"

"I know," Jules quickly replied. "The rabbit is always nibbling. For want of better food it will gnaw the bark of a tree and even the wood. It uses its incisors to cut its food very fine, to gnaw it."

"To gnaw it—that is the right word; hence we give the name of rodents or gnawers to the various animals having incisors of that kind. Such are the squirrel, the hare, the rabbit, the rat, and the mouse, those poor creatures which must gnaw the toughest vegetable substances and fill their bellies with wood, paper, rags even, when there is nothing better for supplying the mill that is kept always going. But it is not merely to satisfy their hunger that these animals are almost incessantly gnawing; there is another reason for their doing it. Their incisors grow all their lives and tend to lengthen indefinitely; consequently, the animal must wear them away by continual friction, as otherwise their crowns would at last so far overlap that they could not be made to meet. Then the poor beast would be unable to seize its food and would perish. In order to be able to eat when hungry, the rat and the rabbit must eat when not hungry, so as to sharpen their incisors and keep them the right length. It is true that they often turn their attention to very poor fodder. A splinter of wood, a straw, a mere nothing suffices to maintain the play of their indefatigable incisors. Remember, children, the expressive term *rodents* (which means *gnawers*), applied to a whole class of animals akin to the rabbit and the rat; remember their curious incisors, for we shall have occasion to speak of them again hereafter. For the present let us finish our examination of the rabbit's teeth.

"The canines are lacking; in their place the jaw shows a bar or, in other words, a large open space. At the extreme back of the mouth are the molars, few in number but strong, with flat crowns and several folds of enamel. In fact, they make an excellent grinding machine.

"In giving you these details concerning the different shapes of teeth in different species of animals, I wished particularly to point out the following truth: Each species eats a particular kind of food for which the teeth are especially formed, so that one might say of any animal, 'Show me its teeth and I will tell you what it eats.' In many instances where we cannot examine the teeth we do not know what such and such a creature feeds on, and in our hasty judgment we mistake a friend for an enemy, a helper for a destroyer. If the animal is ugly we condemn it on the spot and hate it, accusing it of any number of misdeeds. We declare war against it, and never suspect, in our foolishness, that it is a war at our own expense. But there is a very simple precaution by which we can avoid these regrettable mistakes: let us yield to no prejudice, however wide-spread, and before condemning an animal as harmful let us find out what sort of teeth it has. They will tell us the animal's way of living, as you shall soon see for yourselves."

CHAPTER IV

BATS

“WHICH OF you three can tell me what bats feed upon?” asked Uncle Paul the next day.

At this question Emile put on his thinking-cap, closing his eyes and rubbing his forehead; but no ideas came. Nor were Jules and Louis any prompter with an answer.

“Nobody knows? Well, then, so much the better, for you will have the satisfaction of finding it out for yourselves, from the shape of the teeth. The incisors, small and weak, which you see on an enlarged scale in this picture of a bat’s set of teeth—do they look as if they were made for gnawing vegetable substances, after the manner of rats and rabbits? Could they cut any such tough fodder?”

“Certainly not,” replied Jules; “they are too weak to be of much use. And then it seems to me those two sharp, curved fangs must belong to a flesh-eating animal.”

“The long, pointed canines do indicate as much, but the molars show it perhaps still more plainly. With their strong and sharp indented crowns fitting so well into the sharp-edged depressions of the opposite jaw—are those molars designed to crush grain, to grind, slowly and patiently, fibrous substances?”

“No,” said Jules; “they are the teeth of a flesh-eater, not the grist-mill of an herbivorous animal.”

“I am sure now,” affirmed Louis, “that the bat lives on prey.”

“It is a greedy hunter of flesh and blood,” Emile declared. “The cat’s teeth are not more savage-looking.”

“All that is quite correct,” said Uncle Paul. “The teeth have taught you the chief thing about the animal’s habits. Yes, the

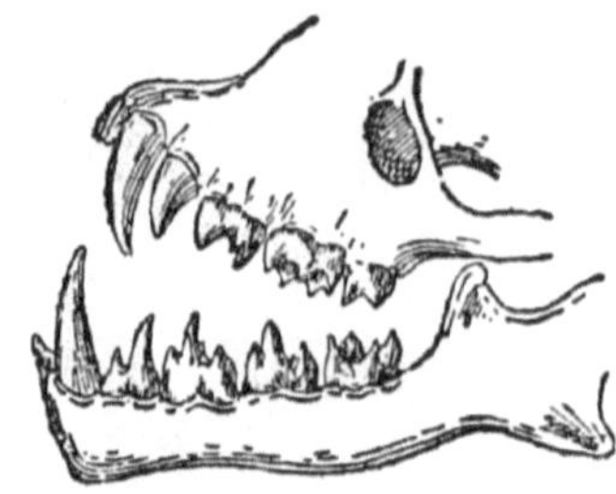

JAWS AND TEETH OF A BAT

bat is a hunter, an eater of live prey, a little ogre always demanding fresh meat. It only remains to find out the kind of game it likes. Evidently the size of the prey must suit the size of the hunter. A bat's head is no bigger than a large hazelnut. It is true the mouth is split from ear to ear and can, when wide open, swallow mouthfuls larger than the smallness of the animal would lead one to suppose. Nevertheless the bat can attack only small creatures. What can it be that it goes chasing through the air when, after sunset, it flies hither and thither unceasingly?"

"Gnats, perhaps, and night-moths," Jules suggested.

"Exactly. Those are its prey. The bat lives on insects exclusively. All are food for its maw: hard-winged beetles, slender mosquitoes, plump moths, flying insects of all sorts; in fact, all the little winged foes of our cereals, vines, fruit trees, woolen stuffs—all those creatures of the air that come in the evening, attracted by our lighted rooms, and singe their wings in the flames of our lamps. Who would undertake to say how many insects bats destroy when they fly around a house? The game is so small, and the hunter is so hungry.

"Notice what happens on a calm summer evening. Lured abroad by the balmy atmosphere of the twilight hours, a host of insects leave their lurking-places and come forth, guests at life's garden party, to sport together in the air, hunt for food, and mate with one another. It is the hour when the sphinx-moths fly abruptly from flower to flower and thrust their long probosces into the depths of the corollas, where honey is stored; the hour when the mosquito, thirsting for human blood, sounds its war-cry in our ears and selects our tenderest spot to stab with its poisoned lancet; the hour when the June-bug leaves the shelter of the leaf, spreads its buzzing wings, and goes humming through the air in quest of its fellows. The gnats dance in joyous swarms which the slightest breath of wind disperses like a column of smoke; butterflies and moths, in wedding-garments, their wings powdered with silvery dust and their antennæ spread out like plumes, join

A Bat in Flight

in the frolic or seek places in which to deposit their eggs; the wood-borer comes forth from its hidden retreat under the bark of the elm; the weevil breaks its cell hollowed out in a grain of wheat; the plume-moths rise in clouds from the granaries and fly toward the fields of ripe cereals; other moths explore here the grape-vines, there the pear trees, apple trees, cherry trees, busily seeking food and shelter for their evil progeny.

"But in the midst of these festive assemblies suddenly there comes a killjoy. It is the bat, which flies hither and thither, up and down, appearing and disappearing, darting its head out this side and that, and each time snapping up an insect on the wing, crushing and swallowing it immediately. The hunting is good; gnats, beetles, and moths abound; and every now and then a little cry of joy announces the capture of a plump June-bug. As long as the fading twilight permits, the eager hunter thus pursues its work of extermination. Satisfied at last, the bat flies back to its somber and quiet retreat. The next evening and all through the summer the hunt is resumed, always with the same ardor, always at the expense of insects only.

"To give you an idea of the multitude of harmful insects, especially of moths, from which the bat delivers us, I will quote a passage from the celebrated French naturalist Buffon, the most graphic historian of the animal kingdom. But first I must tell you that bats are in the habit of making their homes in old towers, grottoes, and abandoned quarries. There, in great numbers, they pass the daylight hours, hanging motionless from the roof, and thence they sally forth at the approach of darkness. The floor of these retreats becomes covered at last with a deep layer of droppings, from which we can learn the kind of food eaten by bats and judge of the importance of their hunting. Now here is what Buffon has to say of a grotto frequented by these creatures:

"Having one day descended into the grottoes of Arci, I was surprised to find there a kind of earth of a singular nature. It formed a bed of blackish matter several feet thick, almost entirely composed of parts of the wings and feet of flies and moths, as if these insects had gathered here in immense numbers, coming together for the express purpose of dying and rotting in company. It was nothing but bats' dung that had been accumulating for years."

"What a curious kind of soil, made up entirely of the remains of dead insects!" Jules exclaimed.

"I will add that sometimes this soil of flies and moths at the bottom of old quarries and caves is abundant enough for the farmer to take account of it and use it as a rich fertilizer. It is called bats' guano."

"To make such heaps of it, then," remarked Louis, "bats must destroy insects by millions and millions."

"Five or six dozen flies or moths are hardly enough for a bat's evening meal; if a few June-bugs should make their appearance, they would be eagerly snapped up. If the band of hunters is a large one, judge of the thousands of harmful insects destroyed in a single season. Next to the birds we have no more valiant helpers than bats; and so I beg you to be friendly to these creatures which, while we are asleep and perhaps dreaming of our rich crops of pears and apples, peaches and grapes and grain, proceed with their silent warfare against the enemies of our harvests, and every evening destroy by myriads moths, mosquitoes, beetles, bugs—in short, the greater part of the insect throng that always threatens us with starvation if we do not keep vigilant watch."

"I see now that the bat does us a good turn," Emile admitted.

"All the same, it is frightfully ugly; and, besides, they say if it touches you it will give you the itch."

"There are any number of other sayings about it that are just as foolish, my boy. One is that the bat pricks with its pointed teeth the she-goat's udders so as to suck her blood and milk; another is that it gnaws the sausages and bacon hung under the chimney mantel; also, that its sudden entrance into a house means misfortune. I have heard persons cry out because a bat had accidentally grazed them with the tip of its wing; and I have seen others pale with terror because they had found one of the innocent creatures fastened by a claw to their bed curtains.

"Here, as in many other things, my dear children, you must take into account the folly of mankind, which is more given to error than to truth. If you were old enough to understand me, I should add that wherever I find a general agreement that a thing is black I think it well to look into the matter and find out whether, on the contrary, it may not be white. We are so stuffed with false notions that very often the exact opposite of the common belief is the real truth. Do you ask for examples? There are plenty of them.

"The sun, we generally say, according to all appearances revolves from east to west around the stationary earth. No, says science, no, it is the earth, on the contrary, that rotates from west to east before the stationary sun. The stars, we say again, are small bright points, little lamps in the arch of the firmament. No, answers science, the stars are not tiny sparks; they are enormous bodies which compare in light and size to the sun itself, a million and a half times as large as the earth. The bat, it is commonly asserted, is a harmful, hideous, venomous creature of ill omen that must be crushed without mercy under the heel. No, affirms science, a thousand times no; the bat is an inoffensive creature that, instead of doing us harm and bringing misfortune, renders us an immense service by protecting the good things of the earth from their countless destroyers.

"No, we should not vent our hatred upon it and pitilessly

kill it; on the contrary, we should like and respect it as one of our best helpers. The poor creature does not deserve the bad reputation that ignorance has given it. Its touch does not communicate either lice or the itch; its teeth do not pierce the goat's udders or attack our stores of bacon; its chance entrance into a room is no more to be dreaded than a butterfly's. For my part I should like to have it visit my bedroom often at night, for then I should soon be rid of the mosquitoes that torment me. All things considered, we have nothing, absolutely nothing to reproach it with, and we are indebted to it for very valuable services. That is the answer of science to ignorant prejudice. Henceforth, then, crush the bat under your heel if you dare."

"I will take good care," said Louis, "never to do such a thing now that I know what an army of enemies we are guarded against by the bat."

"But what a pity," Jules remarked, "that it is such a hideous creature!"

"Hideous?" his uncle repeated. "That is a slander which I hope to make you take back."

"Surely you can't deny that the bat is horribly ugly," persisted the boy.

"Perhaps I can."

"I should like to know," said Emile, "how you can make out that the frightful shape of the creature is beautiful."

"To discuss ugliness and beauty with you, my children," replied Uncle Paul, "is not an undertaking that I should care to enter upon. To follow me in such a discussion you would need a maturity of mind that does not go with your years. Even if you were grown up, it might still be impossible for us to come to an agreement, inasmuch as it is not with the bodily eyes that ugliness and beauty should be judged, but with the eyes of reason ripened by reflection and study and free from the trammels of first impressions, which are generally erroneous. Also, how few possess that intellectual clearness of vision that remains untroubled by prematurely conceived opinions and can thus contemplate things in all the clarity of truth! Trusting the testimony of our eyes and yielding to daily habit, we call beautiful the creatures whose general structure shows a certain conformity with that of the animals most familiar to us and unthinkingly accepted as standards for all future judgments. We call ugly those that differ from these accepted models, and if very unlike we call them hideous. Enlightened reason refuses to be hemmed in by the narrow circle of first impressions; it rises above petty prejudices and says to itself: Nothing is ugly that God has made; everything is beautiful, everything is perfect in itself, as everything is the work of the Creator.

"An animal's form should not be judged by its greater or less resemblance to the forms that are already familiar to us and serve us as standards of comparison, but rather by its fitness for the kind of life for which it was created. Where the structure is in perfect harmony with the functions to be performed, there too is beauty. From this higher point of view ugliness no longer exists; or, rather, it exists all too abundantly, but only in the moral world. Intemperance, laziness, stupid pride—all forms of vice, in short—constitute ugliness and hideousness. To tell the truth, I know of none besides.

"But I must return to the bat, if not in the hope of making you find it beautiful, at least with the certainty of interesting you in its remarkable structure. I will wager, too, that not one of you knows what a bat is."

"It is a kind of bird," declared Emile.

"It is an old rat that has grown a pair of wings," Jules ventured to assert.

"You are both talking nonsense," returned their uncle. "That is the way with us all: we speak at random of animals and persons, giving to one our esteem, to another our scorn, without knowing what they are, what they do, what they are good for. You don't know the first thing about the bat, and yet you overwhelm the poor animal with abuse.

"The bat has nothing in common with birds; it has neither

beak nor feathers; nor is it a rat that has acquired wings in its old age. It is really a peculiar creature that is born, lives, and dies with wings, without in any way belonging to the bird family. Its body has the size, the fur, and somewhat the shape of a mouse; but its wings are bare.

"The most highly organized animals have as a distinctive mark teats or udders, which furnish milk, the first food of their young. These animals do not feed their young family from the beak, as birds do; they do not abandon their offspring to all the hazards of good or ill fortune, careless of their future, as do the stupid races of reptiles and fish. The females rear their young with maternal care, feeding them from time to time with milk from their udders. All the various species that suckle their young, all that are provided with udders, are classed together by men of learning and called mammals, from the Latin *mamma*, a breast or teat. I will add that in the great majority of instances these animals have the body covered with fur or hair, and not with feathers or scales. Feathers belong to birds, scales to reptiles and fishes. As examples of mammals you will immediately think of our domestic animals, the dog, the cat, the cow, the sheep, the goat, the horse, and others."

"I have often noticed," said Emile, "how carefully the cat raises her family. While the kittens press her teats with their little pink paws to make the milk flow faster, the old cat washes them with her tongue and shows her happiness by her soft purring."

"Well, then," resumed Uncle Paul, "the bat is a mammal just as much as is the cat, and like that of the cat its body is protected from the cold by fur, and the female has teats for nursing her little ones. The number of teats varies widely in the different kinds of animals, being greater in the species that have many young at a birth, and less in the others; which is as it should be, in order that the nurslings may all be suckled at the same time. The bat has only two, situated on the breast and not under the stomach. The female bears only a single young one at a time. Emile rightly admires the love of the cat for her kittens; yet the bat is a still tenderer mother. When in the evening she goes out in search of food, instead of leaving her nursling in some hole in the wall after suckling it, she carries it with her, clinging to her breast; and it is while weighted with this load that she chases the nimble moths on the wing. Doubtless the pursuit of prey is thus rendered less fruitful and more difficult; but no matter, the loving mother prefers not to abandon her feeble charge, and allows it to continue peacefully sucking during the evolutions of the hunt. With the deepening darkness the bat regains its retreat, suspends itself from the roof by a toe-nail, and holds its nursling by wrapping it in her wings."

"That is not so bad a way to behave," admitted Jules. "I begin to find the bat less ugly than I thought."

"That is what I just told you," returned his uncle. "Ugliness is begotten of ignorance; it diminishes as knowledge increases. But let us continue our theme."

CHAPTER V

THE BAT'S WINGS

"WINGS, REAL wings, perfectly adapted to flying, are the bat's most striking feature. How can a mammal, an animal whose general structure is that of a dog or a cat for example, possess the flying-apparatus of a bird? How can two organs so entirely different be combined? In the bat's wing, my children, we find an admirable example of the infinite resources at the command of the Creator, who, without adding to or subtracting from the fundamental plan, has adapted the same organs to the most widely different functions. The fore feet of mammals—of the dog, or the cat we will say—are changed into wings in the bat without the addition or the loss of a single part in this incredible transformation. More than that, the human arms, our arms, children—are there represented, piece by piece, bone by bone. You all look at me as if you did not believe it, unable to understand how there can be anything in common between our arms and a bat's wings."

"The fact is," Jules confessed, "it takes all my faith in your words to make me admit that there can be the least likeness between a man's arm and a bat's wing."

"I do not propose to make you admit it because of your faith in me; I propose to prove it to you. Follow along your arm so as to grasp the demonstration better.

"From the shoulder to the elbow the framework of the human arm consists of a bone known as the humerus. From the elbow to the wrist there are two bones of unequal size running side by side the whole length. The larger is the cubitus, the smaller the radius. Then comes the wrist, composed of several little bones which I will not now describe. Next is the palm of the hand, its framework formed of a row of five bones almost alike and each serving to support a finger. Finally, each finger contains a succession of small bones called phalanges, of which the thumb has two, and all the others three each. I will add that two bones serve to attach the arm to the body. One is the shoulder-blade, a broad triangular bone situated on the back behind the shoulder; the other is the collar bone, slender and curved, situated in front and extending from the shoulder to the base of the neck. Those are the collar-bones that you can feel with your hand at the right and left above the breast."

While thus enumerating the parts of the arm, Uncle Paul guided the hand of each listener and made it feel the several bones as they were named. Emile had some difficulty with the learned terms "humerus" and "cubitus," which he now heard for the first time; nevertheless, by paying close attention he found that he could easily remember them. When the boys had all learned the name and the position of each bone in the human arm, their uncle continued:

"Now examine with me this picture of a bat's skeleton. The

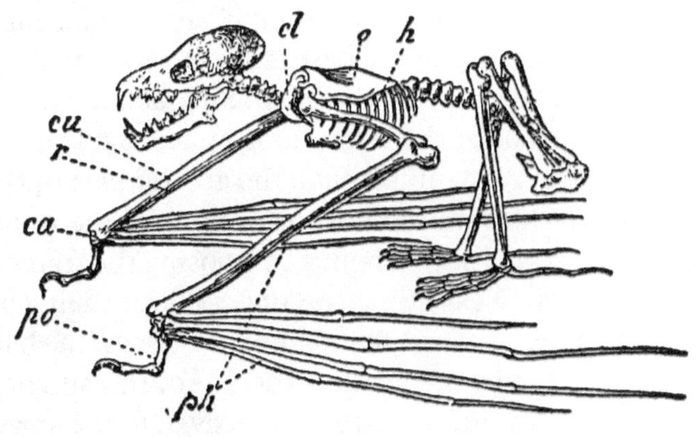

SKELETON OF A BAT
o, shoulder-blade; *cl*, collar-bone; *h*, humerus; *cu*, cubitus;
r, radius; *ca*, carpus or wrist; *po*, pollex or thumb; *ph*, phalanges.

bone marked *o* is the shoulder-blade. As with us, it forms the back of the shoulder, and it is triangular, wide, and flat."

"Then the part marked *cl* is the shoulder, and the bone that goes from there to the base of the neck is the collar-bone?" queried Emile.

"Precisely."

"I see how the rest goes," Louis hastened to interpose. "The bone marked *h* is the humerus, and the elbow is at the angle made by this bone with the next."

"My turn now," put in Jules. "The two bones running side by side from the elbow to the wrist are marked *cu* and *r*. The first is the cubitus, the other the radius. Consequently *ca* is the wrist. But there I get lost."

"The wrist, I told you," explained Uncle Paul, "is composed of several small bones. That structure we find at *ca*, the bat's wrist."

"But, then, the hand?" queried Jules.

"The palm of the hand and the five fingers which it supports are represented by the ribs of the wing and by *po*, which is the thumb. This is the shortest of the five fingers, as with man. It forms no part of the framework of the wing, but is free and is furnished with a hooked nail which the animal uses to cling by and also in walking. Finally, this thumb has two phalanges, as in the human thumb, and at the base is a small bone which in man forms a part of the palm of the hand. So much for the thumb.

"Now let us look at those four long bones that start from the wrist (*ca*) and spread out through the greater part of the wing. Together with the similar but shorter bone of the thumb they represent the series of five bones composing the framework of the human palm. Next come the fingers with their phalanges (*ph*). In short, except for a few slight differences, the bat's wing reproduces, piece by piece, the structure of the human arm."

"Yes," Jules admitted, "it's all there, even to the small bones of the wrist and fingers. Is it possible that a poor bat can pattern after us so closely? The horrid creature copies our arms to make itself wings."

"Your pride need not suffer from this close resemblance, which you will find in different degrees in a multitude of other animals, especially among the mammals, our next of kin in bodily structure. In the formation of his body man enjoys no monopoly; the dog, the cat, the donkey, the ox—each and all of them—share with us a common stock of organs, modified in details and suited to the kind of life of each species. We recognize in the bat's wings the fundamental plan of our arms; we see it also no less plainly in the fore legs of the cat, the dog, and many other animals, and we can trace a rude resemblance to our hand even in the donkey's homely hoof. I tell you these things, my children, not to lessen in your eyes the undeniable superiority of man, but to inspire in you a fellow feeling for animals that are formed like us, suffer as we do, and are far too often the victims of our stupid cruelty. Whoever needlessly causes an animal to suffer commits a barbarous act, an inhuman act, inasmuch as he inflicts torture on flesh like our own; he brutally misuses a body having the same mechanism as our own and the same power of suffering. As to our superiority, it is established preëminently by an exceptional characteristic that places us above all comparison even with creatures that in their physical structure most closely resemble us. This characteristic is reason, the torch that lights us in our search for truth; it is the human soul, which alone knows itself and enjoys the sublime privilege of knowing its divine Author.

"In bats four of the five bones similar to those of our palm are greatly elongated, as are also the corresponding fingers, and they together constitute the four ribs on which is stretched the membrane of the wing, just as silk is stretched on the ribs of an umbrella. Thus it is at the sacrifice of what might have been a hand that the wing is formed. Therefore the scientists call all mammals of like structure with the bat 'chiropters,' meaning hand-winged creatures, from two Greek words signifying hand and wing.

"Of the five fingers one only, the thumb, is left free in the bat, and it is very small. It is furnished, as I said before, with a nail or claw. The four others, destitute of nails, are lengthened to serve as supports to the membrane of the wing. This membrane is a fold of the skin which starts from the shoulder, stretches between the four long fingers of the hand, and then attaches itself to the hind leg, the toes of which are all furnished with hooked nails or claws and do not depart from the ordinary shape of such members. By virtue of the free thumb already described, the wings are able to serve as feet in walking, when these members are folded close to the animal's sides. The bat grips the ground by thrusting in first the right claw and then the left, and pushes itself forward with its hind feet in laborious and awkward leaps. Thus it gets over the ground at what might be called a fast pace, but is soon tired out with the exertion; hence it does not walk except when sure it will not be molested or when it is compelled to do so by its position on a level surface where it cannot launch itself into the air. Then as soon as possible it gains an elevated point, from which it flies off. For in order to unfold the hampering membranes that serve as wings and to throw itself into the air, the bat needs considerable free space, which it cannot get except by hurling itself from a height. Consequently, in the caves inhabited by bats they never fail to secure an unimpeded drop. With the hooked talons of a hind foot they cling to the roof, head downward. That is the way they rest, the way they sleep. At the slightest alarm the claw lets go, the wings spread, and the animal is off."

"What a queer way to sleep," Emile exclaimed, "hanging from the roof by one foot, head downward! And do they stay that way long without getting tired?"

"If necessary, a good half of the year."

When he went to bed that night Emile thought again of the bat's way of sleeping; but he preferred his own.

CHAPTER VI

THE BAT'S SENSES OF SMELL AND HEARING

"**B**ATS ARE nocturnal," Uncle Paul continued the next day; "that is, they leave their lurking-places only at nightfall, to hunt in the evening twilight. As a rule, animals addicted to nocturnal hunting have very large eyes that take in as much light as possible, and thus these animals can see with very little light. Night-birds, such as owls of all kinds, will furnish us a remarkable example a little later. By a singular exception, however, despite their nocturnal habits bats have very small eyes. How, then, are they able to direct themselves in their swift flight, so abrupt in its changes of direction? How, above all, are they aware of the presence of their tiny game—moths and gnats?

"They are guided especially by their senses of smell and hearing, which are extraordinarily acute. What do you say to the bat's ears? What animal of its size can show anything like them? How they flare, like enormous hearing-trumpets, to receive the slightest sound! The bat that bears them has the expressive name of long-eared bat."

"Long-eared bat," repeated Jules; "that's the kind of name I like; it describes the animal and shows what there is about it that is out of the ordinary."

"Such prodigious ears are certainly made to hear sounds inaudible to us by reason of their excessive faintness. They enable their possessor to hear at a distance the beating of a moth's wings and the fluttering of a gnat dancing in the air.

"Other bats which have smaller ears have as a substitute a sense of smell unequaled for its acuteness. The high state of perfection of this sense is the result of the abnormal development of the nose, which covers a good part of the face and gives the animal a very strange appearance. For example, imagine the head of a bat called the horseshoe bat. There is a broad, distended formation of curious shape that occupies almost the whole space between the eyes and the mouth is the nose. It ends above in a large triangular, leaflike expanse; laterally it spreads out in folded laminæ, all together taking the shape of a horseshoe, whence the name of the creature. What odor, however faint, could escape such a nose? The dog, so famous for its keenness of scent, chases the hare without seeing it, guided solely by the odor left behind by the animal, heated in the chase; but how much keener the scent of the horseshoe bat must be when it chases in the same manner a moth that leaves no odor for any nose but its pursuer's! I sometimes wonder whether such a nose, so abnormally developed, may not be able to detect certain qualities that are and always will be unknown to us for want of the means to perceive them. The horseshoe bat's grotesque nose makes you laugh, my little friends; it makes me think. I think of the thousand secrets that nature hides from our senses and that would be as easy for us to learn as they would be valuable if we possessed the scent of a poor bat. Perhaps (who can tell?) the horseshoe bat foresees with its nose the coming storm several days in advance; it may scent the future hurricane, smell the rain-clouds coming from the other end of the earth, know by detecting their odor what winds are about to blow, foretell in similar manner what the weather is going to be; and, guided by perceptions of which we can form no idea, it may make its plans for hunting insects that are sometimes abundant and sometimes scarce according to the state of the atmosphere."

"If the horseshoe bat's nose can do all that," said Jules, "we must agree that it is a first-rate sort of nose."

"I make no positive assertions," his uncle rejoined. "I merely have my suspicions. The only thing that seems to me beyond doubt is that such an organ as the bat's nose serves its owner as a source of sensations unknown to man."

"You say so many wonderful things about it, Uncle," Emile interposed, "that I shall end by thinking the horseshoe bat's nose much more curious than ugly. There's another thing, too, I've just noticed. Why does the creature have such fat cheeks? What a puffed-up face it has."

"With the bat," Uncle Paul explained, "the chase is a short one, lasting only one or two hours—in fact, the short interval between sunset and dark. The remainder of the twenty-four hours is passed in rest, in the quiet of some cavern or grotto. Does the animal, then, have but one meal in all this time? And what if there are evenings when hunting is out of the question, the sky being overcast, the wind too strong, or rain falling, so that the insects keep under cover? The bat would then be subjected to long fasts if it were impossible for it to lay in supplies beforehand. But these supplies must be collected hastily, on the wing, with no interruption to the hunt which lasts so short a time. Hence it is that pouches are indispensable, deep pouches in which the hunter can put his game as fast as he catches it. The cheeks exactly fill this office: they can be enlarged at the creature's will—distended so as to form roomy pockets in which the insects killed with a snap of the teeth can be stowed away. These reserve pockets are called cheek-pouches. Gluttonous monkeys have them. That is where the she-ape, fond of sweets, puts the lump of sugar given her and lets it slowly melt so as to prolong the enjoyment of it. Well, when the bat is out hunting it first satisfies its hunger, and then—especially when its nose, the famous nose that we have just been talking about, predicts unfavorable weather for the following days—it redoubles its exertions and stows away moth after moth in the depths of its elastic pouches. It returns to its quarters with cheeks all distended. Now without fear of famine it can remain idle for several days if necessary. Hanging motionless by a hind claw, it feeds on its store of provisions, nibbling one at a time, as hunger prompts, the insects softened to taste in the reservoir of its cheeks.

"But it is high time we finished with the bats; their history would be too long if I were to tell you all about them. I will only ask Jules what he thinks now of the animal he at first called hideous."

"Frankly, Uncle," answered the boy, "these creatures interest me now more than they disgust me. Their singular wings, formed at the cost of what might have been hands, their prodigious nose and immense ears which make up for their poor eyesight, their cheeks swollen so as to make pouches for their supply of food—all these have interested me very much."

"The cheek-pouches," said Emile, "where the bat puts its game to soak, and the nose that scents the coming storm, seemed to me the most curious things about the animal."

"And I," said Louis, "shall never forget how many enemies bats deliver us from."

"Now you understand," Uncle Paul rejoined, "or at least I hope you are beginning to understand, that bats, being so useful to us in destroying a multitude of ravaging insects, and noteworthy for their singular structure, should not inspire us with an unjustifiable repugnance and still less with a stupid rage to exterminate them. Let us leave in peace these poor creatures that so valiantly earn their living by protecting our crops. Do not let us harm them under the foolish pretext that they are ugly, for their supposed ugliness is in reality an admirable adaptation of bodily structure to the creature's mode of life."

CHAPTER VII

THE HEDGEHOG

I N HIS walled garden Uncle Paul allowed a couple of hedgehogs, which he had brought from the neighboring hills, to wander at large. One evening the children noticed them poking about in a lettuce patch.

"Why," asked Emile, "has Uncle Paul put those animals in the garden and told us to leave them alone if we happened to come across them?"

"No doubt to make war on harmful insects," answered Louis. "Stop, look there! One of them is turning up the earth with its little black snout. Ssh! Let's keep still and see what it's after."

The children crouched down behind a row of peas so as not to be seen. The hedgehog, now scratching with its paws, now rummaging with the tip of its snout, which resembles that of a pig, finally unearthed a big, fat white larva which had probably been clinging to the root of a lettuce plant. The children ran to look at the captured game. The hedgehog, thus taken by surprise, hastened to roll itself up into a ball bristling with spines. In the disinterred worm Jules easily recognized a June-bug larva, one of that ravenous and destructive race that Uncle Paul had already told them about.[1]

In the evening, when they were all gathered together, the hedgehog naturally became the subject of conversation.

"Several years ago," said Uncle Paul, "as I was returning home one evening at a late hour, I chanced upon two hedgehogs coming out from a pile of stones. I tied them up in my hand-

---

1   See *Field, Forest and Farm* by the same author..

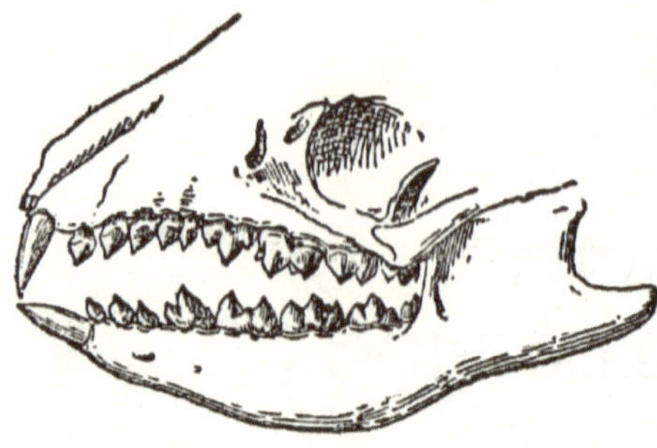

JAWS AND TEETH OF A HEDGEHOG

kerchief so as to bring them home and let them loose in my garden. Ever since then they have never failed to render me certain services that you can appreciate by examining the jaws in this picture."

"Pointed teeth like those," Jules remarked, "were never made for browsing grass. The hedgehog must feed on prey. Its teeth are just right for crunching June-bug worms such as I saw dug up in the garden this morning."

"Notice how sharp the points of the teeth are," resumed his uncle, "both in the upper and in the lower jaw. Those two rows of teeth fit into each other when the animal bites, and they plunge like so many fine daggers into the captured victim's flesh. With this complicated dental mechanism evidently the hedgehog cannot triturate tough food; it must have a kind of diet that is soft, juicy, capable of being reduced to marmalade by a brief chewing. The animal is therefore preëminently a flesh-eater. Several other species, particularly the mole and the shrew-mouse of these regions, have, like the hedgehog, teeth tapering to conical points and interplaying in the two jaws. Their food, too, is about the same as the hedgehog's. All three—hedgehog, mole, and shrew-mouse—live on small game—insects, larvæ, slugs, caterpillars, worms. They belong to the group of mammals known to naturalists as the order of insectivorous animals, or, in other words, the order of insect-eaters. On and under the ground they carry on the same kind of hunt that bats do in the air. In their way of living bats, too, are insectivorous; but their peculiar bodily structure causes them to be placed apart in the order of chiropters. Thus the mammals furnish us two orders of helpers: the chiropters, which hunt on the wing, and the insect-eaters—the insectivorous animals properly so called—

which hunt on and under the ground. To the latter belong the hedgehog, the mole, and the shrew-mouse.

"The hedgehog, the largest of the three, requires the largest and most plentiful prey. Tiny vermin are disdained, but a June-bug larva or a good fat mole-cricket is an excellent find. When they are not buried too deep he digs with his paws and snout to unearth them. You have to-day seen my hedgehogs at work in the lettuce bed. All night they go prowling about the garden, sniffing and rummaging in every nook and corner, and crunching no small number of my foes without doing me much harm. In them I have two vigilant watchmen who make their rounds every night for the greater security of my growing vegetables. However, despite the interest I take in them, I must, to be candid, acknowledge their faults.

"The hedgehog's natural food consists unquestionably of insects; but when a good opportunity presents itself the greedy creature is easily tempted by larger and more highly flavored prey. In its wild state the hedgehog does not hesitate to suck the blood of young rabbits caught in their hole during the mother's absence. The eggs of quail and partridge, too, it esteems as a most delicious feast, but its supreme delight is to wring the necks of a brood of little chickens. One night last year I heard a great commotion in the hen-house. The roosters were raising cries of alarm, the hens were cackling in desperate fright. I ran out to see what the trouble was. One of my hedgehogs had crept in under the door, and I found the rogue regaling himself on some little chickens almost under their mother's wing, she being powerless to help them in the dark. With one kick I sent the assassin rolling outside, and the next day thorough repairs were taken in hand. The holes on a level with the floor were closed up, and since then I have had no further trouble from my insect-hunters. With proper precautions against their thirst for blood, I have two larva-devourers of great value for my garden."

"But won't they do damage of another kind?" asked Louis. "I have heard that hedgehogs climb trees and shake off the ripe fruit, and then roll on it so as to spit it with their spines, after which they carry it off to their holes and eat it at their ease."

"Pay no attention to any such stories, my boy. It is utterly impossible for a hedgehog to climb a tree. Clumsy and stubby as it is, with legs so short and claws useless for climbing, how could it manage an athletic feat that calls for agility, hooked claws, and supple limbs? No, my friend, the hedgehog does not climb trees, neither does it carry off fruit transfixed with its spines. The only vestige of truth in that old wives' tale is that hedgehogs do not live exclusively on prey; if they find fruit that they like on the ground, a very ripe pear or a juicy peach, for example, they munch it with as great contentment as they would a beetle or a June-bug."

"It is also said," Louis added, "that if kept in a house the hedgehog will drive away rats."

"Ah, that I am quite willing to believe. By day the animal crouches in a corner and sleeps, but at night it is on the move, always hunting for slugs, fat beetles, and other insects. Consequently it may well be that its noisy hunt for prey as it goes poking its pointed snout into every hole and cranny frightens the rats and mice and drives them away, especially as the nocturnal prowler exhales a disagreeable odor calculated to betray its presence. Having neither the cat's light paw nor that animal's great patience in lying in wait for game, the hedgehog does not indulge in hunting rats; but if by good luck one falls into its clutches, it is accepted with delight, for the hedgehog's great feast is blood, freshly killed flesh. When I wish to give my two hedgehogs a special treat I throw them a bleeding beef liver or a chicken's entrails. Anything of that sort is eagerly devoured. Tastes so undisguisedly carnivorous tell you what must happen to a mouse caught by one of these animals. I attribute to them the disappearance of some nests of rats that used to trouble me.

"To satisfy its devouring hunger the hedgehog appears to attack all sorts of prey alike, even planting its teeth in a viper without any thought of the reptile's venom; and in still other respects the animal enjoys a remarkable immunity. You have seen the Spanish fly, that magnificent, strong-smelling insect that lives on ash trees and is distinguished by sheath wings of a superb golden green."

"Yes, I remember it," said Jules. "It is used for raising blisters after being dried and ground to powder."

"That is correct. If, then, this powder eats into the skin so readily, what effect ought it to have on the delicate lining of the stomach if introduced into that organ? What animal could swallow it without suffering torture and speedy death? Well, by an exception that I cannot undertake to explain, the hedgehog can feed on this horrible poison without the slightest apparent injury. A celebrated Russian naturalist, Pallas, has seen it make a meal on Spanish flies with no ill results. For a repast of that sort a stomach peculiarly constructed is certainly necessary.

"Once upon a time there was a king, very well known in history, named Mithridates. Being aware that he was surrounded by enemies capable of poisoning him some day, in order to obviate the danger he gradually accustomed himself to the most noxious drugs. By increasing the dose little by little he finally rendered himself immune against poison. The hedgehog is the Mithridates of the animal kingdom; but how far it surpasses the suspicious king! Without practice it dares swallow the poison of the Spanish fly and the viper's deadly venom.

"I like to believe that the hedgehog has not received these exceptional gifts only to leave them unused. It must delight to frequent the haunts of the viper; in its nocturnal rounds in the underbrush it must occasionally come upon the reptile in its retreat and crush its head with those pointed teeth that are so well adapted to such work. What service may it not render in localities infested with this dangerous breed! And yet man rages at the hedgehog, curses it most heartily, and treats it as an unclean beast of no use but to arouse the fury of dogs, which cannot attack it because of its spines. He subjects it to the torture of an ice-cold bath to make it unroll itself; and if the animal refuses to do so he prods it with a pointed stick, goads it, disembowels it."

"We will never meddle with hedgehogs, Uncle Paul," Jules assured him. "We are too much afraid of snakes to drive away this valiant defender."

"What are the hedgehog's spines?" asked Emile.

"Hairs, nothing else, but very coarse, and stiff, and pointed like needles. Together with other hairs, fine, soft, and silky, they cover all the upper part of the body. The under part has only a coat of soft hair; otherwise the animal would wound itself in rolling up into a ball. When the hedgehog scents danger—and it is a very wary beast—it ducks its head under its stomach, draws in its paws, and rolls itself into a ball, presenting everywhere an armor of spines to the enemy. The fox has long been famous for its many ruses; the hedgehog has only one, but it is always effective. Who would dare grapple with the creature when it has assumed its attitude of defense? The dog refuses; after a few luckless essays that make its mouth bleed it declines to go further and contents itself with barking. Sheltered under the safe cover of its spines, the hedgehog turns a deaf ear to these futile threats and remains quiet.

"But if the dog, urged on by its master, returns to the charge, the hedgehog has recourse to a last expedient of war which rarely fails of effect: it discharges its strongly offensive urine, which flows from the inside of the ball and wets the outside. Repelled by the unbearable odor of the ill-smelling beast and pricked on the nose by its spines, even the most eager dog now abandons the attack. The enemy gone, the hedgehog slowly unrolls itself and trots off to some safe retreat."

HIBERNATION

"OUR BATS," continued Uncle Paul, "live exclusively on insects, and these constitute the hedgehog's chief food, but it also hunts larger game or even eats fruit. In winter there are no longer any plump insects to be had, most of them having died after laying their eggs, and the few surviving ones having taken refuge from the cold in hiding-places where they would be very hard to find. The larvæ, too, the hope of future generations, are lying torpid, far out of sight under the ground, in the trunks of old trees, snugly hidden away. The white worm has bored several feet into the ground to escape the frost, there are no more June-bugs for the long-eared owl, no more night-flying moths, and no more beetles for the hedgehog. What, then, is to become of these insect-eaters?"

"They will die of hunger," answered Jules.

"They would indeed all die, were it not for the providential arrangement I am now going to try to make you understand.

"You know the proverb, 'He who sleeps dines,'—a very true proverb in its simple statement of an undeniable fact. Well, the hedgehog, the bat, and other animals put the principle into practice with a wisdom quite equal to that of man. Not being able to dine, for want of insects, they go to sleep; and so deep and heavy is their sleep that to designate it we use a special word, lethargy.

"Another proverb says, 'As you make your bed, so must you lie.' Our dumb animals, never lacking in wisdom in ordering their own affairs, take good care not to forget this proverb, but to adopt wise precautions before abandoning themselves to their long winter sleep. The hedgehog chooses for itself a secure retreat amid the great roots of some old tree stump. Toward the end of the autumn it carries grass and dry leaves to deposit there, and arranges them in a hollow ball, in the middle of which it rolls itself up and goes to sleep. Bats assemble in great numbers in the warm depths of some cavern where nothing can disturb their slumbers. Heads down and bodies packed close together, they hug the walls, covering them with a sort of velvet tapestry; or, clinging to one another, they hang in bunches from the roof. Now the winter may do its worst and the winds may rage; the hedgehog in its warm blanket of leaves and the bats in their sheltered caves sleep a deep sleep until summer returns and with it insects, food, animation, life."

"But don't they eat anything all winter long?" asked Emile, incredulously.

"Nothing whatever," his uncle assured him.

"Then bats and hedgehogs must have a secret. For my part, I eat more in the winter than at any other time, and no amount of sleep would satisfy my hunger."

"Yes, the bat and the hedgehog have a secret in this matter. I am going to tell you this secret, but it is a little hard to understand, I warn you.

"There is one need before which hunger and thirst are silent, however great they may be; a need that is never satisfied, and is always making itself felt, whether we wake or sleep, by night, by day, every hour, every minute. It is the need of air. Air is so essential to the maintenance of life that it has not been left to us to regulate its use as we do in regard to food and drink; and this is so in order that we may not be exposed to the fatal consequences that would follow the slightest forgetfulness. Therefore it is with little or no consciousness on our part and independently of our will that air gains entrance into our body to do its marvelous work there. On air more than on anything else do we live, our daily bread coming only second in the order of importance. Our need of food is felt at only tolerably long intervals; our need of air is felt unceasingly, always imperious, always inexorable. Let any one try for a moment to prevent its admission into the body by closing the entrance passages, the mouth and the nostrils; almost immediately he is suffocated and feels that he would surely die if this state were prolonged a little. And what is true of man is true of all forms of animal life: air is necessary to them all, from the smallest to the greatest.

"What I am going to tell you now will explain this absolute necessity for air for the maintenance of life. Man and also every animal of a superior organization—a classification that includes mammals and birds—have a temperature of their own, a degree of bodily heat peculiar to them, a heat resulting from no external conditions, but from the functions of life alone. Whether under a burning sun or in the freezing cold of winter, whether subjected to the torrid heat of the equator or to the glacial climate of the poles, man's body has a temperature of thirty-eight degrees, centigrade, and cannot be lowered without danger of death. The natural heat of birds attains forty-two degrees in all seasons and in all climates.

"How is it that this heat is always the same, and whence can it come unless from some sort of combustion? There is, in fact, going on within us a perpetual combustion, respiration furnishing the necessary air, and food supplying the fuel. To live is to consume oneself, in the strictest sense of the word; to breathe is to burn. In a figurative sense man has long used the expression 'the torch of life'; but this figurative term proves to be the exact utterance of the truth. Air consumes the torch; it consumes the animal no less; it makes the torch give out heat and light, and it produces in the animal heat and motion. Without air the torch goes out; without air the animal dies. From this point of view the animal may be compared to a highly perfected machine put in motion by heat. It feeds and breathes to produce heat and motion; it receives its fuel in the form of food and burns it in the inmost recesses of its body with the help of the air introduced by breathing. That explains why the need of food is greater in winter than in summer, the body cooling off more rapidly by contact with the outside cold air, and consequently an increased consumption of fuel being required to maintain the normal temperature. A low temperature creates a desire for food; a high temperature lessens the demand. To the hungry Siberians hearty food is necessary; they ask for bacon and other fats, with brandy to drink. But for the people of Sahara a few dates suffice, with a pinch of flour kneaded in the palm of the hand with a little water. Everything that lessens the loss of heat lessens also the need of food. Sleep, rest, warm clothing, all serve to some extent as substitutes for food. And so there is much truth in the saying that he who sleeps dines."

"That may be," Jules assented, "but I don't see how hedgehogs and bats can do without food for four or five months at a time. No matter how soundly I might sleep, I couldn't go without eating so long as that."

"Wait until I finish, and for the present remember this: in every animal life depends on an actual and never-ceasing combustion. Air, as necessary to this combustion as to the burning of wood or coal in our stoves and fireplaces, is taken into the body by breathing. That is what makes breathing so urgent, so incessant. As to the fuel burned, that is furnished by the substance of the animal itself, by the blood made from digested food. Not a finger is lifted by us, not a muscle moved, that does not use up just so much of the fuel furnished by the blood, which itself is made by the food we eat. Walking, running, working, excitement, all forms of exercise or emotion—these literally burn up our blood just as a locomotive burns its coal in dragging behind it the immense weight of a train. That is why activity, hard work, increases our need for food, while rest, idleness, lessens it.

"I will now put to you a question. Let us suppose that there are on the hearth some burning brands, but that they are few and small, and you wish to keep the fire as long as possible. Would you let these firebrands burn freely? Would you take the bellows and blow air on them to increase the blaze?"

"No," replied Jules; "that would be just the way to burn up the brands in no time. They must be covered with ashes. If the air comes to them very slowly and only a little at a time, they will burn gradually and the next morning we shall find the coals still alive."

"That is well said, my boy. To keep up a fire for a long time with a given amount of fuel, the draft must be reduced, the access of air must be largely cut off, but not intercepted altogether, because then the fire would be completely extinguished. Therefore the live coals are buried under ashes, and if the fire is in a stove the door of the ash-pit is nearly closed. With plenty of air, combustion is active but of short duration; with only a little air it is feeble, but lasts a long time.

"As the maintenance of life is the result of a real combustion, any animal obliged to endure a long fast, or in other words to dispense with the regular renewal of the fuel needed in that combustion, must take into its body as little air as possible. It must reduce the draft of its furnace. This draft is respiration, breathing; and so, in order to go without food for months at a time and to make the small amount of fuel held in reserve in the veins last as long as possible, the animal has but one course to follow: it must breathe as little as it can without depriving itself entirely of air, for that would mean the total extinction of the vital spark, just as the complete cutting off of air from a lighted lamp means the speedy extinction of its flame. There you have the hedgehog's and the bat's secret for enduring their long fast through the winter season.

"First of all, every precaution is taken to avoid all loss, all unnecessary expenditure of heat, and to economize as much as possible the reserves of fuel in their poor little veins. The hedgehog wraps itself up warm in a thick blanket of leaves in the heart of a stone-heap or in some hollow tree trunk, while the bats collect in compact groups in the warm shelter of a deep cave. But that is not enough: they must keep quite still, as every movement uses up a certain amount of heat. This requirement is scrupulously observed: their immobility is such that you would say they were dead. And yet all this is still insufficient: respiration must be reduced to a minimum. In fact, their breathing is so weak that the closest scrutiny can hardly detect that they breathe at all. This faint remnant of life is not to be compared, you can well see, to the blazing torch or the brightly burning fire, both of which, enjoying free combustion, send out waves of heat and light. It is rather the feeble glimmer of a night lamp husbanding its last drop of oil; it is the coal that glows faintly under the ashes. So profound is the torpor, so nearly complete the inanition, that were it not followed by an awakening this state would hardly differ in any respect from death.

"The name 'hibernation' is given to this temporary suspension of vitality, or rather this slowing up of life, to which certain animals are subject during the winter. In the number of hibernating animals, or animals that indulge in this long winter sleep, are to be included, besides the hedgehog and the bat, the marmot, the dormouse, the lizard, serpents of various kinds, frogs, and other reptiles. Do you need to be told that in order to assume and maintain this torpid condition in which for whole months food is unnecessary, a special organization is required? Not every creature can hold its breath at will and thus escape the necessity of eating. The dog and the cat might sleep ever so deeply, yet as their breathing would go on almost as actively as in their waking hours, hunger would arouse them before long."

"Just as it would me," said Emile.

"No animals that have an assured supply of food for the winter hibernate, but those that would otherwise perish with hunger in cold weather are saved from destruction by the providential torpor that overtakes them at the approach of the winter season. Their food supply being cut off, they go to sleep. The marmot is wrapped in slumber while the turf on the high mountains is covered with snow; the dormouse when there is no longer any fruit; frogs, toads, snakes, lizards, bats, and hedgehogs, as soon as there cease to be any more insects to feed upon."

CHAPTER IX

THE MOLE

UNCLE PAUL had just trapped a mole that for some days had been uprooting young vegetables and unearthing newly planted seeds in a corner of the garden. He called the children's attention to the animal's black coat, softer than the finest velvet; showed them its snout and made them note its peculiar fitness for digging; pointed to its fore paws, shaped like wide shovels for moving the earth with astonishing rapidity; and remarked on its eyes, so small as to be well-nigh useless, and its jaws armed with savage-looking teeth.

"It is a great pity," said he, "that we are prejudiced against the mole on account of its habit of mining, for there is not in all the world a more pitiless destroyer of vermin."

"I had always heard," Louis remarked, "and had believed until now, that moles lived on a vegetable diet, chiefly of roots, and that they tunneled under the ground to get them."

"To forewarn you of the errors so widely current on the subject of the diet of certain animals, I described to you in some detail the formation of teeth, which always indicate the kind of food eaten. I showed you that one has only to examine an animal's teeth in order to determine whether it is carnivorous or herbivorous. Remember the adage that summed up our talks on the subject: Show me its teeth and I will tell you what the animal eats.

"The mole is a good illustration: it has forty-four sharply pointed teeth, not including the incisors. Do they look like millstones for the leisurely grinding of grain and roots, or sharp tools for making mincemeat of torn flesh?"

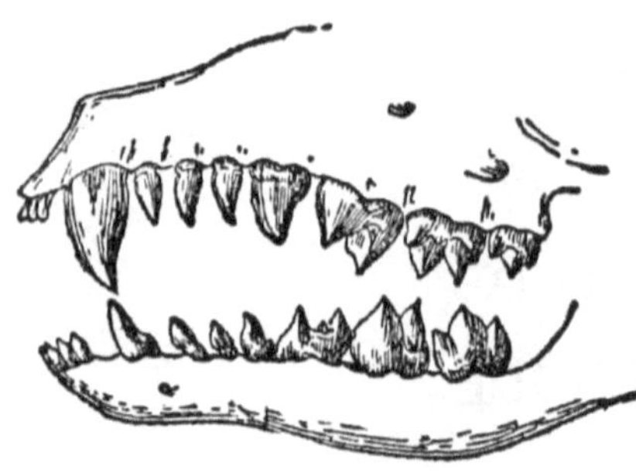

Jaws and Teeth of a Mole

"They are certainly the teeth of an animal that lives on prey," Louis admitted; "the hedgehog and the bat haven't sharper ones."

"To make you sure of this fact," Uncle Paul went on, "I will tell you about some experiments made on the diet of moles. We owe them to a learned French naturalist, Flourens. If after you are grown up you ever have a chance to read his remarkable works, you will find them very interesting and valuable.

"Flourens put two live moles into a cask and, believing them to be herbivorous, gave them for food a supply of roots, carrots, and turnips. As you see, the illustrious naturalist shared the accepted opinion, the false notion just repeated by Louis. But Flourens was soon undeceived. The next morning the vegetables were found untouched, while one of the moles had been devoured by its companion and there was nothing left of it but the skin, turned inside out."

"One of the moles had eaten the other?" cried Emile. "Oh, what a fierce creature!"

"It had feasted on its own kind, a thing that hardly any other animal does. In devouring its comrade it had in the course of the night eaten its own weight of food; and yet the next morning it seemed restless and very hungry. Flourens threw it a live sparrow whose wings he had just clipped. The mole smelt it, walked around it, received a few hard pecks from its beak, then, pouncing on the bird, tore its stomach open and enlarged the opening with its claws so as to plunge its head into the midst of the entrails. With its pointed snout the horrible creature bored into them with frantic delight. In less than no time it had devoured half the contents of the skin, which with its feathers was left whole. Flourens then lowered into the cask a glass full of

Mole

water and saw the mole stand up against the glass, cling to the edge with its fore claws, and drink eagerly. When it had had enough, the animal returned to the sparrow, ate a little more of it, and finally, completely full, lay down to sleep in a corner. The glass and the remains of the bird were then taken out of the cask.

"Hardly six hours later the mole, hungry again, began to smell around the bottom of the cask in search of something to eat. A second sparrow was thrown to it. The mole immediately tore open the stomach to get at its entrails. When it had eaten most of the bird and taken another big drink of water, it appeared satisfied and remained quiet. This was its last meal for the day. Just think, boys, what a quantity of reeking flesh it took to satisfy one mole's hunger! In the night its companion in captivity, and the next day two sparrows! The weight of the food eaten in twenty-four hours was nearly twice that of the eater.

"Was the animal satisfied for long? By no means. The next morning the mole was wandering restlessly about in the bottom of its cask, apparently wild with hunger. Food, quick, quick! or it will die of starvation. The remains of the sparrow left over from the evening before, with a frog which it promptly disemboweled, quieted it for a while. Finally, a toad was thrown to it. As soon as the mole approached to rip it up the toad inflated its body, hoping perhaps to frighten the enemy with its repulsive appearance. At any rate, it succeeded. After sniffing at it, the mole turned away in disgust. Ah! you don't want the toad, you greedy creature; then you shall have turnips, cabbages, and carrots. Plenty of these were given it. But fie on roots! Rather perish than eat turnips! The next morning the mole was found to have starved to death amid the vegetables. It had scorned to touch them with so much as a tooth.

"Had this animal an exceptional appetite, a taste for unusual things, that it should have preferred to die of hunger rather than touch vegetable food? Not at all; it merely followed the preferences of all its kind. Many other experiments have been performed both by Flourens and by other observers. All the moles they have tried to feed with vegetable substances—with bread, lettuce, cabbages, roots, herbage of any description—have starved to death without touching their provisions. On the other hand, those that were fed with raw flesh, worms, larvæ, and insects of various kinds, remained alive.

"Another very simple way to determine positively the kind of food eaten by this animal is to examine the contents of its stomach as it lives in the freedom of its customary haunts. Everything eaten by it must find its way to the stomach. Let us catch a mole, cut it open, and investigate. The stomach is found to contain, sometimes, red pieces of common earthworms, or it may be a pap of beetles, recognizable from the scaly remains that have not been digested; or still again, and rather oftener, we find a marmalade of larvæ, especially the larvæ of June-bugs—undigested bits of mandibles and the hard shell of the skull. In short, one is likely to come upon a mixed hash of all the small creatures inhabiting the soil, such as wood-lice, mil-lipeds, cutworms, moths in the chrysalis state, caterpillars, and subterranean nymphs; but no matter how carefully we search we cannot find a bit of vegetable matter.

"All possible observation points to the same conclusion: despite what is believed by so many it is certain that the mole's diet is confined to animal substances. And could it, I ask you, be otherwise? Would the stomach's contents belie the savage set of teeth you have just seen in the picture? Do not its teeth show that it is a flesh-eater?

"Yes, the mole eats flesh and nothing else; everything proves this. Besides, remember its big appetite, if one may call appetite the raging demands of a stomach that in twelve hours requires a quantity of food equal to the weight of the animal. The mole's existence is a gluttonous frenzy. This frenzy seizes the creature three or four times a day, and it dies of starvation if it has to go without food for more than a few hours. To satisfy its appetite, when its food melts away and disappears almost as soon as swallowed, what can the mole count on? Live sparrows, which it devoured with such zest in the experiments of Flourens, are evidently not for a hunter that burrows underground; at most, some stray frog, found in the field, may fall into its clutches. What, then, is left for it to count on? The larvæ buried underground, and especially those of the June-bug, tender and fat as bacon. That is very little, I admit, for such hunger; but the number to be had will make up for the smallness of the prey. What a slaughter of white worms must take place when the soil abounds in this small game! Scarcely is one meal finished when another begins, and each time, no doubt, other small insects are eaten by the dozen. To free a field of these destroyers of our crops there is no helper equal to the mole.

"A valued destroyer of vermin—that is what we defend when we take the mole's part and give to it, even if somewhat reluctantly, the honorable title of helper. That title, in truth, it only partly deserves. To catch the crickets, the larvæ, the white worms, and the insects of all kinds that it feeds on, the mole is obliged to disturb the roots amid which its prey is to be found. Many that interfere with it in its work are cut; plants have their roots laid bare and are even uprooted altogether; and, finally, the earth dug up by this untiring miner is piled on the surface in little mounds or mole-hills. With such upturning of the soil a field of vegetables may be speedily ruined and a crop of grain badly damaged. One night is enough for a mole to undermine a large tract; for the famished creature is singularly quick in boring the soil where it hopes to find something to eat.

"It is well equipped for making its underground galleries, which often are hundreds of meters long. The body is stubby and almost cylindrical from one end to the other, so as to slip with the least resistance through the narrow passages bored by the animal. The fur is short, thick, and carefully curried so that it shall not catch the dust and may be kept perfectly clean even in the most dusty soil. The tail is very short and the external ears are wanting, although the hearing is remarkably acute. Ears like those of animals that live in the open, would be in the way underground; in the mole they are made very tiny, for the animal's greater convenience. No luxurious outfit does it ask for, but only what is strictly necessary for its work of mining. Eyes wide open so that the dirt could get into them would be a perpetual torment to the creature; and, besides, what use could it make of them in the total darkness of its abode? The mole is not exactly blind, as is generally believed; it has two eyes, but these are very small and set so deep in the surrounding fur that they can be of little use. It is guided by the sense of smell, in which it rivals the pig; and like the pig it has a snout of the right shape for digging up a toothsome morsel. With its snout the pig finds and roots out the savory titbit buried in the ground; the mole in like manner discovers and digs up the plump white worm. To reach it amid a network of roots and under a considerable thickness of soil, the animal has its fore paws, which spread out like large strong hands with exceptionally tough nails. These hands—stout shovels which, if need be, can open a passage through tufa, a soft sort of rock—are the mole's principal tools. As the animal advances, digging with its snout and clearing away with its hands, the earth is thrown to the rear by its hind feet, which are much weaker than the hands but strong enough for the far lighter task. If the mole proposes to return by the same road, the track must be kept clear; accordingly, the earth dug up is thrown outside to form mole-hills at intervals.

"For the present these details will suffice. Now let us take up the much-discussed question of the mole's usefulness. Should we, considering the undoubted services it renders us, let it live in our fields, or ought we rather, on account of its destructive digging, to look upon it as an enemy and wage war on it? Most people seem to feel we should make war on it—war to the death. Some persons make it a practice to destroy every mole they find and there is small pity bestowed upon the little creature unearthed by the spade. But I should like to remind the mole's pitiless enemies that insects do far worse damage, and that for ridding a field of insects nothing is equal to this bloodthirsty hunter. Notwithstanding all opinion to the contrary, I believe that moles in moderate numbers are needed in a field, that it is unwise to destroy them all. Indeed, experience has proved this. I know of regions where the moles have been hunted down and destroyed until not one was left. Now, do you know what was the result? The white worms multiplied so that they ate up everything in the fields. To get rid of the worms it was necessary to let the moles come back and to let them stay so long as they did not become too numerous.

"And there is something else to be said for the mole. Molehills are formed of well-worked earth which, when spread about with the rake, is very good for young grass. Further, the creature's subterranean galleries serve as drains for keeping the soil in a sanitary condition, letting off the extra water just as regular drains would do. On the whole, then, after weighing the arguments on both sides, I am of the opinion that the mole ought not to be banished from our fields unless it multiplies to excess."

"And how about gardens?" queried Louis.

"That is another question. In a few hours a mole can almost ruin a garden. Who would want such a digger among his growing vegetables? You carefully sow your seeds, set out your young plants, even off the ground, and make water-channels; the very next morning—plague take the creature! it has turned everything topsy-turvy. Quick, a spade, a trap, and let us get rid of the pest as soon as possible! Suppose, however, that cutworms and other destructive vermin abound; shall we gain anything by killing the mole? Certainly not. The insects will speedily do more harm than the mole has just wrought; greater mischief is in store, and that is all there is about it. If I had a garden infested with destructive insects, here is what I should do. In the spring I should let loose in my garden half a dozen moles taken alive in the field, and I should then leave them to pursue their hunting in peace. Their work done, the ground cleaned, I should take the moles away."

"You can catch them whenever you want to?" asked Louis.

"Nothing easier. You shall see for yourself."

CHAPTER X

THE MOLE'S NEST—THE SHREW-MOUSE

"ALL THAT you know of the mole's labors is confined to the little mounds of earth, the mole-hills, that it throws up, and the tunnels, of greater or less extent, that it bores just beneath the surface of the soil. These tunnels are hunting-trails, made by the animal in order to search amid the roots for the larvæ it lives on. If the ground is full of game, the mole halts there, probing to right and left, wherever it smells a grub. If the spot is a poor one it prolongs the tunnel or bores fresh ones hither and thither, in every direction, until it finds a place to suit it. But, however abundant the larvæ may be, one vein is soon exhausted, whereupon the old diggings are abandoned and fresh ones undertaken from day to day.

"Near its hunting-ground, thus honeycombed with a succession of tunnels as called for, the mole has a burrow, a fixed abode, to which it retires to rest, sleep, and rear its young. This burrow is a work of art, a strong castle, in the making of which the cautious animal uses great skill, with a view to the utmost possible security. You must not think I am talking about the mole-hills, which are merely the dirt thrown out in the digging. The mole is never to be found lurking beneath these crumbling hillocks.

"Its dwelling is something quite different. It is underground at a depth of nearly a meter, usually beneath a hedge, or at the foot of a wall, or amid the big roots of some great tree. This natural shelter makes it strong so that it will not cave in. Its main part is a chamber (*c*) shaped somewhat like an inverted bottle, carefully rough-coated with loam and made smooth on the inside. It

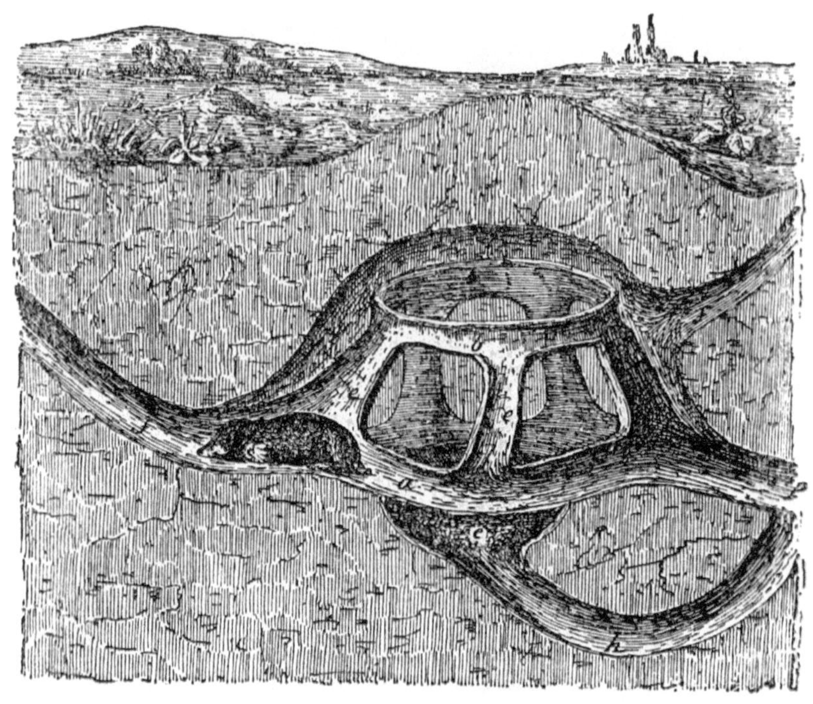

Mole's Burrow

is furnished with a warm bed of moss and dry grass. That is the mole's resting-place, its bedroom, the family nest. Two circular tunnels run around it at a distance: the lower one (*a*) larger, the upper one (*b*) of lesser diameter. They serve as sentry-posts for the safeguarding of the main chamber. Stationed in the upper tunnel, which is reached by three passages leading from the large chamber, the mole listens to what is going on outside. If some danger threatens, half a dozen exits are provided for speedy descent to the lower tunnel, whence there are numerous outlets for instant flight. These lead in all directions, but soon bend back and into the main passage (*p*). If danger overtakes the mole in its inmost retreat (*c*), it escapes by the tunnel (*h*) which leads out from below, winds around, and rejoins the main passage (*p*)."

"I get lost in all those tunnels and passages," said Emile. "The mole's house is very complicated."

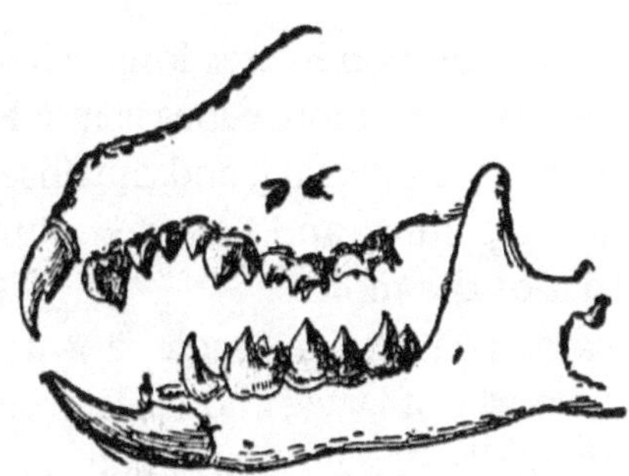

Jaws and Teeth of a Shrew-mouse

"For us, perhaps, but not for the mole. It knows every twist and turn of these winding tunnels, and can get away at very short notice. You think you can catch it in its home, but in a twinkling it is gone and you don't know in what direction.

"The passages for flight, both those that go in all directions from the lower circular tunnel and those that run straight from the chamber, all lead finally into the passage marked *p*, the entrance-way to the mole's abode; and this passage is the main one between the large chamber and the hunting-ground, the permanent highway over which the mole passes to and fro three or four times a day—in fact every time it goes on an expedition or returns home. This passage, meant to last as long as the dwelling remains in use, is much more carefully made than the simple burrows bored from day to day as the mole seeks its food: it is deeper down, wider, smooth and well beaten; no mole-hill is over it; its covering of earth is solid. Yet something betrays it to the searcher's eye. On account of the mole's incessant comings and goings the roots of any plants growing there are more injured than are those over the ordinary tunnels made by the animal; consequently, the grass has an unhealthy, yellowish look. Once this passage is known—and the strip of yellow grass points it out—the mole can be caught at any time. A trap is set inside the tunnel. Obliged to pass through either to get out or to come in, the mole cannot fail to be taken sooner or later."

"That is plain enough," said Louis. "I see now how easy it would be to catch moles again whenever you want to after they have been let loose in a garden to rid it of insects."

"To conclude my account of insectivorous animals," Uncle Paul went on, "I will now tell you about the very smallest of mammals, a tiny creature not more than two inches long. This cunning little animal looks somewhat like a mouse, but is much smaller. The tail is shorter, the head more tapering, and the nose ends in a sharper point. The ears are short and rounded. But the coat is almost the same as that of the mouse.

"The shrew-mouse has the same tastes as the mole: it is an ardent hunter of small game, a devourer of larvæ and insects, as you can see by its finely serrate teeth. Its slender body, made for squeezing into the smallest hole, and its long snout, shaped for prying into the narrowest crannies and crevices, enable it to go wherever vermin may be lurking. Woe to the wood-louse rolled up like a tiny pellet in some crack in the wall, and to the slug hiding under a stone! The shrew-mouse will have no difficulty in catching them, being so small that it could make its home in a nutshell. It will not help them to hide, for the shrew-mouse does not need to see them in order to find them. It detects them by its subtle sense of smell, and hears them if they make the slightest movement. The burrows of the beetles, the warrens of the larvæ, the lurking-places of the tiniest worms hold no secrets from the shrew-mouse. It might be appropriately called the insects' ferret.

"These little creatures are to be found in fields and meadows and gardens, and in winter they come near our houses and make their nests under straw-stacks and dung-heaps. In very cold weather they even find their way into stables, where they live on cockroaches and wood-lice; but at the approach of summer they are off again to the open fields, where they complete the mole's work of extermination. Or they may seek some garden, where they protect the wall-fruit and the vegetable patches from the devouring insect hordes without ever touching any of the growing crops themselves. The teeth of the shrew-mouse are not made for the chewing of vegetable food; like the mole, this tiny creature is carnivorous. Moreover, in their hunting-raids, which are so greatly to our advantage, shrew-mice never do us the slightest injury of any sort, as they never bore tunnels, but merely

SHREW-MOUSE

use the natural cracks in the soil. They cannot be reproached with severing roots or throwing up mounds of earth, as moles do; and yet they are perhaps more an object of general execration than the latter. It is considered a praiseworthy act to crush them every time one gets a chance.

"How has so tiny, pleasing, and useful a creature managed thus to incur the hatred of man? We have here, my children, another instance of the foolish way we accept the first notion that enters our heads, without trying to test it by observation and reason. It is said that the shrew-mouse bites horses' feet and leaves incurable wounds. But how can a shrew-mouse, whose head is at most no larger than a pea, bite a horse and pierce its hide which is the thickness of a finger or more? Again, they say the shrew-mouse is venomous even for man. Some time ago, children, I told you about the viper.[2] You know what its weapons are,—two long, sharp teeth or fangs having little channels through which it introduces a drop of venom into the wound it inflicts. Well, I assure you the shrew-mouse has no weapon like the viper's; it has neither fangs nor a poison-sac, but is wholly harmless to man and horse. Insects alone need fear its fine teeth,—not that they are poisoned in any way, but because they crunch their little victims very neatly.

"I think I see why the shrew-mouse has incurred the charge of being venomous. The pretty little creature exhales an odor; it smells rather strongly of musk. The cat, taking it for a mouse, sometimes chases it, but, repelled by its odor, never eats it. The first to observe this fact said to himself: 'As the cat does not

2   See "The Story-Book of Science."

dare eat it the shrew-mouse must be venomous.' Ever since then this false belief has passed for truth in the country, and no one has taken the trouble to look into the matter more closely; so that the poor little shrew-mouse, one of our most useful and harmless helpers, falls a victim to the stupidity of man, whose gardens it protects."

CHAPTER XI

THE EXPLOIT OF ONE-EYED JOHN

IT HAPPENED one day that One-eyed John caught an owl in his corn-crib, and he had just nailed the live bird to his house door as a bandit of the worst kind, worthy to be exposed to the jeers of all who passed and to dry up on the spot so as to serve as a scarecrow.

John was very proud of his deed; he laughed at the click-clacking of the bird's beak, at the desperate rolling of the eyes as the owl hung there crucified. Its grimaces and contortions, the convulsive efforts of the wings to free themselves from the big nails that pierced them, and the fits of impotent rage expressed by the spasmodic working of the talons put him in the best of humors.

The children of the neighborhood, cruel and heartless as is usual at their age, and still more cruel when grown persons set the sad example, had gathered before the door and were joining in the laugh at the owl's sufferings. John told them that his neighbor, old Annette, had died two weeks before because the owl came three times in quick succession and hooted on the roof of the house.

"Those creatures," said he, "are bad-luck birds. At night they fly into churches and drink the oil out of the lamps; they perch on the roofs of sick people's houses and foretell their death; and they snuggle into a hole in the belfry and laugh when the bell tolls for a funeral."

All this of course frightened the children. "See," said the youngest, pressing close to his brother, "how the owl threatens us with its big red eyes; it must be awfully wicked."

"It's so ugly," said another, "let's hurt it. That will teach it to laugh when people die, and to drink oil out of the holy lamps. John, put its eyes out with this pointed stick, it looks at us so wickedly; and put this piece of glass in its claws so that it will cut its fingers."

And thus each one did what he could to harm the helpless creature; each tried to invent some new torture for it.

Just then Louis happened to come along, and the children called to him to join them in tormenting the owl. More merciful than his comrades, especially since he had fallen into the way of visiting Uncle Paul's house, Louis turned his eyes away from this frightful spectacle and begged John to end the bird's agony instead of making it suffer still further tortures. But the boy's entreaties were all in vain, and he went away much distressed.

As he was going home he recalled something Uncle Paul had said in one of his talks; he had told the boys that when the ignorant crowd agrees to call a thing black it is always well to see whether after all the thing may not be white.

"Here is One-eyed John," said Louis to himself, "One-eyed John, known all about here for his ignorance; he has never in his life opened a book, and he glories in the fact; he can't sign his name; and he rejects with mulish obstinacy every wise suggestion. At this very moment he is urging on the children against that poor owl he has just nailed to his door, and to make them think there is some reason why he should be so cruel he tells them it is a graveyard bird, a bad-luck bird that brings misfortune to people. According to his account the owl is an evil creature, full of malice, and deserves no pity. We must punish it for its wickedness, make it suffer torments as an example to others of its kind, and put it to death without mercy. But what if just the opposite of all this should be true? What if the owl were really a harmless creature or even a very useful one and worthy of our protection? I must find out."

Accordingly, that evening at Uncle Paul's this was the first thing he asked about. At Louis's description of the tortured owl Uncle Paul at once recognized its species.

"The bird that John thought he must nail alive to his door," said he, "is the belfry-owl, also called the barn-owl. The unfortunate creature in no way deserved the frightful treatment it received. I pity it for having fallen into hands made cruel by ignorance. Stupidity and malice go together, they say; and it is very true. He who is ignorant is deliberately cruel. Wild and foolish things are said against the barn-owl, and John repeated them. Having heard them from some one else, he now, in his turn, passes them on to the street urchins who were so eager to put out the bird's eyes. It is not true that the barn-owl flies into churches and drinks the oil from the lamp that is kept lighted night and day in the sanctuary; it is not true that it laughs when it hears the passing-bell; it is not true that its hooting on the roof of a house means that some one in the house will soon die. False are all the sayings about its evil influence and its predictions of misfortune, and any one who believes these absurd stories simply shows that he has no common sense. We are in God's hands, my children, and God alone knows when our last hour is to come. Let us pity those feeble-minded persons who believe the owl knows this tremendous secret; let us pity them, but never let us abuse our reasoning powers by believing that an owl, in expressing after its own fashion, on some house-roof, its satisfaction at having caught a mouse, is solemnly foretelling what is going to happen. Uncle Paul's nephews must henceforth pay not the slightest attention to any such superstitious notions. Let us go on.

"What would you say of John if he had taken it into his head to kill his cat by nailing the animal to the door by its fore paws?"

"I should say," answered Louis, "that if rats ever ate him up it would serve him right."

"What you saw him doing amounts to about the same thing: he was torturing one of the very best destroyers of mice, a bird in form, a cat in habits. The barn-owl went into the corn-crib to guard the poor man's wheat from rats, and John, a prey to superstitious hatred and never thinking of the service the owl was doing him, made haste to nail the useful bird to his door.

"What strange wrong-headedness is it that makes us all, as a rule, destroy the animals that help us most? Almost all our helpers are persecuted. Their good will must be very strong, else our ill treatment would long ago have driven them forever from our dwellings and fields. Bats rid us of a host of enemies, but none the less we look upon them with dislike. The mole and the shrew-mouse purge the soil of vermin, and we dislike them, too. The hedgehog makes war on vipers and white worms, and we make war on him. The owl and various other night-birds are fine rat-hunters, but that does not save them from mistreatment. Still other animals that I will tell you about later do the most useful work for us, and we persecute them all. They are ugly, people say, and for no other reason they are killed. But, blind slayers, shall you not at last have your eyes opened to the fact that because of an unreasonable dislike you have sacrificed your own defenders? You complain of rats—and you nail the owl to your door, where you let its carcass dry up, a hideous trophy! You complain of the white worms—and you crush the mole every time the spade brings one to light. You rip up the hedgehog and set your dogs on him just for fun. You complain of the ravages of moths in your granaries, and if a bat falls into your hands you seldom spare it. You complain, and yet you mistreat all the animals that offer to help you. Blind you are and sadly misguided in your wanton cruelty.

"Regarded merely as it affects his own interests, it is a pitiful piece of work that John has done, but it is far more pitiful in respect to the tortures he has inflicted on the bird. It is not the mark of a man but of a brute to take pleasure in torturing an animal. It is a wicked act and one that good men despise; ignorance is the cause of the act, but ignorance is not an excuse. If an animal is harmful to us, let us get rid of it by killing it, but let us never think of inflicting needless pain, of causing suffering simply for suffering's sake. That would be to smother in ourselves one of the noblest of sentiments, compassion; it would mean the arousing of savage instincts, which too often lead to crime.

He who finds his pleasure in torturing dumb animals cannot take pity on the suffering of his own kind; his heart is hardened and prone to evil. How I pity those poor children who stood by and laughed at the barn-owl's horrible sufferings, and who, led on by the man's example, helped to put out the wretched bird's eyes! How I pity them! Let them beware, let their parents take heed, for there is a bad streak in them."

CHAPTER XII

NOCTURNAL BIRDS OF PREY

"THE BARN-OWL, the horned owl, the gray owl, the white owl, and other similar birds are known under the general name of nocturnal birds of prey. They are called birds of prey because they live by hunting game of various sorts, especially such rodents as rats and mice. They are among birds what the cat is among mammals, untiring destroyers of those fur-covered creatures of which the mouse is the most familiar example to you. Our language has long since taken note of this resemblance in habits by coining the name *chat-huant*, which is applied to some of these birds. They are cats that fly, that hoot, or, in other words, that utter cries like mournful howls of distress. Also, they are nocturnal; that is, they remain during the day in some obscure hiding-place, which they leave only at nightfall to hunt in the twilight and moonlight.

"Their eyes are very large and round and are placed in the front of the head instead of one on each side. A wide ring of fine feathers encircles each eye. The need for these enormous eyes is plainly seen in the birds' nocturnal habits. Being obliged to seek their food in a very feeble light, they must, in order to see with any distinctness, have eyes that admit as much light as possible; that is, the eyes must be such as can open wide.

"But this development of the organs of sight, so useful in the night-time, is a serious inconvenience in the bright light of day. Dazzled, blinded by the sun's rays, the bird of darkness stays in some safe hole and dares not come out. If obliged to issue forth, it does so with extreme caution for fear of hurting itself. It wings its way with hesitation and in short slow flights. Other birds, birds of the day, seeing its uncertainty and awkward-ness, come and vie with one another in offering insults to the clumsy stranger. The redbreast and the tomtit are among the first to hasten to the scene, followed by the finch, the blackbird, the jay, the thrush, and many others. Perched on a branch, the night-bird receives the aggressors with a grotesque balancing of its body, turning its big head this way and that in a ridiculous manner and rolling its great eyes as if thinking thus to terrify its persecutors. But all in vain. The smallest and weakest are the boldest in tormenting it; they assault their victim with beak and claw, pulling out its feathers before the hapless bird can muster courage to defend itself."

"Just think," said Emile, "of a teasing tomtit and a saucy redbreast making sport of an owl blinded by the sun! Why do they behave so?"

"From motives of revenge. The owl loses no opportunity to gobble up those little birds in the night, and shows no more compunction over it than if they were nothing but common mice. Therefore what a frolic it is for the little winged people when by good luck the night-bird strays into the light of day! The pecks fall thick as hail on the sufferer's back, and it is nearly deafened with shrill screams of triumph and insulting cries of hatred. The redbreast pulls out a feather, the tomtit threatens the enemy's eyes, the jay overwhelms it with abuse. The whole grove is in an uproar. But beware when night closes in; then the boldest will lose courage. These same saucy little birds, that come in the daytime and insult the owl, flee from it in wild alarm as soon as darkness allows it to move about and use its powerful talons and hooked beak."

"The redbreast had better get out of the owl's way when the owl can see," said Emile; "it would pay dearly if it tried then to pull out a feather."

"On account of the great size of their eyes, nocturnal birds of prey require a soft light like that of dawn and nightfall. Con-sequently, they leave their lurking-places to hunt for prey either

BURROWING OWL

soon after sunset or just before dawn. Then it is that their raids are most likely to be successful, for they find the small animals either fast asleep or on the point of falling asleep. Moonlight nights are the best for their purposes; those are their nights of veritable joy and feasting, when they can hunt for hours at a time and lay in large supplies of choice provisions. But when there is no moon they have only one scant hour in the early morning and another in the evening for hunting. That means they must fast for hours and that is why they are so greedy when they can get as much food as they want."

"They are very silly to fast like that," Emile declared. "In their place I should hunt all night, even without a moon."

"You say that because you think the owl can see clearly in the blackest darkness. But you are mistaken. To see, we must not merely direct our gaze toward the object to be seen; we must receive into our eyes the light reflected from that object. In the act of seeing, nothing goes out from us; everything comes to us from the thing seen. We do not really throw our glance toward any given object; it is the object that throws its light toward us; or if it does not throw any light, it is for that reason invisible. What I am now saying about human beings applies to all animals. Not one, absolutely not one, can see in the absence of light."

"I had always thought," said Louis, "that cats could see in pitch-darkness."

"Others think so too, but they are much mistaken. The cat can no more distinguish objects, if light is totally lacking, than any other creature can. It has an advantage over us, I grant you: it has large eyes, the pupils of which it can contract and almost close when it finds itself exposed to a bright light that would otherwise dazzle it, or open wide to receive more of the feeble light diffused in a dark room. These large eyes enable it to find its way in places which to us, with our poorer sight, seem pitch-dark. But in reality the darkness is not complete where a cat can manage to see well enough for its purposes. If light is totally lacking, the cat may open its eyes as wide as possible, but it will see nothing, absolutely nothing. In this particular, nocturnal birds do not differ from the cat: their large eyes, made for seeing in a dim light, can see nothing whatever when the night is perfectly dark.

"Now let us follow the bird in its hunt. The night is a fine one for hunting; the air is calm, the moon shining. The hunt begins with a lugubrious war-cry. At that dreaded signal the tomtit hardly feels safe even in the deepest hollow of its tree, the redbreast trembles beneath its shelter of thick foliage, and the finch loses its head with fright. God of the weak, God of the little birds, protect them now! Make the owl, enraged as it still is from the insults of the day, miss them in its search! Blessed be Thy holy name if the rapacious bird turns in some other direction! It skirts the groves and skims over the open plain and the plowed fields. It inspects the furrows where the field-mouse crouches, the stretches of grass-land where the mole burrows, the tumble-down buildings in which rats and mice scamper to and fro. Its flight is silent, its soft wings cleaving the air without making the slightest sound to awaken its intended victims. This noiselessness of flight is due to the structure of the bird's feathers, which are soft as silk and of finest texture. Nothing gives warning of its sudden coming: the prey is seized even before it has suspected the nearness of the enemy. The owl, on the contrary, with its exceptional acuteness of hearing, is kept informed of all that is going on in the neighborhood, its large, deep ears detecting even the rustle of a field-mouse in the grass. If the mouse begins to nibble a rootlet or a grain of wheat, the bird hears the sound of its incisors and pounces on it immediately.

"The prey is seized by two strong claws warmly gloved in down as far as the roots of the nails. Each foot has four toes, three pointing habitually forward, and one backward; but, by a privilege peculiar to nocturnal birds of prey, one of the front toes is movable and can be turned back so that the set of talons is divided into two pairs of equal power whenever the bird wishes to grip, as in a vise, the branch on which it perches, or the victim struggling in its grasp. One blow of the beak breaks the head of the captured creature. This beak is short and very hooked. The two mandibles move with great ease, which enables them, in striking against each other, to give out a sharp rattling sound or clicking by which the bird expresses anger or fright. They stretch wide at the moment of swallowing, exposing a big opening leading into a very large gullet. When they are thus opened, the prey, which has already been kneaded into a compact mass between the claws, disappears entirely as if swallowed up by an abyss. All goes down, including bones and hair. Not a trace is left of the field-mouse, not even its coat of fur. But a single victim is seldom enough, and so the hunt continues. More mice follow the first one, and all are first killed by a peck on the head, all are swallowed whole. If the bird chances upon a fat beetle, he does not disdain it. It is a small mouthful, to be sure, but highly flavored with spices that will aid digestion. At last, having eaten all it possibly can, the owl returns to its lodging in the hollow of some rock, or in a decayed tree trunk, or in some ruined building.

"Now follows digestion. Motionless in the quiet of its peaceful solitude, the bird gently closes its eyes to dream of the fine exploits it has just achieved and to plan others for the following night. Its slumbers are deep and long. In the meantime the stomach does its work. The food swallowed without any preparation or sorting must be divided into two parts, that which is really nutritious and that which is worthless. With the aid of its gastric juice the stomach carefully separates the bones and skins from the nutritious part of its contents. The flesh thus made semifluid disappears, to be converted into blood, and a confused mass remains, composed of skins turned inside out and wearing all their fur, bones as clean as if they had been scraped with a knife, and the hard wing-covers of beetles. This bulky mass could not be passed on by the stomach without danger. How then will the bird get rid of it? Let us watch and find out. Ah, the owl is waking up! Grotesque heavings of the body denote trouble within. The disturbance increases, something ascends through the outstretched neck, the beak opens, and it is all over: there drops to the ground a ball containing skins, bones, scales, fur, feathers—in fact, the entire mass of indigestible matter.

"All nocturnal birds of prey practise this undignified method of freeing the stomach: they throw up in a ball the rejected remnants of what they have swallowed whole. If you ever find yourself near an owl's retreat, examine the ground beneath it: the balls of little bones and hair will tell you from how many mice and other rodents of all kinds these birds deliver us."

"I have seen some of those balls near a rock all white with bird-dung," said Louis.

"Some owl certainly lived there. It was responsible for the dung and the balls of refuse that you saw."

CHAPTER XIII

RATS

"LET US return for a moment to the rodents, the habitual prey of the night-birds. You do not know them all, by any means, but we ought not to pass them by; for if some, like the hare and the rabbit, are useful to us, still more are very destructive. You remember those two pairs of incisors, so long and sharp, that I told you about when I described the rabbit's teeth. All rodents have similar incisors. To keep them sharp and prevent them from overlapping too much by growing too long, which would make it impossible for the animal to feed itself, the rodent must wear them down by constant friction as fast as they grow. Consequently, these terrible incisors have, so to speak, no rest; they must always be nibbling something, no matter what. Thus the harm they do us is much greater than you would suspect from the size of the animal. How much actual food does a mouse need for one meal? Very little, unquestionably. A mouse is so small that a single nut will fill its stomach. Don't think, however, that one day's ravages are confined to that one nut. After the nut is eaten, the animal will proceed, perhaps, to gnaw a hole in a bag, reduce a piece of cloth to tatters, chew up a book, or drill a hole in a board, simply and solely to whet its teeth. And the damage caused by rats and mice in our dwelling-houses is matched by other damage caused by other rodents in the fields. You must make the acquaintance of all these destroyers."

"For my part," Jules confessed, "I shouldn't, if I saw it, know the field-mouse that you told us about in your talk on night-birds."

"I know rats and mice such as we have in the house," said Emile, "but that's all."

NORWAY OR BROWN RAT
(One-third natural size)

"And yet," rejoined his uncle, "I very much doubt whether you have any real knowledge of the rat. I will begin with it.

"The common or black rat is more than twice the size of a mouse. Its coat is nearly black above, and ashy gray underneath. It lives in granaries, thatched roofs, and abandoned ruins. If it fails to find a lodging to its taste, it burrows a hole for itself. It is not a native with us, but is thought to have come from Asia in the wake of the armies returning from the Crusades. To-day the common rat is seldom mentioned in our country; another foreign rodent has come in, the Norway or brown rat, which, being larger than the common rat, has waged war against it and almost wiped out the species. We have not gained by the exchange; quite the contrary, the Norway rat being a much more troublesome creature. The true rat, the black rat, is rare now, especially where the other abounds; and that is why I doubt that any one of you is familiar with it. What you call a rat is more than likely to be one of these Norwegian invaders. Don't forget the color—black—and you will have no difficulty in recognizing the true rat.

"The mouse is much more familiar to you. It has been known from the earliest times all over the world. Need I describe this little rodent, so well known for its liveliness, its wily nature, and its extreme timidity, which makes it scuttle away to its hole at the slightest alarm?"

"We all know the mouse very well," Jules assured him.

"The Norway or brown rat, also known as the sewer-rat, is the largest and most troublesome of all European rats. It attains a length of nearly a foot, without counting the tail, which is scaly like the mouse's and a little shorter than the body. The largest and strongest Norway rat can cope with a cat. Its presence in Europe dates only from the middle of the eighteenth century, and it seems to have been brought from India in the hold of ships, which it commonly infests. It has now spread all over the world. Its coat is reddish brown above and ashy gray underneath.

"Norway rats frequent storehouses, cellars, sewers, slaughter-houses, and dumping grounds. Everything is food to these filthy and audacious creatures, and they even dare to attack a sleeping man. In large towns they multiply so fast as to cause serious alarm. The vicinity of the slaughter-house of Montfaucon in Paris is so undermined with their innumerable burrows that the buildings there are in danger of collapsing. To preserve them from this disaster it is necessary to protect their foundation against the attacks of the rodents by means of a deep enclosing belt of broken glass bottles."

"What attracts them in such numbers to these places?" asked Jules.

"The abundance of food, the dead bodies of slaughtered horses. In one night, if left in the slaughter-house yards, dead horses are devoured to the skeleton. During severe frosts if the skin is not removed in time the Norway rats get inside the body, stay there, and eat all the flesh, so that when a thaw comes and the workmen begin to skin the animal, they find inside the skin nothing but a host of rats swarming among the bare bones."

"But don't the people there have any cats to protect them?" asked Emile.

"Cats! The Norway rats would eat them alive, my boy, in no time. They have something better, however—dogs, both terriers and bulldogs, that run the rats down in the sewers with astonishing cleverness and break their back with one bite. The bulldog—that's the kind of cat you need for such mice. This hunt in the sewer, moreover, must be frequently repeated, for Norway rats multiply with frightful rapidity, and if we were not careful the town would sooner or later be endangered; the horrible creature, strong in its numbers, would devour all Paris. In December of the year 1849 two hundred and fifty thousand rats were destroyed in a few days as the result of a single hunt.

"In the country the Norway rat frequents the banks of foul streams; it enters kitchens through sink-holes; it gets into hen-houses and rabbit-warrens by undermining the walls. It haunts cellars and stables, but rarely makes its way into high granaries, doubtless because of its liking for filthy drainage and any kind of offal, which can be found only on ground floors and in basements. It pounces upon eggs and young fowls, and even has the boldness to suck the blood of full-grown poultry and rabbits. When it cannot get animal food, which is its first choice, it will eat grain and vegetables of all kinds. No sort of food is rejected by this filthy glutton. To get rid of it you can hardly count on the cat, for usually pussy is afraid to attack it. Nor are night-birds strong enough to battle with it, except the eagle-owl, which does not abound in any numbers. The trap and poison are our only remaining means of overcoming this redoubtable foe.

"The field-mouse is a little larger than the ordinary mouse. Its coat, which closely resembles that of the Norway rat, is reddish brown above and white underneath. Its eyes are large and prominent, its ears nearly black, and its feet white. Its tail, which is very long, like that of the common mouse, is thinly covered with hair and is black toward the end. The field-mouse frequents woods, hedges, fields, and gardens. It cuts down the stalks of grain to get at the ears, of which it nibbles a few kernels and wastefully scatters the rest. In its quest for food it unearths newly planted seeds, takes a taste of the young shoots that have just come up, gnaws the bark of shrubs, and feasts on growing vegetables. Its ravages are all the more serious because it lays up provisions against a time of need. In storage chambers more than a foot underground, beneath some tree trunk or rock, it collects grain, hazelnuts, acorns, almonds, and chestnuts, often going a considerable distance to get them. One such store-room is not enough; it must have several, for it has a way of foolishly forgetting where its treasure is buried. In winter the field-mouse ventures to approach our houses and makes its way into our cellars where fruit and vegetables are kept, or it establishes itself in great numbers in our granaries.

"The dwarf rat or harvest-mouse is the smallest rodent

HARVEST MOUSE AND NEST

of France. It is a graceful creature, smaller than the common mouse, and of a yellowish tawny color, which is brighter on the rump than elsewhere; but the belly, breast, and throat are a beautiful white, and the tail and feet a light yellow. The ears, which stand out but very little beyond the fur of the head, are rounded and hairy, and the eyes are prominent. The dwarf rat lives exclusively in grain-fields and feeds on grain. After the harvest it takes refuge in the stacks of grain, especially in oat-stacks, but is never bold enough to enter houses. I am telling you about this pretty little rodent not so much because I begrudge it the few grains of oats it steals from us as because I wish to acquaint you with its nest.

"Other rats rear their young either in a hole in a rock or a wall or in a burrow dug for the purpose. The harvest-mouse, however, scorns these stifling quarters; it must have an aërial nest like that built by birds. So it brings together several wheat-stalks as they stand in the field, interlaces them with bits of straw, and builds, half-way up from the ground, a nest as beautifully made as any bird's. This nest is spherical, interwoven with leaves on the outside and padded with moss on the inside. It has only one little side opening, through which the rain cannot enter. Suspended at the height of several feet on the flexible support of the grain stalks, it swings to and fro with the slightest wind."

"How, then," asked Emile, "does the little mouse manage to get in and out of its nest?"

"It climbs up one of the stalks, being so small that this serves it perfectly as a ladder."

"If I ever come across a harvest-mouse I sha'n't have the heart to do it any harm. It may go on eating oats in its pretty little nest, for all I care; I sha'n't try to stop it."

"Here," concluded Uncle Paul, "I will end my account of the chief representatives of the rat family in these regions. They are five in number: the black rat, the mouse, the Norway rat, the field-mouse, and the harvest-mouse."

CHAPTER XIV

MEADOW-MICE[3]—HAMSTERS— DORMICE

"A NOTHER KIND of rodent now calls for our attention: it is the family of meadow-mice, commonly confounded with rats. Meadow-mice are easily recognized by their short, slightly hairy tail.

"The meadow-mouse is about as large as a common mouse. Its coat is of a yellowish hue mixed with gray above and dirty white underneath. The tail is only one-quarter as long as the body. The eyes are large and prominent, the ears rounded, hairy, and standing out but little from the fur. The head is large and less pointed than that of the ordinary mouse.

"In its rapid and abundant breeding the meadow-mouse is one of the farmer's chief foes. It overruns grain-fields especially, cutting down the stalks to nibble the ears. After harvest it attacks clover roots, carrots, potatoes, and the products in general of our kitchen-gardens. In winter it digs under the furrows to eat the seeds sown there. If the soil is so frost-bound as not to permit it to reach the buried seed, it retires to the stacks of grain, where it does great damage. It never makes its way into our dwellings. Meadow-mice appear to emigrate from one country to another in colonies when the country they have ravaged can no longer supply them with food; at any rate, from time to time, once or twice in a decade, they suddenly appear in countless droves that are a real scourge to the country visited. The best destroyers

3   The French *campagnol* is translated in this book by *meadow-mouse*. The term *vole*, another rendering, is purely British and too uncommon in America to warrant its use in these pages.—*Translator.*

of these creatures are nocturnal birds of prey, as is proved by the presence of their skulls, bones, and skins in the balls that are thrown up by these birds after digestion. Some say diurnal birds of prey, buzzards in particular, are equally fond of them. It is not at all uncommon to find in a buzzard's crop as many as ten or more meadow-mice.

"The underground meadow-mouse is much less common in France than the one just described, from which it differs in its gray-and-blackish coat, its somewhat smaller tail, and its tiny eyes. But the greatest difference is in its habits. The first-mentioned lives in the fields, especially in grain-fields, while the second frequents meadows and kitchen-gardens. It feeds on various kinds of vegetables, such as celery, artichokes, carrots, potatoes, and cardoons. It seldom shows itself out of its underground tunnels, and on account of its habit of lurking beneath the surface it is called the underground meadow-mouse.

"The amphibian meadow-mouse is commonly known by the name of water-rat. We can easily tell it from the black rat, which is of about the same size, by its red coat, its short tail (which is not quite half the length of its body), and its larger and less pointed head. It burrows under the banks of streams, ditches, and marshes, where it feeds chiefly on roots, but does not disdain small fish when it can catch them. It is a good swimmer and diver. Sometimes it makes its way into kitchen-gardens, where it does the same sort of harm as the underground meadow-mouse, and into orchards, where it gnaws the base of young trees.

LEMMING

"The lemming is never seen around here. It frequents the coasts of the Arctic Ocean in Norway and Lapland. I will tell you something about it on account of its curious way of traveling from one country to another, of which our meadow-mouse offers us a far less striking example. The lemming, with its very short and hairy tail, its big head, and its stocky body, has the appearance of a small rabbit. Its coat is red marbled with black and brown.

"At the approach of severe cold weather, and sometimes with no apparent reason, the lemmings leave their haunts in the high mountain chains of Norway and set out on a long journey toward the sea. The emigrating horde, composed of myriads of individuals, trot in a straight line over all obstacles, never allowing themselves to be turned from their course. In traveling in a line, one after another, says Linnæus, the great Swedish naturalist, they trace straight parallel furrows, two or three fingers deep and several ells apart. They devour everything eatable that obstructs their passage, all roots and herbage. Nothing turns them from their course. Let a man appear in their path, and they slip between his legs. If they come to a haystack they gnaw a tunnel through it; reaching a rock, they skirt it in a semicircle and then resume their original direction. Should a lake be encountered on their route, they swim across it in a straight line, however wide it may be. If a boat is in their way in the middle of a body of water, they clamber over it and jump into the water again on the other side. A swiftly flowing river does not stop them: they plunge into the foaming current even if they all perish."

"They must be very obstinate," said Emile, "to prefer to drown rather than turn their procession out of a straight line."

"Animals sometimes show these examples of obstinacy, which we cannot understand, but which might easily be explained if we knew the motives that make them act thus. Perhaps by deviating from a straight line the lemmings might lose their way, a way provided with no finger-posts, but indicated simply by instinct. However, we will leave them to pursue their long pilgrimage, from which few will return, so numerous are the dangers and the enemies awaiting them on the way. Let them cross their

HAMSTER

rivers and lakes while we return to the rodents of France.

"The hamster abounds in central Europe, notably in Alsace. It is also called the Strasbourg marmot or rye pig. It is almost as large as the black rat, but is more stocky. Its tail is short and hairy, its fur red on the back, black under the belly, with yellowish spots on the flanks, a white spot on the throat, and another on each shoulder.

"Hamsters live on roots, fruit, and especially cereals, of which they store up a large supply. Each animal digs a burrow composed of several rooms, the largest of which is used as a granary. There they store rye and wheat, beans and peas, vetch and linseed. The hamster hoards like a miser, laying up far more than it will ever need, simply for the satisfaction of hoarding. In some of its store-rooms as much as two hundredweight of provisions may be found. What can a creature no bigger than your fist do with all these supplies? Winter comes, and the hamster shuts itself up in its underground quarters, assured of food and lodging, and grows big and fat. If the cold is very severe it goes to sleep like the marmot."

"And what about the two hundredweight of grain collected, a kernel at a time?" queried Emile.

"The whole supply simply spoils and is so much waste; but little does the hamster care; he begins all over again the next year. The animal's special business is, first and foremost, to ravage fields, as is proved by the pile of grain it stores up, out of all proportion to its needs. It hoards food to destroy it, far more than to be sure of something to eat, being very different in this way from most hibernating animals. In the midst of all its stores of food, if the winter is very cold, it is overtaken by the same torpor that saves the hedgehog and the bat from death by starvation. This miser has not even the excuse of want. Happy are those regions that it does not rob! Let us pass on to other rodents."

"There are, then, still more of these greedy animals?" Jules inquired.

"Yes; they are somewhat like insects: after they are all gone there are still some left. The world seems to be a pasture delivered over to the mandibles of larvæ and the incisors of rodents.

"Dormice, of many varieties, live in the woods and orchards and eat fruit. These rodents have the agility, elegance of form, and rich fur of squirrels. They make their home in hollow tree trunks, holes in walls, and crannies in rocks. During the winter, when fruit is lacking, they remain in a deep sleep.

"The dormouse proper is found in Provence and Roussillon. It is a pretty creature, reminding one of the squirrel. Its tail is long and thickly covered with hair; its fur ashy brown on the back and whitish under the belly. At night it ravages the fruit trees, and no one knows better how to pick out the pear, the peach, or the plum at just the right stage of ripeness. You have, let us suppose, looked over your fruit with satisfaction and decided to give it one more day of sunshine to bring it to perfection. The next morning you go out to gather the harvest and, lo and behold, it is gone; the dormouse has been there before you.

DORMOUSE

"The garden dormouse is smaller, being about as large as the black rat. Its coat is a pleasing mixture of red, white, and black, the back being red, the belly, paws, cheeks, and shoulders white, and the parts about the eyes and down the sides of the neck black. This animal is scattered all over France. It lurks about dwellings, in gardens, and among vines and shrubbery, living chiefly on fruit, which it ruins in great quantities, tasting first one choice specimen and then another, without finishing any of them. Garden dormice spend the winter several in one hole, where they sleep all curled up amid the supplies of walnuts, almonds, and hazelnuts that they have laid up."

"Then if they sleep," said Emile, "they don't need any food."

"Pardon me, my boy; they do need food, and badly, though not while sleeping, but when they wake up. This awakening takes place at the beginning of spring, when the sun is first warming up the earth. At that time of year there is no fruit to be had; and the garden dormice, after their fast of several months, have a tremendous appetite, as you can easily imagine. What would become of them now, poor little things, if it were not for their supply of nuts?"

"Those little dormice are very prudent," Emile remarked. "They know that at the end of their long winter's sleep they won't find any fruit in the orchards, and so they lay up provisions beforehand. But why don't they put by apples and pears if they are so fond of them?"

"Because apples and pears would spoil, whereas almonds and hazelnuts keep very well."

"That's so. I hadn't thought of that, but the little dormouse had."

"No, it does not think of it, either. It does not know that pears spoil and nuts keep, because it has never tried to keep pears. It does not foresee that when it wakes up, the fruit trees will not be bearing fruit, will hardly have their first leaves; it does not know how long it would have to wait to find a pear to nibble; it knows nothing of all these things, which it is now about to become aware of, perhaps for the first time, through experience. Some one else thinks for the dormouse and gives it the prudence to store up nuts in a hole in the wall; some one who understands, foresees, and knows everything. And that some one is God, the Father of the man who plants the pear-tree, and Father also of the little dormouse that is so fond of pears."

CHAPTER XV

HORNED OWLS

"WE HAVE glanced in a cursory way at a number of our rodents that are harmful to crops. I pass over in silence the pretty squirrel, a lover of walnuts and beechnuts, and the industrious beaver, an animal which may still be found, here and there, along the Rhone. The hare and the rabbit, too, I willingly give over to the hunter's rifle. What protection have we from the devouring hunger of the others—the rats, the field-mice, and the meadow-mice? How are we to hold them in check? In our homes we have the cat; outside we have the army of feathered cats—the nocturnal birds of prey. I will divide these latter into two classes, to make it easier to distinguish the various species. One has the head adorned with two tufts of feathers—plumicorns is the term sometimes used—while the other class lacks this ornament. Horned owls come under the first classification; hornless owls, or those that may be called simply owls, come under the second.

"The largest of the horned owls is the eagle-owl. 'It can easily be recognized,' says Buffon, 'by its burly form, its enormous head, its large and cavernous ears, the two egrets surmounting its head to a height of more than two inches and a half, its short hooked beak, black in color, its great clear eyes with their fixed gaze and large black pupils, encircled by an orange-colored ruff of feathers, and its face surrounded by hairs—or, rather, little rudimentary white feathers bordering a ring of other little feathers that are curled—also by its black hooked claws of great strength, its very short neck, its reddish brown plumage spotted with black and yellow on the back, its feet covered with thick down and reddish feathers to the very roots of the nails, and, finally, its hair-raising cry of *whee-hoo, hoo-hoo, hoo-hoo, poo-hoo,* which it sends forth in the silence of the night when all the rest of the world is still. Then it is that it awakens its intended victims, fills them with vague alarm, pursues and catches them, and carries them off to the caverns where it has its hiding-place. It lives among the rocks or in old deserted towers in the mountains, rarely descend-

AMERICAN LONG-EARED OWL

ing into the plains and never willingly perching on trees, but rather on the roof of some sequestered church or ancient castle. Its favorite prey consists of young hares, little rabbits, field-mice, and rats, of which it digests the fleshy substance and throws up the hair, bones, and skin in round balls. The eagle-owl makes its nest in some rocky cave or in a hole in some lofty old wall. Its nest is nearly three feet in diameter, and is made of small dry branches interwoven with flexible roots and padded with leaves inside. Only one or two, or rarely as many as three, eggs are found in this nest. In color they somewhat resemble the bird's plumage, and in size they are larger than hens' eggs.' "

"Those two things like horns that the eagle-owl has on its head—are they ears?" asked Emile.

"No, my boy, they are egrets, upstanding feathers that give the bird a warlike appearance. Its ears are not visible, being hidden by the plumage. They are very large and deep, which explains why the eagle-owl's hearing is so wonderfully acute."

"The eagle-owl," Louis here observed, "eats field-mice and

rats, for which it is to be thanked; but it also eats young hares and young rabbits. Isn't that a pity?"

"For the hunter, I admit; but for the farmer it is quite another thing. Don't forget that the hare and the rabbit belong to the order of rodents; they have incisors which spare nothing in the fields. If they were left to breed in peace they would prove a serious menace to our crops. History tells of countries so ravaged by rabbits that it became necessary to send an army to help the inhabitants get rid of them. We shall never reach that condition, I am sure; but it is no cause for regret that the eagle-owl, jointly with the hunter, keeps the animals within tolerable bounds. Moreover, the bird is very scarce everywhere. One pair of these birds in a year is the most that you will find in the mountains about here. An extensive hunting-ground is required by such big eaters if they are not to starve one another out.

"I have a more serious complaint to bring against the eagle-owl: when it cannot find its favorite game—meadow-mice, field-mice, and rats—it contents itself with bats, snakes, toads, lizards, and frogs, and thus deprives us of some of our best protectors. Be assured, once for all, that while we have some irreproachable helpers, there are also others that from our point of view are guilty of a good many misdeeds. Bear in mind the mole, which throws up the earth and cuts the roots of plants in its war on insects. No animal gives a moment's thought to man—except the dog, who is our friend even more than he is our servant. No other pays any heed to our interests; all work for themselves and their young. If their instinct prompts them to destroy only species harmful to us, so much the better: they are excellent helpers; but if they hunt both harmful and helpful species, we must balance the total good against the total harm that they do. If the good tips the scale, let us respect the animal: it is a helper. If it does more harm than good, let us declare war on the creature: it is a ravager. The eagle-owl catches in the fields such formidable hoarders of grain as field-mice and hamsters; in gardens, dormice and other lovers of fruit; in the neighborhood of our houses, ordinary mice and rats, and even the horrible Norway rat. There you have the plea for the defendant. On the other hand, the hunter charges the bird with killing a certain number of young rabbits incautiously taking a taste or two of wild thyme by moonlight, and with appropriating a few young hares that would otherwise be eaten by human beings. For my part, I accuse it of feeding its young on the serviceable toad, the useful snake, and the cricket-eating lizard. There you have the prosecutor's charge. But, the balance being struck, the bird's services are found to outweigh its misdeeds, and I declare that the eagle-owl deserves well of the farmer."

"It is a unanimous verdict," declared Jules.

"The common horned owl, or lesser eagle-owl," Uncle Paul continued, "is much like the bird we have been discussing, only it is far smaller, being very little larger than a crow, while the other is the size of a goose. It is the commonest of all the nocturnal birds of prey in these regions. In the night hours throughout the summer it keeps repeating, in melancholy accents, its long-drawn and doleful cry of *cloo-cloo*, which can be heard a long way off. Just as it takes flight it gives a sort of bitter sigh, made no doubt by the air expelled from its lungs by the effort of the wings at the moment of flying off. In the daytime, confronted by human beings, this bird wears a dazed and foolish expression. It snaps its beak, stamps its feet, and moves its big head abruptly up and down and from side to side. If attacked by too strong an enemy, it lies down on its back and threatens its foe with claws and beak. It inhabits ruined buildings, caves in rocks, and the hollow trunks of old trees. Seldom does it take the trouble to build a nest of its own, preferring to patch up one that has been deserted by a magpie or a buzzard. There it lays four or five round white eggs. I will remark in passing that the eggs of nocturnal birds of prey are not oval like hens' eggs, but more nearly round. The hunting habits of the horned owl are like those of the eagle-owl: it has the same liking for rodents such as field-mice, rats, ordinary mice, and meadow-mice; it pounces upon young rabbits in the same manner, after patiently watching for them at the mouth of the burrow. Now let us pass on to another species.

"The short-horned owl, or large sparrow-owl, resembles the lesser eagle-owl in plumage and size. The two egrets or plumicorns are very short, and they seldom stand erect as in the two preceding species. Because of the shortness of these 'horns,' the large sparrow-

Virginia Horned Owl

owl is often taken for a hornless owl. This species is seldom seen near dwelling-houses, preferring rocks, quarries, and ruined and solitary castles. It builds no nest, but is content to lay in a hole in some wall or rock two or three white eggs, shiny and round, and about as large as pigeons' eggs. Its usual cry is *goo*, uttered rather softly; but if rain is coming the cry is changed to *goyoo*. Its diet is mostly confined to field-mice and meadow-mice.

"The red owl is of about the blackbird's size. Its plumage is ashy gray mottled with red and marked with little flecks of black running lengthwise and fine gray lines running around the body. It is the smallest and prettiest of our nocturnal birds of prey. When its fine egrets stand up well on the forehead they give it a bold and martial air that goes well with its eagerness for the chase."

"In the picture," Emile pointed out, "its horns are standing up."

"When the bird is in one of its peaceful moments; there is nothing to arouse it, nothing to attract its attention. It will withdraw into itself and is thinking of the fine feast it had when it last went hunting. It is digesting that feast. But let a mouse come and scratch anywhere near, and the red owl immediately ruffles its forehead—the first sign of attention. It straightens up and spreads out its egrets—a sign of the closest possible attention. It has heard, it has understood. Off darts the bird and the mouse is caught.

"The smaller rodents are its delight. It seasons them with beetles and June-bugs—especially the latter which are an aid to digestion. When larger game is lacking it contents itself with a frugal meal of insects, hoping to make up for it soon with a good dinner of meadow-mice.

"Red owls are great travelers. They assemble in companies, sometimes to migrate for the winter and seek a warmer clime, sometimes to search out a district where there is plenty of game, when their present haunts no longer offer enough to suffice them. If field-mice are on the increase in some particular region and are ravaging the fields of grain and hay, the red owls hear of it, I don't know how. They spread the glad tidings, all club together, and start for the lands where feasting awaits them. With such zeal do they apply themselves to the work of extermination that in a few weeks the fields are cleared of the infesting hordes.

"Red owls nest in hollow trees and clefts in rocks. Their eggs, from two to four in a nest, are of a shiny white."

CHAPTER XVI

OTHER OWLS

"**O**WLS NOT belonging to the horned class lack, of course, the egrets or plumicorns characteristic of the latter. The largest of the hornless owls is the howlet or tawny owl, which is about as large as one of our domestic hens. The predominating color of its plumage is grayish in the male and reddish in the female, a difference that sometimes causes them to be mistaken for separate species. On this background color is a sprinkling of light brown spots, running lengthwise of the body and less numerous on the breast and stomach than elsewhere. The wings are marked with several large, white, round spots. The head is very large and nearly round, the face sunken in the surrounding feathers and partly concealed by them. The eyes, likewise sunken, are brown and surrounded with small gray feathers.

"The name howlet is connected in its derivation with the word howl, and the bird called by that name is indeed remarkable for its cry, not unlike a wolf's howl. When at the close of a somber winter day the wind whips the snow and moans in the trees, one may often hear a frightful cry, prolonged and mournful, rising from the dark depths of the forest—*hoo-hoo, hoo-hoo, hoo-hoo.* Then in the lonely cottage the frightened mother makes the sign of the cross, while her little ones press close to her, crying, and saying, 'The wolves are coming.' Don't be uneasy, good people; it is not a wolf, it is an owl *hoo-hooing,* sounding its war-cry from the top of some hollow oak and getting ready for its nightly rounds.

"In summer-time the howlet lives in the woods. It hunts by preference field-mice and meadow-mice, which it swallows whole, afterward throwing up the skin and bones rolled into a ball. The little birds that worry it so unmercifully in the daytime, whenever they get a chance to come upon it unawares in the sunlight, are not safe from its beak in the hours of darkness if the night-bird can pounce upon them after first frightening them with its terrible *hoo-hoo*. Keep as still as mice in your hiding-places, you finches and red-

Gnome-owl with Captured Mouse

breasts and tomtits, and don't betray yourselves by giving voice to your alarm. Let the owl *hoo-hoo* as much as it pleases. If you make a sound you are lost.

"If the fields prove disappointing as a hunting-ground, the owl makes bold to approach dwelling-houses and finds its way into barns, there to play the part of cat and thus make good the title of 'hooting cat' which has been given it. For patience and skill in catching rats and mice it rivals Raminagrobis[4] himself. It is a guest to be treated with respect when hunger compels it to visit our granaries. After completing its nightly rounds it returns to the woods early in the morning, hides in the densest thickets or in the trees having the most abundant foliage, and there passes the day silent and motionless. In winter its home is always in the hollow of some old tree trunk. It lays its eggs in the abandoned nests of magpies, crows, buzzards, and kestrels; and these eggs, of a dingy gray color, are about as large as a pullet's, but nearly round.

"The belfry-owl, also known as the barn-owl, is an ungainly

4   A name given to the cat in La Fontaine's "Fables."—*Translator.*

bird rather smaller than the howlet. Its plumage, however, is not wanting in elegance, being red on the back, sprinkled with gray and brown and prettily dotted with white points alternating with dark ones, and white underneath, with or without brown spots. The eyes are deep-set and each is encircled by a ring of fine white feathers almost like hair. A little collar bordered with red frames the face. The beak is whitish, and the claws are covered only with a soft white down, very short, under which the pink flesh can be seen. This bird has none of the proud bearing of the eagle-owl and the red owl; it carries itself awkwardly with an embarrassed, almost shamefaced look. Humpbacked and with wings hanging down, face sad and scowling, and legs long and ungainly—such is the barn-owl's appearance in repose. As if to complete its ungraceful attitude, the bird, whenever anything disturbs it, teeters from side to side in a ludicrous fashion, with haggard eyes and wings slightly raised."

"And what is the teetering for?" asked Jules.

"No doubt to frighten its enemy. In time of danger the barn-owl utters a harsh, grating cry—*craa! craa! craa!*—which often frightens away the enemy. The owl's habitual cry in the silence of the night is a mournful, heavy breathing not unlike the snoring of a man sleeping with his mouth open. To these cries add the darkness of the night, the near neighborhood of churches and cemeteries, and you will understand how the innocent barn-owl has managed to frighten children, women, and even men; you will be able to see why it has the reputation of being a funeral bird, the bird of death, summoning to the cemetery one of the persons living in the house it visits. The French name, *effraie* (fright), has reference to these superstitious terrors; it designates the bird that frightens with its nightly chant those who are foolish enough to believe in ghosts and sorcerers."

"It may practise its chant on our roof as much as it likes," Jules declared boldly; "it won't scare me a bit."

"Nor would it scare any one else if everybody would listen to reason instead of putting faith in ridiculous stories. Fear, like cruelty, is the daughter of ignorance. Train your reason, accustom yourselves to see things as they really are, and foolish fears will be banished.

"The barn-owl also goes by the name of belfry-owl, because it likes to make its home in old church towers. Sometimes it will enter a church by night to hunt mice. Those who first came upon the ill-famed bird near the altar did not fail to accuse it of drinking oil from the lamp or, rather, of eating it when it is congealed by the cold. The charge itself proves its own falsity, as oil cannot congeal in a lamp that is always kept burning. But the slanderers do not trouble themselves about a little thing like that when they wish to blacken the bird's reputation. They will continue for a long time, if not forever, to regard the owl as a profaner of holy lamps. In Provence they will always call this bird the oil-drinker.

"In reality, the barn-owl lives on rats and mice, which it catches in barns and churches; on field-mice, meadow-mice, and dormice, which it hunts in gardens and fields. Here, beyond a doubt, we have a service rendered that ought to make people forget its false reputation, make them like and protect it as it deserves. Will the bird that gives us very real help and is guiltless of a single offense ever be declared innocent? I very much doubt it. Superstition is so deep-rooted that there will never be lacking a One-eyed John to nail a live owl to his door.

"The barn-owl likes to live in inhabited regions. The roofs of churches, summits of steeples, high towers—these are its favorite haunts. All day it remains crouching in some dark hole, from which it does not come out until after sunset. Its manner of taking flight deserves mention. First it lets itself fall from the summit of its steeple like a dead weight, and it does not spread its wings until after a rather long vertical drop. It then pursues a zigzag course, making no more noise than if the wind bore it along. It is fond of nesting in abandoned ruins, in the hollow trunks of worm-eaten trees, occasionally in barns, high up on some beam. But it builds no nest to hold its eggs, which are laid on the spot that may have been selected, with no leaves, roots, or hair to serve as bedding. The laying takes place toward the end of March and is limited to five or six white eggs remarkable for their oval shape, an exceptional shape for nocturnal birds of prey. The little ones, with their large eyes, beak stretched open for food, and rumpled down, are the ugliest creatures imaginable. The mother feeds them with insects and bits of mouse-flesh.

"The smallest of our hornless owls is the sparrow-owl. Like the red owl, it is about the size of a blackbird. It is dark brown in color, with large white spots of a round or oval shape. The throat is white, and the tail is crossed by four narrow whitish stripes. The sparrow-owl has a quick and light bearing, and it sees by day much better than other night birds; therefore it sometimes chases small birds, but rarely with success. When it has the good luck to catch one it plucks it very clean before eating it, instead of following the gluttonous example of the horned owls and the howlet, which swallow such prey whole and throw the feathers up later. Its hunting expeditions are much more fruitful when directed against field-mice and common mice, which it dismembers before eating. Other owls make but one mouthful of their prey; the sparrow-owl tears to pieces the animal it has caught, perhaps so that it may enjoy the flavor more. To express astonishment, surprise, fear, the barn-owl waddles in a most ridiculous manner; but the sparrow-owl adopts another method: it bows its legs, crouches down, and then abruptly rises, lengthening its neck and turning its head to right and left. You would say it was moved by springs from within. This performance is repeated over and over again, each time accompanied by a clacking of the beak. In flight the bird's habitual cry is *poo, poo, poo*; at rest it says *ay-may, aid-may*, repeated several times in quick succession in a tone almost human.

"The sparrow-owl lives in deserted buildings, quarries, old

and dilapidated towers, but never in hollow trees. It frequents the roofs of churches and of village houses. Its nest consists of a hole in a rock or a wall, where it lays four or five round white eggs somewhat speckled with red."

CHAPTER XVII

THE EAGLE

"IF IT were my purpose to give you a systematic and scientific account of birds, instead of acquainting you with the various species useful to agriculture, I ought to have begun with birds that hunt by day and to have postponed my talks on those that hunt by night; in other words, the eagle, the falcon, and the hawk should have been described first. But should you ask me why, I should be rather at a loss for a satisfactory answer. For want of a better let us content ourselves with this one: the first do their work by day, the second at night. But the eagle and the others of that group live at our expense, while the horned owl and its kind render us a great service by holding in check what would else be a disastrous multiplication of rodents. Consequently, in point of usefulness, the night-bird comes first.

"But this is contrary to all usage, both scientific and popular, which puts the eagle first in the list of birds. Do we not say of the eagle that it is the king of birds? Why has this title been given to the fierce bandit, the murderer of lambs? I should be puzzled to answer this question did I not know man's inclination to glorify brute strength even though he himself may be its victim. You, my children, will find that out only too soon, to your sorrow. Plunder on a grand scale appeals, alas, to something in our faulty human nature that makes us excuse it; nay, more, that makes us glorify it; whereas productive toil, useful to all, leaves us cold or even disdainful. The falcon is a ravisher of our hen-houses, a bloodthirsty marauder of our dove-cotes; and we hold it in high esteem, calling it a noble bird. Shall we, then, never learn to judge animals and men by their true worth, their real usefulness? Let us hope that as so many fine minds have worked, are working, and always will work to bring about this miracle, you, my children, will some day follow their example. Work for this end with all your power, and blessings be upon you if you succeed in giving some additional strength, however little it may be, to this common effort put forth by all men of light and leading.

"I shall discuss but briefly the birds of prey whose activities are confined to the daylight hours. They are nearly all bandits, noth-

GOLDEN EAGLE

ing else, living at our cost by robbery and murder. From the fact that they hunt by day, never at night, they are called diurnal or day birds of prey. The brightest light does not dazzle them. It is even said of the eagle and others of this class that they can look straight at the sun, and this is credited to them as an added title of nobility. But there is no great merit in this performance when once you know how they shade their eyes in accomplishing it. They have three eyelids to each eye: first, two like ours, an upper and a lower, which close in sleep, and then a third, which is semi-transparent and is withdrawn completely into the corner of the eye when the bird has no use for it, but when needed comes out from under the other two, which remain open, and serves as a curtain. If the light is too bright or the bird wishes to look toward the sun, it has merely to draw over the eye this third eyelid, this eye-shade, through the semi-transparency of which the rays of light enter the pupil in a much subdued intensity. There you have the whole secret of the eagle's bold look in facing the sun."

"I could do as much if I shaded my eyes with a curtain," Emile declared.

"All these birds are furnished with a very strong beak having hooked mandibles for dismembering their prey. Their claws are composed of four separate talons to each foot, three of these talons pointing forward and one backward. The talons are long, recurved, and grooved on the under side, the grooves having sharp edges that they may the better cut into flesh. The eagle's bearing is bold, its looks stern, and its flight marvelously powerful. Eagles like to circle about in the air, to soar with scarcely a movement of the wings in the upper regions of the atmosphere beyond our view. Nevertheless, even from this immense height they can distinguish what is taking place on the earth's surface below. They explore every farm with their piercing eyes and inspect every poultry-yard. Let a suitable prey show itself, and instantly the bird swoops down with whistling wing, faster than lead would fall. The unwary fowl is snatched from under the farmer's very eyes.

"Fortunately, the eagle, the chief of these bandits, is a very rare bird. In form it is large, measuring a meter and more from the tip of the beak to the tip of the tail, and it is covered with brown plumage. Its extended wings measure a span of nearly three meters. Its fierce eye, overshadowed by a very prominent eyebrow, glows with a somber fire. The eagle's nest is known as its aery, and is flat instead of bowl-shaped like other birds' nests. It is a sort of solid floor made of interwoven twigs and covered with a bed of rushes and heather. It is commonly placed on the face of some steep and forbidding precipice and between two rocks, the upper one of which overhangs and forms a kind of roof for the nest. The eggs, two in number—sometimes, though rarely, three—are of a dingy white spotted with red. The young eaglets are so greedy that at the time of their rearing the aery is strewn with bits of bleeding flesh. Some neighboring ledge of rock serves the parents as slaughter-house and cutting-up bench. It is there that the hares and rabbits, partridges and ducks, lambs and kids, seized in the plains and carried in rapid flight to the lofty heights where the eagle makes its home, are torn to pieces in order to be fed to the ever-hungry eaglets.”

“Is the eagle really strong enough,” asked Emile, “to carry off a lamb like that? I had heard it, but couldn’t believe it.”

BALD EAGLE

“Nothing is less open to doubt,” his uncle assured him. “It would carry you off if it found you alone in the mountains.”

“I could defend myself with a stick.”

“Possibly; but let me tell you an incident, one of many to be found in the pages of an author whose word we may believe.

“Two little girls, one five years old, the other three, were playing together when a medium-sized eagle suddenly swooped down upon the elder and despite her companion’s cries, and in the very face of some workmen who came hurrying to the spot, snatched her up into the air. Two months later a shepherd found, on a rock half a league distant, the body of the child half devoured and dried up.

“What do you think now of the eagle, the king of birds?”

“I think it’s a brigand of the worst kind,” affirmed Jules.

“Would you like to see an eagle in the act of hunting, witness its fierce joy when it buries its hooked talons in the quivering flesh of its prey? Then listen to this fine passage from the pen of that ardent lover of birds, Audubon. The scene is laid far from here, in America, and the eagle belongs to a different species from ours; but never mind, the ways of these bandits are the same everywhere.

“ ‘To give you some idea of the nature of this bird, permit me to place you on the Mississippi, on which you may float gently along, while approaching winter brings millions of water-fowl on whistling wings, from the countries of the north, to seek a milder climate in which to sojourn for a season. The Eagle is seen perched in an erect attitude, on the highest summit of the tallest tree by the margin of the broad stream. His glistening but stern eye looks over the vast expanse. He listens attentively to every sound that comes to his quick ear from afar, glancing now and then on the earth beneath, lest even the light tread of the fawn may pass unheard. His mate is perched on the opposite side, and should all be tranquil and silent, warns him by a cry to continue being patient. At this well known call, the male partly opens his broad wings, inclines his body a little downwards, and answers to her voice in tones not unlike the laugh of a maniac. The next moment, he resumes his erect attitude, and again all around is silent. Ducks of many species, the Teal, the Wigeon, the Mallard and others, are seen passing with great rapidity, and following the course of the current; but the Eagle heeds them not: they are at that time beneath his attention. The next moment, however, the wild trumpetlike sound of a yet distant but approaching Swan is heard. A shriek from the female Eagle comes across the stream,—for she is as fully on the alert as her mate. The latter suddenly shakes the whole of his body, and with a few touches of his bill, aided by the action of his cuticular muscles, arranges his plumage in an instant. The snow-white bird is now in sight: her long neck is stretched forward, her eye is on the watch, vigilant as that of her enemy; her large wings seem with difficulty to support the weight of her body, although they flap incessantly. So irksome do her exertions seem, that her very legs are spread beneath her tail, to aid her in her flight. She approaches, however. The Eagle has marked her for his prey. As the Swan is passing the dreaded pair, the male bird, in full preparation for the chase, starts from his perch with an awful scream, that to the Swan's ear brings more terror than the report of the large duck-gun.

" 'Now is the moment to witness the display of the Eagle's powers. He glides through the air like a falling star, and, like a flash of lightning, comes upon the timorous quarry, which now, in agony and despair, seeks, by various manœuvres, to elude the grasp of his cruel talons. It mounts, doubles, and willingly would plunge into the stream, were it not prevented by the Eagle, which, long possessed of the knowledge that by such a stratagem the Swan might escape him, forces it to remain in the air by attempting to strike it with his talons from beneath. The hope of escape is soon given up by the Swan. It has already become much weakened, and its strength fails at the sight of the courage and swiftness of its antagonist. Its last gasp is about to escape, when the ferocious Eagle strikes with his talons the under side of its wings, and with unresisted power forces the bird to fall in a slanting direction upon the nearest shore.

" 'It is then, reader, that you may see the cruel spirit of this dreaded enemy of the feathered race, whilst, exulting over his prey, he for the first time breathes at ease. He presses down his powerful feet, and drives his sharp claws deeper than ever into the heart of the dying Swan. He shrieks with delight as he feels the last convulsions of his prey, which has now sunk under his unceasing efforts to render death as painfully felt as it can possibly be. The female has watched every movement of her mate, and if she did not assist him in capturing the Swan, it was not from want of will, but merely that she felt full assurance that the power and courage of her lord were quite sufficient for the deed. She now sails to the spot where he eagerly awaits her, and when she has arrived, they together turn the breast of the luckless Swan upwards, and gorge themselves with gore.' "[5]

"Poor swan!" was Emile's pitying comment.

---

[5]   Audubon: "Ornithological Biography," I. 160–162.—*Translator.*

CHAPTER XVIII

HAWKS AND FALCONS

"WHAT ARE we to do with enemies like the eagle?" asked Louis when Uncle Paul had finished Audubon's account of that bird's fierce and destructive rapacity.

"Destroy them," was the reply, "destroy them by every possible means, for we can count on no assistance from other than human helpers. Eagles are the tyrants of the air, and no other bird dares attack them. The destruction of their nests is the surest way to put an end to the ravages they from time to time commit among our flocks. But it is an enterprise not without danger to make one's way to the eagle's aery and wring the necks of the young birds. The shepherds of the Pyrenees go about this work in couples, one armed with a double-barreled rifle and the other with a long pike. At daybreak, when the eagle is already away hunting, the two nest-destroyers climb to the top of the steep declivity where the aery is situated. The first man, the one armed with the rifle, posts himself on the rocky summit to fire at the eagle if it returns, while the second, his pike fastened to his belt, clambers down from rock to rock to the aery and removes the eaglets, which are still too young to offer serious resistance. But at their first cry of distress the mother hastens to the rescue and hurls herself furiously at her enemy, who receives her with blows of his pike until his comrade brings her down with a well-aimed shot. The male, until then soaring among the clouds, now descends like a thunderbolt and is on the hunter's head before the man has time to use his pike. Fortunately a second bullet from the rifle-man stationed above breaks the bird's wing."

Red-shouldered Hawk

"What if he had missed the bird?" asked Jules.

"Then it would have been all over with his companion. His face torn by the eagle's beak and his eyes pecked out, he would have fallen to the foot of the precipice, a mangled corpse. No, it is hardly a holiday diversion to go bird-nesting among the haunts of the eagle."

"I'm sure I shouldn't care to undertake it," was Jules's comment.

"Next to the eagle the goshawk is the largest of our diurnal birds of prey. It is a magnificent creature about the size of a well-grown rooster, brown above and white underneath, with numerous little dark stripes running around the body. The eye is adorned with a white eyebrow, the beak is blue-black, and the feet are yellow.

"The goshawk is the scourge of pigeon-cotes, for which reason it is also called the pigeons' falcon. It selects for itself a lofty perch on some tall tree and there keeps a watchful eye on the flocks of pigeons foraging in the fields. Woe betide the luckless one that forgets for a moment to be on its guard. The bird pounces upon it in oblique flight, almost skimming the surface of the ground, and in less than no time the pigeon is seized and carried off to some lonely rock, where the ravisher plucks its feathers and tears it to pieces while still warm. If the farmer is not on the lookout the goshawk attacks the poultry and does great harm. At the mere appearance of the bird's shadow the rooster raises a cry of alarm and the little chickens hastily take refuge under their mother's wing, while she, her feathers ruffled and her eyes blazing, sometimes succeeds in frightening off the

Cooper's Hawk

enemy by her show of boldness. For lack of pigeons and barnyard fowls the goshawk hunts young hares, squirrels, and small birds, and in time of famine it will even eat moles and mice. Wooded mountains are its favorite abode, and it builds its nest in the tallest oaks and beeches. Its eggs, four or five in number, are slightly red or bluish and spotted with brown.

"The common sparrow-hawk is about as large as a magpie. Its plumage somewhat resembles the goshawk's, being ashy blue on the back and white underneath, with brown stripes running cross-wise. The throat and breast are reddish, and the tail is barred with six or seven dark bands. The legs and claws are of a beautiful yellow, and are long and slender.

"The sparrow-hawk is a hunter of pigeons, which it tries to catch off guard by flying around the pigeon-cote and by watching from the concealment of some tree-top. The lark, the thrush, and the quail often fall into its clutches. Its flight is low and oblique like the goshawk's, the wings of both being too short and too rounded at the tip to permit of lofty flight or sudden charges. The young, just out of the nest and as yet inexperienced in the cunning of the chase, are for a while trained by the parent birds for the career they are to follow; and indeed it is no rare occurrence to see the whole family hunting in company. The sparrow-hawk nests in tall trees and lays four or five white eggs ornamented with brown spots, which are larger and more numerous toward the big end of the egg. Both the goshawk and the sparrow-hawk, when they are attacked by an enemy stronger than themselves, do as the horned owl does: they lie on their backs and brandish their claws.

"Of all our diurnal birds of prey, falcons are the most courageous and the best equipped for flying. As a distinctive characteristic they have a sharp tooth on each side of the tip of the beak,

GERFALCON

which itself is very powerful and curves downward in a notable manner from the very outset. Their wings are pointed at the tip and when folded they extend beyond or at least as far as the end of the tail. All falcons soar in their flight when hunting. To this class belong the common falcon, the hobby, and the merlin.

"The common falcon, which is as large as a hen, can be recognized by a sort of mustache or black spot it has on each cheek. Its back is of a dark ashen hue crossed by narrow stripes of a still deeper shade; the throat and breast are pure white, with black markings running lengthwise; the stomach and thighs are light gray tinged with blue and striped with black; and the tail shows alternate stripes of dingy white and of black. The beak is blue with a black tip, and the eyes and legs are a beautiful yellow. But it should be added that the plumage of the common falcon varies a good deal with age, and not until the bird is three or four years old does it agree with the description I have just given.

"The summits of the wildest and loftiest crags are the falcon's home, whence it goes forth to hunt pigeons, quails, partridges, chickens, and ducks. It rises and soars some time in the air, searching for its victims, and then swoops down upon them like a missile hurled from the sky. With astonishing boldness it makes its way into the farmer's pigeon-cotes and chases the pigeons themselves under the very eyes of passers-by, in the middle of crowded streets. It will even snatch partridges from before the hunter's rifle and from under the hunting-dog's nose. Its cry is strong and piercing, and it flies unwearied at the rate of twenty leagues an hour for hundreds of leagues; but its walk is jerky and awkward because its hooked claws, furnished with long and recurved nails, rest insecurely on the ground. The falcon nests on the southern face of rocky precipices, the nest itself being clumsily built and holding three or four eggs of a reddish hue spotted with brown.

"The hobby is smaller than the common falcon. It is brown above and whitish beneath, with thighs and the lower part of the stomach red. Its boldness is equaled only by the falcon's, for it gives chase to larks and quails even when the hunter is in the act of shooting them, and dashes into the midst of the fowler's net to seize the decoy birds. It perches on tall trees and nests in their branches. Its eggs are whitish with a few red spots.

"The merlin is the smallest of the diurnal birds of prey, being scarcely larger than a thrush. It is brown on the back, and whitish with brown spots underneath. Its nest, which is seldom found in our part of the country, is built in the hollow of a rock and contains five or six whitish eggs marbled at the larger end with brown and dingy green.

"Despite its smallness it is a bold bandit. Little birds are terror-stricken at the mere sound of the merlin's wings in their neighborhood. Even the partridge is not safe from its attacks. It begins by separating one of the birds from the rest of the covey, and then, circling about above it in a spiral, which grows smaller and smaller, it descends until it can reach its victim with its claws and knocks it down with a blow on the breast.

"Such are the principal diurnal birds of prey that we have to make war upon without mercy. Up and after these savage bloodsuckers, destroyers of game, ravagers of poultry-yards and pigeon-cotes! Take your gun, vigilant farmer, watch for the falcon and the goshawk, and let fire at those brigands! Destroy their nests, break their eggs, and wring the necks of their young, if you wish to save your chickens, ducks, and pigeons."

KESTRELS, KITES AND BUZZARDS

"THE KESTREL belongs to the falcon family, as may be seen from the small, sharp tooth on each side of the tip of the beak. It is rather a handsome bird, about the size of a pigeon, red in color, with black spots, and a white tip to the tail. The beak is blue and the legs are yellow. The kestrel is the most widely scattered bird of prey and the one most often seen near human habitations. Its favorite haunts are old castles, lofty towers, and belfries. One often sees it flying with untiring wing around these buildings, uttering the while a piercing cry, *plee, plee, plee! pree, pree, pree!* which it sends forth to frighten the sparrows snuggling in holes in the wall, so that it may seize them when they fly out. It carefully plucks the little captured birds before eating them; but it has another kind of prey which gives it less trouble, and that is the mouse, which it enters open barns in order to catch, also the fat and savory field-mouse, which it spies from on high when holding itself motionless in the air in one position with tail and wings gracefully extended. What will it do with its catch? Will it skin the creature for the sake of clean-

HAWK-OWL OR KESTREL

liness, as it plucks the sparrow? No, the common mouse and the field-mouse are dainty morsels of which the kestrel would be loath to lose a single drop of blood. The rodent is swallowed just as it is, whole if small, piecemeal if large. After digestion the skin and bones are thrown up through the beak in the form of little balls, just as in the case of the owl.

KITE

"The kestrel nests in old towers, abandoned ruins, hollow rocks. Its nest, made of twigs and roots, holds four or five rust-colored eggs marbled with brown.

"We will pass now to the kite, which is different from all other birds of prey, with its broad and forked tail, its very long wings, its rather slender claws, and its very small beak, a beak not at all in keeping with the bird's size, which exceeds that of the falcon. This beak makes the bird cowardly to excess, frightened by the slightest danger, put to flight by a mere crow.

"If pressed by hunger, however, the kite will venture into the neighborhood of pigeon-cotes and poultry-yards in order to seize young pigeons and little chickens. Fortunately, the hen, if she has time to gather her brood under her wings, can scare the invader away by simply showing her anger. For want of poultry, the kite, which is hated by thrifty country people, attacks reptiles, rats, field-mice, and meadow-mice; and if it can get nothing else it will content itself with carrion, such as dead sheep and spoiled fish.

"The kite's extended wings measure more than a meter and a half from tip to tip, and its flight presents a fine spectacle. When the bird sweeps in wide circles through the upper atmosphere, it is as if it were swimming, gliding without the least apparent exertion. Then all at once it stops in its flight and remains suspended in one position for a quarter of an hour at a stretch, held there by an invisible movement of the wings.

"The kite is of a deep red hue on the back and rust-colored on the breast and stomach, with a whitish head and the large wing-feathers black. Its cry resembles a cat's mewing. It builds its nest in tall trees or, still oftener, in the hollows of rocks. Its eggs, commonly three in number, are white shading into dingy yellow and speckled with a few irregular brown spots.

"The birds known as harriers have a small semicircular collar of fine thick feathers projecting from each side of the face and reaching from beak to ear, much like the ring around the hornless owl's eyes. In the contour of the breast, in the long legs and wings, and in the still longer tail, they have something of the falcon's appearance and bearing; while in their large head and in the little collar around the face they are not unlike the nocturnal birds of prey. Harriers frequent marshes and the banks of stagnant bodies of water, where they lie concealed among the rushes in order to seize any small rodents, reptiles, or insects that may come within their reach. The farmer has no complaint to bring against them, as they show proper respect for his little pigeons, chickens, and ducklings. Indeed, they are welcome visitors on account of their strong liking for field-mice. Unfortunately, the hunter accuses them of killing game, especially water-fowl, hares, and rabbits.

"In this connection it is to be noted that the weasel, a small carnivorous quadruped with a thirst for blood, is wont to make its way into warrens in quest of young hares and rabbits, in order to suck their blood, after which the dead bodies are left behind some bush. These murderous operations do not escape the harrier's vigilance. In its leisurely flights it keeps a sharp eye on the surroundings of all warrens in the woods, for the purpose of carrying off any dead bodies and feasting on the weasel's leavings. That it may occasionally be at fault and mistake a live rabbit for a dead one, I should not dare deny; but after all

I forgive it willingly enough, and in consideration of its war on field-mice I should be inclined to bestow upon it the honorable title of farmer's helper.

"If we may feel some uncertainty about harriers, there is no such doubt concerning buzzards. In them we certainly have very valuable helpers, large eaters of field-mice and meadow-mice, and great destroyers of moles, those tireless burrowers whose numbers must be kept within strict limits. Buzzards have a short, wide beak, curving downward from the base; wings very long, but not pointed, reaching almost to the tip of the tail; strong legs, and the space between the eyes and nostrils bristling with hairs.

"Buzzards are fond of repose and phlegmatic by nature; or it might be more accurate to say that they are endowed with a remarkable capacity for patient and motionless waiting, a gift very necessary for the successful hunting of the field-mouse, which must be watched for by the hour at the mouth of its burrow. For half a day at a time, if need be, the buzzard lies in wait without making the least movement or giving the slightest sign of impatience. One would take it to be asleep. Then, all of a sudden, the bird falls to hacking the soil with its beak and tearing the turf with its powerful claws. A disemboweled mole is brought to light, or perhaps a field-mouse is the prize, and in either event the victim is no sooner caught than swallowed.

"Now do you know what reputation the buzzard has won by this habit of long and motionless waiting so indispensable in the quest of game with the acuteness of hearing characteristic of the mole and of rodents? The reputation of stupidity. We say of a person of limited intelligence that he is as stupid as a buzzard. Here again is an instance of that wrong-headedness which makes us think little of so many of our helpers and glorify those that prey upon us. Stupidity is the name we give to the buzzard's peculiarities, and for no better reason than that the bird spares our poultry-yards and rids us of troublesome rodents; whereas we speak of the eagle, which steals our lambs, and of the falcon, plunderer of chicken-coops, as courageous, noble, and splendid.

"The common buzzard is a large brown bird with a whitish throat, stomach-feathers marked with little lines alternately brown and white, and tail crossed by nine or ten dark stripes. Its beak is whitish at the base and black at the tip, its eyes and legs yellow. This species nests in tall trees, the nest being made of interwoven twigs and lined with wool and hair. It lays but three eggs at most, which are whitish and irregularly sprinkled with dingy yellow spots. It is the common buzzard especially that has won the reputation of stupidity with its leisurely flying and its patience in watching for prey. It usually watches on some mound of earth. Observers who have studied its habits say that sixteen is about the number of mice it commonly eats in one day, which makes nearly six thousand a year."

"That's the kind of bird we should like to have about our houses if we could only tame it," remarked Jules.

"There is nothing to prevent our trying it," his uncle rejoined. "The buzzard's disposition is good enough. Other observers, who have studied its hunting of field-mice, estimate that it eats nearly four thousand of these in one year. From this number you can form some idea of the multitude of little rodents a whole flock of buzzards would be able to destroy. But we must not give the bird too much praise. I know that it does not hesitate, when occasion offers, to seize and carry off a wounded young hare; and I also know that when the snow is on the ground and the buzzard is pressed by hunger, it will pounce upon any stray chicken that may have got out of the poultry-yard. But what are these few acts of theft when compared with the thousands of rodents of all kinds that it clears away from our fields? Whatever the season of the year, one cannot open a buzzard's crop without finding common mice, field-mice, and meadow-mice there by the dozen. If I owned a field that was ravaged by these rodents, I should lose no time in planting a few stumps there to serve as perches and watch-towers for buzzards in their patient hunt for their favorite game.

"There is another variety of buzzard, the hawk-buzzard, that does us good service in its fondness for larvæ, caterpillars, and insects generally, particularly wasps."

"What, those wasps that hurt so when they sting?" asked Emile.

"Yes, my boy; this buzzard feasts on the wasps whose sting is so painful to us; it swallows them without

Rough-legged Buzzard

a thought of their sting, just as the hedgehog devours the viper and never worries about its venomous fangs. The bird attacks their nests with its beak and pulls out the nymphs from their cells, carrying them, fat and tender, to its little ones.

"This buzzard is a somewhat smaller bird than the common buzzard. Its back is brown, its throat light yellow with brown stripes, and its breast and stomach white sprinkled with dark heart-shaped spots. The tail is crossed by three wide dark bands, the beak is black, and, finally, the head of the old male is bluish-gray. The bird nests in woods, in tall trees, and its eggs are rather small, being yellowish-white in color, but with so thick a sprinkling of large brown spots as sometimes almost to hide the color underneath.

"The feather-legged buzzard has legs covered with long feathers, as in certain species of pigeons bearing the same qualifying name. It frequents river banks, uncultivated fields, and woods, and lives on field-mice, moles, reptiles, and if need be on insects.

"Here let us bring to a close our talk on birds of prey. I have told you about the more important ones, both diurnal and nocturnal, about their habits, their food, and the services or the harm they do us. It is now for you to add to what these brief

SNAKE-BUZZARD
(Also called short-toed eagle)

talks have taught you, by observing the things that come under your eyes every day. Do not fail to examine with some care the buzzard as you see it perched on a mound and patiently watching for a field-mouse; also the kestrel as it flies screaming around the belfry and pounces, sometimes on a mouse, sometimes on a sparrow; and the kite, too, as it soars on motionless wings in the blue sky. You will get from this sort of study, first, a great deal of pleasure, and, secondly, knowledge that will be highly useful if you ever have a farm or a garden."

"It seems to me," said Jules, "that you have left out the very commonest of the birds of prey, the crows."

"Crows are not birds of prey," replied Uncle Paul. "They have not the hooked beak, the clutching claws, or the sharp, curved nails of birds formed for a life of rapine. I will tell you about them to-morrow; or, rather, I will begin with that one of the crow family known as the raven."

CHAPTER XX

THE RAVEN

"THEIR BLACK plumage and similarity of shape make us mistake all sorts of birds for crows. Let us begin with one of these, the raven. This bird is of good size, being about as large as our domestic rooster, and it has a hoarse cry, uttered slowly,—*craa, craa, craa*. It is the raven that has won such a reputation with children from that famous fable about the raven and the fox."

"Yes, I know," Emile hastened to interpose; "you mean the one that begins, 'Master Raven, perched on a tree, held a piece of cheese in his beak.' Where do you suppose he got that cheese?"

"History remains silent on that important question, but my opinion would be that he stole it from some window-sill where the farmer's wife had put out some newly made cheese to dry in a little wicker basket."

"The fox says good morning to Mr. Raven, and praises his plumage," continued Emile; "and he goes on: 'How trig and trim you are, how handsome you look to me!' And so on and so forth. How could the raven help having a swelled head after such flattery?"

RAVEN

"That fox was certainly a cunning rogue. To make sure that the bird will listen, instead of beginning with flattery that might have aroused his intended victim's suspicions (for the bird was not altogether lacking in common sense), he began by praising what is really not without merit. On a near view the raven is seen to be not by any means of a dead black; it shows glints of purple and blue on the back, and a flickering greenish tinge on the stomach, the total effect being that of some highly polished metal. At the first flattering words you may be sure the raven cast a complacent glance at its costume and, seeing it brilliant with blue, purple, and green, found it quite as rich as the fox declared it to be. So now the bird was well prepared—ready for the fulsome flattery that was to follow. The fox would have it believe the offensive odor clinging to it from eating so much carrion to be the aroma of musk, and its hoarse croaking to be melodious warbling. But just there was the difficulty, to make it croak and thus open its mouth, which held the cheese."

> "And if that voice of thine
> Can match thy plumage fine,
> Thou art the very phenix of all the woods around,"

quoted Emile.

"Yes, that's it," said Uncle Paul. "Do you see how the sly rascal is making headway? He would have the raven believe itself a singer, mistake its raucous *craa, craa* for the note of the nightingale. Had he begun with any such extravagant compliment, he would have defeated his own ends; but he very cleverly led up to this supreme flattery and, to pique the raven's foolish vanity still further, gave a doubtful tone to his admiration. 'I know,' was what he seemed to the bird to say, 'that your voice is widely celebrated; but what I am not so sure of is whether it matches your splendid plumage, whether you can really sing in a manner worthy of so magnificent a costume. I must hear you, and if your vocal performance equals your outward appearance, then you will indeed prove yourself to be the paragon of birds, the very phenix of these forests.' 'Ah, you doubt it?' said the raven to itself; 'well, then, listen to this operatic trill: *craa, craa, craa.*' "

Emile again took up the fable:

> "And so to prove it could
> Its boastfulness make good,
> It opened wide its beak and thus let fall the cheese,
> Which Master Fox did seize——"

"Not so fast!" his uncle interrupted him. "Master Fox could not have gone on talking with the cheese in his mouth; he could not have pointed the moral in that neat little lesson with which the fable ends. I can see him putting his paw on the prize while he licks his chops and looks tauntingly at the shamefaced bird. 'My good sir,' he says, 'let me call your attention to the fact that you are a conceited nincompoop.' "

"He doesn't call the bird Mr. Raven any more, now that he's got hold of the cheese," Emile observed.

"No; to call him that was all very well in the beginning; it flattered the bird. But now the fox makes fun of his dupe and calls him 'my good sir' in a tone of patronizing condolence. To express pity for those we have cajoled and deceived—is not that the very perfection of roguery? There we have, most assuredly, a fox that will make his way in the world. Read in La Fontaine, the incomparable story-teller, the abominable tricks Master Reynard plays later on the goat, the wolf, and many others; or, better, wait a while and we will read them together next winter before the open fire. For the present we will leave the raven of the fable and try to learn something about the real raven's manner of living.

"Ravens do not flock together as crows do, but live alone or in pairs on rocky heights and in the tallest trees. The society or even the near neighborhood of its fellows is unbearable to a raven. With angry peckings it drives away from its chosen district any of its kind that may try to establish themselves there, even though they may have been born in the same nest. If the intruder is merely a bird of passage, it is conducted with menacing demonstrations to the frontiers of the domain and is jealously watched until it disappears in the distance. Crows, social creatures, are treated in the same way. The raven asks to be left alone, quite alone, on its bare rock, and woe to the ill-advised intruder that disturbs its solitude! It builds its nest in the topmost branches of a solitary tree or, still more to its liking, in some fissure that offers itself in the perpendicular face of a rocky precipice. The nest is made of sticks and roots on the outside, and of moss, hair, rags, and fine grasses within."

"I should like to know," said Jules, "what ravens' eggs are like."

"Birds' eggs are usually remarkable for their beauty, both in shape and in color; and for this reason, if for no other, they merit our attention. But it is no idle or merely ornamental accomplishment to be able to distinguish one from another, to know whether any given egg belongs to a useful species that should be respected or to a harmful species that should not be allowed to breed in the vicinity of our fields and gardens. With this end in view I have already told you the characteristic marks of the eggs of our principal birds of prey, some of which eggs should be destroyed without any consideration, while others should be protected. As this is a matter that interests you, I will continue in the same way and will describe the eggs of those birds that we are still to talk about.

"Know, then, that ravens' eggs are much more beautifully colored than might be expected from the somber plumage of the bird. They are bluish green, with brown spots. This background of bluish green, sometimes lighter and sometimes darker, occurs again, together with the brown spots, in the eggs of crows, magpies, jays, blackbirds, thrushes, and fieldfares, birds that resemble one another closely in their bodily structure, despite their marked differences in size, plumage, and habits. The eggs of certain blackbirds and fieldfares are of a magnificent sky-blue color.

"The raven is an omnivorous creature: fruit, larvæ, insects, sprouting grain, flesh, whether in a fresh condition or otherwise, all suit it equally well; but its favorite fare is carrion, which it knows how to find a long way off, guided by sight and smell. Wherever there is a dead animal, there the raven makes its appearance and contends for the loathsome quarry with dogs. The habit of gorging itself with this infected food gives it a repulsive odor. For lack of dead prey—the sort most acceptable to its tastes, its great appetite, and its cowardice—the raven hunts such live prey as young hares and young rabbits, and other small and destructive rodents. It pilfers from birds' nests both eggs and new-born birds, a succulent banquet for its young; and it even has the boldness to carry off little chickens from poultry-yards. Without offering the slightest plea in its favor, I leave the raven to the hatred it has always incurred by reason of its funereal plumage, its forbidding aspect, its sinister croaking, repulsive odor, filthy greed, and savage disposition."

CHAPTER XXI

THE CROW

"IN FRANCE we have four kinds of crows: the black crow, the mantled daw, the rook or harvest crow, and the jackdaw or little belfry crow.

"The black crow has the same plumage and the same general appearance as the raven, but is one-quarter smaller. During the summer these birds live in pairs in the woods, which they leave only to get something to eat. In the spring their food consists of birds' eggs, especially the eggs of partridges, which they know how to puncture skilfully so as to carry them to their young on the point of the beak. Like the raven, this bird is fond of decayed flesh and little birds still covered with down. Crows attack small, weak, or wounded game, and venture into poultry-yards to carry off any unwary ducklings or little chickens that may have strayed away from their mothers. Spoiled fish, worms, insects, fruit, seeds, according to season and locality, fill their crop. They especially like nuts, which they know how to break by letting them fall from a sufficient height.

"In winter black crows gather in large flocks, either in an unmixed company or together with rooks and mantled daws. They go wandering about in the fields, mingling with the flocks and sometimes even alighting on a sheep's back to hunt for vermin under the wool. They follow the plowman to feed on the larvæ turned up by his plowshare; and they explore the seeded ground and eat recently sown grain made tender and sweet by germination. Toward evening they fly together to the tall trees of some neighboring wood, where they chatter noisily as the sun sets, and smooth their feathers, and finally go to sleep. These trees are meeting-places where every evening the crows gather from different quarters, sometimes from several miles around. At daybreak they divide into flocks of greater or less size and disperse in all directions to hunt for food in the tilled fields.

"At the end of winter this company is broken up, the crows pair off, and each pair chooses in the neighboring forests a district a quarter of a league in extent, from which every other couple is excluded, this arrangement ensuring sufficient sub-sistence for each establishment in the bird colony. The nest is built in some tree of medium size, and is made of small twigs and roots interwoven and rudely cemented with loam or horse dung, a mattress of fine rootlets being laid inside. If some bird of prey happens to come too near this nest, its owners assail the intruder with fury and crack its skull with a blow of the beak."

"Good for you, brave crows!" cried Emile. "Your enemies will think twice before they come and bother you."

"I admire the courage of crows in protecting their young," Uncle Paul admitted; "but I cannot forgive them their plunder-ing of poultry-yards, their thefts of young birds and eggs, and their upturning of seeded ground. We must then include the black crow among bandits that are to be destroyed.

"In the same class, too, we must place the mantled daw, so called from the sort of grayish-white cloak that reaches from the shoulders to the tail both in front and on the back. The rest of the plumage is black, with glints of blue, like the raven's. This bird comes to us toward the end of autumn, joins the company of black crows and rooks, and may be seen searching our fields for larvæ and sprouting grain. On the seashore, where its num-bers are much greater than in the interior, it lives on fish and mollusks cast up by the waves or left by fishermen. Only under dire necessity will it touch carrion, the favorite food of the black crow and the raven. In March the mantled daw leaves us, to go and breed in the North.

"The rook, which is a little smaller than the black crow, has the latter's plumage, but with more of a violet and coppery luster. Its beak, too, is more nearly straight and has a sharper tip. It is readily distinguished from the crow and the raven by the characteristic mark of its occupation, the skin of its forehead and around the beak being bare of feathers and looking white and powdery, like a scar. Is the bird born like that? Not at all. Just as a workman handling rough and heavy objects makes his hands callous, so the rook acquires by its work the rough and scaly skin so noticeable on its forehead. It is a tireless digger and its beak is its pick, which it thrusts into the ground as deeply as it can. From constant friction with the soil the forehead and the base of the beak lose their feathers and become bald, or even have the skin itself worn away so as to leave a rough scar. The rook's object in this toilsome operation is to capture white worms and all the destructive larvæ that are such a scourge to our cultivated fields. I saw some rooks one day hard at work in a waste tract of land, lifting up and turning over the stones scattered here and there. So eager were they that they sometimes threw the smaller stones as high as a man's head. Now guess what they were looking for so busily. They were looking for insects and all sorts of vermin. In this work of turning over stones and digging in the soil rooks cannot fail to injure their tool, the beak, and they must rub the feathers off from its base.

"I should have a high opinion of these birds if they contented themselves with hunting insects; but unfortunately they have a decided fondness for sprouting seeds, a dainty dish that they exert all their ingenuity to procure. It is said that they bury acorns and leave them in the ground until they begin to sprout and have lost their bitter taste, when they dig them up and eat them."

"What a bright idea!" Emile exclaimed. "The hard, bitter acorn is buried in the ground to get mellow, and when the rook thinks it has stayed there just long enough he has so good a memory he can go and find it again and dig it up. By that time it is just right to eat, soft and sweet and a fine feast for Mr. Rook."

"So far there is nothing to find fault with," said Uncle Paul.

"A bushel more or less of acorns is a small matter, and I willingly hand them over to the rooks to dispose of in their curious fashion. But other sprouting seeds suit them equally well, especially wheat, which they can so easily procure in winter in the recently sown fields. When I see a flock of rooks sedately pacing the furrows and plunging their beaks in here and there where the ground is softened by a thaw, I know well enough those birds might pretend they were hunting for June-bug larvæ, but he would be a simpleton indeed who accepted this explanation at that time of year, when the worms are all too deep in the ground for the rook's beak to reach them. It is wheat they are really after, and as rooks go in very large flocks, which may even darken the sky in their flight, you can easily understand that such reapers make short work of their harvest. Nor is that all: in the autumn rooks consume great quantities of walnuts and chestnuts, and in the spring they dig up potato fields to obtain the newly planted tubers."

"Couldn't they live on dead animals, as the black crow and the raven do?" asked Louis.

"No; a rook, however hungry, will not touch a dead animal. It must have seeds and fruit or larvæ and insects; and as it chooses one or the other of these kinds of food, the rook is our foe or our friend. So there are two opinions about the bird. Some persons, remembering only its thefts, would wage a relentless war against it, feeling that each rook destroyed means a bushel of wheat gained. Others, mindful chiefly of its destruction of larvæ and insects, maintain that the rook deserves kind treatment at the farmer's hands because it rids his fields of vermin, following the plowman to pick up white worms in the furrows and plunging its sharp beak into the ground for the grubs of the June-bug. For these excellent reasons they declare the rook worthy of our protection."

"Then which of the two opinions are we to accept?" was Louis's query.

"To my thinking, neither of them, but something half-way

between, as in the case of the mole. If white worms abound, let us bear with the rook, as it makes war on these enemies of ours; but if we have no need of its help, let us chase the bird from our fields. In our warfare on destructive insects we have two real helpers, the mole and the rook; but unfortunately we have to weigh their ravages against their services. Accordingly, let us treat them with forbearance if we have a worse ill to dread, but rid ourselves of their presence if our fields are in good condition.

"All the year round the rook lives with its own kind. It goes in flocks to seek food, and in flocks it chooses its breeding-place. Sometimes a single oak has a dozen nests, with as many in each of the trees around, over a large tract of ground. There is great commotion in this aërial city at the time of nest-building, for rooks are very clamorous and also much given to stealing from their neighbors. When a young and inexperienced couple suspend building operations for a moment, to go and get further material for construction, the neighbors pillage the half-completed nest; this one carries off a little stick, that one a blade of grass and some moss, to use in their own work. On their return the robbed ones are thrown into a terrible passion, accuse this one and that one, take counsel with friends, and attack the robbers furiously if the theft has not been cleverly concealed. Experienced couples never leave the nest unguarded, but one stays and watches while the other goes for building material.

"The jackdaw or little belfry-crow is all black and about the size of a pigeon. Like rooks, these birds fly in flocks and nest with their own kind. High towers, old castles, and the belfries of Gothic churches are their favorite abode. Their nests, which are made of a few sticks and a little straw, sometimes are placed each by itself in a hole in the wall, and sometimes are very near together in huddled groups. The jackdaw when flying keeps uttering a harsh and piercing cry. It feeds on insects, worms, larvæ, and fruit, but never on decayed flesh. It renders us some service by clearing trees of caterpillars, but I complain of it for hunting the eggs of little birds. Although jackdaws are always to be found about our old buildings, they nevertheless move from place to place, usually in large flocks, sometimes of their own kind exclusively, at other times in company with rooks and mantled daws."

CHAPTER XXII

WOODPECKERS

In front of Uncle Paul's house there is a grove of beeches several centuries old, its branches interlacing at a great height and forming a continuous canopy supported by hundreds of tree trunks as smooth and white as stone columns. In the autumn that is where Emile and Jules go and hunt in the moss for mushrooms of all colors to show to their uncle, who tells the boys how to distinguish the edible from the poisonous kinds. There, too, they hunt for beetles: the stag-beetle, whose large fat head bears enormous branching nippers; great black capricorn-beetles that may be seen at sunset running along the dead branches and clinging to them, as they go, with their jointed antennæ, which are longer than the insect's body; and long-horn beetles, likewise furnished with antennæ of unusual length, and also remarkable for their wing sheaths richly colored with blue or yellow or red, with spots and stripes of black velvet.

GREATER SPOTTED WOODPECKER

A multitude of birds of many kinds make this grove their abode. There the quarrelsome jay fights with one of its own species for the possession of a beechnut; there the magpie chatters on a high branch and then flies down and alights in a neighboring field, jerking up its tail and looking around with an air of defiance; crows have their evening rendezvous there; and there the woodpecker hammers away at old bark to make the insects come out so that it may snap them up with its viscous tongue. Listen to the bird at its work: *toc, toc, toc!* If it is interrupted in its task it flies away with a cry of *teo, teo, teo*, repeated thirty or forty times in quick succession and resembling a noisy burst of laughter.

"What bird is it that seems to be making fun of us with such loud laughter as it flies off?" Emile and Jules asked each other one day when they were watching from their window the woodpeckers and the jays at play in the branches of the old beech trees.

Jacques, their uncle's gardener, heard them as he was watering the cabbage bed. After finishing a series of little trenches to carry the water to all parts of the bed, he came up to the window for a talk with the boys.

"That bird you see there," said he, "with green plumage and a red head, is a woodpecker. It has several different cries. If it is going to rain it says *plieu, plieu*, in a long-drawn and plaintive tone. When at work, in order to keep up its spirits it every now and then gives a harsh cry, *tiackackan, tiackackan*, so that the whole forest echoes with it. In the nesting season it gives a quick *teo, teo, teo*, just like what you heard a moment ago."

"Then it has its nest now in the beech grove?" asked Jules.

"It is at work on it, for all the morning I've heard it hammering away with all its might. You see, it makes its nest in a hole that it hollows out by pecking the trunk of a tree with its beak. It's a fine beak it has, too, so hard and pointed that the bird is always afraid of going too deep into the wood. So after two or three good hard pecks it skips round to the other side of the trunk to see if it hasn't bored clear through."

PICULET
(A small soft-tailed
woodpecker)

"Bah! you're only in fun," returned Jules.

"Not at all," protested Jacques; "it's what I've heard said, and I've often seen the woodpecker hurry round to look at the other side of the trunk."

"But the bird must have some other reason than just to see whether or not the tree is bored through. I'm going to ask Uncle."

"Ask him, too, if he knows the ironweed that the woodpecker rubs its beak on to make it harder than steel."

"Your ironweed sounds to me like a fairy tale."

"Well, I'm only telling you what I've heard. I don't know anything about it, myself; but they say it's a very rare weed and that the woodpecker goes to look for it in the mountains so that it may harden and whet its beak on it. And anything you touch to that weed becomes as hard as the best steel. What a find that would be for my scythe and my hedging-bill, my sickle and grafting-knife! I know many a man that would give a bag of gold for the woodpecker's secret."

The young cabbage plants had by this time received enough water, and it was now the lettuce's turn. Jacques went back to his work and left the boys to puzzle over the question whether or not there was any truth in this story of the woodpecker's fear lest it might bore through the tree trunk with each peck of its beak. They brought the matter up that evening in their talk with their uncle.

"There is both truth and falsehood in what my good Jacques told you," he said. "The true is what he saw with his own eyes, the false what he repeats from hearsay among the country folk. He told you correctly about the woodpecker's different cries, which he knows so well from having heard them over and over again; and he was right about the bird's way of running around to the other side of the trunk that it has just struck several times with its beak. All the rest is false, or, rather, an amusing legend with a basis of fact which we will now examine.

"Woodpeckers live solely on insects and larvæ, especially those species of insects and larvæ that are found in wood. The large grubs of capricorn-beetles, stag-beetles, long-horn beetles, and others are their favorite dish. To get at them they have to clear away the dead bark and bore into the worm-eaten wood beneath. The instrument used in this rough work is the bird's beak, which is straight and wedge-shaped, square at the base, fluted lengthwise, and shaped at the point like a carpenter's chisel. It is so hard and durable that, in order to account for a tool of such perfection, some simple-minded wood-cutter made up the story that has been repeated ever since, the childish story of the ironweed. Need I tell you that there is nothing in the world that by its mere touch can give to objects the hardness of iron or steel?"

"I had my doubts," Jules declared, "when Jacques was telling us about it; I couldn't believe in his wonderful weed."

"The woodpecker has no need to rub its beak against anything to give it the hardness necessary for the work to be done; it is born with a good strong beak, to begin with, and keeps it to the end, and that beak never has to be retempered. It is the continuation of a very thick skull which can withstand rather violent shocks, and it is operated by a short, strong neck which can keep up its hammering without fatigue even should the bird wish to bore into the very heart of a tree trunk. After it has drilled its hole the woodpecker darts into it an exceedingly long tongue, worm-shaped and viscous—that is, coated with a sort of mucilage made by the saliva—and armed with a hard barbed point with which it transfixes the larvæ that have been uncovered.

"To climb the trunk of the tree to be operated upon and, for hours at a time if need be, to stay there where larvæ seem to be lurking, the woodpecker has short, muscular legs which end in stout claws, each foot having four talons or toes, two pointing forward and two backward, armed with curved nails of great strength. The bird's way of standing on the vertical surface of a tree trunk is made possible not only by the division of its talons as I have described them, with their strong nails clinging to

Three-toed
Woodpecker of Java

rough bark, but also by a third support furnished by the tail. The large tail feathers are stiff, slightly bent downward, worn at the tip, and supplied with rough barbs. When the woodpecker starts in on what promises to be a long job, it plants itself firmly on the tripod of its tail and two feet and holds itself steady even in positions that would seem to be highly uncomfortable. Without fatigue and without pause it can strip an entire tree trunk of its dried-up bark.

"The objects of its persevering search are the insects hidden under this bark. It can tell by the sound made when it strikes the tree with its beak whether or not the wood is decayed and full of insects, a hollow sound being of good omen to the bird. If the wood does not give out this hollow sound, the woodpecker knows that further drilling at that point would be but so much labor wasted. In the first case it strips off the bark, makes the wood beneath fly this way and that in a shower of little chips, clears off the worm-hole dust, and finally reaches the plump grub in its snug retreat. In the second case it strikes two or three well-directed blows to start the dry bark and frighten any insects that may be lurking underneath. Immediately this insect population runs in alarm, some to the right, others to the left, toward the opposite side of the tree trunk; but the woodpecker, knowing well enough what is going on, reaches the other side in time to nab the fugitives."

"Now," said Jules, "I understand what Jacques was saying. The woodpecker doesn't run around the tree to see whether or not it has bored through to the other side, but to gobble up the insects that are trying to get away. I thought the woodpecker must be very silly to think it could drill right through the trunk of a tree with one peck of its beak; but now that I know the real reason of what it does, I see that it's a wonderfully clever bird."

"I assure you once more that animals have more intelligence than they are given credit for. Let us beware of seeing an evil meaning in habits and aptitudes that we do not understand. Is it not said of the buzzard that it is a stupid bird, just because it shows such patience in watching and waiting, perfectly motionless, for the field-mouse it suspects to be lurking under the ground? And here we have the woodpecker accused of being so foolish as to think it can pierce a tree trunk with one blow of its beak, merely because it runs around to capture the insects fleeing to the other side! Bear this in mind: there is in animals no foolishness except what we ascribe to them from our own point of view. Whenever we are able to discover the real motive, we always find their actions perfectly logical. And that is only what might have been expected, for an animal has no choice in its acts, but is made to perform them according to its mode of life as determined from the beginning by Divine Wisdom. Man alone is free: by a sublime privilege he is left to choose between good and evil, between sound reason and blind passion. He seeks and chooses, at his own risk and peril, the true or the false, the just or the unjust, the beautiful or the ugly. But animals, having no spiritual battles to fight as we have, are now what they have always been and always will be; they do to-day what they did yesterday and will do to-morrow; for centuries and centuries they go on doing the same thing without improvement or deterioration, and with an unfailing sense given them by God.

"Woodpeckers spend their lives running around tree trunks from top to bottom in order to start the old bark that shelters insects, and exploring all fissures with their long, pointed tongue, which is pushed down into every hole where worms may possibly be hiding. These birds are placed in our forests as keepers. They inspect sickly trees in particular, trees honeycombed by vermin, and they examine carefully the diseased parts. Occasionally they may chance to attack a healthy part, especially in making their nests, and they may thus injure the tree by drilling into the live wood. But this damage is more than atoned for in the long run, and so I do not hesitate to bestow upon our woodpeckers the title of forest-preservers, a title earned by their assiduous warfare on insects injurious to wood. Seldom do they leave their timber-yard—the trunk and the main branches of the tree—and descend to the ground, except when they chance to find an ant-hill, the inmates of which they devour with delight. They place their nests at a considerable height from the ground, deep down in a round hole bored with the beak in the heart of some tree trunk. The bedding consists of moss and wool, and the eggs, four to six in number, are in every instance white, smooth, and as lustrous as ivory."

CHAPTER XXIII

MORE ABOUT WOODPECKERS

"THE COMMONEST of our woodpeckers is the green wood-pecker, which is about as large as a turtle-dove. Its plumage has a richness rarely seen in that of any of our other birds. The top of the head and the nape of the neck are of a magnificent crimson; two mustaches of the same hue adorn the bird's face; the back is green, the breast and stomach yellowish white, the rump yellow, and the large wing-feathers black with regular marks of white on the edge. The female has less brilliant coloring than the male and its mustaches are black instead of red.

"It is the green woodpecker that you heard in the grove this morning, giving its cry of *teo, teo, teo*. I will not go over what Jacques has already told you about its different cries. The green woodpecker is passionately fond of ants, and when it discovers an ant-hill it posts itself near by and stretches its long viscous tongue across the path the ants follow. You know these little creatures' way of marching in long files, one or more, following the exact path taken by the leaders. The woodpecker's viscous tongue is extended across this line of march. The ants from behind come up, hesitate a moment before the barricade, and then venture upon the tongue, in order to follow their friends marching on ahead as if nothing had happened. Immediately we have one ant caught, then four, then ten, all struggling in the sticky mucilage covering the tongue. The woodpecker does not move, but remains quiet until its tongue is quite covered. Nor has it long to wait. Soon the living trap, laden with game, is withdrawn into the beak. Ah, that was a luscious mouthful! Without leaving the spot the ant-eater repeats this performance again and again, laying its tongue on the ground and then draw-ing it in black with ants, until its hunger is satisfied."

"Animals know more than one would think, as you said a while ago," Emile remarked. "That trick of the woodpecker's shows it plainly enough. Instead of picking the ants up one by one, which would be very slow work with such small game, the woodpecker takes them dozens at a time. It lays its tongue across their path on the ground, draws it in again when it is all plastered over with ants, and the thing is done. And the mouthful is well worth the trouble. Who would have thought of making a trap of one's tongue, a trap that catches game with glue?"

"But its passion for ants," resumed Uncle Paul, "does not make the woodpecker neglect its duty as keeper of forests. It goes climbing up tree trunks, tapping the sickly parts, and pecking away with blows that at a distance sound like hammer strokes. If a passer-by interrupts it at its work it does not immediately fly away, but runs around the trunk like a squirrel, and from the other side sticks out its head a little to see who or what is coming. If the intruder advances, the woodpecker goes on around the tree, always keeping on the opposite side until it becomes frightened, when it flies off, making the woods ring with its sonorous *tiackackan, tiackackan*. It flies with swift darts and bounds, swooping down, then rising, describing a series of undulating arches in the air.

"For its nest it bores out a deep hole in soft-wood trees such as firs and poplars. Male and female work with lusty blows of the beak, taking turns at the hardest part of the task, the pierc-ing of the live wood of the trunk, until the worm-eaten center is reached. Chips, wood-dust, and decayed fragments are dug out with the feet, and at last the hole is deep enough and slanting enough to exclude the light of day. The young ones leave the nest before they can fly, and they may be seen exercising near it, learning to climb, to run around the trunk of their tree, and to cling to it upside down. You will be amused to watch them if you ever have the good fortune to be present at the frolics of a young family of woodpeckers.

"The great spotted woodpecker is about as large as a thrush. It has a wide red stripe across the nape of the neck, the upper part of the body is prettily spotted with pure white and deep black, and the under part is white as far as the abdomen, which is red, as is also the rump. The female has no red on the nape of the neck. The food of this bird is the same as the green woodpecker's. It strikes the tree with quicker, smarter blows, and if disturbed in its work it remains motionless in the shelter of a large branch with its green eyes fixed on the object of its distrust. Its cry is a kind of hoarse, grinding *trer-rer-rer-rer*.

"The variegated woodpecker much resembles the great spotted woodpecker in plumage, but is a little smaller. It is adorned with a red cap which covers the whole of the upper part and the back of the head, while the great spotted woodpecker has only a stripe of this color on the nape of the neck. Both these birds are found in the large wooded districts of France, and they live on the same diet,—insects, wood-boring larvæ, and ants. Also, because of their velvet costume of black and white and their scarlet cap, they are both to be ranked among the prettiest birds we have.

"Let us add to them the little spotted woodpecker. It is smaller than a sparrow, and its dress is that of the great spotted woodpecker. This bird is found almost exclusively in the fir forests of the East and of the Pyrenees.

"The wryneck is closely akin to the woodpeckers in the structure of its feet, whose four toes or talons are divided into two pairs, one pointing forward and the other backward, and in its very long and viscous tongue which it pushes into ant-hills or stretches out on the ground to receive the insects as they pass. It is a small bird, being no larger than a lark. Its plumage is watered with black, brown, gray, and russet, somewhat like the woodcock's, but with tints better defined and more beautiful in their combined effect. The wryneck is a great eater of caterpillars, and it is also passionately fond of ants, which it catches as does the woodpecker, with its sticky tongue laid on the ground across their path. Its name comes from the habit it has of twisting its neck and looking backward with a sort of slow and undulating movement like a snake's."

"Why does it imitate a snake like that?" Emile inquired.

"It is its way of expressing surprise and alarm; and perhaps it also hopes to frighten its foe with the motions. At any rate, it is sometimes successful. If a birdnest-hunter climbs up to its hole to steal its little ones, the wryneck emits, from the depths of its retreat, a sharp hissing and begins to make snake-like movements with its neck. The young birds, still featherless, imitate their mother to the best of their ability, and succeed so well that the hunter thinks he has thrust his hand into a nest of writhing and twisting flat-headed vipers. Thoroughly frightened, the boy clambers down, not without leaving some shreds of his breeches on the way."

"Serves the rascal right, too," declared Emile.

"The wryneck reaches us in April and leaves toward the end of summer. It haunts the outskirts of woods and visits gardens and orchards for caterpillars. It nests in a hole in a tree trunk and gladly avails itself of the woodpecker's abandoned quarters after furbishing them up a little to suit itself. The eggs, which are white and polished like the woodpecker's, rest on a simple little bed of wood-dust that the bird dislodges from the walls of its hole with a few blows of its beak.

"Despite the structure of its feet, the wryneck does not climb tree trunks and rarely even perches on them, preferring to stay on the ground and hunt caterpillars or stretch out its tongue in the ants' path, which has given it, in the South, the name of stretch-tongue.

"The nuthatch, on the contrary, though differing from the woodpecker in the formation of its claws, is a first-rate climber and spends its life running about on the trunks of trees, inspecting every crack and cranny for insects and pecking at the old bark. Three of its talons point forward, the fourth alone being turned in the opposite direction; but for firmness of support the last is worth two of the others, so thick and powerful is it, and the nail at the end so strong and hooked. The beak resembles the woodpecker's, being straight, fluted lengthwise, and sharply pointed. It is an excellent tool for digging into wood and getting out the worms. The tongue cannot be projected like the woodpecker's to catch insects with its glue, nor does the tail serve as a support.

"The nuthatch examines old trees with painstaking care, going up and down the trunk repeatedly, or around it in a spiral, and sometimes visiting a branch above or below or on one side. Every crack is explored with the point of the beak, to the accompaniment of the bird's resonant cry, *tuee, tuee, tuee*, repeated again and again in a penetrating tone. Very few insects can escape so careful a search. If grubs are lacking, the nuthatch makes a frugal meal of a hazelnut. First it fixes the nut firmly in the fork made by two branches, and then it hammers away at it, encouraging itself the while by uttering its cry, until the hard shell is pierced and the kernel exposed."

"It must take the bird a long time to crack a hazelnut with its beak," was the opinion of Jules.

"No, it is done very quickly, the beak is so hard and pointed. Very quickly, too, a caged nuthatch will break through the woodwork of its prison and make an opening large enough to escape through. Not even the woodpecker has a better carpenter's chisel.

"The nuthatch is about as large as a sparrow. All the upper part of its plumage is of a bluish ash color, the throat and cheeks are white, and the breast and stomach red. A black stripe, starting from the corner of the beak, passes over the eye and down the side of the neck. This bird nests in a hole in a tree trunk and it knows how, if need be, to make the opening of the nest smaller with a little moistened clay. Its eggs, from five to seven in number, are laid on moss or wood-dust and are of a dingy white dotted with red. It gets its name of nuthatch (which means nuthacker) from its way of hacking the nuts it is so fond of."

CHAPTER XXIV

CLIMBERS—THE HOOPOE

"I HAVE been telling you about woodpeckers and the nuthatch, insect-eaters with chisel-shaped beaks for cutting into trees and getting out the worms hidden in the wood. Then I spoke of the wryneck, which does not use its beak for hacking old tree trunks, but can, like the woodpecker, stick out its tongue on the ants' path and catch the insects with the glue of its saliva. Now we come to some more insect-eaters, but their work is less laborious than that of the woodpecker. They do not hack and hew tree trunks, but merely seek their prey in the cracks and crannies that serve as its refuge. For this kind of hunting they have a long and slender beak that curves slightly downward.

"As their name implies, climbers show great agility in climbing. Their beak is very narrow, the better to penetrate the cracks in the bark of trees, and it is bent like an arch and has a fine point. Their feet have three talons pointing forward and one, much stronger, pointing backward. We have in France two climbers, one of which is furnished with a tail composed of a few long, stiff feathers that serve as a support to the bird in climbing, as the woodpecker's tail serves that bird, while the other is not thus equipped.

"The so-called common climber is a tiny bird with whitish plumage spotted with brown above and tinged with red on the rump and tail. Its life is a most laborious one. It frequents woods, orchards, and the trees of our public promenades, where you may see it always busily engaged in examining every square inch of the surface of tree trunks in order to thrust its slender beak into the cracks of the bark and catch any lurking gnats, bugs,

Hoopoe

caterpillars, or cocoons. It runs down the trunk as fast as it runs up, which woodpeckers cannot do, their progress always being upward, either in a straight line or spirally. It ascends in little leaps and bounds, and helps itself along by propping its tail against the tree. Arrived at the top of the trunk, it descends quickly and begins the same operations on the next tree. At every step it cheers itself up with its sharp, flute-like cry. At nightfall it retires into some hole in a tree trunk. There, too, it makes its nest, which is formed of fine grasses and bits of moss held together by threads from spiders' webs. Its eggs, from five to seven in number, are pure white with red spots.

"The wall-climber, or scaler, makes its way up the perpendicular faces of rocks, ramparts, and old walls, prying out all the various insects and their eggs that may be lurking in the fissures. With its large claws it clings to these vertical surfaces and does not use its tail as a support. This bird, which is of about the size of a lark, has unusually beautiful plumage of a light ash color, with touches of bright red, black, and pure white on the wings. The throat is black, and so is the tail, the latter being edged with white at the tip. The richness of its coloring and the habit it has of remaining stationary in its flight before the rock or other surface it is exploring, just as butterflies hold themselves motionless on their wings while they suck the honey of flowers with their trumpet, have given it the expressive name of butterfly of the rocks. It inhabits the Alps, the Pyrenees, and the Jura Mountains. In winter it visits old buildings in our towns.

"The hoopoe is especially remarkable for its double row of long red feathers edged with black and white, which, at the bird's pleasure, are made to lie down toward the back or stand upright on the head and spread out as a handsome crest. The rest of the plumage is wine-colored, except the tail and wings, which are black. The wings are also ornamented with white stripes running across them.

"In size this bird is about as large as a turtle-dove. It lives alone and prefers to remain on the ground usually, rarely perching unless on the lower branches of trees. Its favorite haunts are moist fields, which it walks over at a sedate pace, every now and then erecting its beautiful crest either from satisfaction at having found a savory mouthful or because of being startled by something, for it is a very timid bird. With its long beak it digs in the ground for grubs, beetles, and crickets; or it gathers ants on its viscous tongue. When it has had enough it withdraws to some low branch and there digests its food at leisure. At the mating season it says, *poo, poo*, whence without doubt comes its familiar nickname of poo-poo.

"Elegant though it is in appearance, the hoopoe is not at all particular about the condition of its nest, which it makes in the interior of a worm-eaten tree trunk. It lines the hole with a mortar composed of clay and cows' dung, whereon it places a little bed of dry leaves and moss. This nest, so deep and so hard to keep clean, ought to be cleared out daily, but the parent bird does nothing about it, leaving the filth to accumulate until it forms a rampart all around the nest. This barricade may serve as an excellent defense against the birdnest-hunter, who would naturally hesitate to thrust his hand into the foul mess; and so I will not censure the bird too severely for its poor housekeeping.

"The hoopoe is with us only in summer. Toward the first of September it crosses the Mediterranean to pass the winter under the warmer skies of Africa."

CHAPTER XXV

THE CUCKOO

IN AN old pear-tree with dense foliage, at the foot of the garden, a black-headed warbler had built its nest. Day by day
Jules had watched the bird as it brought blades of dry grass,
one by one, and wove them into the shape of a cup, after which
it furnished the interior with a hair mattress. Then came the
eggs, to the number of five, light chestnut in color, marbled with
darker streaks. Parting the branches very gently in the mother's
absence, and standing on tiptoe, Jules had peeped into the nest,
but of course without touching anything; he had merely cast a
rapid glance at the pretty cluster of five eggs lying together at
the bottom. The laying was over, his uncle told him; now would
begin the incubation, and in a few days five little creatures, blind
and featherless, would at the slightest rustling of the foliage
stretch their yellow beaks wide open in mute appeal for food.
Already Jules was looking forward to the good time he would
have in watching, from a distance, the bringing up of the brood,
and was planning how, when the little birds should have grown
a trifle larger, he would put some small caterpillars and worms
on the end of a stick and drop them into the nest for the young
ones to eat. Then before long the new-fledged warblers would
leave the nest and the garden would have five more caterpillar-
destroyers repaying with their services and joyful songs the
kind-hearted attentions of their boy friend.

That was what Jules was eagerly looking forward to yesterday, but to-day he returns from his visit to the nest with a
troubled look on his face. A strange thing has happened: with
the warbler's five eggs there is a sixth one, a little larger and of

a different color. Whence comes this strange egg? Who put it in the nest, and why?

Uncle Paul, on being consulted, went to the nest and came back with the egg.

"Your warbler's nest, my dear child," he said, "has had a fortunate escape; but for your visit this morning the young birds would have been lost almost as soon as they were hatched. This egg that I have brought back is a cuckoo's egg."

"But I don't see how it came to be in the warbler's nest or what danger it threatened to the young birds that are coming."

"You will see when I tell you the cuckoo's habits. It is a curious story. The cuckoo is the bird that in early spring, when the meadows are sprinkled with violets and the trees are just putting forth their leaves, keeps repeating its cry of *cuckoo, cuckoo*, in a clear and plaintive tone."

"I have often heard it," said Jules, "singing on the edges of woods, but have never been able to get a good look at it."

"I have seen it flying away," Emile put in, "and it seemed to me pretty large."

"The cuckoo is at least as large as a turtle-dove," their uncle continued. "Its plumage is ashy gray on the back and white underneath, with numerous brown crosswise stripes resembling those seen on many birds of prey. The wings are long, as is also the tail, which is spotted and tipped with white. Despite its likeness to the goshawk and sparrow-hawk, the cuckoo is not to be classed as a bird of prey. Its talons lack the necessary strength, and its beak, which is rather long, is flattened and only slightly curved. Those are neither the hooked claws nor the savage beak of a bird living the life of a murderer. The cuckoo's food consists entirely of insects and caterpillars. You remember the processionaries of the oak tree, those frightful black caterpillars that spin large silken nests against the trunk of a tree and bristle with barbed hairs that cause such terrible itching if you touch them?"

"Yes," answered Jules; "and you told us that the cuckoo eats those caterpillars."

"It feasts on them, as it does on all hairy caterpillars; but the hairs are rolled up into a ball in the stomach and thrown up through the beak. As a greedy devourer of insects and caterpillars the cuckoo deserves protection; the only regret is that a multitude of little birds most useful to us should be destroyed by it. Let us consider the facts of the case.

"The female cuckoo never builds a nest, nor does she know how to hatch out her own young; but let us plead the best excuse we can for her. Her breast seems to be so formed as not to impart enough warmth to eggs to make them hatch; and, more than that, she lays so often throughout the summer as to leave her no time for making a home of her own. In short, this bird never knows the joy of taking care of her young. It is not because she will not hatch her own eggs, but because she cannot. She has to leave this work to other birds."

"Then the cuckoo's egg I found in the garden nest was left there for the warbler to take care of?" Jules inquired.

"Precisely. Now see by what wonderful planning the strange egg comes to be adopted by another mother. Bear in mind that the cuckoo lives exclusively on insects. The young cuckoo must have caterpillars. Where will food of this sort be found if not in the nests of birds that feed on insects, as for instance warblers, redbreasts, tomtits, nightingales, stonechats, wagtails, and others? It is to just these nests that the cuckoo goes. Sometimes it may chance to lay its eggs in the nests of birds that live on seeds, such as linnets, bullfinches, greenfinches, or yellow-hammers; but even then the choice is wise; for if the foster-parents are eaters of seeds they bring up their young on worms, which are easier to digest, and so the little cuckoo finds in these nests food suited to its needs. But the cuckoo's eggs are never laid in the nests of quails, partridges, or other species whose young are granivorous from the beginning. In a brood whose habitual diet was not theirs the changelings would surely die of hunger."

"But how," asked Jules, "does the cuckoo know what nests to choose and what ones not to choose, when it lays its eggs?"

"If it knew why it laid its eggs where it does, I should have to admit that the cuckoo's sagacity surpassed man's; but it does not know at all the reason for its choice. A wise Providence has arranged everything for the bird. The egg—which, judged by the cuckoo's size, should be as large as a pigeon's or a turtle-dove's—is hardly as big as a sparrow's, so that it can easily find a place in the warbler's or even the wren's tiny nest without arousing the adoptive mother's suspicions. Moreover, this egg is variable in its color, as if the better to harmonize with the coloring of those with which it will be incubated, whether in this or that or the other nest. Sometimes the cuckoo's egg is ash-colored, at other times red, green, or pale blue. It may closely resemble the sparrow's eggs, or it may be mottled with spots of smaller or larger size, in lesser or greater numbers; or, again, it may be marbled with black streaks. But, despite these variations, it is always easy to see the difference between the cuckoo's egg and the others in a nest. If one of the eggs is found to differ from the others in shape and color, that one certainly came from the cuckoo. By that sign alone I recognized the egg we have here from the warbler's nest."

"The other five," Jules declared, "are as like one another as so many drops of water; but the sixth, which you have there, is very different."

"And that is why I am sure it belongs to the cuckoo," replied his uncle.

"The cuckoo seems to me," said Louis, "very large to be able to get into such a small nest as the warbler's, the redbreast's, or the nightingale's, so as to lay its egg there."

"That is not what the bird does. The egg is laid on the ground, anywhere; then the mother takes it up in her beak, puts it in a sort of pocket at the base of her gullet—a pocket provided for that purpose—and flies through the neighboring thickets on the lookout for a place for its final reception. When she finds a nest to suit her she stretches her neck over the edge, opens her beak, and lets the egg gently drop among the others. That done, the cuckoo flies away and never returns to learn the result. Other eggs are placed in the same way, here and there, one by one, in different nests."

"And do the owners of the nests make no objections?" asked Jules.

"If they are at home they receive the cuckoo with angry pecks and chase her away; but she usually succeeds in choosing the right moment and approaches the nest by stealth when the owners are absent."

"But when they come back they must see at least that there is a strange egg in the nest and throw it out."

"Not at all. Whether or not the mother bird perceives that there is an egg too many, I could not say. But at any rate, as there must be cuckoos in the world, things are so arranged that their species shall not become extinct, and all the eggs in the nest are watched over and hatched with impartial care, until the last young bird is out. At first all goes well enough: the young ones need but little food, and for one more the parents can easily find enough worms. All are fed alike, with no more for the children of the house than for the stranger.

"But pretty soon the young cuckoo is found to be growing faster than the others; it will soon need for itself alone all the food that its foster-parents can possibly secure with the utmost industry; it is always opening its wide beak, always complaining of hunger. Moreover, it is cramped for room in the little house of hair and wool. Its featherless body, squatting there flat and red, its large head, its bottomless abyss of a beak, its big, bulging eyes, all give it the appearance of a toad sitting at the bottom of the nest. There is no longer room in the house for all its inmates, nor yet enough food to live on. Then a dreadful deed is done. The young cuckoo slips under one of the little birds, takes it on its back, which is hollowed as if for the purpose, and holds it there by slightly raising its wings. Dragging itself backward to the raised rim of the nest, it rests a moment, and then throws the burden over."

"The horrid creature throws out of the nest the little one of the bird that feeds it?" exclaimed Emile incredulously.

"Yes, in cold blood, so as to have more room for itself. With the tips of its wings it feels around for a moment to make sure the little bird is gone, and then returns to the bottom of the nest to go through the same process with another. And so they all go, one after another, to the very last; all are thrown out of the nest."

"I'd like to be there to catch him at it—the scoundrel!" was Emile's comment.

"What becomes of the poor little things pushed out of their own home by the ungrateful young cuckoo? If the nest is high above the ground all perish, crushed by their fall, and the ants immediately begin to suck their blood. If it is low, some live and take refuge in the moss, where the mother comes to console them and bring them something to eat. The cuckoo remains in sole possession of the nest."

"And the horrid toad will starve to death there," said Jules. "The father and mother, now that their brood is destroyed, won't bring it anything more to eat."

"That is where you are mistaken. They continue to feed it liberally, as if nothing had happened; they perform wonders to satisfy its big appetite; they do not allow themselves a minute's rest in their efforts to fill that beak that is always open and is wide enough to swallow the nurses themselves."

"Then the warbler isn't afraid of her greedy nursling that might gobble her up any moment?" queried Jules.

"Although she is its mother only by chance, she is devoted to it. She comes joyfully with a caterpillar at the end of her beak while the cuckoo gapes at the edge of the nest, as ugly as a little monster. With no tremor of fear the warbler delivers the mouthful by putting her head into the yawning gulf. The gulf closes, swallows, and yawns again, demanding something more, and all haste is made to satisfy its needs."

"Kind warbler!" murmured Jules. "What self-denial in order to bring up the ugly rascal that has ravaged her nest!"

"So it has to be," Uncle Paul rejoined, "or we should long ago have been left with no cuckoos in the world to help us get rid of the processionary caterpillars of the oak-tree."

"All the same, I don't like that bird." And with this Jules took up the cuckoo's egg he had found in the garden nest. "May I?" said he to his uncle, with a gesture.

"Yes, I have no objection," answered Uncle Paul, who preferred five warblers in his garden to one vagabond cuckoo. And *smack* went the egg as the boy dashed it to the ground.

CHAPTER XXVI

SHRIKES

"ALL SORTS of absurd stories have been made up about the cuckoo and its curious habits, and thus fable has added to the actual facts, which are in themselves strange enough. Even to-day there are in circulation any number of fairy tales on the subject of this bird. I will tell you a few of them in order to put you on your guard against these childish notions.

"First, they say cuckoos change their nature twice a year, being cuckoos in the spring and sparrow-hawks the rest of the year. According to this account, the bird comes to us from some distant country in April in its first form on the back of a kite that is so accommodating as to serve it as a mount. This mode of travel is adopted by the cuckoo to spare its own wings, still too weak to carry it. Undoubtedly the bird's plumage—which, as I have told you, resembles in its brown crosswise stripes on the breast the plumage of certain birds of prey—has fostered this popular belief in the changing of the cuckoo into a sparrow-hawk and of the sparrow-hawk into a cuckoo. People have allowed themselves to be deceived by this variegated dress. When the bird sings in April and May it is a cuckoo because it has the cuckoo's cry; but when it falls silent in summer it becomes a sparrow-hawk because it has the plumage of one. So the cuckoo is changed into a sparrow-hawk, and when spring comes again the sparrow-hawk is changed into a cuckoo once more. For thousands and thousands of years this nonsense has been believed by most people.

"The cuckoo is a migratory bird: it remains with us from April to September, but departs for Africa at the approach of winter. To explain its reappearance in the spring some one invented the story of its being carried on the back of a kite; but I need not assure you that there is not a word of truth in this fairy tale. The cuckoo is always a cuckoo, and it returns from warmer climes on its own wings, as does the swallow. Another legend is that the cuckoo turns into a toad."

"Isn't that because the cuckoo, when it is young and before it has any feathers, is very ugly and looks like a toad?" asked Jules.

"Exactly. And, finally, the bird is accused of discharging on plants a fatal saliva that breeds insects. The truth of the matter is that a tiny insect, light green and shaped somewhat like a grasshopper, is in the habit of pricking the stems of plants with its sucker to make the sap run; and this sap presents the appearance of a white foam that looks like saliva. The insect takes its position in the midst of this cool and foamy froth to shelter itself from the heat of the sun and to drink at its leisure. There you have the real facts in the case. 'Cuckoo-spit' is the name popularly given to the insect. It does little harm to plants. In reality, then, the supposed harmful saliva of the cuckoo is merely an ingenious means employed by an inoffensive little creature to keep itself cool. Many other ridiculous stories are told about the cuckoo, but it would be only a waste of time to dwell on them. Let us get on.

"We have already had occasion several times to speak of our doubtful helpers, those co-workers whose valuable services are offset by certain grave offenses. You have just seen how that devourer of hairy caterpillars, the cuckoo, is guilty of the blackest ingratitude toward the warbler, its nurse, in brutally throwing out of their nest the little birds which would have become model caterpillar-destroyers. That is a rather high price to pay for the destruction of oak-tree processionary caterpillars. To finish the list of these birds whose conduct deserves, from an agricultural point of view, both praise and blame, I will tell you about the shrike, a great insect-destroyer, but also a barbarous slaughterer of small birds.

SHRIKE

"Despite their diminutive size—the largest shrike being hardly as big as a thrush—these birds have the fierce boldness of the most powerful birds of prey. They will even pursue any falcon that ventures near their nest. Their diet consists chiefly of large insects; but unfortunately they also pounce on little birds, greedily devouring their brains and afterward tearing their flesh to shreds and eating it too. For this life of rapine they have a strong hooked beak, toothed toward the tip of the upper mandible, and powerful talons ending in sharp nails that resemble in miniature the claws of birds of prey. We have in this country four species of shrikes.

"The common shrike is of the size of a blackbird, and its plumage is ashy gray above and white underneath. A wide black stripe, starting from the beak, continues around the eye and runs down over the cheek. The wings and tail are black, ornamented with white. The bird likes to perch on lofty tree-tops, where it keeps repeating its cry of *truee, truee*, in a piercing tone. In flying from tree to tree it looks as if it were going to alight on the ground; but presently it rises again, describing a graceful curve in the air. Its food consists chiefly of field-mice and large beetles, but occasionally of small birds which it catches on the wing. It likes to build its nest in tangled and thorny hedges, and lays from four to six eggs, reddish in color and encircled toward the large end by a ring of brown spots. Similar rings are found placed in the same way on the eggs of our various other shrikes and furnish a distinctive and easily recognizable characteristic mark.

"The black-headed shrike can be recognized, as its name indicates, by the wide black stripe that encircles the forehead.

This bird is of about the lark's size and has the plumage of the common shrike except on the stomach, which is reddish. The eggs, white tinted with red, have the ring at the large end formed of numerous little spots, red, brown, or violet in color.

"The red shrike is slightly smaller. The top of its head and the back of its neck are bright red, the stomach and rump white. Otherwise the plumage is like that of the two species just described.

"The red-backed shrike is the smallest and the best-known of our shrikes. It is ash color on the head and rump, chestnut red on the back, and light red underneath. A black ring encircles the eye, the throat is white, and the large tail-feathers and wing-feathers are black.

"These last three shrikes that I have named can at will imitate the various cries of small birds, and they make use of this talent, it is said, to lure them to their destruction. The red-backed shrike is especially expert in this. It first hides in some dense shrubbery and then imitates the song of whatever species it hears chirping in the neighborhood. The imprudent ones come at its call, which they think proceeds from one of their own kind, and the red-backed shrike pounces on them as soon as it has them well within reach. But this trick succeeds only with inexperienced little birds, the older ones knowing it and taking care not to be deceived. The captured bird is skinned before being eaten, and that is the origin of the French name (*écorcheur*, flayer) given to this fourth species of shrike. The others, however, share this habit. As they lack the faculty of rolling the feathers into a ball and throwing them up after digestion, as do the hornless owls, these birds take the precaution to prepare the game beforehand by tearing off the skin in shreds. It is a quick way of plucking their victim. Notwithstanding its talent in imitating the calls of other birds, the red-backed shrike is not so lucky as to make dupes every day. In case of failure the shrike contents itself with common mice, field-mice, grasshoppers, June-bugs, and fat beetles. Such is the shrike's passion for beetles that when it has eaten all it can it continues to hunt them just for the fun of hunting; and, not knowing what to do with the captured insects, it impales them on the thorns of bushes. Perhaps that is its way of stocking its larder with food and letting it acquire a strong flavor like venison, a flavor much to its taste.

"The other shrikes also have this mania for laying up reserves of beetles stuck on thorns, reserves which the bird does not always come back for, and which often dry up on the spot without being touched. But this waste of game is of little consequence, as the final result is always to our advantage: we are delivered from a multitude of foes by these eager hunters. When they do us such service shall we count it an unpardonable crime that they sometimes allow themselves the pleasure of feasting on little birds? For my part I should be very reluctant to do so. I pity with all my heart the poor little bird that foolishly lets itself be caught by the shrike; but I also have a lively sympathy for the beautiful tree which, if bereft of its defenders, would soon be given over to the worms and honeycombed with holes all packed with filth.

"The red-backed shrike frequents groves, orchards, and gardens. It nests in thick hedges, sometimes in the interlacing branches of apple trees. Its eggs are white tinged with red. The ring at the large end is composed of brown, gray, and greenish spots. In building its nest the bird uses a kind of everlasting that grows abundantly in the fields and has stems all covered with a white cotton-like fluff. The inside of the nest is furnished with a couch of little twigs and fine rootlets interwoven and comfortably overlaid with wool, down, and horsehair. The other shrikes use in their nests the same materials, especially the everlasting with its white fluff."

CHAPTER XXVII

THE TITMOUSE

" A T LAST we come to some caterpillar-destroyers that are never anything but helpful. First of all there is the titmouse, also known as the tomtit.

"It is a graceful little bird, lively and quick-tempered, always on the go, flying continually from tree to tree, carefully inspecting the branches, hanging from the tip ends of the slenderest of them in all sorts of positions, often head downward, swaying this way and that with its flexible support and never letting go its hold, while it examines all buds that it suspects of containing worms, and tears these buds to pieces in order to get at the grubs and insect eggs they contain. It is calculated that a titmouse consumes three hundred thousand insect eggs a year, and certainly few birds have larger families to provide for! Twenty or more little ones all huddled together in the same nest are not too great a strain on the parent's energy and industry. The mother bird has to examine buds and the fissures in the bark

TUFTED TITMOUSE

of trees in order to find grubs, spiders, caterpillars, worms of every kind, and feed a score of beaks always open and demanding food in the bottom of the nest. She comes with a caterpillar, the brood is all excitement, twenty mouths fly open, but only one receives the morsel, leaving nineteen still expectant. Then away flies the titmouse again without an instant's pause, to seek more food. Thus back and forth she flies, without rest and without weariness; and by the time the twentieth mouth is fed the first one is again open, and has been open a good while, clamoring for more.

"I will leave you to guess how many worms are eaten in a day by such a household; and I will also let you reach your own conclusions regarding the value of these birds as caterpillar-hunters among our fruit trees. Complaint is made, I know, that they tear open the buds and destroy them; but the harm they do is only apparent. When they pluck a bud it is to get out some tiny larva lodged between two scales, and not to harm the young leaves or flowers that are forming. It is better that this wormy bud should perish; it would not have produced anything, and the enemy lodged within it would have produced countless others to ravage the tree the next year."

"Then the titmouse does not feed on vegetable matter?" asked Louis.

"No, except perhaps occasionally on a few seeds, such as those of hemp. The bird requires animal food; small insects of all kinds, their eggs and larvæ, suit it best. Its appetite for prey is so keen that it has the courage to attack little, disabled birds or those caught in snares, pecking at their skulls and greedily devouring their brains. It is true that the titmouse is remarkably courageous despite its smallness of size; it is extremely quick and quarrelsome, and a regular little ogre in time of famine. Its beak is conical, strong, short, and pointed; and its claws end in hooked nails designed for seizing their victims, like the talons of birds of prey. With these the bird grasps its food and conveys it to its beak, like the parrot.

"At the end of the brooding season the tomtits all assemble in companies of one or two families each and travel together by short stages. These companies appear to have a leader, prob-ably the father or the mother, and every now and then they are called together from one tree to another, after which they separate again, only to reunite once more at the leader's summons. Their flight is short and irregular: they scatter through the woods, gardens, fields, and orchards, inspecting trees and bushes on the way and picking up larvæ and insects.

"The titmouse family is made up of many species. We have eight in our country, but I shall speak only of the principal ones.

"The coal-tit is the largest, being of about the redbreast's size. It is bluish gray on the back and yellow underneath. The head is of a beautiful glossy black, and a wide stripe of the same color runs down the middle of the chest and stomach and around the eyes, which are also set off by a large white spot. The large wing-feathers are edged with ashy blue.

"This bird is very common in copses and gardens, and is the one we hear in autumn repeating, as it examines the bark of fruit trees, its cry of *titipoo, titipoo, titipoo.* At times this cry has a harsh sound like the rasping of a file, and this has given to the bird, in some neighborhoods, the name of locksmith. It nests in a hollow tree trunk, lining its quarters with some soft, silky material, chiefly fine feathers. Its laying consists of about fifteen white eggs spotted with light red, especially toward the large end. Its family demands not fewer than three hundred caterpillars a day, or their equivalent in vermin of some sort. What the gardener, the nurseryman, and the forester owe this valiant caterpillar-destroyer by the end of the year cannot be calculated. Yet I have seen these very persons angrily thrust an arm into the hollow trunk of an old apple-tree to pull out the coal-tit's nest and throw the whole thing to the winds,—eggs, feathers, and little birds only a day old. And they thought they were doing something worthy of praise, for according to them the coal-tit eats buds. But I declare that the coal-tit does not eat buds; it eats the little larvæ lodged in the bud's scales, and its instinct never allows it to molest healthy buds, which contain nothing of any value to the bird. Leave it in peace, then, to pluck the wormy buds, which it can very easily tell from the sound ones.

"The coal-tit sometimes eats hemp-seed or hazelnuts, picking out the edible part with a dexterity of beak and claw—I had almost said hand—possessed by no other bird. The sparrow, chaffinch, goldfinch, and others crush the hemp-seed between their mandibles; the coal-tit grasps it in its claw, carries it to the beak, and makes in the shell a small round opening through which it picks out the meat. The hazelnut is managed with the same skill.

"The blue tit is a beautiful little bird that keeps company with the coal-tit and frequents orchards. It is olive-colored above and yellow underneath, with the top of the head an azure blue, the forehead white, and the cheeks white framed in black. A little collar of black also encircles the back and sides of the neck. The large feathers of the tail and wings are edged with blue. This titmouse, so elegant in plumage, so graceful in its bearing, always running about over the bark of tree trunks and around the branches, always hanging from the flexible boughs, and always pecking and searching, is no whit inferior to the coal-tit in its talent for catching caterpillars. It has been seen in a few hours to clear a rosebush of two thousand plant-lice. Caterpillars and the eggs of insects, especially of those that attack fruit, are its chief food. It is very fond of little birds' brains, but if need be can get along with hemp-seed. Like the coal-tit, it nests in a hollow tree trunk, its nest being nothing but a heap of small feathers. No other species raises a larger family. The eggs are more than twenty in number, white with reddish spots, especially at the large end.

"Two other tomtits, of less value as caterpillar-destroyers, build their nests with much art. They are the long-tailed titmouse and the penduline.

"The first of these is different from all other tomtits in the length of its tail, which forms more than half the length of the body. This bird lives in the woods during the summer and visits our gardens and orchards only in the winter. It is a small bird, scarcely bigger than a wren, reddish gray on the back and white underneath, with a tinge of red on the stomach and with white nape and cheeks.

"The nest is occasionally built in the fork of some branch in bush or hedge, a few feet from the ground, but oftener it is attached to the trunk of a willow or a poplar. Its shape is that of an elongated oval or, rather, an enormous cocoon enlarged at the base, with an entrance on the side about an inch from the top. The outside is made of lichens such as grow on old tree trunks, having thus the appearance of bark and deceiving the casual observer. Filaments of wool bind the whole compactly together. The dome or roof, ingeniously contrived for shedding rain, is a thick felt of moss and cobweb. The inside is like an oven with a bowl-shaped bottom and high arched top. Its shape and the thick layer of soft feathers lining it make the nest warm and cozy. From sixteen to twenty young birds are packed into the narrow space, which does not exceed the hollow of the hand. By what miracle of orderly arrangement do these twenty little creatures and their mother manage to find room for themselves in this tiny abode, and how can tails of such length develop there? It would be impossible to find anywhere a more economical use of space."

"How I should like to see the twenty little tomtits snuggling together in that tiny nest!" Emile exclaimed.

"I have had that good fortune," said his uncle, "and even now I am strangely moved whenever I think of those twenty little heads stretching up from the bottom of the nest, trembling and with open beaks as if their mother had come. I looked for a moment through the opening of the nest at the tiny creatures, and then withdrew. The parents were already at hand, ruffling their feathers with anxiety. Fear nothing, little birds, so watchful of your family; Uncle Paul is not one to commit the crime of touching your nest."

"Nor Emile, either," chimed in the boy.

"Nor yet Jules or Louis," added the last-named.

"I hope not, indeed; for otherwise Uncle Paul would tell you no more stories.

"The penduline's nest is still more remarkable. This titmouse

LONG-TAILED TITMICE

is found hardly anywhere except along the banks of the lower
Rhone. It hangs its nest very high, from the tip of some swaying
tree branch by the waterside, so that its young are gently rocked
by the breeze from the water. The nest is a sort of oval purse
about as large as a quart bottle and pierced on the side near the
top by a narrow opening that would hardly admit a man's thumb.
To enter its nest the tomtit, small though it is, must stretch the

elastic wall, which yields a little and then contracts again. This purse-shaped abode is made of the cotton-like fluff that flies off in May from the ripe catkins of poplars and willows. The bird gathers this material and then weaves it together with a warp of wool and hemp. The resulting fabric resembles the felt of a coarse hat.

"I am at a loss to understand how the bird manages to weave with its beak and claws a stuff superior to any that the unaided human fingers could produce; and yet it does this with no instruction, with no hesitation, and with no hints from the work of others. At its very first attempt the titmouse puts to shame the studied art of our weavers and fullers. The top or roof of the nest includes in its structure the tip of the branch from which it hangs and also the little twigs growing out of that tip end which serve as a framework for the vault; but the foliage emerges from the sides of the nest and furnishes shade from the sun's heat. Finally, to secure the nest more firmly, cordage of wool and hemp binds the upper part to the branch and below is worked into the woof of the felt. The inside is lined with poplar fluff of the best quality. It takes a pair of pendulines three weeks of the hardest work to make this marvel."

"Doesn't the rain ever get through the covering of the nest?" Emile inquired.

"No; the felt is so thick and so closely woven that even with the hardest rain not a drop of water can leak into the cotton-lined interior."

"How comfortable the little birds must be in their snug nest! The wind rocks them gently over the water, and from their little window they can see the river flowing below. What is this clever penduline like?"

"It is ash-colored, with brown wings and tail, and a black stripe across the forehead. Its dress is simple, you see, as is always the case with those that possess real merit. The blue tit has rich plumage, but when it comes to nest-building it can only pile feathers on top of one another at the bottom of a tree-hollow. The penduline is of modest appearance, but it builds the most wonderful nest it is possible to find. To each his portion, talent or fine clothes."

"All of us here choose talent," declared Jules.

"Never, my children," urged Uncle Paul, "be untrue to that sentiment."

"We should have to forget your teachings," the other replied, "before we could do that."

"And what are the eggs like?" asked Emile.

"Emile is bound to have all I can tell him about the penduline. Does this builder of felt nests interest you, then, so very much?"

"Yes, it does," Emile assured him.

"Well, the eggs are quite white and rather long. There are three or four of them to a nest."

"No more than that, when the other tomtits have twenty?"

"No more; but to make up for it there are two layings a year."

CHAPTER XXVIII

THE WREN AND THE KINGLET

"A NOTHER HIGHLY talented architect, past master in the building of nests, is the wren, known in learned language as the troglodyte. If you ask me the meaning of this strange name I shall reply that it is a Greek word signifying 'dweller in holes.' Some inventor of names, more in love with Greek than desirous of being understood, thought he was doing a fine thing when he gave this big name to the little bird that worms its way into small holes as a mouse would. Perhaps my description will be more easily understood than his hard name. The troglodyte or wren is a fluffy bunch of plumage resembling that of the woodcock. With trailing wings, beak to windward, and tail erect over its rump, it is always frisking and hopping about, uttering the while its cheery cry of *teederee, teeree, teeree*."

"I know that bird," Jules broke in. "It isn't much bigger than a walnut, and every winter it comes flying about the house, hunting in the woodpile and in holes in the walls, and darting into the thickest parts of bushes. From a distance you would take it for a bold little rat."

"That is it, that is the wren. In summer it lives in densely grown woods. There, under the arch formed by some large upward-curving root coated with a thick fleece of moss, it builds a home for itself in imitation

WINTER WREN

of the penduline's nest. The materials it uses are bits of moss, which make the nest look like its support. It forms them into a large hollow ball with a very narrow opening on one side. It is lined with feathers. Occasionally the wren builds its nest in some chimney or a pile of fag-ots, a thick clump of ivy or a natural cavity in the bank of a shady stream.

GREAT CAROLINA WREN

The laying consists of about ten white eggs dotted with red at the large end.

"When the weather turns cold, the bird leaves the woods and approaches our farm-houses. You can see it then, always busy and on the move, prying into dark holes in woodpiles, old walls, dead trees, and thick bushes, looking in every crack and cranny for all kinds of vermin that take up their winter quarters in the fissures with which old bark is furrowed and in the cracks that occur in weather-beaten mortar. To gain an idea of their unceasing activity in this sort of research, you have only to watch them once as they go prying into a heap of brush, flying in and out on all sides of it without a moment's pause for rest."

"Yes," assented Jules, "but it is so tiny a creature it can't do much work."

"If the wren hunted big game, certainly at the end of the day it would not have captured its prey by the dozen. What could such a little thing do with a June-bug? It would not come to the end of such a supply of food for several days."

"And the June-bug would be too hard for its beak, too," remarked Jules.

Long-billed Marsh Wren

"What it needs is the smallest of caterpillars and the tiniest of gnats, which make a more delicate mouthful and are better adapted to the bird's small throat. I need not remind you that the worst foes to our crops are the smallest. A grub too tiny to catch the eye endangers our cereals, and others equally small ravage our fruit while it is still in the bud. How much does it take to destroy a blossom that would produce a pear the size of your two fists? One single larva just visible to the naked eye. Well, the wren attacks these tiny foes of ours that are all the more troublesome because we cannot see them easily. Now guess how many little caterpillars a day the wren needs for feeding its brood. Observers whose patience I admire have calculated the number."

"Let us say ten caterpillars to each little bird," replied Jules, "and ten little birds in the nest. That would make a hundred caterpillars a day, and it is certainly a lot."

"A lot! Ah, how far out you are in your reckoning! The mother wren brings something to her little ones at least thirty-six times an hour. She feeds them a mixed diet of insects, larvæ and eggs. At the end of a day the number of insects destroyed, of one kind and another, amounts to one hundred and fifty-six thousand. That leaves your paltry hundred a long way behind, my dear Jules."

"Then the caterpillars must be very small, or the brood of wrens would die of indigestion."

"Undoubtedly they are exceedingly small, and then a great many are not even hatched yet; but the result as far as we are concerned is just as important, so many eggs devoured meaning so many ravagers the fewer a little later."

"Supposing," said Louis, "that the wren takes only the worms that attack pears, that would be one hundred and fifty-six thousand pears the little birds would save for us in one day?"

"Evidently."

"But that is beyond belief."

"I admit that the result is very great in comparison with the means employed. A tiny bird that nobody notices goes pecking here and there, and we find that at the end of the day the caterpillar-eater has destroyed, either in the egg or in the nymph-stage or in the final form, thousands of insects which, if allowed to live, would have deprived us of enormous basketfuls of fruit and hundreds of bushels of grain. If we were to estimate the value of the crops saved by insectivorous birds, it would be a fabulous sum. Leave them, therefore, in peace, my children, and do all you can to protect them; for these busy little creatures ward off famine from our homes.

"While we are on the subject let us speak of another little Tom Thumb of a bird, another caterpillar-destroyer as energetic as the wren. It is called the kinglet, that is to say, the little king, on account of the crown of golden yellow edged with black that encircles its head. It is the smallest of our birds. It is olive-colored above and yellowish-white beneath. Its beautiful crown feathers can stand up like a crest.

"The kinglet breeds in the cold countries of Europe, and especially in the fir forests of Norway. Its nest is a little ball no bigger than your fist, open at the top, artistically fashioned outside with moss, wool, and spiders' webs, and lined with the softest down. It rests flat on some fir branch at an inaccessible

GOLDCREST
(An American species of kinglet)

height. The eggs, from six to eight in number, are of a uniform flesh color.

"Although very delicate in appearance, the kinglet stands the cold with great hardihood. It comes to us from the land of its birth in small flocks when the autumnal fogs are gathering and the leaves are falling. These flocks of five or six birds at most scatter through the woods, public promenades, and orchards, to examine the cracks in bark, to explore the heaps of dead leaves, and to inspect the buds while clinging to the tips of the smallest branches. Not even the tomtit shows itself a more expert gymnast in hanging with head downward and working in all sorts of attitudes. The task of destroying caterpillars is accompanied by a continual little rallying cry: *zee-zee-zee, zee-zee-zee.*

"The kinglet has great confidence in mankind. With no sign of fear even when within hearing of the footsteps and conversation of persons walking about, it continues its evolutions, its hunting, its *zee-zee-zee.* It will let one come close, almost near enough to reach out a hand and take hold of it. But the knowing little creature, although it appears not to see you because it is so busy, darts suddenly away and mounts to the upper branches to carry on its work at a safer distance."

CHAPTER XXIX

SWALLOWS

"WE HAVE whole tribes of helpers that devote themselves to the patient search for insect eggs in the cracks of tree bark and in piles of dead leaves, for larvæ between the scales of buds and in the worm-holes in wood, and for insects lurking in narrow crevices where they hide from their pursuers. These invaluable assistants of ours embrace the magpies, nuthatches, wrynecks, climbers, tomtits, wrens, kinglets, and many others. In the kind of hunting here referred to the bird is not obliged to chase the game, to vie with it in swiftness; it is enough to know how to find it in its hiding-place. For this a sharp eye and a slender beak are necessary; wings are only of secondary importance.

"But now we come to other species of birds that hunt in the air, chase their game on the wing, pursuing gnats and flies and butterflies, moths and mosquitoes and beetles. They require a short beak, but one that opens very wide and is pretty sure to catch insects as they fly—a beak, in fine, that may be depended on to work almost of itself and without an instant's pause in the bird's flight; a beak that, above all, is so sticky inside that as soon as an insect's wing grazes this viscous lining it is caught fast in the glue-like substance. The beak of the bat, that other hunter of insects on the wing, the bat's beak, I say, opening from ear to ear, may serve as a model in respect to the width of its opening. But above all else the hunter must have swift wings that never tire, that can fly as fast as the prey which is trying so hard to escape, that can follow the bewildering zigzags of a moth manœuvering to save its life. A cleft beak that opens wide and wings that are strong and tire-less—such must be the equipment of the bird that pursues its prey in the open air.

"Chief among these hunters is the swallow, which may be called the daylight bat, as the bat is the twilight swallow. Both chase fly-ing insects, following them in their endless dodgings and dou-blings and snapping them up with yawning beak, then passing on without an instant's delay to the

White-bellied Swallow

pursuit of others. But how much more pleasing in appearance, how much swifter in flight is the swallow than that hunter, the sad-looking bat! While we may compare their work and their way of hunting, we cannot compare them in anything else. Buf-fon quotes Guéneau de Montbéliard as saying:

" 'The air is the swallow's appropriate element, and it is the nature of the bird to be ever on the wing. It eats flying, bathes flying, and sometimes even feeds its young when flying. It glides through the air with no effort, with perfect ease, conscious of being in its own domain. It explores aërial space in all its dimen-sions, as if to enjoy it to the utmost, and its delight in the act is expressed by little cries of rapture. It may be seen giving chase to flying insects and following with supple agility their evasive and tortuous course; or it may leave one to pursue another and snap up a third in passing; or, again, it lightly skims the surface of land and water to catch any that may be gathered there for the sake of coolness and moisture; or, finally, it may in its turn be driven to flee with all speed before the lightning-like onset of some bird of prey. Always in full control of its movements even when flying at topmost speed, it is continually changing its course, describing in the air a bewildering maze whose paths cross, interlace, recede from and approach one another, meet, wind, ascend, descend, interweave, and mingle in a thousand different ways and after a plan so complicated as to defy representation to the eye by the art of drawing and scarcely to lend itself to description for the imagination through the medium of speech.'

"We have three kinds of swallows in France, of which the best known is the martin, black above with glints of blue, and white beneath and on the rump. It builds its nest in window-corners, under the eaves of roofs, and on the cornices of buildings. The materials it uses are fine soil, chiefly that which is deposited by earthworms, after digestion, in little mounds over our fields and gardens. The swallow carries it, a beakful at a time, mixes it with a little viscous saliva to make it stick together, and lays it by courses until it takes the shape of a hemisphere attached to the wall and provided with a small opening at the top. Bits of straw give additional firmness to the masonry; and, finally, the interior is lined with an abundance of little feathers. The laying consists of four or five pure white eggs without any spots.

"The nests are used year after year by the same pairs of birds, being recognized by them on their annual return in the spring and made as good as new with a few repairs. If some are left vacant by reason of the owners' death in distant lands, new couples profit by the fact."

"Don't they ever quarrel over the old nests?" asked Jules.

"Very seldom. Swallows like to live in colonies, and their nests touch one another sometimes to the number of hundreds on the same cornice. Each couple recognizes its own nest without the slightest hesitation, and scrupulously respects others' property in order to have its own respected. There is among them a deep feeling of joint responsibility, and they help one

SWALLOW'S NEST

another with as much intelligence as zeal. Occasionally it happens that a nest is no sooner finished than it gives way, either because the mortar used is not strong enough or because the masons were in too great a hurry and had not the patience to let one course dry before laying another, or for some other reason. On hearing of the disaster the neighbors hasten to console the unlucky pair and help them to rebuild. All set to work, bringing the best mortar, straw, and feathers, and in forty-eight hours the nest is rebuilt. Left to themselves, it would have taken the owners a fortnight to repair the damage."

"That's the kind of friends in need I like to see!" declared Emile.

"But I have something still better to tell you. Let us suppose a swallow has been so careless as to become entangled in a mesh of loose threads, and the more frantically it struggles to escape the more firmly it binds its fetters. With wings and claws held fast it is in danger of perishing. Uttering piteous cries, it calls on its comrades for help. All hasten to give aid, noisily making plans for relief and working away with beak and talons until they finally unsnarl the tangle and free the captive. The happy event is then celebrated with chirpings of delight. That is what I saw with my own eyes, right here in the garden, one day when Mother Ambroisine was bleaching some of the linen thread she spins on her distaff.

"An author[6] of note tells us that he once witnessed something similar. These are his words: 'I saw a swallow that had unfortunately, I know not how, caught its foot in a slip-knot tied in a string, the other end of which was fastened to a roof gutter. The bird's strength was exhausted and it hung, crying, from the end of the string, with an occasional effort to escape. All the swallows in the neighborhood had assembled, to the number of several thousand. They formed a veritable cloud, each one uttering cries of alarm and pity. After considerable hesitation

6   Dupont de Nemours.

one of them hit on a plan for freeing their luckless companion and communicated it to the others, whereupon they all set to work. A space was cleared and every swallow within hail came, one after another, as in a ring-game, and gave in passing a peck at the string. These blows, all delivered at the same point, followed one another with only a second's interval or less. Half an hour of this work sufficed to sever the thread and liberate the prisoner. But the entire company of birds, with a few exceptions, stayed there until night, chattering away incessantly, though no longer in anxious tones, but rather as if in mutual congratulation and animated comment.'

"Again: 'An insolent sparrow invades a swallow's nest and likes it so well it wishes to stay. The owners assail the intruder, but the latter, having a stronger beak and being also protected by the ramparts of the nest, easily repulses their attacks. Ha! so you won't budge, then? We'll see about that. One of the two swallows remains to hold the blockade while the other goes for help. The neighbors hasten to the spot, consider the situation, deliberate on means to be employed, and finally conclude that it is out of the question to hope to dislodge by force an enemy so securely entrenched in the nest as in a strong redoubt. There is but one opinion: the invader cannot be ousted from the nest, but the proprietors must at least be avenged. No sooner said than done. While a few courageous ones posted at the opening intimidate the interloper with their cries, the others fetch a supply of their usual mortar, soil moistened with saliva, and little by little close the entrance to the nest.' "

"Who was the fool that time?" cried Jules, in high delight.

"It certainly was the sparrow, sealed up in its narrow prison and left to perish."

"Caught, you nest-robber!" Emile exclaimed, clapping his hands.

"The chimney-swallow or house-swallow, also called barn-swallow, has chestnut-red forehead, throat, and eyebrows, a black back with violet sheen, and a white breast and stomach.

Its name of house-swallow is given to it because it seeks man's neighborhood and even nests inside our houses, especially where there is but little commotion or noise. Open and empty rooms, sheds and coach-houses, the eaves of roofs, the under side of balcony floors, and the inside of tall chimneys are its chosen nesting-places. The nest itself is made of moistened clay mixed with straw and hay and furnished inside with feathers and dry grass. It is in the shape of a half-cup wide open at the top. The eggs are five in number, white with small brown and violet spots.

"The house-swallow is the most interesting of the tribe. It is the farmer's cheery companion and the guest of the barn, while the martin prefers towns and the cornices of monuments. Its characteristic cry is a sweet little song which the father, perched on the edge of the nest, keeps repeating to the brooding mother to beguile the long hours of incubation. This bird is found all over the world. It reaches us after a long migration about the first of April, twelve days before the martin and a month ahead of the swift.

"The sand-martin is smaller and of less frequent occurrence than the other two swallows of which we are speaking. Its back is mouse-gray in color, as are also its cheeks and a wide stripe across the chest, while breast and stomach are pure white. With its beak and claws—poor tools for such rough work did not energetic good will supply the deficiency—it tunnels into steep sand-banks by the waterside, or into the face of cliffs and the walls of quarries, making a hole with a narrow entrance and extending in a winding passage for nearly two feet. At the further end a little space is hollowed out and furnished with a thick bed of straw, dry grass, and feathers, all heaped together with no art. There are laid five or six slightly translucent white eggs. The sand-martin perches only on rocks, to which it clings easily with its long and pointed claws. It haunts the water's edge, which it explores in rapid flight, darting to and fro and snapping up the gnats attracted by the coolness."

"It is said," remarked Jules, "that swallows take long journeys."

"Yes, all our swallows migrate every year, not from a love of wandering but from necessity. Many other birds, particularly those that live on insects, do the same. Swallows, like bats, live entirely on flying insects, and when cold weather comes these are lacking. What does the bat do then to keep from starving?"

"It goes to sleep," answered Emile.

"Yes, it closes as tightly as it can the draft in the vital stove—that natural stove, you know, that gives us heat, movement, and animation by burning up our blood with the help of air. The bat almost stops its breath in order to economize the fuel stored up in its little veins and make it last until the reappearance of insects at the approach of summer. In a word, it goes to sleep in the depths of some grotto, falling into an unconsciousness resembling death. Birds, however, cannot thus save their fuel. Their little stoves are always burning away under forced draft, because of the violent exercise of flying. Their temperature, summer and winter, is forty-two degrees, centigrade, whereas man's is only thirty-eight. When such a fire has to be kept going, imagine if you can take a six months' nap because there was nothing to eat in the larder. It is quite out of the question. What, then, do birds do?

"Unable to do as the bat does, they form a bold resolve: they leave their native land, which is about to be stripped of flying insects by the cold, and go far away, sad to leave but not without the hope of returning some day. They migrate, the strong helping the weak, the old and much-traveled ones guiding the young and inexperienced. They form in flocks and fly southward to Africa, where abundant food and a warmer sun await them. With no compass but instinct to direct their course, they cross the sea, the vast expanse of water in which only an occasional islet offers them a halting-place. Many perish in the crossing, and many arrive faint with hunger and spent with fatigue, but they do arrive at last."

"It must be a trying time for the swallows when the day for starting comes," Jules observed.

"A very trying time indeed, for the bird has to tear itself away from its beloved haunts, the place where it was born, to face the fatigues and dangers of a tremendous journey, a journey never before taken by the greater number of the emigrants. In a general assembly the date of departure is fixed for about the end of August in the case of martins and sand-martins, and later, even as late as October, for house-swallows. This being arranged, the martins gather for several successive days on the roofs of high buildings. Every now and then small groups detach themselves from the rest and circle about in the air with anxious cries, taking a last look at their birthplace and bidding it farewell; then they return to their companions and, we may imagine, fall to chattering about their hopes and fears as they prepare for the journey by a careful examination of their plumage, which they oil a feather at a time. After several repetitions of these touching farewells a plaintive twittering announces the fateful hour: they must start. Launching themselves on their desperate adventure, they take flight in a body toward the south.

"House-swallows, when the time for their departure approaches, hold a consultation on some leafless tree, and almost always in the rain. The emigrating flock numbers three or four hundred birds."

CHAPTER XXX

SWIFTS AND NIGHT-JARS

"THE SWIFT is that large black swallow that flies in flocks on summer evenings and utters a shrill cry as it passes. Hunting insects on the wing is its occupation. It has a very short beak that opens wide, a big gullet, always coated with a glue that holds the captured game, long and pointed wings which enable it to cover in continuous flight eighty leagues an hour, and piercing eyes capable of seeing a gnat at a hundred meters' distance, or even farther. Every insect that ventures into the upper air is lost: the swift's open beak is a living trap, a trap that advances rapidly to swallow up the tiny prey.

"If the bird has little ones, it sometimes stows away its prey in its cheek-pouches and, when they are full, returns to its nest to feed these provisions to the hungry mouths waiting to be filled, discharging through its beak the accumulated flies, moths, and beetles.

"What a slaughter of twilight-flying insects takes place when the screaming flocks of swifts fly hither and thither, circling about in the calm glow of sunset! What an onrush of whirring wings!

EUROPEAN SWIFT

What dash and eager-
ness! How animated the
scene! Some fly merely
as chance dictates, let-
ting themselves glide
gently through the air
for the mere pleasure
of the motion; others
describe intertwining
circles without number;
others, again, soar aloft
on motionless wings or
let themselves fall from

Rock Swift

dizzy heights as if wounded and helpless; still others follow a
straight course, racing toward some distant goal and then returning for a fresh start; and, finally, there are those that go whirling
in noisy companies about some lofty building. But what of this
one that darts across our vision in such hot haste? It flashes
past with three strokes of the wings and is lost in the haze of
the distance. What impetuosity, children, what amazing speed!"

"I have often wished I could fly when I was watching those
birds," said Emile. "If I only had their wings to carry me to
those blue mountains we see from here, how I should like to
go flying to the top of that highest peak and then come back as
quickly as I went!"

"That wish, my boy, is common to us all; every one must
envy the swift its wings, but certainly no one would ever think
of envying it its feet."

"Why?"

"Because they are so misshapen and the legs are so short that
they cannot be used for walking. All four toes point forward.
That tells you the swift does not perch, being unable to grasp the
supporting branch, but must cling to walls for a brief rest, after
which it must take flight again, starting with a falling movement
as bats do. Guéneau de Montbéliard tells us this:

" 'Swifts have to be on the wing a great part of the time. They never voluntarily alight on the ground, and if by some accident they fall to earth they cannot rise again into the air without extreme difficulty, by dragging themselves up on to a little mound or by climbing with beak and claws upon a stone from which they can spread their long wings. If the ground is quite level they either lie prone on the stomach or sway from side to side with a balancing motion, or they manage to struggle forward a little by beating the earth with their wings. After repeated efforts they sometimes succeed in flying off. The earth, therefore, is to them a great danger that must be avoided with the utmost care. Any state between swift motion and absolute rest is hardly possible with them. Violent exercise in the air and perfect quiet in their place of retreat—these two, as a rule, make up their existence. The only variation known to them is to hang on to some wall near their hole and then drag themselves into the nest by clambering along with the help of beak and any chance support that they can find. Usually they enter their retreat in full flight. After passing and repassing its entrance more than a hundred times, all at once they dart in so quickly that they are lost to sight before you know whither they are gone. You feel almost inclined to believe they have vanished into thin air.'

"Their nest is nearly always placed in a deep hole in the wall and at a great height. It is made of hemp threads, little wisps of tow, bits of straw, feathers, rags, and cotton-like down from poplar and willow catkins. These materials are stuck together with the viscous saliva that constantly oozes from the swift's throat and serves as glue to entangle captured insects. The bird spreads it over the nest and thoroughly moistens the successive layers. In drying this saliva hardens and takes on the shiny appearance of gum, giving consistency and even elasticity to the whole structure. If you squeeze the nest between your two hands it will shrink up without breaking, and when the pressure is removed it will resume its former shape.

"The swift, then, furnishes its own adhesive cement, but whence does it obtain the other materials it needs, such as tow, rags, straw, and feathers? Of course it is not so foolish as to go and pick them up from the ground, where it might find them as other birds do; for if it touched the ground it would certainly come to grief. Therefore it resorts to cunning. As it reaches us rather late in the season, it takes advantage of such holes as it finds already abandoned by the sparrows, and there it finds abundant materials which it uses in its own way by sticking them together with its glue. If the sparrows have not yet broken up housekeeping, it boldly invades their nests, steals bits of flock and tufts of hair, straw, and feathers, a little from one and a little from another, and makes with these its own nest in another hole in the same wall. The female lays from two to four eggs, pure white and rather elongated. Swifts seldom stay more than three months with us. Arriving after the swallows early in May, they leave at the end of July.

"The white-breasted swift differs from the bird I have just described in being larger and having a white breast and stomach. It is found in the region of the Alps and of the Pyrenees and frequents the Mediterranean shores, especially where the waves beat against high, steep cliffs. Middle and northern Europe are not visited by this bird. Its flight is even swifter than that of its black cousin, and it flies habitually at a great height, descending only when bad weather threatens. It builds its nest at the summit of high, steep rocks, making it of straw and moss stuck together with the glue from its own throat.

"The night-jar closely resembles the swift, hav-

NIGHT-JAR

ing, like that bird, a short beak which is very broad at the base and opens very wide, while from the gullet comes a sticky saliva for holding fast any insects that are caught. Its size is about that of the thrush; its plumage is light, soft, and shaded with gray and brown; its eyes are large and prominent and very sensitive to light; the base of its beak bristles with long, stiff hairs; and its legs are short, but at the same time not ill adapted to walking.

"As indicated by the sensitiveness of its eyes, which cannot endure the full light of day, and by the softness and lightness and gray color of its plumage, which resembles that of the hornless owl, the night-jar is a twilight bird: it is the swift of the evening, flying and hunting only when the sun is near setting. By the fading light of a summer evening it may be seen scanning the ground in low flight to and fro over its surface, after the manner of the swallow. It flies with mouth wide open, so that the air in striking the throat produces a low and continuous humming like that of a spinning-wheel."

"And is it from that humming sound that it gets its name of night-jar?" asked Jules.

"Precisely. But it does not make this humming sound for the mere love of hearing it; its object is to snap up the twilight-flying insects as it passes with distended beak. Big beetles sporting in the evening air, June-bugs, and other plump winged creatures disappear in the viscous gullet, while small butter-flies, moths, gnats, and mosquitoes become entangled by the dozen in the fatal glue. If the game is large, the bird swallows it at once, whole and still alive; if small, it waits until it has caught a certain number and then swallows them all in one mouthful."

"But does it really swallow big beetles and June-bugs alive?" Emile asked.

"You can readily understand that in its headlong chase the bird has no time to dismember its captives. Pouncing upon the insect with wide-open beak, snapping it up, and gulping it down—all this it does as it flies, without a moment's pause.

No sooner is the plumpest prey captured than down it goes, alive and struggling, into the bird's crop."

"A dozen of that sort of game must stir up a big rumpus in the bird's crop," was Emile's opinion.

"Almost any other creature in the night-jar's place would have its digestion ruined by a brisk company of coleopters kicking about in the stomach and tickling its walls with their rough and prickly legs; but I am inclined to believe the bird has the means of quieting them immediately by smothering them with its digestive juices. As it carries on the business of stuffing its crop with large live beetles, it ought to know the secret of how to prevent their making a hole in its stomach. But that does not lessen my admiration for its digestive powers. No creature enjoys a more remarkable immunity from dyspepsia.

"On a near view the night-jar is not a pretty bird. Its flat skull; its tremendously yawning beak, which seems to split the whole head in two; its wide-open gullet, red and slimy and powdered with the remains of moths recently devoured; its large and prominent eyes—all these give it somewhat the appearance of a toad. That is why it is sometimes called the flying toad. Another common name for it is goat-sucker, based on a false belief as to one of its habits. It likes to visit pastures and sheepfolds, where it chases the beetles to be found there. Noting its frequent appearance among the sheep and goats, shepherds imagined it came there to suck their milk. If they had watched it more closely they would have seen the absurdity of any such notion. A bird suck? What nonsense! But the more ridiculous an idea is, the more likely it is to spread, and the absurd name of goat-sucker is better known in many places than the appropriate and expressive one of night-jar.

"This bird comes to us from warmer lands toward the beginning of May, and leaves us in September. It builds no nest, imitating in this various nocturnal birds of prey. Some hole in the ground or among broken stones, at the foot of a tree or a rock, and usually taken just as it happens to be, suffices to hold the bird's eggs, which are two or three in number, white with tawny and bluish spots.

"In closing let me beg you to remember what we owe these big-throated birds that hunt insects on the wing, and more especially the swifts and swallows, who defend our granaries and gardens, our wardrobes and our very persons. What would you think of any one who, possessing the terrible secret of creating by the bushel moths, gnats, mosquitoes, weevils, and other destructive insects, should let loose a swarm of these creatures in the air about us?"

"I should say hanging was too good for him," answered Louis.

"But that is exactly what any one does who kills a swallow. It is true he does not create moths and mosquitoes and other insects, but he saves the lives of those that the swallow would have eaten, and thus he is guilty of as grave an offense as if he had created them on purpose to turn them loose on us. He does a wicked deed, for he receives with deadly shotgun the pretty, joyous creature, messenger of spring and sunshine, that comes trustfully asking his hospitality and the permission to build its nest under the eaves of his house. He causes famine, for he encourages the multiplication of those devouring hordes that levy every year on our farm products a tax that amounts to thousands of millions of francs in its total sum and is constantly increasing as insect-eating birds decrease. A wicked deed, I say, a deed which causes famine—that is what is really done by the murderer of swallows."

CHAPTER XXXI

THE BIRD'S BEAK

"THERE ARE many other small birds that live almost exclusively on insects, and in so doing render a great service to agriculture. A full account of them all would take too long; and, besides, you are familiar with the greater number, seeing them daily in the woods, fields, orchards, and gardens. I will confine myself, therefore, to the chief difference between insect-eaters and birds that live on seeds and grain; and then a glance at some of the habits of the most important species will complete our rapid review.

"The food of small birds falls into two classes, seeds and insects. Certain birds require millet, hemp-seed, pips, and similar seeds of all kinds, while others need grubs, larvæ, insects. The choice of one or the other sort of food is determined by the shape of the beak, just as a mammal's diet depends on the structure of the animal's teeth. The molars of the horse and the ox call for forage to grind under their flat, wide crowns; but those of the wolf and the cat, with their sharp edges, need flesh to cut to pieces. In the same manner the bird's beak, according to

BEAKS AND CLAWS OF BIRDS OF PREY
1, golden eagle; 2, gerfalcon

whether it is shaped this way or that, whether large or small, thick or slender, strong or weak, requires hard seeds that crack under the mandibles and in opening yield their kernels, or the tender grub that is swallowed without having to be crushed. Show me your teeth, we said to the mammal, and I shall know what you eat. Show me your beak, we might now say to the bird, and I shall know whether you live on insects or seeds.

"The beak of the bird that lives on seeds or grain—that is, the granivorous bird—is thick, conical, wide at the base, and strong in proportion to the hardness of the seeds it has to crack open; but the beak of the bird that lives on insects—that is, the insectivorous bird—is thin, slender, delicate, and weak in proportion to the softness of the insects it catches. In our everyday speech we note this difference by applying to the small granivorous birds the general designation grosbeak, while the insect-eaters are often called slender-beaked birds. Let us remember these two expressive words and formulate the general principle thus: Seeds for the grosbeak, worms for the slender beak.

"And now without further delay we will put the rule into practice. Here is a bird whose diet is perhaps a matter of uncertainty to you. If I ask you what, to judge from the shape of its beak, is its customary food, shall you be at a loss how to reply?"

"That strong beak, so wide at the base, must be meant for crunching the very hardest seeds," was Jules's opinion.

"Yes," Emile chimed in, "that bird certainly lives on seeds; it is written all over its big face."

"It is, indeed, a consumer of all kinds of seeds; it is the greenfinch of our copses, greenish underneath and with a yellow border to its tail. The dominant color of its costume, green mixed with yellow, has given it the name of greenfinch. And this one?"

"Seeds for the grosbeak, worms for the slender beak," repeated Emile. "The beak has no strength; it is rather long but thin; the bird is an insect-eater."

"And one of the greediest, for it belongs to the family of war-

BEAKS AND CLAWS OF WADING-BIRDS
1, stork; 2, heron; 3, crane

blers, those delightful songsters that would be afraid of getting hoarse if they ate dry, farinaceous grain. To keep their vocal cords flexible these artists must have the gentle lubricant furnished by caterpillars and the succulent flesh of larvæ. They take good heed not to touch coarse seeds, which would injure the voice. This bird is the reed-warbler, which lives on dragon-flies, small June-bugs, mosquitoes, and horse-flies, snapping them up on the wing. It builds its nest among the reeds in willow thickets. It is reddish brown above and yellowish white underneath.

"Finally, let us look at this third one."

"Another slender beak," said Emile; "another insect-eater."

"Yes; you see it isn't difficult. The bird has three names among us: washerwoman, wagtail, and little shepherdess. Washerwoman, because it frequents the waterside in company with those that wash linen; wagtail, because it wags its tail at every step it takes; and little shepherdess, because it likes the society of shepherds and flocks. It is ash-colored above, white underneath, and black on the back of the head and also on the throat and breast.

"Wagtails go hopping along in a lively manner over the sand at the water's edge, looking for little worms. Every now and then they fly up a few feet into the air, balance, pirouette, and alight again on some slight elevation. They may also be seen skipping across the fields among the sheep and standing on the backs of the latter even in the shepherd's presence, in order to get the parasitic insects lurking under the wool. They live on small slugs, moths, flies, and larvæ.

"Midway between birds eating only seeds and those eating only insects must be placed, in respect to their food, those that have a mixed diet and eat, according to season, place, and circumstances, insects and seeds, larvæ and berries. Their beak has neither a strong, conical structure like that of purely granivorous birds, nor a delicately slender form like the beak of the insect-eaters, but is between these two extremes. This beak, instrument of general utility, is found in the lark, that bringer of gladness to our plowed fields; in the thrush and the blackbird, lovers of grapes and juniper-berries, but not less fond of insects; in the oriole, that superb black and yellow bird so appreciative of cherries flavored with toothsome larvæ; and in the starling, devourer of figs, grapes, insects, slugs, and various kinds of seeds.

"The starling is a magnificent bird almost as large as a blackbird, brilliant with glints of metallic luster on a dark background. Its color is black with greenish sheen on head and wings and violet on breast and back. Most of the feathers are adorned with a reddish-white spot at the very end. It nests under the roofs of buildings, in dove-cotes, and in hollow tree trunks. The nest, composed on the outside of straw, and within of dry grasses and feathers, contains four spotless whitish eggs. Starlings come to us in the autumn. They fly in large flocks, whirling about like grain winnowed in a sieve and sending forth piercing cries from high up in the air. They alight in marshes and damp meadows, where they destroy much vermin."

CHAPTER XXXII

INSECTIVOROUS BIRDS

"**N**ow let us go back to the principal slender-beaked birds, eaters of insects only and consequently our greatest helpers. They are all small in size, delicately and gracefully formed, and modest in dress. Among them we find the sweet singers that make the woods echo in spring with the refreshing songs of the opening season.

"First there is the nightingale, clothed all in brown except the under parts, which are whitish in color. Listen to it some

NIGHTINGALE

calm evening in May. All is quiet, so we need not lose a note of the bird's hymn. It begins with a few timid and tentative phrases, thus:

> *Teoo-oo, teoo-oo, teoo-oo, teoo-oo,*
> *Shpe, teoo-oo, tokooa.*

Then it becomes more animated:

> *Teo, teo, teo, teo, teo,*
> *Koo-oo-teoo, koo-oo-teoo, koo-oo-teoo, koo-oo-teoo,*
> *Tskoo-o, tskoo-o, tskoo-o, tskoo-o,*
> *Tsee-ee, tsee-ee, tsee-ee, tsee-ee, tsee-ee, tsee-ee.*

Here the phrasing becomes more marked, the melody quicker:

Dlo, dlo, dlo, dlo, dlo, dlo,
Koo-e-oo, trrrrrrritz!
Lu-lu-lu, le-le-le-le, lee-lee-lee-lee.

Enthusiasm then bursts all bounds and the bird indulges in the most brilliant roulades; but our harsh alphabet is powerless to show the sounds that come from this wonderful throat.

" 'The nightingale,' says Buffon, 'begins with a timid prelude in weak and almost wavering tones, as if wishing to try its instrument and win the attention of those within hearing; but presently, gaining assurance, it gradually becomes animated and displays all the resources of its incomparable organ. Bursts of melody, lively volleys of rippling song in which clearness is equaled only by volubility, low and voiceless murmurs inaudible to the listener, but calculated to increase the brilliance of the notes about to be heard, vivid and rapid trills that sweep the gamut and are articulated with force and even with a certain hardness of effect not unpleasing to the ear, plaintive cadences softly modulated, notes struck without art but full of soul, enchanting and poignant chords that seem to come from the very heart and to convey a touching significance— such are the impassioned strains by which, in a tongue doubtless full of sentiment, this natural songster appears to try to charm its mate or, rather, to contend before her with his jealous rivals for the prize of supreme excellence in song.'

YELLOW WARBLER

WHEATEAR

"I have seen unfeeling barbarians cut short this pretty romance with a shot from a gun. They say that half a dozen nightingales make an excellent broiled dish. Horrors! What a frightful brute is man when he thinks of nothing but his stomach!

"The nightingale builds its nest in bushes and rather near the ground, sometimes even among the roots. Coarse grasses and oak leaves are used for the outside, tufts of fleece and horsehair for the inside. The female lays five dark-green eggs.

"With the nightingale, though less wonderful as singers, are to be classed the warblers, thirty or more species of which can be counted in Europe. All live on flies, caterpillars, small beetles, spiders, and larvæ of various kinds. Their nests are constructed with much art. Some nest in trees and hedges in our gardens; others prefer thickets and lonely groves; still others choose holes in tree trunks and walls. Others, again, build on piling that projects above the water in marshes; that is, they unite three or four slender reeds with a ligature and build their nest on this swaying support. Others, finally, content themselves with a little hole in the ground. Among the best-known of these birds is the black-capped warbler, so named on account of the black hood that covers the top of the head and the nape of the neck. You remember it is one of the cuckoo's victims, as was proved by the egg found a few days ago, in the nest at the foot of the garden. Then we must include the babbling warbler, lover of copses, orchards, and gardens; the little red warbler, which visits our fruit trees and says, *zip-zap, zip-zap, zip-zap*; the marsh-warbler, which builds its nest among the marsh reeds; and the Alpine warbler, guest of chalets and tuneful songster of high, snowy mountains.

"Now let us look at the fallow-finch or whitetail, which flies from clod to clod in our fallow fields (whence its name of fallow-finch), and in flying spreads its white tail, a target for the huntsman and the reason for its second name. It is ash-colored on the back and reddish white underneath, with black wings and eyebrows. It frequents cultivated fields to catch the grubs turned up by the plow. Its nest,

EUROPEAN ROBIN

placed under a clod of turf, amid a pile of stones, or in a hole in some dry wall, is made of moss, grass, and feathers. The eggs, five or six in number, are light blue. The fallow-finch's chosen haunts are dry, rocky uplands, where it may be seen in the autumn in large flocks, flying from one rock to another and from one clod to another, keeping close to the ground.

"By the fallow-finch's side let us place the stonechat, a little, lively, active bird always seen perched on the topmost branch of a bush or bramble, where it repeats, with frisky movements, its short cry of *ooistratra, ooistratra*. If from this place of observation it sees an insect on the ground, it flies down, seizes it, and returns in a trice to its perch by a short curving flight like that so characteristic of the shrike. Its plumage is brown, with red breast and black throat. The sides of the neck, together with the wings and the rump, are ornamented with

AMERICAN ROBIN

Song-thrush

white. Stonechats frequent hedges that border sown fields and dry pastures, and are never seen, any more than are fallow-finches, in damp lands along the banks of rivers. They build their nests, in which they lay five or six greenish-blue eggs, among the roots of bushes, in crevices in rocks, and among piles of stones.

"I should count it almost a crime to omit here the robin redbreast, in my opinion the most pleasing of our smaller birds in its wide-awake manner, its gentle look, and its friendly curiosity, which makes it come and pick up the shepherd's crumbs when he is eating his lunch. At the first dawn of day it begins its lively song, uttering now and then a note or two that recall certain parts of the nightingale's more elaborate performance. Who does not know its alert cry from the depths of some clump of bushes, *treet, tee-ree-tee-teet, tee-reet, tee-ree-tee-teet*, and its call to some passing member of its kin, *oo-eep, oo-eep*?

"The redbreast is greenish brown above, bright red on the throat and breast, and white on the stomach. It nests in the densest woods amid the moss-grown tree roots, and its nest, made of leaves, horsehair, tufts of wool, and

Red-winged Thrush

feathers, contains from five to seven whitish eggs spotted with red.

"In winter the redbreast leaves the forest, draws near our farms, and even ventures into our houses in quest of food. God forbid, boys, that you should ever betray its confidence when, on a stormy winter's day, it

Varied Thrush

comes discreetly tapping with its beak on the window-pane, asking hospitality. Welcome the poor little famished creature, and it will pay you a hundred times over with its gentle warbling and its zeal in defending the fruits of the earth.

"But enough about the slender-beaks. You ought by this time to appreciate the immense help we receive from these legions of insect-eaters which share the work of the fields, hedges, meadows, gardens, woods, and orchards, and wage incessant warfare on every sort of vermin that would destroy our harvests unless others than ourselves were constantly on the watch—others cleverer and endowed with sharper eyesight and greater patience for the unending hunt, and also having nothing else to do. I am not exaggerating, I assure you; without our insectivorous birds we should soon suffer from famine. Who, then, except an idiot with a mania for destruction, would dare touch the nests of these birds of the good God that enliven the country-side

Thrush-tit

with their varied plumage and protect us from insects? There are, I well know, unruly boys who, tired of their books and lessons, delight to play truant and make a pastime of climbing trees and searching hedges in order to toss the new-born birds out of their nests to a miserable death and to smash the eggs. The rural guard is on the watch for these wicked thieves, and the law punishes them, that our fields and orchards may enjoy the birds' protection and continue to produce their sheaves and their fruit."

CHAPTER XXXIII

GRANIVOROUS BIRDS

"IT MIGHT at first seem that I ought to be as lenient toward those who hunt granivorous birds as I have just shown myself severe toward the destroyers of insectivorous birds; for can it be denied that birds given to a vegetable diet are harmful to our crops, that they plunder our grain-fields and devour great quantities of seeds, buds, fruit, and young garden plants? Some of them know how to extract the wheat grains from the ear, and others boldly come to get their share of the oats thrown to the poultry in our barnyards. Others, again, prefer the juicy flesh of fruit and know before we do when cherries are ripe or pears are mellow, so that when we come to gather in the harvest all that we find is merely what they have left. There are even some that have a queer-shaped beak for splitting fruit open and dividing it into quarters so as to get at the pips, which are to them the very choicest of titbits. Look at this one's beak and tell me if you have ever seen a more singular tool."

"The two mandibles cross each other," said Jules. "Instead of meeting they go criss-cross like the blades of an old pair of scissors out of order."

"What can such a rickety beak be good for," Emile asked, "with its tips pointing one up and the other down? It will never be able to pick up a seed from the ground."

"Consequently, it does not get its food from the ground. Its manner of proceeding is more complicated.

"First I will say that the bird is known as a crossbill, from the position of the two mandibles. This odd arrangement is not the result of an accident to the bird, as for instance a sprain following some violent effort; it is not a crippled beak, nor is it a rickety beak, as Emile calls it, but a beak in its natural and perfect state. The bird is born with this odd beak and has never had any other. It is even extremely doubtful whether it would consent to make a change if it had the opportunity, so useful a tool is this beak for the work it has to do. The crossbill has a fondness for pine seeds above all other food. Take a pine-cone and lift the scales with the point of a penknife. You will find behind each scale two seeds full of oil and smelling slightly of resin. They are the titbits the bird is after. But how get at them under scales so hard and so firmly held in place? In vain would the grosbeak hammer at these scales with its strong tool; it would never succeed in opening them. Even we ourselves with the aid of a knife find it difficult. But the crossbill makes play of this hard work. It inserts the tip of one mandible under the scale and, using the other as a fulcrum, pries with a turning movement until the scale is lifted and the seed laid bare; and the whole thing is done in next to no time. A key turning in the lock does not push the bolt more easily."

"I must change my mind," Jules acknowledged, "about this beak that at first seemed to me so awkward; it is a first-rate key to force the lock of a pine-cone."

"And it is not less useful," proceeded his uncle, "in quartering apples and getting out the pips. I should not like to have crossbills by the dozen in any orchard of mine; they would soon tear all the fruit to pieces. Fortunately, it is not our level plains that these birds choose as their haunts, but cold, mountainous regions covered with dark forests of cone-bearing evergreens. Their plumage is bright red more or less tinged with green and yellow. Crossbills breed in the coldest countries of Europe and build their nests even in midwinter. Their materials are moss and lichens, made to shed the melting snow by a coating of resin.

"I shall enter no plea for the crossbill: its taste for apple and pear seeds is a serious matter; but I will mention certain things that seem to plead for the granivorous birds as a class. First,

LINNET

the greater number of these birds feed on wild seeds of no value to us even if not actually harmful to our cultivated fields. We weed our tilled land, clearing it of all plants that exhaust it to no purpose. Many granivorous birds also weed, in their own way: they gather the seeds that would otherwise infest the soil. For example, must we not acknowledge the services of the goldfinch, which, when thistles have matured, alights on their prickly heads and searches for the seeds amid the thistle-down? I need not describe this pretty little bird, so well is it known to you all."

"It has a splash of red on its head," said Emile, "with yellow, black, and white on its wings."

"Yes, that is the goldfinch. Its nest, which is one of the most carefully built to be found anywhere, is placed in the fork of some flexible branch. The outside consists of mosses and lichens with a padding of down from thistles and other plants bearing seeds that have silky tufts, as for example the groundsel and the dandelion. The inside, artistically rounded, is lined with a thick layer of horsehair, wool, and feathers. The eggs, five or six in number, are white with reddish-brown spots, chiefly at the large end. The goldfinch merits our gratitude: it cheers us with its singing and works diligently at weeding lands infested with thistles and groundsel.

"I will say as much in favor of the linnet, which feeds on all kinds of small seeds in our fields and to that extent follows the honorable trade of weeding. At the same time I will not hide its liking for linseed, which has given it the name it bears. It is very fond of hemp-seed, also. But hemp and flax are not found everywhere, and the bird manages to get along very well without them by gathering a quantity of other seeds, more or less harmful to agriculture. It likes to breed in hilly country, choosing some thickly grown juniper-tree or bush. Its nest contains five or six white eggs with red spots. Its plumage is brown with a dash of crimson on head and breast.

"To the part of weeders, seed-eating birds add a second even more praiseworthy one. Seeds, it is true, furnish their customary food; but most of the birds devour a great number of insects when these are plentiful and easy to find. If they lack the patience to hunt for worms in their most hidden retreats with the painstaking care of the slender-beaks, they at least profit by those that fortune places within their reach. A few grubs to season their regular diet of seeds are a godsend to them; and, moreover, their favorite seeds may by some mischance be lacking in their neighborhood. Not every day can the goldfinch find thistle-seeds nor the linnet flaxseed. What, then, is to be done except to have patience and in the meantime eat insects?

"Last but not least, in their young days when, weak and featherless, they are fed from the parents' beak, many granivorous birds are brought up on insects. The reason is plain enough. You can readily understand that the delicate crop of a young bird just out of the shell has not the strength to digest hard, dry seeds. It must have something more nourishing, something smaller and, above all, more succulent, such as a marmalade of grubs prepared in the mother's beak. A few days later, with the first growth of down, will come little soft caterpillars served whole; then tougher insects will prepare the stomach for the more difficult digestion of seeds. I select a few examples at random.

"The chaffinch, the gay chaffinch, is well known to be a granivorous bird, a lover of millet and hemp-seed. Now, what does it give its little ones while they are still in the nest? It gives them hairless caterpillars and tender larvæ, chosen as being the easiest food to digest. I can say the same of the greenfinch, a bird with plumage midway between green and yellow; of the bullfinch, known by its red breast and stomach; and of the various buntings that come in the winter in flocks, pecking around our straw-stacks. These last, however, feed perhaps more than the others on seeds, as they have on the inside of the upper mandible a small, hard excrescence intended expressly for crushing them.

"I might add to these examples, but prefer to conclude with a bird that is one of the most familiar to you, the sparrow. Here, certainly, we have an undoubted seed-eater. It raids our dove-cotes and poultry-yards and steals the food of our pigeons and poultry. It goes a-harvesting in the grain-fields before our reapers have begun their task. A great many other misdeeds are laid at its door. It strips cherry trees, plunders our gardens, forages for sprouting seeds, regales itself on young lettuce, and nips the first little leaflets of green peas. But when hatching-time comes this bold pilferer is transformed into a helper inferior to none. At least twenty times an hour the father and the mother, by turns, bring a mouthful to their young ones, and each time it consists of either a caterpillar or an insect large enough to require quartering, or perhaps a larva as fat as butter; or it may be a grasshopper or some other small game. In one week the brood consumes about three thousand insects, including larvæ, caterpillars, and grubs of all kinds. I have counted in the immediate vicinity of a single nest of these birds the remains of seven hundred June-bugs besides small insects without number. Behold what a store of food is needed for raising only one brood! What quantities of vermin, then, must all the broods of a community devour! After such services let him who will presume to raise a hand

EUROPEAN HOUSE SPARROW

against our sparrows; as for me, I leave them in peace as long as they do not become too troublesome.

"My closing word is this: eaters of seeds and eaters of insects, grosbeaks and slender-beaks, some in greater degree, some in less, all come to our aid. Peace, then, to the little birds, the joy of the country-side and the protectors of our crops!"

CHAPTER XXXIV

SNAKES AND LIZARDS

"I PROPOSE to-day to undertake the defense of reptiles, which many people fear and dislike, even look upon with horror. I have shown you what services are rendered by bats despite the repugnance we feel for them. These animals, regarded by us as hideous and treated as enemies, I have brought you to look upon as valuable helpers, veritable swallows of the night, devoted to the extermination of twilight insects. As soon as reason illuminates the darkness of prejudice the detested creature is found to be a very useful animal. In like manner I shall now try to make you separate the false from the true in respect to the reptiles. Let us begin with the snake.

"If to explain our dislike for bats we mention their strange and repulsive appearance, we have not the same excuse in regard to snakes. Their slender form is not lacking in grace, the suppleness they display in their undulating movements is pleasing to the eye, and their scaly skin is decorated with well-defined colors that are prettily arranged. Our aversion, then, must be otherwise explained. Some serpents are venomous; they are armed with a formidable and death-dealing weapon. Certainly it is not for these that I ask your favor. Indeed, if it were in my power to exterminate them all I would gladly free the earth of their presence. But others—and these are far more numerous—are not venomous and consequently are perfectly harmless unless they are large enough to hurt us by muscular force, which is not rare in the hot countries of the equator, but never to be feared in our part of the world, where the largest snake is not so strong as a mere child. Thus it is that some are much to be

HEAD OF SNAKE,
showing Forked Tongue

feared on account of their venom, while others, at least those of this region, are not in the least dangerous. But we are all too prone to lose sight of this difference in serpents. The evil reputation of the one with venomous fangs is fastened on all the others, so that we abhor them all alike because we believe them all to be venomous. In France we have only one venomous serpent, the viper, and all the others, large as well as small, are perfectly harmless and we will refer to them simply as snakes.

"In one of our former talks[7] I told you about the viper, describing its form and coloring, the structure of its venomous apparatus, and the effects of its bite. I here repeat the principal facts then related, in order to give you now a connected account of our serpents as a class.

"All serpents dart back and forth between their lips, with extreme rapidity, something that looks like a black thread, of great flexibility and ending in a fork. Many persons believe this to be the reptile's weapon, the sting, as they call it, whereas in reality it is nothing but the tongue—a quite inoffensive tongue, which the creature uses for catching insects to feed upon, and also for expressing in its own peculiar fashion the passions that agitate it. This last it does by shooting the tongue swiftly in and out between the lips. All serpents without exception have a tongue, but in our country it is only the viper that possesses the terrible apparatus for injecting venom.

"This apparatus is composed, first, of two fangs or long, sharp teeth, situated in the upper jaw. Unlike ordinary teeth, these fangs are not fixed firmly in their sockets, but can at the creature's will stand up for attack or lie down in a groove of the gum and remain there as harmless as a stiletto in its sheath. In this way the viper runs no risk of wounding itself. The fangs

7   See "The Story-Book of Science."

are hollow and pierced near the point with a very small opening through which the venom is discharged into the wound they give. Finally, at the base of each fang is a small pocket or sac filled with a venomous liquid. It is to all appearance a perfectly harmless liquid, odorless and tasteless, so that you would take it for nothing but water. When the viper strikes with its fangs, the venom sac discharges a drop of its contents into the tiny channel perforating the fang, and the liquid is injected into the wound. It is by mixing with the blood that the venom produces its terrifying effects."

"I remember all that very well," said Jules, "and also what you said must be done to prevent the mixing of the venom with the blood in general that circulates through the body."

"And I also told you that the viper haunts by preference warm, rocky hills; it lurks under stones and in underbrush. In color it is brown or reddish, with a dark zigzag stripe along the back and a row of spots on each side, each spot fitting into one of the angles made by the zigzag stripe. Its stomach is slate-color and its head rather triangular in shape, being broader than the neck and running to a blunt point at the mouth. The viper is timid by nature and attacks man only in self-defense. Its movements are abrupt, irregular, and sluggish."

"What does it live on?" Jules inquired. "Does it eat nothing but little insects that it can catch with its tongue?"

"Its chief food consists of larger prey, which calls for the use of its venomous weapon. Small field-rats, field-mice, meadow-mice, moles, sometimes frogs and even toads, are its usual victims. The animal attacked by the reptile is first stung with the venomous fangs, whereupon it is immediately overcome with agony. As soon as the prey is dead the viper twines its folds about the lifeless body, squeezes it tightly, and subjects it to a sort of kneading process in order to make it smaller; for the victim must be gulped down in one mouthful even if it exceeds the serpent itself in size. This preparation finished, the gullet opens to its utmost width and the two jaws, seeming almost to fly apart, seize with their sharp teeth, which point backward toward the throat, the head of the mole or field-mouse or whatever the small game may be. A flow of saliva then streams over the body to make it slip down more readily, but it is so large a mouthful that the viper manages to swallow it only by a violent effort. The throat dilates and contracts, the jaws move alternately from right to left and from left to right, to coax the unwieldy mass downward, and so it is that this laborious swallowing is protracted sometimes for hours, sometimes for a whole day. Indeed, it not seldom occurs that the forward half of the prey is already undergoing digestion in the stomach while the hind quarters still stick in the throat or protrude from the mouth.

"Let us pass on to the common snakes. These have no venomous fangs in the jaw; their teeth are small and even and lacking in strength, useful as an aid in holding the captured prey and helping in the swallowing of it (which is as difficult as with the viper), but incapable of inflicting a serious wound. These creatures, too, are extremely timid, fleeing at the slightest alarm; but if retreat is cut off they put on a bold front to impose on the enemy, coiling themselves in a spiral, erecting the head, swaying this way and that, hissing, and trying to bite. There is no need, however, to be afraid; a scratch of no more importance than a pin-prick would be the worst that could befall one. You would suffer far greater injury by thrusting your hand into a bramble-bush."

"If it isn't any more dangerous than that," Jules declared boldly, "I shan't mind taking up snakes in my hands."

"I do not tell you this to encourage you to capture these creatures and make playthings of them; on the contrary, I wish you to leave them alone, but I also desire to remove an unwarranted fear, the fear of snakes that is so prevalent in country districts. Fear, always an evil counselor, never does a good deed in prompting one to throw stones at a harmless creature found in a hole in the wall. The passer-by attacks it with his stick if he sees it crossing the road, and the mower in the hayfield cuts off its head with his scythe. Were they not listening to a foolish fear and yielding to an unreasonable dislike, they would leave the poor thing in peace and no one would be the worse for it, as snakes not only are harmless, but they render us excellent service by destroying numerous insects and small rodents such as meadow-mice and field-mice. From this point of view, snakes deserve protection and not the hatred that is commonly felt for them."

"But," objected Louis, "they say snakes can charm birds by their gaze and draw them into their open mouth by first overcoming them with their poisonous breath. Helpless, the bird plunges headlong into the creature's horrible gullet."

"There is a grain of truth in what you say, but far more untruth, the result of popular superstition which deliberately credits the serpent with sorcery. In the first place, the breath of a serpent, or of any reptile whatever, has nothing poisonous about it, nothing magically attractive, nothing supernatural. You all have too much common sense to make it necessary for me to dwell on these ridiculous tales. There remains only the belief that the bird is charmed by the reptile's hard, fixed gaze. The marvel of this amounts in reality to very little.

"Some of our snakes are very fond of birds' eggs. They climb trees, search out the nests, and eat the eggs when the mothers are not there to protect them. More than one human nest-robber who thought he was seizing a jay's or a blackbird's brood has put his hand instead on the cold coiled body of a reptile in the bottom of the nest. I have even known instances in which the plunderers, seized with horror at this unexpected encounter, fell backward from the tree-top and did not come out of the adventure without broken bones. A warning to others. The larger snakes do not content themselves with eggs, but devour the young birds as well, even those that are outside the nest when they can catch them, which fortunately is not easy. Imagine an innocent little bird surprised by a snake in the underbrush. The poor little thing suddenly sees before it a mouth horribly wide open and glittering eyes regarding it steadily. Scared almost to death, the bird loses its head and is powerless to take flight. In vain it beats its wings, cries plaintively, and finally falls from the branch, paralyzed and dying. The monster lying in wait catches the poor thing in its mouth.

"The power to charm that serpents are supposed to have is therefore in reality only the power so to terrify a bird that it cannot fly. We ourselves, on being suddenly confronted by an appalling danger—do we always retain the presence of mind necessary to face it? Are there not plenty of persons that get bewildered, lose their wits completely, and make matters worse by acting foolishly? The charm exerted by serpents all comes down simply to that. I am inclined to believe that a bird, on being surprised by a snake, usually is able to overcome the first feeling of terror and to take flight as soon as it sees the reptile's horrible gullet yawning to receive the expected prey; and so the serpent's attempt to paralyze its victim has a chance to succeed only with very young and inexperienced birds. What paralyzes with fright an ignorant young nestling hardly affects a bird that is master of itself; what terrifies a child or a person of weak character makes little impression on a man capable of keeping his head in time of danger. Acquire the habit, children, of keeping calm in times of danger or excitement, and you will avoid many calamities and escape many perils, just as the bird that does not lose its head escapes the snake lurking in ambush to catch it.

"One of our common snakes is the water-snake, so called because it likes damp places and frequents still water, where it shows itself a good swimmer in its pursuit of little fish, water insects, and tadpoles. It lays its eggs usually in dunghills, where they will be hatched out by the heat. These eggs are of an elongated oval shape, with a soft shell resembling wet parchment. In size they are about as large as a magpie's eggs. They are joined together in a string by a semi-liquid viscous substance. On stirring a heap of dung, country people often turn up with their forks these soft-shelled eggs whose origin is unknown to them and from which, to their great surprise, come young serpents. They declare them to be roosters' eggs, unnatural eggs, magic eggs that produce snakes instead of chickens; and it would be difficult to convince them that this is not true. As for you, my children, if you ever happen to hear any one speak of eggs laid by roosters in dunghills and producing serpents, remember that they are simply the eggs of the water-snake.

"Put no faith, either, in still another fable current in our villages. According to this, all snakes have a consuming desire to enter the mouth and then the body of any one sleeping on the cool grass. To rid the patient of this inconvenient guest the serpent must be lured from its retreat by the smell of warm milk. Of course this is pure nonsense, as no animal can wish to take refuge in the human stomach, where it would be digested, reduced to pap, by the same process that digests our bread.

"One often meets in hay-fields or even in hay itself a small reptile differing from the snake in structure. It is known as the slow-worm or blind-worm. Its head is small and merges into the body without narrowing into a neck; furthermore, the tail is blunt, so that the two ends of the body are of nearly the same shape and leave us for a moment in doubt as to which is the head and which the tail. The slow-worm is covered with very smooth and shiny scales. The back is silvery yellow and marked from one end to the other by three black lines which change, as the worm grows older, to a succession of dots and even disappear entirely at last. The stomach is blackish. On being disturbed the slow-worm forcibly contracts, stiffens, and becomes almost as rigid as a lizard's tail.

"Many people believe that this little creature is venomous, and even to touch it or meet its eye is thought to be very dangerous. But its evil reputation is quite undeserved. The slow-worm is really the most harmless of reptiles: it does not even offer to bite in its own defense, but contents itself with

SERPENTIFORM LIZARD

stiffening until it is as rigid as a wooden rod. It lives chiefly on beetles and earthworms.

"Now to conclude this brief account of snakes: vipers excepted, not one of our serpents is venomous, none can harm us, the bite of none is in the least dangerous. Snakes do us no injury whatever; on the contrary, they help us by destroying a multitude of insects and small rodents. Let us, then, conquer an unreasonable horror and hatred and suffer these helpers of ours to live in peace.

"Equal consideration should be shown to lizards, those agile hunters of insects and even of small fur-bearing game such as rodents. Who does not know the little gray lizard, lover of sunny walls? It lies in wait for flies, darting its tongue in and out as if in play; and it ransacks one hole after another in quest of insects. It is the protector of wall-fruit.

"When on a fine spring day the sun shines warm on some wall or hillside, the lizard may be seen stretched out comfortably on this wall or on the new grass covering the hillside. It steeps itself delightedly in the healthful warmth; it shows its pleasure by gentle undulations of its relaxed tail and by its shining eyes; and presently, perhaps, it darts like an arrow to seize some small prey or to find a spot still more to its liking. Far from fleeing at the approach of man, it seems to regard him with friendliness; but at the slightest alarming sound, as the fall of a leaf, it rolls over, falls, and remains motionless for some moments, as if stunned by the fall; or else it darts away, vanishes from sight, reappears, hides again, then comes forth once more, turns and twists until the eye can hardly follow it, folds itself over several times, and finally retires to some shelter to recover from its fright.

"As useful as it is graceful in form, the little gray lizard lives on flies, crickets, grasshoppers, earthworms, and nearly all insects that prey upon our fruit and grain; thus it would be much to our advantage if the species were more widely scattered. The greater our supply of gray lizards, the faster should we see the enemies of our gardens disappear.

"The green lizard so common everywhere—in hedges, on the skirts of woods, in thickets having an undergrowth of wild grass—attains a length of three decimeters. The back shows an elegant embroidery of green pearls set off with black and yellow dots. This little creature is marvelously swift of foot, darting into the midst of underbrush and dry leaves with a suddenness that always takes one by surprise and causes at first a little start of fear. When it is attacked by a dog it throws itself at the assailant's snout and plants its teeth with such determination that it will let itself be carried along and even killed rather than relax its hold. But its bite is not at all venomous; it merely punctures the skin without leaving in the wound any kind of poison. In captivity it becomes very tame, very gentle, and willingly lets itself be handled. Its food consists chiefly of insects.

"The olive-growing districts of France have another lizard, larger, stronger, heavier, and more squat in form than the common green lizard. The people of Provence call it the glass-bead, but scientists give it the name of ocellated lizard from the small black spots scattered like little eyes (*ocelli*, in Latin) on the bluish-green background of the creature's back. This lizard haunts dry hillsides exposed to the full heat of the sun. It bores for itself a deep hole in some sandy spot, generally under the shelter of a projecting stone. Trusting to its formidable bite, it is very bold. Not only does it leap at dogs' snouts, but it will even attack man if it finds itself too hard-pressed. This courage has won for it a terrible reputation among country people, who think it very dangerous, more venomous than even the viper.

"Now, Uncle Paul, who knows this lizard as well as he knows the bottom of his own pocket, who has watched its movements for whole days in order to learn its habits, who has examined its teeth very carefully so as to be able to report with authority on its bite, and who has even let himself be bitten by it in order to leave no doubt on the subject—Uncle Paul, I say, declares that this dreaded lizard does not deserve the reputation it bears. It is not venomous in the least; it bites hard, it is true, nipping the skin and even taking away a piece, but without poisoning the wound; in a word, it is no more to be feared than the common green lizard. Its food consists of beetles, grasshoppers, and small field-rats; and therefore, despite the fear it inspires, I have no hesitation in placing the ocellated lizard in the class of helpers."

CHAPTER XXXV

THE BATRACHIANS

"I have kept until the last the ugliest and the least esteemed of our helpers, the toad. With it must be classed the frog and the tree-toad because of their close resemblance to it in form and, still more, because of the similar change all three undergo in developing from the egg to the full-grown animal. Common language gives the name of reptile, from a Latin word meaning to creep or crawl, to the snake and the toad, the lizard and the frog, and all similar hairless animals having either no legs at all or very short ones and crawling on the stomach. Science, however, makes a difference; it limits the name reptile to the snake, the lizard, and other animals having a scaly skin and hatching from the egg in the form they are to keep; and it gives the name batrachian (from the Greek *batrachos*, a frog) to the toad, frog, tree-toad, and some others, which have a naked skin and whose first shape gives place later to a different one. Reptiles do not undergo a complete change; batrachians do. Just as the butterfly is first a caterpillar, quite different in structure, its way of living, and its diet from what it finally becomes in its perfect state, so the toad, the frog, and the tree-toad begin their

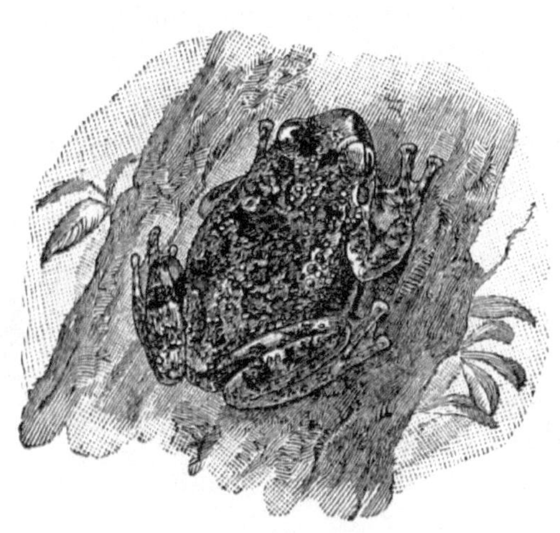

AMERICAN TREE TOAD

existence as tadpoles with none of the structure and habits they are finally to have.

"Tadpole or big-head, that is the word to indicate the batrachian in its transitory state. A very large head merging into a plump stomach that ends abruptly in a flat tail—such is the animal in the beginning. It has no limbs, no organs of locomotion unless it be the tail, which whips the water to push the creature forward and serves as oar and rudder at the same time. The toad tadpole is small and entirely black; the frog tadpole is much larger, silvery on the belly and grayish on the back. All tadpoles inhabit still waters, as ponds or pools warmed by the sun; but for toad tadpoles even shallow puddles or wagon-ruts with a few inches of rain will suffice, where they can gather in black rows or stretch themselves flat on the stomach in the tepid mud at the water's edge. Frog tadpoles, however, thrive best in ponds of some extent, with various water-plants and sufficient depth for diving and swimming. Like fish, tadpoles breathe the air that is in water; and like them, also, they die if kept out of water a short time. Thus they are real fish as far as breathing is concerned. But in their final form batrachians breathe atmospheric air and die of suffocation in water. They are land animals in that state, and breathe like other land animals.

"You have very often seen frogs and toads in the water, and no doubt you think they could live there indefinitely. Undeceive yourselves: they go to the water only to lay their eggs or to escape from some danger or to bathe in hot weather, but they could not remain under water any length of time without dying. They have to come up at intervals to breathe, which they do by getting at least the nostrils out. Here we have a difference between the tadpole and the full-grown batrachian,

HYLAPLESIA TINCTORIA
(A frog-like toad of tropical America)

between the larva, so to speak, and the creature at its maturity: the tadpole lives in water and perishes in the air, whereas the frog that comes from it lives in the air and perishes in water.

"And there is a still further difference: the tadpole lives exclusively on vegetable matter, its mouth is equipped with a sort of small horny beak to browse the foliage of water-plants, and in its big belly it has a very long intestine coiled about several times so as to prolong the passage of the food through the body and thus make sure that all the juices it may contain are extracted. The mature batrachian exchanges this horny beak for real jaws furnished with irregularities that serve as teeth, it lives solely on an animal diet, especially on insects, and its intestine is short because the food it eats is easy of digestion and readily yields what nourishment it contains.

"To turn a tadpole into a frog or a toad it is not enough to change its respiratory and digestive organs; new organs form, organs of which there was not the least sign when the creature was hatched, while still others disappear without leaving any trace. The tadpole is born absolutely without legs. After a while the hind legs appear, later come the fore legs, and still later the tail shrinks and vanishes."

"I remember seeing tadpoles," said Jules, "some with two legs, some with four; but every one of them had a tail."

"When the tail has disappeared the animal is no longer a tadpole, but a young toad or frog."

"Does the tail come off itself, or does the animal pull it off?" Emile inquired with eager interest.

"Neither the one nor the other. The tail is too valuable when the change takes place to be thrown away in that reckless fashion. It contains a store of material suitable for making something else in the bodily organism. When the legs begin to put forth, when the organs of digestion and those of respiration begin to take a new form, these new creations, these transformations, require material with which to build. Fleshy substance is needed for the up-building of the body just as bricks and mortar are needed for the construction of the house. Of course the tadpole eats to make flesh and to provide a reserve for the work of transformation; but this method of accumulation is slow, and therefore, to save time, the organs useless to the future animal are destroyed, bit by bit, and their material is used in the construction of new parts. It is thus that the tail disappears. The blood circulating through it gradually eats it away, dissolves it, as we might say, at the proper time and carries elsewhere the fluid substance, which, turned again into flesh, helps to form the legs or other parts of the remodeled organism."

"What a deal of economy in getting rid of a tadpole's tail!" exclaimed Emile. "Not a particle of it, even if no bigger than a pin's head, must be thrown away, for it might be used to make the little toe on one of the feet."

"Yes, my boy, a wonderful economy, an economy careful of every atom of matter in order that life, the divine worker, may not fail to have at its disposal, undiminished by waste, the resources committed to its keeping by the Creator for works that are unceasingly being destroyed and then restored on a new plan.

"I should add here that certain batrachians keep the tail as long as they live. To this class belong the salamanders, one species of which, the terrestrial or land salamander, is extremely ugly. In form it is half-way between a toad and a lizard, and its color is black with large bright-yellow spots. It is from one to two decimeters long. It haunts damp places near springs and eats insects and earthworms. Despite its repulsive appearance it is perfectly harmless.

"The tadpole of the salamander breathes through fine tuft-like appendages which spread out in the water on each side of the neck. These tufts are called gills, and they correspond to the fish's breathing organs or gills, which are likewise situated on each side of the neck under the tiny flap commonly called the ear. Tadpoles of the frog and the toad have, for the first few days, fringed gills floating out freely; but in a short time they are drawn in under the skin and become invisible like the gills of fish.

"Frogs have a slender form not devoid of a certain grace. Their hind legs are very long and powerful, being especially good at jumping, the frog's customary mode of progress. First gathering itself together, the animal suddenly relaxes like a spring and throws itself forward by a vigorous thrust of the thighs. The hind toes are very markedly webbed; in other words, they are united by a membrane as are the toes of swimming birds, the duck in particular. This arrangement of the toes so as to form a broad paddle or oar, together with the suppleness of the hind legs, which are alternately drawn up against the sides and then forcibly extended, makes the frog an expert swimmer.

"The common or green frog is spotted with black on a green background, and it has three yellowish stripes on the back, the belly also being yellow. It abounds on the banks of all still waters, and to it we owe the noisy croaking that comes from every ditch on a summer evening.

"The red frog is spotted with black on a reddish background, and is easily recognizable by the black stripe running from the eye over the ear. It likes cool places such as damp meadows and fields and underbrush. It is less fond of the water than the one just named, and it croaks much less.

"Both live on live prey, as for example aquatic larvæ, worms, flies and other insects, and snails, and they never touch vegetable matter; therefore they are good helpers in our gardens.

"Tree-toads—or, less correctly, tree-frogs—differ from ordinary frogs in having viscous cushions at the end of their toes, which enable them to climb trees, where they hunt insects. They stay all summer in the foliage and go to the water only to lay their eggs. Their cry, which gains force from a sort of pocket that shows plainly under the throat, is very loud and raucous. The tree-toad that we have around here, the common tree-toad, is of a beautiful delicate green hue on the back and yellowish-white on the belly."

CHAPTER XXXVI

THE TOAD

"WHAT SHALL I say in defense of that poor creature, the toad, whose very name is enough to excite disgust? It is really loathed by all. It seems to us the ugliest and most disgusting of animals. What has it done, poor thing, to deserve the dislike every one feels for it?

"It is ugly, the plaintiff asserts. Its flabby form is a shapeless lump, thrown together as if in careless haste, and its flattened, dirt-colored back is strewn with livid warts. Its legs, too short for symmetry or for effectual service, are unable to lift out of the mud its swollen stomach, which drags on the ground. Its big head merges into a hideous mouth, and heavy eyelids open to show large and prominent eyes which stare stupidly. If some danger threatens, it puffs itself up, forming under its skin an air-cushion which resists blows with its flabby elasticity.

"It is venomous, the plaintiff further declares. Squatting in the mire at the bottom of some dark hole, it absorbs the unwholesome humors of the slime for use in filling the warts on its back with a milky venom which oozes out and moistens the entire body in time of peril. It also squirts into the eyes of any one who

Toad

attacks it a liquid, its urine, which burns and stings. It infects the atmosphere with its foul breath. From its gullet drips a fluid that poisons the grass and fruit over which the animal passes, so that its track is as fatal as its appearance is loathsome. In a word, the toad is ugly and venomous; then war without mercy on the hideous creature that infects earth, air, water, and by its very appearance disgusts the beholder! There you have the charges against the toad.

"Now what shall I say in my turn, in defense of the poor creature? I shall tell the truth, the simple truth, and the charges made against it will be reduced to nothing.

"As to the ugliness of the toad I will not say a word; all are welcome to their own opinion on that subject. I only ask you to recall our talk about bats."

"I don't think the toad so horribly ugly," Jules ventured to assert. "Its golden-yellow eyes are full of fire, its voice is sweet, almost flute-like, while the frog's croak is anything but musical. I admit that the toad's bloated body is not graceful; but, after all, it has some good points."

"Little toads hopping about among the reeds at the edge of the pond," said Emile, "are pretty to look at, and they make me laugh when they tumble heels over head every time they jump. I have taken them up in my hand, but I wouldn't touch big toads; I am afraid of them."

"I wouldn't either," Jules agreed, "for fear of their venom."

"Ah, the venom! That is the serious side of the question, and not the creature's ugliness, which is open to discussion. The toad has the beauty appropriate to it, the beauty of a toad, and it cannot have any other without ceasing to be what it is.

"On being molested toads perspire through the warts that cover their skin a thick and viscous fluid that looks somewhat like milk. This secretion has a nauseous, burning taste and is unbearably bitter."

"Some one, then, has tasted the milky sweat that oozes from the toad's warts?" asked Jules.

"Yes, scientists have tasted it in order to tell us the truth about it, just as others have done with the viper's venom. We must respect highly these courageous investigators, who are willing to make any sacrifice if only they may add to our knowledge and relieve our sufferings."

"The toad sweats this milky liquid when tormented; is that the way it defends itself?" Jules further inquired.

"It hopes to defend itself by the horrid odor of its sweat and by its intolerably bitter taste; but this sweat is put to no further use. The animal would be truly dangerous if it could inject its sweat into our blood as the viper injects its venom through its fangs into the wound already made by them. I will now relate a few experiments made by the scientists I just referred to.

"A drop of the toad's milky fluid is introduced with a pointed steel instrument into the flesh of a little bird. In a few minutes the bird staggers as if intoxicated, shuts its eyes, gasps, and falls dead."

"Really and truly dead?" asked Emile.

"Really and truly dead," his uncle replied. "A dog is treated in the same manner, but with a stronger dose. In less than an hour the animal dies in a frightful frenzy."

"Then this white sweat of the toad must be a perfectly horrible venom," Jules remarked.

"Travelers tell us that certain South American Indian tribes poison the tips of their arrows with this venom. First they impale alive on a long stick a number of these animals, and then put them near the fire to make their warts sweat. The fluid that oozes out is collected in a large leaf, and into this fluid the savages dip their arrow-heads, a wound from which is then likely to prove fatal."

"Isn't it the truth, then," asked Jules, "that toads are venomous?"

"Yes and no. Applied in any way but by injection, the toad's sweat is harmless; to act as venom it must mix with the blood through a wound. But I will not repeat what I have already told you about the viper's venom. The toad is powerless to make the slightest wound in our flesh, and therefore it is absolutely impossible for it to harm us. It possesses a poison without being able to make any use of it except to bedew its own body by perspiring, thus repelling its enemies by the horrid smell and taste of this sweat. You can handle a toad without any sort of risk if you wish to; wash your hands immediately afterward if they have become moistened by the contact, and there will be no further trouble. Unless the foolish fancy should seize you to collect a little of the venomous liquid on the point of a penknife and then prick yourself with the knife till you drew blood, I can assure you positively that the toad would cause you no injury whatever."

"That is plain enough," Jules admitted, "for the toad has no means of making a wound to receive the venom from its warts; but they tell of other kinds of venom such as urine thrown to a distance and drivel running from the mouth."

"No drivel runs from the toad's mouth, nor is there any truth in the animal's poisoning fruit and grass with its saliva. That is pure calumny invented to blacken the detested animal."

"And the urine?"

"The toad, when molested, discharges its urine as a means of defense, but not to any distance. You would have to hold your face close to the animal to receive the discharge in the eyes. If that should happen to some careless person, a temporary redness of the eyes would be the utmost result. But no one would think of putting his face so close to the animal, and so there is no cause for alarm on that score."

"What about the creature's terrible breath?" was Jules's next inquiry.

"Another calumny on a par with that about the saliva. Its breath is no more harmful than any other animal's. So there is absolutely nothing left of the charges brought against the toad. The poison it sweats in moments of danger to drive away its enemies cannot injure as venom injures, because the animal has no means of injecting it into a wound and mixing it with the blood, as venom must be mixed to take effect. The discharge of its urine falls too short to be dangerous, and even if it should reach its mark its effect would be so slight that it is not worth considering. Does any one give a thought to the hedgehog's urine when that animal sprays itself with this liquid on being molested? The toad's similar mode of defense is no more to be feared. The other complaints, such as the swelling of one's hands after touching the animal, air poisoned by its breath, fruit and vegetables infected by the saliva and the creature's tracks, all come from people's prejudice, their imagination, which has given the poor batrachian a bad reputation.

"The toad is harmless, but that is not enough to entitle it to our consideration. It is also a very useful helper, a devourer of beetles, slugs, larvæ—vermin of every description, in short. After spending the day under a cool stone or in some dark hole, it leaves its retreat at nightfall to make its rounds, hunching itself along on its big belly. Here is a slug making such haste as it can toward the lettuce bed, there a cricket chirping at the mouth of its hole, and there again a June-bug laying its eggs in the ground. Very softly the toad approaches and in three mouthfuls gobbles them all up with a gurgle of satisfaction. Ah, those tasted good! And now for some more.

"It continues on its way, and by the time it has finished its rounds, at daybreak, you may imagine what a multitude of worms and other small prey the glutton has stowed away in its capacious stomach. And yet this useful creature is stoned to death because it is ugly! My children, never commit any such act of cruelty, at once foolish and harmful; do not stone the toad, for you would thereby deprive the fields and gardens of a vigilant guardian. Let it go its way in peace and it will destroy so many insects that you will in the end find it less ugly than you had thought.

"So well known is the toad's usefulness that in England the animal is an article of commerce. Toads are bought in the market at so much a head, carried home carefully so as not to come to any harm, and then allowed the freedom of the garden or placed in a hothouse, a crystal palace, perhaps, where wonderful plants are grown. The toad's business is to lie in wait for beetles, slugs, and other destroyers that might nibble the valuable plants; and it does its duty with zeal. What a change of fortune for the maligned creature when it finds itself living in a warm atmosphere and surrounded by the most splendid flowers procured at great expense from all parts of the world and now exhaling the most fragrant odors! As a finishing touch to the honor done the poor thing in its floral palace of glass, there is offered the tribute of poetry, that flower of the human imagination and invention. Listen to this.

"A wretched toad with head split open and one eye gouged out by some cruel hand was painfully dragging itself along through the mud of a public highway, when four small boys chanced to spy it as they were passing.

> "They spied the toad,
> And one and all sent up a gleeful shout:
> 'Come on, come on, let's kill the ugly lout!
> But first we'll have some fun.' They laughed their fill,
> As boys will laugh, hard-hearted, when they kill.
> They pricked and goaded with a pointed stick,
> Devising each in turn some cruel trick,
> Flushed with their sport, egged on by passers-by,
> While for the martyred toad none gave a sigh.
> Poor ugly thing! But nature made it so;
> For this alone its blood was caused to flow.
> It tried to flee; one foot was severed quite,
> Which gave the heartless band renewed delight.
> Its gouged-out eye hung down; half-blind it sought
> Some sheltering reeds; its efforts came to naught.
> Its mangled form had been, you would have sworn,
> Through some machine, to be so rent and torn.
> And, oh, to think that hearts can be so base
> As to wish ill to one in such sad case,
> And to so great a load of suffering sore
> To undertake to add one torment more!
> Well-nigh exhausted now, hope almost gone,
> The half-dismembered creature still toiled on.
> E'en death itself would not, for pity's sake,
> So hideous a thing consent to take;

Or thus it seemed, and so with antics rude
The toad's tormentors still their sport pursued.
Attempts to snare it next were made in vain:
It dodged, and sought a rut half filled with rain;
And, by its muddy bath somewhat restored,
Withstood the missiles that upon it poured.
Ah, what a sight was there, the beauty fresh
Of childhood, and its joy in bleeding flesh!
Such sport as theirs there surely ne'er had been:
'Come on,' they called, 'come John, come Benjamin!
And bring a stone, a big one, and we'll see
If Master Toad is quite as smart as we.'
Accordingly a massive stone was found,
Of ponderous weight, unwieldy, large, and round;
But cheerfully the lads their muscles strained,
With ends so laudable to be attained.
Just then, by curious chance, there passed that way
An over-loaded, heavy-rumbling dray.
An aged donkey, deaf, half-starved, and lame,
Was harnessed to the cart—the more's the shame—
And on its back a pannier also bore.
A long day's march behind and home before,
The patient beast trudged on with labored breath,
Though each step more seemed like to be its death.
Its toil-worn frame was so exceeding thin
You would have said 'twas naught but bones and skin.
It bore full many marks of cruel blows,
And in its eyes one read the tale of those
That suffer hardship without hope. Meanwhile
Its master heaped upon it curses vile,
Nor spared the cudgel; but the road was deep
In mire that clogged the wheels, the hills were steep.
Creaking and groaning in lugubrious tones,
The dray, thus pulled by thing of skin and bones,
Moved slowly forward till at length the road
Descended sharply, and thus eased the load;
But this now crowded on the nigh-spent beast
With force sufficient (so it seemed, at least)
To hurl him headlong. And yet, strange to tell,
The donkey paused, unheeding blows that fell
From wrathful hand. The boys broke off their play,

Content to yield the donkey right of way.
'Stand off!' they cried; 'let go there, Dick and Bob;
Let go the stone, the cart will do our job
With much more sport for us, so stand aside!'
All stood alert to see what should betide
Their wretched victim. But far otherwise
The thing fell out before their wondering eyes
Than they had thought: the donkey, bruised and lame,
At sight of woes that put his own to shame
Spared not himself, but gathered all his strength
And held the loaded cart until, at length,
Although remonstrant blows rained on his back,
He turned the dray from out the beaten track.
The grinding wheels, diverted, harmless pass,
And tortured toad is saved by tortured ass.
The driver cracks his whip, pulls at the reins,
And now the dray once more the road regains.
At that, one of the group engaged in play
(The very one who tells you this to-day)
Let fall the stone he'd been about to cast
Just as the laden wain came rumbling past;
And as he dropped it, lo, in accents clear
A mandate from on high fell on his ear,
A mandate that was quickly understood,
For it was brief, these simple words: 'Be good.'[8]

"In closing I repeat, with the great poet: 'Be good.' Be good if you wish God to love you; be good that you may grow up to be noble-hearted men; be good to one another, helping one another; be good to the animals that give us their fleece, their strength, and their life, and those that protect the fruits of the earth for us by keeping vigilant guard over them. Be kind to them all, even to the humblest among them, the toad, which serves us uncomplainingly and asks in return no pay but a pitying glance."

8   From *"Le Crapaud"* ("The Toad"), by Victor Hugo.—*Translator.*

CHAPTER XXXVII

INSTINCT

J ULES AND Emile had put a caterpillar into a glass and brought it to their uncle, who made it the subject of a little talk to his young hearers.

"Examine the creature closely," said he. "Its skin is delicate, so delicate that even a light touch hurts it; but here on the head, at the point called the skull, it has the hardness of horn, forming a sort of cap or helmet which can without injury endure friction with the hard texture of wood. The head is the part of the creature that opens the way, and it is therefore protected by armor, while the rest of the body, as it follows the head, does not need this casing of horn."

"I understand," said Emile; "the creature works its way along by scratching and tunneling with its feet."

"No, my boy; the feet are not used for boring through wood. The caterpillar has eight pairs. The first three pairs, or those nearest the head, have quite a different shape from the others: they are slender and pointed, and it is they that in the change that takes place later become the butterfly's legs, though in doing so they grow much longer and take another shape. Hence they are called the true legs. The next four pairs are placed toward the middle of the body, and the last pair is at the very end. These five pairs bear the name of false legs because they completely disappear when the caterpillar gives place to the butterfly or moth. They are short and wide, and are furnished beneath with numerous little hooks by which the caterpillar clings to the walls of its abode. The stiff hairs covering the body are also used for locomotion, the caterpillar wriggling and squirming in its tunnel somewhat as does the chimney-sweep in helping himself with knees and back as he makes his way up the inside of a chimney."

"Then what does the caterpillar use for boring through the wood?" asked Jules.

"The tool for chipping away the wood consists of two curved fangs or teeth, almost black, one on each side of the mouth, which open and shut like a pair of cutting nippers. They are called mandibles and are in reality jaws or, more properly, teeth which, instead of meeting in a vertical plane as do ours, come together horizontally or sidewise. For precision of movement these mandibles are superior to our best cutting nippers, and for hardness they are almost equal to steel. They seize the wood, bit by bit, patiently and untiringly; they cut, saw, tear away a little at a time, and so bore a tunnel just large enough for the caterpillar to pass through."

"And what becomes of the wood-dust?" Jules further inquired. "I should think it would block the way, the passage being so narrow."

"The wood-dust passes through the creature's body; the caterpillar eats it, and after digestion has taken from it the very small amount of nourishment it contains, it is ejected behind, molded into tiny pellets. Digestion in a caterpillar is soon accomplished. Just think of it: wood is an extremely meager fare, and so the worm must keep on eating its way forward, cutting, gnawing, digesting. To acquire the fatness necessary for the coming change the creature must have a good-sized pear-tree limb or lilac trunk to work on.

"The wormhole dust left behind by the boring worm sometimes betrays the insect to its enemies. Whenever you see any of this dust left by digestion coming out at some little orifice in the bark of a pear-tree, apple-tree, or other tree, you may know the borer is at work, and the branch where he is at work should be cut off immediately, to prevent more serious harm. If the caterpillar has not gone too far, a pointed iron wire may be thrust into the opening and an attempt made to kill the creature in its hole. But as the passage is very winding, this method is by no means certain of success."

"Couldn't the wire be pushed in through another opening?" queried Jules.

"But, my boy, you don't suppose the caterpillar is so simple as to make windows here and there in its dwelling and so make it easy for its foes, of which it has many besides man, to attack it! If it should take a fancy, let us say, to go out and get a little fresh air some fine day, a sparrow might spy it and carry it off as a choice titbit for its brood under the roof tiles. All these dangers it knows; or, rather, it guesses them vaguely, for every creature, even to the smallest worm, knows how to protect itself and preserve its species. Unquestionably it lacks the reasoning faculty, which belongs only to man; but it none the less acts as if it reasoned out its own interests with an accuracy that astounds the thoughtful observer. As a matter of fact, my dear children, Another has already reasoned for it, and that Other is the universal Reason in and by whom all live; it is God, the Father of men, and also the Father of lilacs and of the caterpillars that gnaw them. The creature knows, then, without ever having learned; it is master of its art without having been taught; and at the very first trial, with no experience to rely on, it does admirably the thing it was intended to do. This gift bestowed at birth, this unfailing inspiration that guides it in its work, is called instinct.

"In its butterfly state the leopard-moth takes very little food, at the most a few drops of honey from the opening flowers. Its proboscis, so slender and so delicate, is fitted to get this food. Now that it no longer has its strong mandibles, how can the moth imagine that wood is eatable? Is it possible that it remembers what it liked as a caterpillar? Who can say? Moreover, how can the moth tell what trees have wood suitable for the larvæ, when we ourselves must have a certain degree of education in order to know the commonest varieties? The moth, with no previous education, never mistakes a plane-tree for a pear-tree, a box-tree for a lilac, an oak for an elm. Thus the eggs are always laid on the right sort of tree, never on any other. Where man might make a mistake, the insect never errs.

"The young larva comes out of the egg. What does the poor little thing know from experience of the hard trade it is to follow? Nothing, absolutely nothing. No matter; as soon as it is born it attacks the wood it rests upon and hollows out a shelter for itself with the least possible delay. This most urgent business being attended to, it now leisurely gnaws its way ahead, nibbling a little here and a little there and shaping its course according to the quality of the wood. The passage lengthens, increasing in diameter as the creature grows, and sometimes ascending, sometimes descending, sometimes running horizontally quite through the trunk or branch. The mass of the wood may be attacked with little system and without economy, for the larva is assured of food enough in any event. One precaution, however, it invariably takes: it never bores through the bark, for fear of betraying its presence to hostile eyes. But how does the larva, working in total darkness, know when it is getting near the bark and must turn back? What gives it the fear it has of showing itself? What makes it so careful to remain in the heart of the wood and thus avoid the vigilant sparrow it has never seen? It is instinct, the inspiration that protects all animal-kind in the fierce battle of life."

CHAPTER XXXVIII

THE GRAIN-WEEVIL

UNCLE PAUL had sent old Jacques to town to buy the drug they were going to apply to Simon's wheat. Meanwhile he took occasion to tell his young hearers about the wheat-devourer that was to have the benefit of the drug. The handful of grain left by Simon was in a plate on the table. The little weevils were running about in frantic endeavors to escape, while Emile with a straw was pushing them back into the middle of the plate, where they cowered among the kernels of wheat. Louis and Jules were also there, all attention to what was going on.

"This ravager of our granaries," began Uncle Paul, "is called the grain-weevil, or, in Latin, *calandra*. It belongs to the order of coleoptera or beetles. Its defensive armor is a hard brown casing finely engraved. It has no membranous wings under the elytra or wing sheaths. Hence it is unable to fly, but it runs fast enough and it clings to objects with a firm grip. You see how busy Emile is kept with his straw in preventing the prisoners' escape. The grain-weevil is about four millimeters long, its body is of a uniform blackish brown, and its head ends in a long snout, a kind of slender trum-

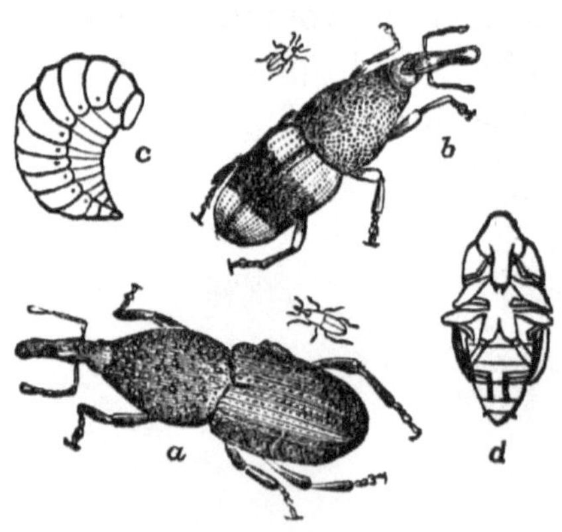

GRAIN-WEEVILS
a, corn-weevil; *b*, rice-weevil;
c, larva; *d*, pupa.

pet. The corselet or thorax is long, marked with fine pricks or dots, and the wing sheaths are delicately furrowed. The insect's most striking characteristic is its long, trumpet-shaped snout."

"It seems to me," said Jules, "I have seen other beetles, and rather large ones, too, with the head ending in a trumpet like that."

"I've found them on hazels," added Louis, "and they had a long, slender beak that would make you think the insect was smoking a long pipe."

"The trumpet beetles form a numerous class, and they are all weevils, but their mode of life varies for the different species. Some attack fruit trees and grape-vines. We will speak of them one of these days.

"With its pointed snout the grain-weevil makes a tiny hole in a kernel of wheat, and in this it lays an egg which it makes fast by means of a sticky liquid from its own body. Then it passes immediately to other kernels and treats them in the same way, until its store of eggs is exhausted. And all this is done with such delicate nicety that the sharpest eyes would fail to detect any trace of these mischievous germs in the kernels. But a weevil knows very well when a kernel has already received an egg, from whatever source, and never does it commit the blunder of laying a second one there, for the grain of wheat is too small for more than one eater. To each kernel its larva, to each larva its kernel, and no more.

"Soon the eggs hatch. The tiny worm punctures the envelop of the grain and through the almost invisible opening makes its way into the mealy substance within. There it is at home, in perfect quiet, peacefully devoted to the pleasures of feasting. For its own exclusive use a grain of wheat, a whole grain of wheat! Thus it grows big and fat. In five or six weeks the flour is all eaten up, but the bran remains, for the clever larva is careful not to make a hole in it; it will need it to serve as a cradle during the coming change. The gnawed kernel appears quite whole, when as a matter of fact it is hollow and lodges a weevil. In this hiding-place the larva turns into a nymph, and the latter into a perfect insect. Then the fully developed weevil tears open the bran covering and leaves its home to explore the pile of wheat, select certain ungnawed grains, and lay its eggs in them, eggs that will in time produce a new population of ravagers."

Here Uncle Paul picked out a few grains, one by one, and submitted them to his hearers' scrutiny.

"What do you see that is at all unusual in those grains?" he asked. "Look at them well."

"I have looked and looked," Emile replied after a little, "and I don't see anything."

"I don't see anything, either," said Jules.

"Nor I," added Louis.

"Those grains, boys, have no flour in them, despite their fair outside appearance; the weevil has emptied them."

"But how can you tell so easily?" asked Jules.

"A kernel inhabited by the grain-weevil yields to the pressure of a finger and is also lighter in weight than one that is sound. From appearance alone one cannot tell infested kernels from uninjured ones, as the outside looks the same in both cases. Thus, without extreme vigilance, the inroads of the weevil pass unperceived until the developed insects show themselves; and then the evil is beyond remedy. Didn't Simon think he had a fine lot of wheat when there was hardly anything but the bran left? A very simple experiment suffices to prove the condition of the wheat. Throw a handful of it into water and all the sound kernels will sink to the bottom, all the unsound ones float on the surface. We will perform this experiment with the wheat on the plate if Jules will go to the spring and bring a glass of water."

The water was brought and Uncle Paul threw the wheat into it. A few grains sank, many floated. These latter were opened with the point of a pin, and in some was found a little soft white worm, without legs, but furnished with strong mandibles. It was the larva of the grain-weevil. In others there was a white nymph, and in a few was the perfect insect all ready to leave its snug abode.

"To judge by the number of grains that floated," Jules remarked, "Simon's pile of wheat, even if it is not a very big one, must contain millions of weevils. It must have taken a lot of the creatures to produce such an immense family, mustn't it?"

"Not so many as you might think. How many eggs do you suppose one weevil lays?"

"A dozen, perhaps."

"Ah, how far out you are in your reckoning! In the course of one season a weevil lays from eight to ten thousand eggs, from which spring as many larvæ, each gnawing a grain. A liter measure[9] contains, on an average, ten thousand grains of wheat. To feed the family of one weevil, therefore, nearly a liter of wheat is needed. Suppose there are a thousand pairs of these insects in a granary; that would be enough to destroy ten hectoliters of wheat, rye, barley, or oats; for they attack all kinds of grain impartially."

---

9   A liter is slightly more than a quart, a hectoliter a little more than one hundred quarts.—*Translator.*

CHAPTER XXXIX

THE COMMON CATERPILLAR

"I REMEMBER," said Jules, "one Sunday last winter—it was some time in December or January, I think—the mayor had just posted a notice on the door of the town hall, and the people were reading it as they came from church. The notice was something about caterpillars, and the mayor had ordered their nests to be destroyed."

"Yes," rejoined Uncle Paul, "the mayor had in mind, luckily for us, the caterpillar law."

"What! Is there a law about caterpillars, with a fine for disobeying it?"

"Yes, my boy, there is a law about caterpillars, and I thank the legislature that had the wisdom to pass it. God grant it may become a more general statute and include a greater number of our insect enemies, the June-bug especially, and that it may be strictly enforced!"

"But that would put people out, to have to leave their business and go and hunt for caterpillar-nests and burn them. At least, that's what One-eyed John said when he read the mayor's notice."

"Leave their business, you say? Is it leaving one's business to go and save the crops when they are threatened? Laws, my young friend, are rules made for the general good, and we should all obey them scrupulously. If there are any narrow-minded objectors or stupid grumblers—any One-eyed Johns, in short—that choose to take offense, so much the worse for them: they will have to obey in any event, for the common interest is not to be compromised by the foolishness of a few.

"The mayor's notice had especial reference to a caterpillar whose ravages are, in some seasons, truly calamitous. So abundant is this caterpillar in central and northern France that it is called, briefly, the common caterpillar. It is encountered everywhere, on fruit trees and forest trees, in garden walks and on plants and hedges, and even on the bark of trees, sometimes in countless legions.

"It is dark brown in color with six rows of little tubercles or pimples of the same hue, each bearing a tuft of long, red hair. The ring-like segment to which is attached the last pair of false legs, and also the following segment, have each a plump red nipple which can at the caterpillar's pleasure recede under the skin or stand out prominently. The butterfly developing from this caterpillar is pure white except on the abdomen, which is brown. Furthermore, the female has a thick tuft of red hair at the end of the abdomen. Its purpose is shown when the eggs are laid: after these are deposited, to the number of three or four hundred, the butterfly rubs off the hair and places it over the eggs. The laying takes place in July and the eggs, deposited in a little heap on a leaf, are rose red."

"But if they are on a leaf," objected Emile, "they must fall from the tree when the leaves fall, and then the wind might blow them away."

"The butterfly that lays its eggs on a leaf knows very well what it is about. On the other hand, those butterflies that lay eggs that are to go through the winter and hatch in the spring are very careful not to entrust their eggs to a leaf, which will soon fall to the ground. They make their eggs fast to the bark. But whence do they get their knowledge of the future? Who told them the leaves would fall and therefore would be insecure resting-places for the eggs? They do not learn this by experience, for they have never seen the autumnal shedding of leaves, having been born when the foliage is already well advanced for their nourishment, and laying their eggs and dying while it is still on the trees. If, then, experience cannot account for it, we must ascribe the insect's mysterious foreknowledge to the incomprehensible inspiration of instinct, which sees the invisible and knows the unknown because there is a Sovereign Intelligence that knows all and orders all.

"Our common caterpillar likewise is led by instinct when it lays its eggs on a leaf, for long before the fall of that leaf they will hatch, in the last fortnight of July."

"A cunning rascal, that caterpillar," said Emile; "it knows the order of the seasons as if it had the almanac by heart."

"I haven't told you all. Another motive acts in determining the butterfly's course. In laying its eggs on a leaf the insect places them where the young caterpillars are sure to find food close at hand when they come out of the eggs, so that they will not have to go running about over the branches, a dangerous thing at their tender age. All anxiety as to food supply is thus removed at the outset, and this assurance against famine is so much to the good in this world of chance and uncertainty, whether for men or caterpillars."

"If the butterfly reasoned it all out," said Jules, "it couldn't do any better."

"Perhaps not so well, my child. Are there not plenty of people, alas, that show far less foresight? The butterfly leaves to its young a leaf as a heritage, a leaf to eat, whereas the spendthrift, the idler, leaves to his family nothing but poverty and suffering. He has not even the wisdom of an insect."

CHAPTER XL

CATERPILLARS AT TABLE

❝IN THE latter part of July the eggs hatch and through the covering of down appear, here and there, little heads pushing aside the fluff that is in their way. The first caterpillar hatched out crawls forward and begins to browse on the upper surface of the leaf, grazing it lightly and without eating through to the under surface or touching the veins; it feeds only on the pulpy matter forming most of the leaf's thickness. As the hatching continues, another little caterpillar advances and takes its place beside the first, then a third, a fourth, and so on until the whole width of the leaf is occupied. In this way is formed the first row of browsing caterpillars, all with heads in a straight line and leaving in front a certain unoccupied space. The next caterpillar to emerge from under the matting of down begins a second row by taking its station at the tail of one of the preceding ones, after which others place themselves at the right and left. This row completed, a third is formed in the same manner, and then others, so that in a short time the entire surface of the leaf except the forward end is covered with rows of eaters. If one leaf is not enough for the whole brood, the later comers establish themselves in like order on neighboring leaves.

"There they are, then, all at table. The strictest discipline prevails in this leafy dining-hall: each caterpillar gnaws what is directly under its mandibles, without turning to right or left, as that would take from its neighbor's share; without advancing ahead of its own line, as that would mean using the supplies of the future; and without falling behind, as that would throw the rear ranks into confusion. Under these conditions a few mouthfuls and no more fall to each caterpillar. That is very little for a larva's appetite. It must have more, but how obtain it? Scatter abroad on other leaves, haphazard? Undoubtedly there is plenty of room for all on the tree. But that would be highly imprudent: they must keep together, for union is the strength of the weak; they must keep together to be able to offer some sort of formidable appearance to their enemies. It would be equally objectionable for each to be a law to itself and gnaw where it chose on the same leaf. The resulting confusion would cause waste, and also it would be very difficult for each to get its proper share, some stuffing themselves and others near by dying of hunger. In such absence of law and order they would come to blows and fight desperately for a footing on the leaf, so that civil war would soon thin their ranks, for there is no worse counselor in such emergencies than the stomach. Order is the only solution of their problem, order which safeguards human as well as insect communities."

"What do they do, then?" asked Jules.

"We are coming to that. Each caterpillar, as I said, gnaws only the spot directly within reach. In this way there is left unbrowsed, first the part covered by each body, and then the forward part of the leaf, which is still unoccupied. The first row of caterpillars advances one step and finds a second ration in the part thus reached; but at the same time it uncovers in the rear a crosswise strip one step wide, which the second row now advances to feed upon, while in its turn it leaves a similar strip free for the third row; and so on. One step forward for the whole troop puts each row in possession of the strip left uncovered by the preceding row. As for the first row, it feeds little by little on the forward part of the leaf, designedly left unoccupied in the beginning. When step by step the very end of the leaf is reached, each caterpillar has gnawed a strip as long and as wide as its own body. By that time the first meal is finished. You see that with order and economy a hundred and more caterpillars all have a place in the dining-hall on the surface of the leaf, and all have as nearly equal rations as if these had been allotted by weight and measure."

"Animals with their instinct are wonderful creatures, Uncle," observed Jules. "Every day brings some fresh surprise."

"It is not the creature itself that is to be wondered at, my dear child; the marvels it accomplishes are not the fruit of its reflection. A grub just out of the egg can have no ideas on method, economy, coöperation, when in order to acquire these ideas man needs the full maturity of his reason. Our tribute of admiration should be paid to the Infinite Wisdom which governs the world and leads a brood of caterpillars browsing the surface of a leaf.

"Their first hunger appeased, the caterpillars construct a shelter from rain and the heat of the sun. On its gnawed side the leaf is dryer than on the other, and consequently has of itself taken a kind of concave shape by curling up, which makes it serve excellently for the floor and walls of the new abode. As for the ceiling, that is to be of silk. From one raised edge of the leaf to the other the caterpillars stretch threads to strengthen their shelter and serve as framework for the roof, and finally they weave a fabric on this network of threads. Thus is erected a tent under which the caterpillars take refuge for the night after roaming over the foliage most of the day, feeding sometimes on one leaf, sometimes on another. Thither also they retire when the heat is excessive or the weather threatening. It is a shelter hastily constructed and not of enduring quality, besides being too small to hold them all. So other tents are made of other gnawed leaves, and the caterpillars live for a while divided into small families.

"But with the first rain-storms of autumn, in September or October, a large building is constructed for housing the whole colony through the winter. It is a bulky mass of dry leaves and white silk, with no definite shape. The inside is divided with silk partitions into numerous apartments to which there is access through holes that pierce, systematically, the several partitions. Each enclosure thus has its doors which, without being directly opposite each other, yet provide free circulation. In short, this common nest, though made of extremely fine silk, is substantial enough to be proof against wind and weather, for the caterpillars use many webs, placed one over another and each containing a great number of threads. With the coming of the first cold weather all shut themselves up, the doors are barricaded with silk, and everything is made snug for the winter. Now let the wind blow and the snow fall! Curled up together and snuggling against one another, the caterpillars sleep the deep sleep produced by the cold, lying torpid in their house of silk until the warmth of opening spring awakens them and sends them forth to browse on the growing leaves."

"And don't they eat anything all winter?" asked Emile.

"All winter as well as a part of the autumn and spring they take no food whatever. Their fast lasts six months, and it is an absolute fast that must leave them with very empty stomachs."

"They must be awfully hungry when they wake up."

"So hungry that they make a dash for the tender young leaves and opening flowers, and in less than no time strip an orchard bare. If the nests are very numerous whole forests are browsed to the last leaf."

"And then?"

"To prevent these ravages the mayor's notice is heeded. Some time in the winter these terrible bags of dry leaves and silk are detached from the trees, hedges, and bushes, and the nests with their occupants are burned. In spring it would be too late: the caterpillars would all have left their quarters."

CHAPTER XLI

ENEMIES OF THE GRAPEVINE

ONE MORNING Jules was sent to the mill to give notice that his uncle's wheat was ready to be ground. After he had left the village his road ran along beside a vineyard that showed signs of neglect, weeds and thistles springing up unchecked. Nevertheless the vines were pleasing to the eye in the spring freshness of their tender green shoots, with their clusters of blossoms still in the bud and their delicate tendrils reaching out for something to cling to. Here and there leaves of faded and ragged appearance, with others that were dried up and shriveled, took away somewhat from the general effect; but they were not very numerous and Jules failed to notice them at first. Afterward, for the last half of the way along the vineyard, these withered leaves became so abundant that the young vine shoots looked as if they had been swept by a fire.

"Some ravager is at work here," said the boy to himself, for his eyes were daily becoming more keenly observant. "Let's look into this a little."

The vines were pitiful to behold, their young shoots showing more and more toward the growing end, where the grape clusters were forming, dried and crumpled leaves, some

LEAF-HOPPER (A GRAPEVINE-EATER)
a, with wings spread; *b*, with wings closed; cross shows natural size.

of these being rolled up like cigars. Under closer scrutiny there was often to be seen an insect with a long beak, a weevil of a brilliant metallic green color. Without question this beautiful weevil was the cause of the mischief. Insects and cigars, especially the former, sparkling creatures in the bright light of the sun, were soon collected by Jules as specimens to take home. Just then One-eyed John, the owner of the vineyard, came along.

"What are you doing there?" he demanded.

"Catching a few of these insects that are ruining your vines," the boy replied.

"Let me see them."

"Here they are."

"And you say they are ruining my vines?"

"I think so. I have just seen some of them making these cigars."

"Oh, bosh, you silly! Do you think they would take the trouble to make cigars out of leaves? They don't smoke. It's the moon that has burned my vines, the moon."

And so, satisfied with his explanation, One-eyed John turned on his heel and went off, whistling a tune. But he would stop whistling when, three years later, he had to pull up those vines, exhausted as they were by the cigar-rollers. Nevertheless he would not take back what he had said: the moon had caused all the mischief.

Returning from the mill, Jules picked up Louis on the way and brought him back to share in the benefit of what Uncle Paul might have to say concerning the specimens Jules had collected.

"The insect found on the vine," said he, after examining one of the brilliant creatures, "is a weevil. You all remember that this name is given to various beetles with a head tapering into a sort of trumpet. This one is the *rhynchites*, as entomologists call it, or the vine-grub, as it is known to vine-growers. It is of a magnificent lustrous green on the back, and underneath it shines like gold. Some dark-blue ones are also found, but they are more rare. The male has on each side of the thorax a little pointed protuberance directed forward. The larva is a small, white, legless worm that begins life in a roll made by the mother with a vine leaf. In the month of May she begins operations by cutting the stem of the leaf three-quarters through to arrest the flow of sap, so that the leaf may wither and be the easier to roll. Then the weevil rolls it up and lays three or four eggs in its folds. When in the process of drying the leaf has assumed the color of tobacco, you would take it for a cigar hanging from the vine. The young larvæ soon abandon this first shelter, let themselves fall, and burrow into the ground, where they finish developing. The vine-grub saps the vigor of the vine by destroying its leaves, and therefore the cigar-like rolls should be picked off and burned in May or June. In this way the infant insects are destroyed in the cradle and much future damage is prevented."

"Along with the shiny green weevil that rolls vine leaves into cigars I found this other insect," Jules announced, displaying the creature.

"That is not a weevil, as you can see from the shape of its head, which has no tapering beak. Its wing sheaths are chestnut red, the rest of the body being black. It is known as the eumolpus or, more commonly, the vine-fretter, or, in our language, the scrivener because in gnawing the surface of the vine leaves it traces fine lines that look somewhat like intricate handwriting. It attacks in the same way the stems of grape leaves and of grape clusters, the young shoots of the vine, and the grapes themselves. If the insects are numerous, all these incisions and lacerations cause the vines to wither away and produce but little fruit, and that of poor quality.

"The larvæ of the vine-fretter live in the ground, and to destroy them the soil thus infested is turned over in the winter, as exposure to the cold kills the grubs. When the insects are fully developed it is exceedingly difficult to rid the vines of them. At the slightest alarm the little creature, busy with its destructive writing on the leaves, draws its legs up under its belly and lets itself drop to the ground, where it cannot be easily seen because of its dull hue; and it also keeps perfectly still, playing dead."

"Does it think it can escape by not moving?" asked Emile.

"Doubtless, because then, even if it should by any chance be discovered, it would probably be mistaken for a grain of earth."

"Wouldn't it be better for it to fly away or run away than to play dead?"

"Its flight is too heavy and its legs too short. All insects that cannot take instant flight and are without means of defense do as does the vine-fretter in time of danger: they remain perfectly motionless. Nearly always this expedient succeeds with them because their color, commonly a dull one, causes them to be confounded with the soil."

"Ah, the sly rogues!"

"Well, then, this ruse of the vine-fretter must be turned to account by us in our efforts to exterminate the insect. Under the vine we stretch a cloth, after which a sharp blow is given to the main stem. The vine-fretters let themselves fall, they play dead, but they can be seen on the cloth and not one escapes the sad fate awaiting it."

CHAPTER XLII

CLEVER MISCHIEF-MAKERS

"HERE IS another weevil I have to show you," began Uncle Paul the next day. "What do you think of it? Note its shiny violet coat with glints of blue that bring out the delicate down with which the whole body is covered. The purple of our richest silks is not so magnificent."

"Oh, the pretty little thing!" cried Emile. "What can it do with its beautiful clothes?"

"Nothing to our advantage, my boy. Fine clothes do not make useful citizens, either among insects or among men. The bee's dress is a modest brown, and the bee works at honey-making; the dress of the weevil I show you here is very handsome, but the elegant creature lives at our expense. If you have in your garden any fine plums or pears or apples, it gets ahead of you in harvesting the crop; it does not even wait for the fruit to ripen, so fearful is it of being too late. In June it punctures with its pointed snout the young apple or pear or plum and lays an egg in the unripe flesh. The fruit thus treated feeds the larva for some time, and then dries up and falls off. Then the worm emigrates, leaves the plum that has nourished it, and buries itself in the ground to reappear the next spring as a perfect insect."

"I should like to know the name of this plum-pricker; I'd teach it to behave if I got hold of it."

"It is called, very inappropriately, the *rhynchites bacchus.*"

"Bacchus, if I remember rightly," said Jules, "is the god of wine."

"Exactly; and that is where the word is out of place here. No doubt the first observers confounded the weevil of our orchards with that of our vineyards, giving to the former the name that should belong to the latter. But the mistake has been made and we can't do anything about it now. Let us keep the names as they are, but not confound the two weevils so different in appearance and habits. The weevil that rolls the vine leaves is hairless and of a golden-green color; the other is all covered with hairs and its color is a lustrous violet. To avoid confusion in our talk, why should we not call this latter insect the plum-weevil, or the pear-weevil?"

"That would be a good name for it," assented Louis.

"I shall just call it the plum-pricker," declared Emile.

"There is no reason why you should not," his uncle agreed. "Now let us pass on to another member of the family. See what widely dissimilar habits there are in a group of insects in which the expert eye can nevertheless perceive close resemblances, I might almost say a near relationship. Some roll grape or oak or poplar leaves; others puncture fruit with the beak; this one here that I am going to tell you about severs—partly, never wholly—the tips of young and tender shoots of various fruit trees. Hence they are commonly known as bud-cutters. It is a weevil, but much smaller than that of the grapevine. The adjective conical is given to it on account of the shape of its thorax or breastplate, which tapers a little toward the front like a sugar-loaf. It is rather lustrous and of a blue color shading into green.

"It shows remarkable cleverness in its operations. Establishing itself in spring on a pear, cherry, apricot, plum, or hawthorn tree, indifferently, it selects one by one the shoots that suit it, and in the not yet unfolded terminal bud it bores with its beak a tiny hole, in which it lays an egg. But it appears that the young larva requires a diet especially prepared for it, one that is slightly decomposed, and not the bitter juices of the vigorously growing shoot. Have not we ourselves similar tastes? Do we eat medlars and sorb-apples just as they come from the tree? No indeed; they must first be left to ripen on straw, even to decay a little."

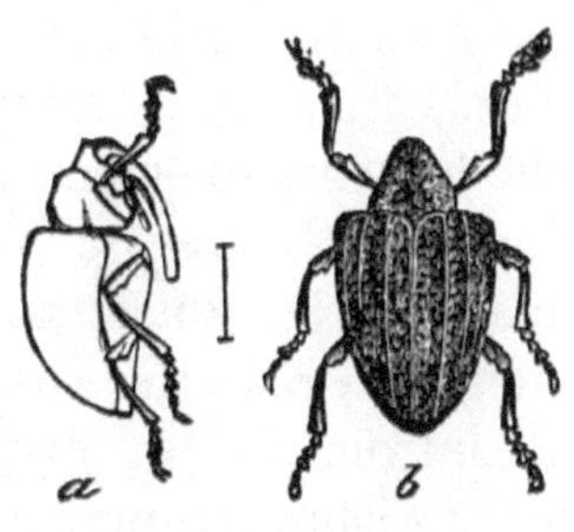

QUINCE-WEEVIL
a, side view; *b*, view from above; line shows natural size.

"Then they are first-rate," was Emile's pronouncement; "but before that they are horrid."

"That is what the larva of the weevil would say about the shoot on which it has just hatched out. Before being treated it is bitter, it rasps the throat and sets the mandibles on edge; after treatment it is delicious."

"Yet it doesn't put the branch to ripen on straw as we do medlars?"

"No. In most cases larvæ show no ingenuity whatever; they eat like gluttons and without a thought for anything but eating. You know well enough that giving oneself up to gorging is hardly the way to improve the mind. For these larvæ, then, a ready-made pap has to be provided, as otherwise, not knowing how to prepare it themselves, they would stupidly starve to death. And who prepares the food and makes it just right for them? The mother, if you please, the mother whose great and only occupation it is to provide for the future needs of her unborn young. She makes it her business to find for them food that not only has no nourishment in it for herself, but which she dislikes; she denies herself the enjoyment of flowery fields and summer sunshine to devote all her energies to arduous labors that are of no advantage to her personally; and when she has spent her little span of life at this hard task she retires into a corner and dies content: the table is set, the young larvæ will not lack for food.

"When you see the weevil on a vine leaf, sparkling like a precious gem, do not think it is there to enjoy itself. It is spending itself in the difficult undertaking of sawing the leaf half-way through at the stem, after which it will roll the leaf into a sheath to serve as lodging and first food for the larvæ. Its whole life of two or three weeks is given to this work. How can it benefit the insect itself to saw leaf stems and make the leaves wither in the sun and then roll them up? In no way whatever; the weevil does not eat these leaves or lodge in the sheath made by rolling one of them up. It spends its energies in this work solely for the larvæ that are to be hatched out after its death. Have you ever reflected, my children, on this perpetual miracle,—the miracle of a mother living only for her little ones, little ones that she is destined never to see? I will not conceal from you that every time I think of this maternal foresight, this laborious preparation for a future unknown to the mother herself, I feel myself deeply moved. The All-seeing Eye is there.

"In a way peculiar to itself the conical weevil makes ready the pap that is to feed its family. The larvæ, as I said, require the mild juices of a shoot that has been deprived of its natural vigor. What does the mother do to put the branch in the proper condition? Under the spot where the egg is laid she cuts away the bark and some of the wood in a circle, with her fine mandibles, leaving the shoot supported only by the central portion of the stem. The sap no longer circulating beyond this girdle, the leaves affected soon wither and the entire tip of the shoot turns black and acquires that state of decay best liked by the new-born grub."

"I knew how to ripen medlars on straw," said Emile, "but I should have been puzzled to tell how to ripen a branch of a tree. What curious creatures those are, with their clever ways of doing things! One can do one thing and another can do another, and it is always ingenious and never the same."

"It is vexatious that all too often the insect's labors involve harm and loss to us. When a fruit-tree has been operated on by the conical weevil you can see, in the month of May, the tips of the shoots hanging withered and blackened, after which they dry up and fall."

"Do the larvæ stay in the tips of the fallen branches?" asked Jules.

"What would they do there? Food would fail them, and so they bury themselves in the ground to finish their growth and pass the winter there snugly and safely. In the spring their metamorphosis takes place."

"Then to guard against insect ravages for the next year," said Louis, "the withered shoots that hang from the trees should be collected and burned while the larvæ are still there."

"Yes, that is the best thing to do."

CHAPTER XLIII

NUT-WEEVILS AND FLOWER-WEEVILS

"HA, YOU rascal, I've caught you at it now, eating my hazel-nuts!" cried Louis one day on seeing a weevil piercing with its long beak a still tender young nut. "I've caught you at it. But first I'll learn all about you, and then we'll have a reckoning."

The weevil was placed in a paper cornucopia together with some pierced hazelnuts, and in his first spare moment Louis hastened to Uncle Paul's house, his cheeks flushed with excitement. Little Louis was very fond of hazelnuts, and to catch in the very act the insect that attacks them was a very serious matter, to his thinking. In the evening Uncle Paul had his usual audience around him to listen to his account of the hazelnut-weevil.

"Here is the little insect Louis has caught," he began. "Look at its beak a moment."

"What a nose!" exclaimed Emile. "Oh, what a nose! It is as slender as a hair and very long and turned back at the end."

"Doesn't it look as if it were smoking a long pipe, as I said the other day?" asked Louis.

"See, Uncle," Emile pointed out, "how close together its eyes are; they almost touch each other, and the insect seems to be squinting. How funny it is, with its nose like a pipe-stem and its squinting eyes!"

NUT-WEEVIL
a, view from above; *b*, side view;
line shows natural size.

"Where is its mouth?" asked Jules.

"At the very end of what Emile calls its long nose," his uncle replied.

"How does it manage to eat? Food must have a hard time getting through that stem not so big around as a thread."

"Yes, how does it manage to eat?" Emile chimed in. "I should be in a terrible fix if I had to take my food through a straw as long as myself."

"The weevil is obliged to exercise moderation; at the most it drinks with its beak only a few drops of sap from the hazelnut-tree it inhabits. But if the weevil is temperate in its diet, the larva of the weevil eats with a good appetite: it demands the whole kernel of a hazelnut, and it is on purpose to give the larva this food that the weevil is provided with the long beak that astonishes you. The perfect insect, I repeat, lives much more for its future family than for itself, its equipment being designed with reference to the future of its young. If the weevil had to think merely of its own food its trumpet would be highly inconvenient; but it must above all look out for the well-being of its larvæ, and to make provision for that, the creature's long and slender beak is a wonderful tool, serving as a fine gimlet for boring through the nutshell so that the egg may be laid in the very meat itself and the larva be hatched out in the lap of plenty."

"That must be a long, hard job for so fine a gimlet," Jules remarked.

"Not at all. The tiny mandibles at the end of the trumpet bite the shell almost as easily as an edged tool of steel would do it; and moreover the weevil chooses its time. It is in May, when the hazelnuts are beginning to grow and their shells are soft, that the task is undertaken. The insect attacks the nut at the base through the green covering called the cup. As soon as the hole is made, an egg is laid inside the nut and in a week the larva is hatched out. It is a legless worm, white with a red head. As the grub eats very little at first, the hazelnut continues to grow and its kernel to ripen, though gnawed little by little. When August comes, the store of provision is exhausted and the wormy nut lies on the ground. Then the worm, its mandibles strong by this time, makes a round hole in the empty shell and, leaving the nut, buries itself in the ground, where it undergoes transformation the following spring.”

“When I am cracking nuts with my teeth,” said Emile, “I once in a while bite into something bitter and soft.”

“That is the grub of the weevil.”

“Pah! The nasty thing!”

“How can I keep the creatures off my hazelnut trees?” asked Louis.

“That is very simple. Gather the wormy nuts, which sooner or later fall to the ground just as does fruit attacked by insects. If they are not pierced with a large hole the worm is still there. By burning them you destroy the weevils of the following year.”

“But this year’s weevils will be left.”

“No, for it is a rule that insects die soon after laying their eggs.”

“You haven’t told us the name of this hazelnut-eater,” said Jules.

“It is called the hazelnut-balaninus or hazelnut-weevil, and you can easily recognize it by its very fine, long, and recurved beak, as also by the yellowish-gray down that covers the whole of the insect.

“Another balaninus, smaller but of the same shape and color, lives in acorns in its larva state, and is known as the oak-balaninus. A third, not very often seen around here, lives in cherry-stones. It is the cherry-balaninus.”

“How different they all are in their ways of living!” Jules remarked. “The grain-weevil gnaws the kernels of grain; the vine-weevils and fruit-weevils roll leaves or prick pears and plums or cut the buds; and now here are the nut-weevils that attack the hazelnut-meat, the cherry-stone, and the acorn. Are there any that eat flowers?”

“Indeed there are. No part of a plant is spared by insects.

The apple-tree, the pear-tree, and the cherry-tree have each its peculiar weevil that in its larva state lives at the expense of the flower buds. These ravagers are called by a Greek name meaning flower-eaters. See this apple-tree weevil, the one most familiar to us. It is brown, with a small white stripe edged with black and placed slantwise on the end of each wing sheath. Beginning in April, it spreads over the apple trees and pierces the flower buds with its fine beak, laying an egg in each one. A week later the larva is hatched out, and immediately the little worm begins to gnaw the flower that is curled up in the bud. Only the outside covering is left intact by this devourer. Of course a bud that has had its heart eaten out cannot blossom, and so flower and fruit are both lost. The damaged buds, being gnawed only within, keep their shape and take in drying the appearance of cloves."

"Those cloves that Mother Ambroisine puts in stews?" asked Emile.

"The same."

"What are cloves?"

"They are, as I have already told you,[10] the buds or unopened flowers of the clove-tree, an aromatic bush growing in hot countries. They are gathered before opening and are dried in the sun."

"I see why buds pricked by the flower-weevil look like cloves. In both cases they are buds that have dried up without opening."

"The larva of the flower-weevil, like those of weevils in general, is a tiny legless worm, white in color. It does not leave the bud it has gnawed when this falls from the tree. The larva of the nut-weevil leaves its nut by boring a hole through the shell, that of the conical weevil leaves the fallen shoot, the vine-weevil lets itself drop out of its rolled leaf, and all three bury themselves in the ground to pass the winter in safety and be transformed the following spring. The larva of the flower-weevil is more expeditious: its change into an insect takes place as soon as it has eaten its bud, so that there is no need for it to leave its quarters. As animals never do anything without a purpose, the

10   See "The Secret of Everyday Things."

grub remains shut up in the dry bud. Six weeks after the egg is laid the larva emerges transformed into a perfect insect and flits from one apple-tree to another all summer. Then comes the winter."

"That must be a trying time," said Jules.

"Many perish, but others survive, hidden under moss, in the cracks of bark, or among dry leaves. Indeed, there are plenty of them left to destroy the buds on our apple trees when spring comes.

"The flower-weevil of the pear-tree and that of the cherry-tree resemble the one I have just shown you, and their habits are exactly the same.

"It is not easy to get rid of these flower-destroyers. If one had only a few trees to take care of, and those easy to get at in every part, one could if necessary gather and burn the dry buds inhabited by the larvæ. By this painstaking process some of the following year's fruit might be saved; but not even so should we get rid of all the flower-weevils, as these insects fly well and far and they would come from the surrounding region after we had destroyed all our own. Besides, the gathering of injured buds is impracticable on a large scale."

"Will these little flower-eaters come to be masters of our orchards?" asked Jules. "Will they destroy our apples and pears in the bud, and can't we do anything to prevent it?"

"They would indeed be masters had we not vigilant guards, sharp-eyed helpers, that from sunrise to sunset lie in wait for insects and hunt them with a patience, skill, and industry that none of us would be capable of."

"You mean the birds?" said Emile.

"Yes, the birds. When you see on an apple-tree in bloom a little bird hopping from branch to branch, warbling and pecking, thank God, my children, for giving us the charming creature that with every peck of its beak delivers us from an enemy."

CHAPTER XLIV

ENEMIES OF CLOVER

"Would you like to see another little creature that by reason of its very smallness and its countless numbers braves our wrath and commits ravages that can be checked only by our agricultural helpers, the foes of our foes? Here it is."

"I see it, with its long beak," cried Jules; "it is another weevil."

"Oh, how tiny it is!" exclaimed Emile. "Surely it can't eat very much."

"It is small, but so numerous that to feed its larvæ it requires whole fields of clover; not the entire plant, but only the blossom, as with the larvæ of the flower-weevil."

"What gluttons! They think they must have blossoms, tender and sweet-smelling."

"It is the clover-weevil, and it measures scarcely three millimeters in length. The body, of a uniform black, is slightly globular behind. You know clover well enough, with its blossoms massed in a round head. Well, the clover-weevil lays its eggs on the flower-head before the blossoms open."

"Without boring into each flower separately to lay its eggs in?" Jules inquired.

"The weevil does not take that trouble. The larvæ must manage for themselves. As soon as it is hatched out each one pierces the base of the flower that suits it and works its way inside. Once there, it eats the heart of

CLOVER-WEEVIL
(Line shows natural size)

the bud, especially the part that would have become fruit, the little pod with its seeds. That done, it takes on its insect form.

"Another weevil, equally small and equally numerous, runs neck and neck with this one in destroying clover blossoms. It is black, with yellow legs. Both abound in cul-

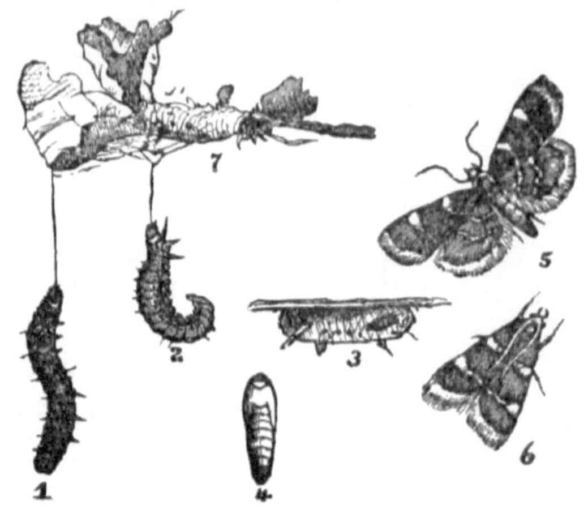

CLOVER-HAY WORM
1, 2, larvæ; 3, cocoon; 4, chrysalis;
5, 6, moth with wings spread and closed;
7, worm covered with silken web.

tivated fields. In winter they can be found gathered at the foot of trees, waiting for the clover to bloom before they go to work.

"You might think these two weevils enough to destroy this useful forage plant; but there are others still, some larger and some smaller, and all eager to get at the poor clover. It would almost seem as if insects had agreed to attack especially those plants that are useful to man. They set to work, by threes, by fours, by tens, and even by hundreds if need be, to carry out their ruinous operations, some on the flowers, others on the roots, and still others on the leaves and stems of our most valuable plants. The grapevine has its caterpillars, beetles, and lice; wheat feeds destroyers still more numerous and varied, such as weevils, moths, white worms, gnats, and many others; and for the pear-tree alone we can count five hundred ravagers, perhaps more."

"Do they want to starve us, then?" Jules again inquired.

"What shall I say? They go to work in a way to frighten one. You ask their motive. I will try to show you some other time; but now let us finish our talk on the enemies of clover.

"This one, here in my hand, is known by the learned as the clover-hylast. It is a tiny brown beetle with truncated wing sheaths like those of the bark-beetle, which it closely resembles. In fact it belongs to the same family. While the clover-weevil is busy destroying

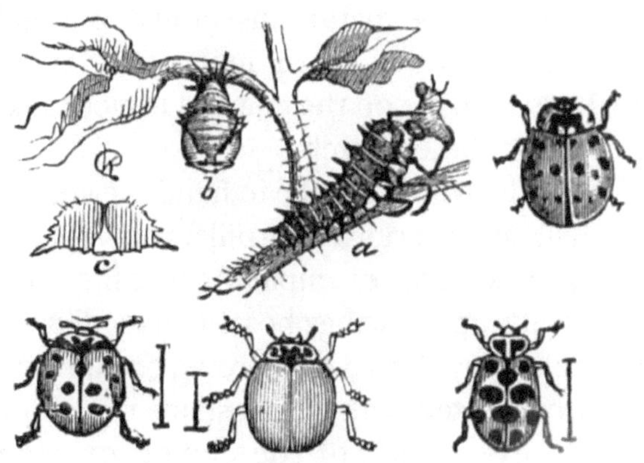

LADYBIRDS

a, larva; *b*, pupa; *c*, first joint of larva, enlarged; *d*, beetle; below, from left to right, nine-spotted ladybird, trim ladybird, and spotted ladybird, with lines showing natural size.

the blossoms, this creature stays in the ground and gnaws the roots of the plant.

"We have now the roots, the blossoms, and the young shoots devoured. Who will look after the leaves? 'I,' replies a little beetle with a rounded back and a flattened stomach, and called the globular lasia; 'I will do it so that man shall not find anything to mow after we get through with the clover.'

"You are familiar with the ladybird or ladybug, that little red beetle with tiny black spots on its back, the good God's insect. Never molest it when you find it in the garden. It works for us, going from one plant to another, devouring lice, those pot-bellied creatures that in countless swarms infest the tender shoots of plants and suck the sap. The ladybird eats our enemies, plant-lice; it dotes on them. Do not disturb it.

"The insect known as the globular lasia is of the same family as the ladybird, and like the latter it is round and red and has black spots, but they are placed differently and usually number about a dozen on each wing sheath. The larva is yellow and all bristling with little hairs that stand up like tiny thorns. Both the larva and the mature insect live, not on lice, but on leaves, whether of clover, vetch, lucerne, or some other plant. The marks they make on the gnawed leaves look like furrows made by a four-toothed comb.

"Finally, who is to take in hand the stems of the clover? This task will fall to various caterpillars equipped with good teeth and strong jaws, as for example the glyphic noctua, a rather pretty moth with upper wings bearing irregular spots encircled each by a light-gray thread on a brown background, and lower wings brightly spotted with a light shade of yellow.

"On every part of the clover, on stems and blossoms, leaves and roots, ravenous devourers are now installed. Have I exhausted the list? By no means. There are others in plenty, if only to take the leavings of those I have named."

CHAPTER XLV

CABBAGE-EATERS

ONE DAY Jacques came in from the garden with a cabbage root all covered with warts having the shape and size of a pea. In each wart was a little worm.

"Some of the cabbages are withering away," announced the old gardener, "though there are no worms on the leaves. I think the trouble comes from the warts on the roots."

"You have guessed right, my good Jacques," replied Uncle Paul. "Leave me that root and pull up all the cabbages that appear to you to be affected. Of course you will burn all the diseased roots. By so doing you will arrest the evil in the beginning, as the insect causing the mischief is rare with us. The important thing is not to let it multiply in the garden, even if we have to throw away many of the cabbages in exterminating it."

Uncle Paul's instructions were followed, and no more warty roots have been seen since. Next day the cabbage's enemies were the subject of conversation.

"Cultivated plants," said Uncle Paul, "are more exposed to the ravages of insects than the same plants in a wild state, because they are of a finer flavor, tenderer, and of more luxuriant growth. Let us first consider the cabbage, now that Jacques has furnished us the occasion.

"Look at this root, quite covered with ugly warts, hollow inside. I open one. What do we find within? A small worm, a larva that would, if left undisturbed, develop into a weevil with a beak that lies down on the breast between the forelegs when the insect curls up and plays dead. This weevil is known to men of science as belonging to a genus called *ceuthorhynchus*, a name formed from two Greek words and meaning snout-hider. It is black, with grayish hairs on the back and white scales on the belly. Its thorax has a deep furrow and its wing sheaths are ornamented with fine parallel grooves.

"It lays its eggs about the beginning of summer. The insect works its way down to the root and punctures it here and there with its beak, laying an egg in each puncture. In flowing around the wounded part the sap of the plant forms a knob or fleshy wart in which the larva grows until the end of October, when the worm leaves this nest to bury itself in the ground, safe from the cold, and undergo transformation. The punctured root exhausts its energies in bleeding sap to form the warts occupied by the larvæ, so that the cabbage rapidly withers away; and in this manner the cabbage-weevil makes itself an enemy much to be feared, especially in England where it is extremely common. Nor does it confine its depredations to cabbages; it attacks turnips also, and radishes and rape."

"This weevil seems to eat a good many things," said Jules. "I thought each kind of insect always fed on one particular plant."

"You were not far wrong, my boy. In most cases insects have very exclusive tastes, each confining itself to one kind of plant and disdaining all others. Sometimes, however, they vary their diet, and as they are connoisseurs, very well up on vegetable flavors, in changing their food they choose plants having nearly identical nutritive properties, taste, and smell. Do not we ourselves find in the radish and the turnip something of the smell and taste of the cabbage?"

"That's so," assented Louis.

"We find more or less similarity in the qualities characteristic of a great many other plants grouped together by botanists in the family of *cruciferæ* and including, for instance, the cress, the radish, and colza."

"Botanists, cruciferæ—I don't know very well what those are," said Emile.

"No, those are strange words to you. Botanists are learned

persons who spend their time studying plants and who tell us their names and properties, differences and resemblances, where they grow and when they blossom, with other matters of that sort."

"And cruciferæ?"

"That word means cross-bearers and is applied to a large group of plants with blossoms having four pieces or petals placed two by two, opposite each other, so as to form a sort of cross. A good example is the colza blossom. Plants with cross-shaped flowers include the cabbage, rape, turnip, radish, clove, colza, cress, and many others."

"They are all cruciferæ?"

"Yes, all cruciferæ. But their likeness is not confined to the shape of the blossom; their inner properties also, such as smell, taste, and the rest, are the same, or very nearly so. Consequently, the cabbage-weevil, as knowing a little creature as can be found, goes to the turnip when there are no cabbages to be had, to the colza if turnips also are lacking, or to other plants still, but always to some member of the cruciferæ family. Other insects show this same peculiarity, each species having its particular group of plants and going from one to another without ever making a mistake as to family."

"Then they are expert botanists, I should say," Jules remarked.

"One might almost think so; at least they show in their choice so keen a discernment that often men of science go to school to them to learn the various degrees of relationship in the plant world."

"Oh, Uncle Paul, you are joking!" exclaimed Jules.

"Joking? Listen. You know the nasturtium, that beautiful orange-colored flower ending at the bottom in a kind of horn; and you know the mignonette, that sweet-smelling plant that Mother Ambroisine grows in the window."

"Yes, I know them."

"Then tell me whether you find between mignonette,

nasturtium, and cabbage any resemblance, any sign of plant-relationship."

"No, indeed! Those three plants are wholly unlike one another: their flowers haven't the same shape, nor their leaves, nor yet their fruit."

"Well, my dear boy, you, who rather pride yourself on knowing something about flowers, really know much less about them than a poor little green caterpillar very common in our gardens; and many persons of far more learning than you could take lessons from this same caterpillar. It feeds indifferently on various cruciferæ, such as the cabbage, rape, and the turnip; but it also feeds on the nasturtium and the mignonette. Why? You must ask the scientists who make a thorough study of plants and are determined to find out the minutest details concerning them. They would tell you that there is something in their innermost structure, something invisible to our untrained eyes, that makes the nasturtium and the mignonette very nearly akin to the cruciferæ without looking like them. It is enough to puzzle anybody, I admit. A worthless caterpillar has, from the beginning of the world, eaten mignonette as well as turnip, cabbage as well as nasturtium, and has been familiar with plant-relationships unsuspected by science until our own time."

"I should like to see this caterpillar that knows so much about plants."

"Your desire shall be gratified without delay."

CHAPTER XLVI

A DESTRUCTIVE FAMILY

THEY WENT out to the garden and Uncle Paul hunted for some time in the cabbage bed before he found what he wanted.

"Here is the caterpillar we were talking about," he announced at last. "It is of a delicate green color with three yellow stripes running lengthwise. Now you must make the acquaintance of the butterfly. Jules, go and bring me the net."

Uncle Paul had a large gauze net, the mouth of which was attached to a hoop of coarse iron wire fastened to the end of a long stick. That was his butterfly-net, and in his leisure moments he used it for catching butterflies, that he might destroy them before they laid their eggs on the plants in the garden. The more butterflies destroyed, the fewer hundreds of caterpillars a little later. Jules came back with the net, but the chase did not accomplish the desired result, though another butterfly was caught very much like the one they were after.

"We must be content with this," said Uncle Paul. "My butterfly-hunting of the last few days seems to have left us none of the sort I am looking for; so we will not waste any more time.

"The insect I have just caught is known as the cabbage-butterfly. Its wings are white, the forward ones having black tips and two or three spots of the same color in the middle."

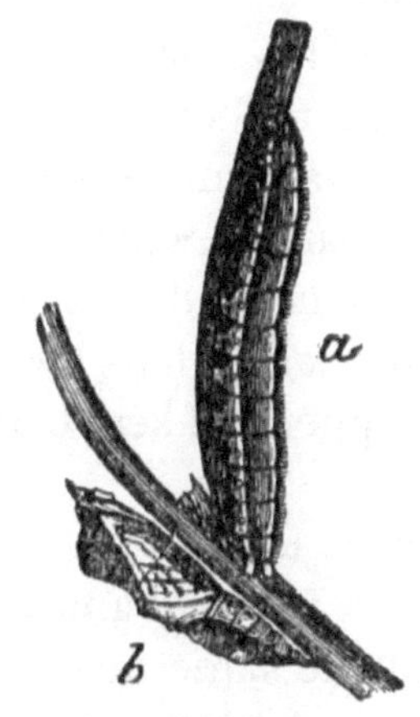

EUROPEAN CABBAGE WORM, NATURAL SIZE
a, worm or larva; *b*, pupa.

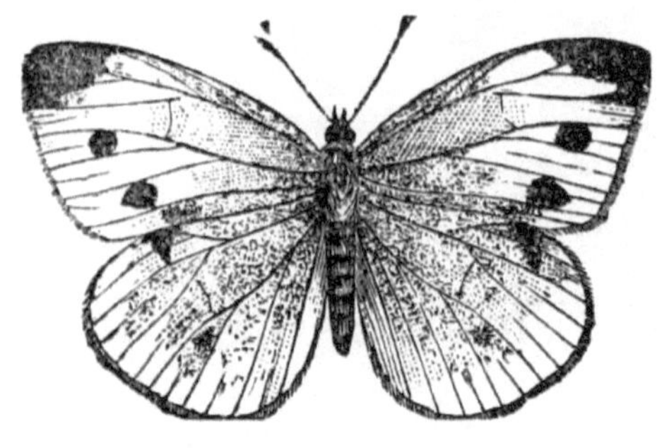

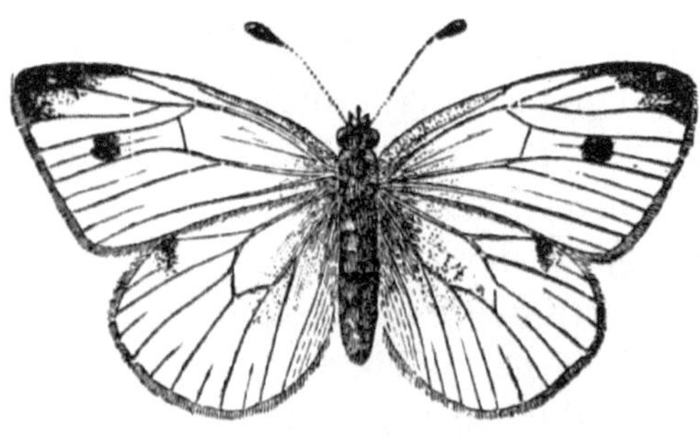

European Cabbage Butterfly,
natural size
(female above, male below)

"I see that butterfly everywhere," declared Emile.

"It is in fact one of the most widely prevalent species. Its caterpillar is greenish, marked with black dots and three longitudinal yellow stripes. It does not spin a cocoon for its metamorphosis. The chrysalis is spotted with yellow and black, and is found near where the caterpillar lived, suspended from a wall or a tree in a very ingenious manner. Before shedding its skin the caterpillar emits its small supply of liquid silk, gluing the end of its tail to the spot it has selected and then spinning a fine band which it passes across its body, fastening the two ends at right and left on the stone or the bark to which it is clinging. These preliminaries concluded, the chrysalis stage is reached, the chrysalis being held firmly in place with its lower end glued to the supporting object and its upper half kept from falling by the silk band."

"Without any cocoon to protect it?" asked Emile.

"Without any cocoon whatever; hence it is called a naked chrysalis. Many other caterpillars adopt the same method: having only a scanty little drop of liquid silk, much too small a quantity for spinning a cocoon, they content themselves, when their metamorphosis approaches, with gluing their tail to some object and supporting themselves further with a narrow band. It is to be noted that butterflies from caterpillars that do not spin cocoons all have very slender antennæ ending abruptly in a rounded protuberance or swelling, and that they fly by day in the brightest sunshine. They are butterflies proper, as distinguished from moths. These latter have the chrysalis enclosed in a cocoon, and their antennæ are sometimes of a feathery appearance, sometimes spindle-shaped, or they may take the form of elongated clubs, or, finally, they may be thread-like, tapering but little toward the end. They fly mostly in the evening twilight, or even in the night. Compare the antennæ of the cabbage-butterfly with those of the silkworm-moth or the leopard-moth and you will see how easy it is to distinguish a butterfly from a moth, a cocoonless from a cocoon-spinning insect."

"Then that's all you have to do—just see whether the antennæ end in a little round swelling," said Jules.

"With something on the antennæ," repeated Emile, "no cocoon; without that, a cocoon. How easy it is!"

"As the youngest and giddiest of my hearers has understood my explanation so well, I will pass on. Let us return to the butterfly whose caterpillar is so interesting to Jules because it eats indifferently cabbages, turnips, radishes, nasturtiums, and mignonette. This butterfly is very much like the cabbage-butterfly. It too is white, with black spots on the forward wings, but not of so deep a shade. Furthermore it is about a third smaller. It is called the radish-butterfly. To distinguish these two species, so much alike in coloring and both feeding on the same plants, gardeners call the former the big cabbage-butterfly, and the latter the little cabbage-butterfly."

"I know those butterflies," Jules interposed. "Many a time I've seen both kinds on the flowers in the garden, and I got them mixed because there is hardly any difference in their color. Now I shall know how to tell them apart. The larger one is the cabbage-butterfly, the smaller the radish-butterfly."

"You must bear in mind that the words cabbage and radish used to designate the two butterflies do not mean that the caterpillar of the one eats exclusively cabbages and that of the other only radishes. As a matter of fact, the names could be reversed without any impropriety, for both caterpillars, as occasion offers, feed on either the cabbage, the radish, the turnip, or some other cruciferous plant. But let it be noted also that these two terms have been chosen as substantially true to the facts, though likely to mislead if taken in too literal a sense.

"The same remark applies to a third species, the turnip-butterfly, whose caterpillar feeds not only on the leaves of turnip plants, but also on those of the nasturtium, the mignonette, the radish, cabbage, and many other crucifers. It is of about the size of the radish-butterfly, and its wings are white with greenish veins underneath. The forward wings have also black spots on their upper surfaces. The caterpillar is slightly hairy and of a uniform green color with no yellow stripes running lengthwise."

CHAPTER XLVII

FLIERS WITH WINGS OF GAUZE

QUESTIONED AS to the means to be adopted in order to protect from their insect enemies the various plants he had mentioned in his last talk, Uncle Paul was forced to acknowledge the inadequacy of any preventive measures at our command.

"For protecting a few square yards of cabbage-patch from these devourers," he explained, "a rigorous search for worms and an incessant chase after butterflies on that particular piece of land might prove effective; but how keep watch over acres and acres, with butterflies and moths of many kinds flying all about and alighting every moment to lay their eggs? The cost of any such watchfulness would far exceed the value of the crop. And so it is in general, with all raising of farm products on a large scale: when once the enemy is in possession it is all but impossible to drive him out if we depend on our own resources, however much we may spend in the attempt. Because of their infinite numbers the insects always have the advantage of us. But fortunately there are others fighting for us, and they wage valiant warfare against our insect foes, especially against worms and caterpillars."

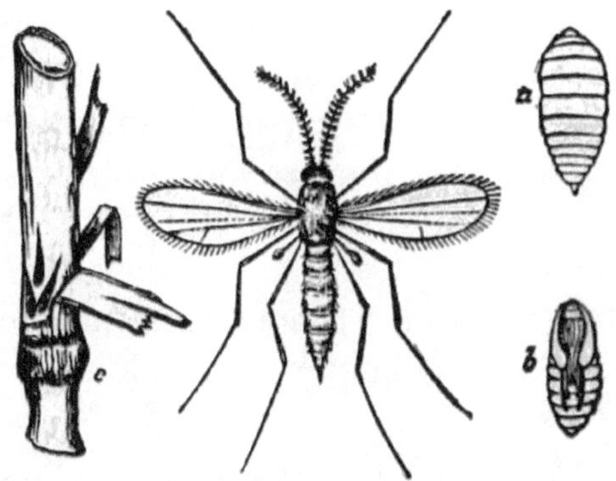

HESSIAN FLY
(Belonging to the order of Diptera)
a, larva; b, pupa; c, infected wheat-stalk.

"You mean the birds?" asked Jules.

"Yes, and other equally useful helpers that you have never heard of, notwithstanding the immense service they render us. I refer to the insects belonging to the order known as *hymenoptera*."

"Hymenoptera? I've never heard that word before."

"And for that reason I hasten to explain its meaning to you. You are familiar with the honey-bee, the bumblebee, and the wasp. Like butterflies, they have four wings for flying; but these wings, instead of being covered with scales—those scales that come off on your hand and look like dust—are simply membranes of a transparent or gauzy appearance. Hence the name hymenoptera that is given to these insects, a Latin name that may be translated as 'membranous-winged creatures.' Furthermore, they have at the end of the abdomen a very fine sting which comes out of its sheath when the irritated insect seeks to defend itself by pricking the venturesome fingers that have seized it. In other species this sting is represented sometimes by a kind of saw or cutlass, sometimes by a blade, more or less long and slender, hidden in a fold of the stomach or else projecting and open to view. Well, insects thus armed with a sting, a saw, or a blade, and having four membranous wings as fine and transparent as those of the honey-bee, the bumblebee, and the wasp, are called hymenoptera. They form an order just as butterflies and moths form the order of lepidoptera, and insects with sheaths protecting the lower pair of wings form the order of coleoptera."

"The grasshopper," Jules observed, "has a kind of sword on the end of its body, but it hasn't the bee's fine, transparent wings."

"Therefore it is not one of the hymenoptera."

"The grasshopper doesn't hurt any one with its sword, does it?" asked Emile.

"No; it uses this tool simply for placing its eggs in the ground where they are to hatch. It is a sort of conveyor for the eggs, and is called a terebra. The saw, the blade, the cutlass, and other like implements that terminate the body of various insects have also this name. They serve to deposit the eggs in suitable places where the larvæ can find food. But this implement, dangerous though it looks, never stings when the insect is molested; it is not a defensive weapon. Only the honey-bee, the bumblebee, the wasp, and some others have for their defense a sting that inflicts a painful wound."

"So painful," Emile interrupted, "that I still remember how once, when I wanted to see what was going on in the beehive, I was stung by the bees."

"The wasp's sting is much worse," remarked Louis. "When I was gathering the grapes last year I took hold of a bunch where there were some wasps, and my hand was swollen all day and pained me so I should have cried if there had been nobody around."

"How wonderful that such small creatures really hurt like that!" Jules exclaimed. "I should like to know why."

"I will tell you. The sting of these insects is a slender lancet, hard and sharp-pointed, a kind of dagger finer than the finest needle. It is situated at the end of the abdomen. In repose it is not seen, being concealed in a sort of scabbard let into the creature's body; but in time of danger it comes out of this scabbard. Now, it is not exactly the wound made by the sting that causes the smarting pain you know so well. This wound is so slight, so subtle, that we cannot see it, and we should hardly feel it if it were made by a needle or a thorn as fine as the sting. But the sting communicates with a venom-sac lodged in the insect's body, and through a tiny channel running the length of the sting there is injected into the very heart of the wound a minute quantity of a highly dangerous liquid. After this injection the sting is withdrawn, while the venom remains in the wound; and that is what causes the pain.

"Learned men who have studied this curious subject relate the following experiment, which was performed in order to prove that it is the venomous liquid introduced into the wound, and not the wound itself, that causes the pain. When one pricks oneself with a very fine needle the pain is of no consequence and passes almost immediately. Well, the prick of a needle, insignificant in itself, can be made very painful indeed if the little wound is poisoned with venom from a bee or a wasp. The learned men I just spoke of dipped the point of a needle into the bee's venom-sac and with the needle thus moistened lightly pricked themselves. The pain that followed was severe and protracted, even severer and of longer duration than if the insect itself had stung the experimenters. This difference is to be explained by the fact that the needle, large in comparison with the insect's sting, introduced into the wound much more venom than the sting itself could have conveyed. Now you understand, I hope, that it is the injection of the venom into the wound that causes all the mischief."

"That is plain enough," assented Jules.

"The bee's sting is barbed," continued Uncle Paul; "that is to say, it is furnished with teeth somewhat like those of a saw and pointing backward. In its haste to fly away after stinging, the bee does not always succeed, on account of these teeth, in drawing out the sting from the wound it has inflicted; and thus the sting is wrenched from the bee's body, to the endangering of the insect's life. The venom-sac is left behind also; it is that little white globule one sees outside the wound and at the base of the sting. If the person stung, hastening to extract the sting, is awkward enough to press on the little sac, a great part of the venom is likely to be injected into the wound, with a corresponding increase of pain. This is a warning to you, whenever you are stung by a bee, to draw out the sting cautiously and to be careful not to press on the venom-sac."

CHAPTER XLVIII

BENEFICENT PARASITES

CONTINUING THE subject of the day before, Uncle Paul laid emphasis on the distinction between those hymenopterous insects that sting and those that do not.

"At the end of the abdomen," said he, "the one class have a poisoned weapon for self-defense, as in bees and wasps, while the other class are furnished simply with the implement called a terebra, sometimes concealed in a fold of the skin, sometimes standing out in full view, and used, not for stinging, but for introducing the creature's eggs into such places as will provide the nourishment required by the future brood. Insects of this latter class are called by the general name of *ichneumons*. This morning Emile caught one, which I will show you."

"I found it on a flower," said Emile, "and I wrapped a handkerchief round my hand for fear of being stung. The thing it has sticking out at the end of its body looks rather dangerous."

"The precaution was needless," his uncle assured him. "No ichneumon, however long its terebra may be, can sting your hand. The hymenopters that are to be feared have their sting hidden, and they bring it out only at the moment of attack."

"Those three thread-like things as long as the insect's body—what are they for?" asked Jules.

"The two lateral ones unite and form a scabbard for holding and protecting the middle one, the most important of the three, for it is used to deposit the eggs at the point chosen as suitable by the insect."

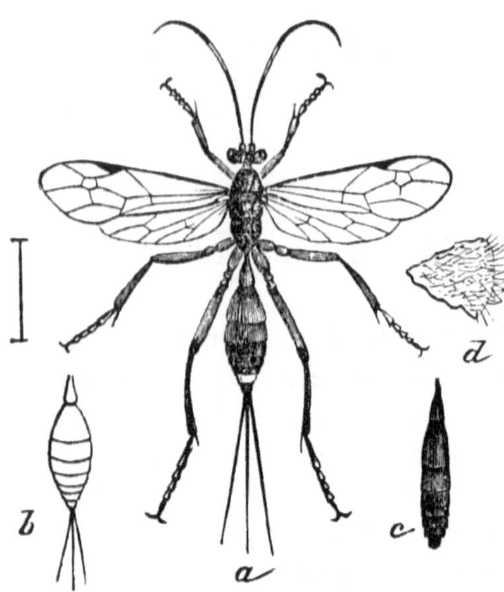

ICHNEUMON FLY
a, female fly; *b*, enlarged abdomen of female; *c*, enlarged abdomen of male; *d*, enlarged portion of wing.

"I've seen ichneumons very much like this one," said Louis, "with the terebra stuck right into the thick bark of a poplar. They must have been laying their eggs in the wood under the bark."

"No, they were doing something better than that. The larvæ of ichneumons live in the bodies of other larvæ, which they devour little by little without killing them until the very last. They are carnivorous larvæ: they must have fresh meat that is renewed about as fast as they eat it. The ichneumons Louis speaks of were engaged in depositing their eggs in the bodies of plump worms that live in the wood of the tree and turn into beetles."

"But these beetle-worms," Jules pointed out, "were not in sight. They were under the bark and perhaps in the wood itself."

"The ichneumon does not need to see them to know where they are."

"Does it hear them then?"

"No more than it sees them. The worm stays quietly in its little tunnel, being careful not to make any noise that will attract the attention of its enemy."

"Then the ichneumon must at least smell them."

"That is very doubtful. A live larva has no odor. And, besides, the most difficult part is not to find out whether or not a suit-

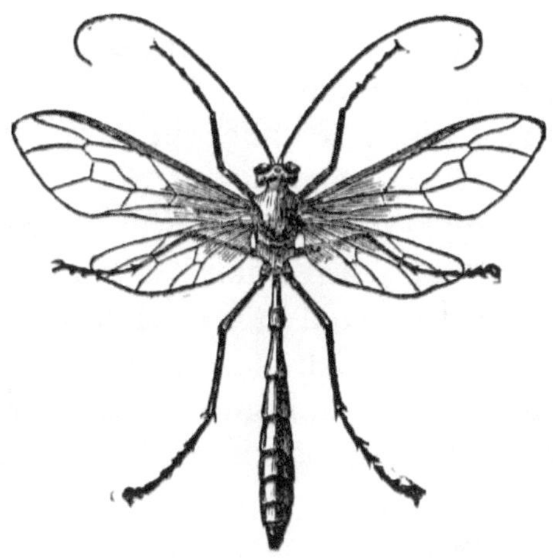

Long-tailed Ophion, natural size
(One of the *Ichneumonidæ*)

ably plump larva is there under the bark, at such and such a depth; it is also necessary to ascertain whether another ichneumon egg has not already been laid in the body of the coveted worm, as one larva would be insufficient for two nurslings. An egg deposited in some fat worm is not seen, heard, or felt; that is very evident. Nevertheless the ichneumon never plunges its terebra through the bark into a larva already occupied. What guides it? I do not know; nobody knows. Instinct has ways and means unsuspected by our wisdom. An ichneumon alights on the trunk of a tree. The perfectly healthy bark betrays to the sharpest eyes no sign of what the hymenopter is after. Never mind; the insect soon satisfies itself as to whether or not the place is a good one for its purpose. It makes a careful examination, tapping with its antennæ and keeping up a continual vibratory movement. A spot is chosen. The insect plants itself firmly on its legs, draws up its abdomen, and, holding its terebra in a vertical position, plunges the point of it into an imperceptible fissure in the bark. The little auger pierces the bark, though not without effort and occasional pauses, for there are difficulties to be overcome; nevertheless it goes as far as its length permits. The end is attained; the point of the instrument penetrates the flesh of the worm hidden under the bark. The egg being deposited in the incision thus made, the insect withdraws its blade carefully, so as not to break it, and proceeds to lay eggs in the bodies of other larvæ."

"Then the great length of this blade," Jules remarked, "though at first it seems unhandy for the creature, is on the contrary perfectly fitted for the work to be done. With too short a terebra the ichneumon couldn't reach the larvæ under the bark and even in the wood itself."

"From the length of the terebra one can estimate at what depth, as a rule, the eggs are laid. Ichneumons with a long terebra lay their eggs in larvæ protected by a thick layer of bark or wood or earth or other material; those with a short terebra seek larvæ living in the open air, such as caterpillars for example. However, if the caterpillar is covered with long hairs, thus keeping the ichneumon at a distance from the skin of its victim, a long implement is still necessary to convey the eggs into the flesh. But for smooth-skinned caterpillars without any defense the ichneumon is furnished with a very short terebra, often invisible when not in action, so that the end of the insect's abdomen must be pressed in order to make the egg-conveyer show itself, be it lancet, saw, fine blade, or other instrument of that sort.

"The ichneumon on the hunt is one of the most curious sights imaginable. Caterpillars are peacefully browsing on leaves. An ichneumon comes along, flies about over them, selects the ones that look best for its purpose, and never fails to exclude those that already have eggs in their bodies. At the sound of their enemy's wings the terrified caterpillars stop eating and begin to move their heads in a startled manner from side to side, doubtless in the hope of frightening off the foe. But the latter pays no attention to these vain threats; it alights on the caterpillar of its choice and, so quickly that you hardly have time to see the operation, darts its terebra and lays an egg in the wound."

"And doesn't the caterpillar make any resistance?" asked Emile.

"It performs some lively antics, but that is all. The poor creature cannot defend itself against an enemy in the air, a winged enemy that can always keep at a safe distance and is always ready to fly away. The other eligible caterpillars in the group are attacked in the same manner, one by one, until the ichneumon has laid all its eggs."

"Each caterpillar gets only one egg?" asked Jules.

"That depends on the size of the egg-layer. If it is large it lays but one egg in each caterpillar, so that the larvæ may each have enough food; if small, it lays several."

"And then what happens?" Emile inquired.

"The ichneumon gone, the pricked caterpillars soon recover their composure and resume their eating. The prick, not being poisoned with venom, causes very little pain; besides, it would take a good deal more than that to affect their appetites. All goes well for a few days, as long as the eggs are unhatched."

"Do those eggs hatch in the caterpillar's body?"

"Yes."

"And as soon as they have hatched do the little larvæ set to work devouring the caterpillar's inside?"

"That's the way of it."

"What an awful stomach-ache for the poor caterpillars!"

"Nevertheless, even with such pain as may result from the gradual consumption of their flesh, the caterpillars continue to eat as if nothing had happened, the satisfaction of their appetite making them forget their sufferings, so imperious is their need of food. And furthermore, for a reason that I will explain, the parasitic worms observe a certain caution in their ravages.

"In the body of every animal are certain organs more indispensable than others for the maintenance of life, and if they are injured, even though slightly, death follows. Such are the heart and brain in the higher animals. In a caterpillar's body there are, it is true, no heart or brain like those of animals higher in the scale; but there are analogous organs just as necessary to the ongoing of the vital functions. If the ichneumon's larvæ, in eating their victim's flesh, were to injure these vital organs, the caterpillar would quickly die, and the larvæ would perish too, for they must have fresh meat, not decayed flesh. It is a question of life or death to them whether the grubs avoid biting in the wrong place or not. The caterpillar must live in order that they may live; it must prolong its miserable existence until they are ready for their metamorphosis. So the little parasites scrupulously respect any organ indispensable to the maintenance of life and feed on the rest; guided by instinct, they distinguish admirably between what they may attack and what they must let alone. A time comes, however, when because of their approaching transformation they do not need to exercise further self-restraint, and they accordingly devour the parts until then left intact. Thereupon the caterpillar dies, being reduced to an empty skin which the larvæ promptly abandon in order to spin their cocoons and turn into nymphs and finally into ichneumons.

"Sometimes the caterpillar is spared until it has shut itself up in a case and turned into a chrysalis, with the result that the larvæ inhabiting the caterpillar find themselves, without any labor on their part, provided with snug quarters for the winter. Out of every such wormy chrysalis, consumed to the skin, there emerges in the spring, not a butterfly, but a swarm of ichneumons."

"Last autumn," said Jules, "I found in the garden a large brown cocoon, and I hoped to see a beautiful butterfly come out of it; but this spring, to my great astonishment, out came a swarm of little flies."

"What you took for flies was a brood of ichneumons. Yet there are flies, real flies, that lay their eggs in the bodies of caterpillars, just as the hymenopterous butterflies do with their terebra."

"With their strange way of living on other creatures," observed Louis, "ichneumons must destroy lots of caterpillars."

"They destroy so many that often, if you take a hundred caterpillars haphazard from cabbages or other growing vegetables, you will find not more than two or three that are sound and in a condition to undergo metamorphosis."

"Can those that have eggs in them be told from the rest?" asked Louis.

"Easily. The point pierced by the ichneumon's terebra is surrounded by a little black spot. When you are gathering caterpillars it is well not to crush those that you see are pricked, nor yet those that look diseased and have a loose skin. They are ichneumon-feeders, and their preservation means so many more swarms of ichneumons the next summer for the destruction of caterpillars."

CHAPTER XLIX

APPLE-EATERS

"PLEASE TELL us about the worm we find in apples and pears," was Louis's request one day when the children were gathered about their uncle.

"That worm, my lad," he began, "as I have already briefly explained, is the grub or larva of a small moth."

"Seems to me," interrupted Jules, "the moth is responsible for a good deal of mischief."

"Yes, moths do more harm than any other insects; but not as moths, for these never give us any cause for complaint, being content to suck a little honey through their slender trumpet from the flowers growing on every side. It is in the larva state, with appetites of the most varied sort, that they commit their ravages. I have already told you about worms that gnaw wood and those that eat woolen stuffs, those that browse the foliage and those that attack roots. Now we come to some that give their attention to fruit.

"The best-known of these is the worm that lives in apples and pears. We usually call it the apple-worm, and its moth is known as the apple-pyralis. The term pyralis is new to you; it comes from a Greek word meaning fire, and was long ago ignorantly applied to the apple-moth because that insect was supposed to eat fire as its regular diet. Its forward wings are ash-gray streaked crosswise with brown and ornamented at the tip with a large red spot encircled by a golden-red border. The rear wings are brown. When the fruit is just beginning to form, the pyralis lays an egg in the blossom end of apple or pear, no matter which, and the little worm that soon comes from this egg takes up its abode close to the seeds. The narrow channel by which it entered skins over so that the wormy fruit appears intact for some time. Meanwhile the worm is living in the lap of luxury, with an abundance of its favorite food all around; but it must have a passage communicating with the outside so as to get air and make the abode sanitary, encumbered as it is with refuse and excrement. Accordingly the worm bores a little tunnel through the flesh of the fruit to the skin and through this also; there the tunnel ends in a round hole. Through this passageway the larva receives fresh air and throws out from time to time the chewed and digested pulp, in the form familiar to us as reddish wormhole dust. The translucent quality of its skin causes the worm to vary in hue according to the color of what it eats, being sometimes white, sometimes brown or yellow, and sometimes pink. It is ornamented with little black tubercles or pimples arranged in pairs. The head and the first ring-like section of the body are brown.

"Apples and pears containing worms continue to grow; indeed, they ripen sooner than the others, but it is a sickly maturity that hastens the fall of the fruit. As a rule, the larva in wormy fruit that has fallen to the ground is by that time fully grown; accordingly, it leaves its domicile by the passage already made and creeps into some crevice in the bark of a tree, or sometimes it retires underground, after which it makes for itself a shell of silk mixed with fragments of wood or dead leaves, and turns into a moth the next year, when all the young apples and pears are ready to receive its eggs for the new generation.

"In plums and apricots is found a worm closely resembling that infesting apples and pears; another occurs in chestnuts, and a third in pea-pods, the tender young peas furnishing excellent food for the intruder. All these worms are the larvæ of moths commonly named from the fruit or vegetable they infest. The pea-worm, after it has devoured the best part of the pod's contents, passes into another pod by boring a round hole. Its moth appears in June, and the larva in July and August. Consequently, spring peas are never wormy, while those of late summer very often are. This example shows you how, in certain instances, a crop can be saved by hastening or delaying the sowing, according to the time when the ravagers may be expected to appear."

"But no such plan can be carried out with chestnuts," said Emile. "That is plain enough, for chestnut trees bear their nuts at a fixed time, and we can't hurry them up or keep them back. The chestnut-moth comes just when the table is set for its young ones. What disgusting-looking worms they are, too—all red and soaked in their own juice in the chestnut-meat!"

"We can't do anything, either, for the apple trees and the pear trees, can we?" Louis inquired.

"Not much. Some people gather the wormy apples and pears fallen from or still on the trees, and crush them to kill the worms inside. That makes so many enemies the fewer for the following year; but again it has to be admitted that, left to our own resources, we could never defend ourselves against the pyralis and other similar moths that produce larvæ from which hardly anything is safe. Fortunately the swallow catches these moths on the wing, bats chase them assiduously in the twilight, and the little gray lizard snaps them up when they alight on the trunks of trees. These are so many friends, protectors of our gardens and orchards."

"The moths you call by that queer name, pyralis—are there a good many of them?" asked Jules.

"There are numerous species, and each species is represented by countless legions of individual moths. Some of these attack fruit; I have just told you about the principal ones. Others have a different mode of life, and of these I will speak to-morrow. But they are all very small moths, and some are beautifully colored. Their antennæ are fine and their wings, rounding at the shoulders, spread out in the form of a cape and are folded together in repose like the two halves of a sloping roof; that is, they incline to right and left. Their grubs have a smooth and shiny skin. These worms draw back quickly when molested and let themselves fall to the ground, deadening the shock of the fall by means of a silk thread that holds them suspended by the lip."

"That's a clever trick," Emile observed. "As soon as the worm is frightened it glues the end of the thread to something and down it drops, but gently and only as fast as the thread is let out by the spinneret."

"This morning," said Jules, "Mother Ambroisine was picking over some dried peas. A few were pierced with a round hole, and others had a little brown insect spotted with white. Peas, then, have two enemies: the pyralis-worm that eats fresh fruit and the insect I am speaking of that eats them dry."

"The insect that eats dried peas is a small beetle, a weevil with a wide and very short snout. It is known as the pea-weevil. Another weevil eats beans, and still another lentils. It is always the larva that does the mischief. Once arrived at the perfect state, the weevil bores a round hole in the seed and gets out. These weevils have the same habits as the grain-weevil. They are destroyed by the use of sulphide of carbon, or simply by the action of heat if the seeds they infest are not to be sown, for the temperature required to kill the insects and their larvæ would also destroy the germinative principle of the seed."

CHAPTER L

LEAF-ROLLERS

"MANY OF the moths bearing the name of pyralis have a curious habit in their larva state, of rolling up the leaves of trees, or of folding them lengthwise, or of uniting several in the form of a sheath by means of silk threads, so as to make a shelter in which they may nibble away in safety at the interior of their green abode. For this reason they are called leaf-rollers. The one best known, on account of the damage it does, is the grapevine-pyralis.

"It is a small moth with yellow wings having the metallic sheen of copper and crossed by brown stripes. Its larva is greenish, bristling with short hairs and having a head of a dark lustrous green color. In August the moth lays its eggs on the vine leaves in little slabs of twenty at most. Hatching takes place in September. At this advanced season of the year caterpillars do not eat; they suspend themselves by a thread and wait for the wind to drive them against the vine or one of its supports. As soon as they get a foothold on the desired object they take refuge in cracks in the bark and fissures in the wood, and there they lie torpid through the winter. At the reawakening of vegetable life and the first pushing forth of the new vine shoots they leave their winter quarters, invade the vines, and entwine with silk threads the young grape clusters and the tender leaves, after which they feed upon them with an appetite sharpened by a fast of five or six months. With such ravenous eaters devastation proceeds apace, and in a few weeks, if the worms are numerous, the most flourishing vine is reduced to a pitiful condition and all hope of a harvest is abandoned. The ravages wrought by this moth

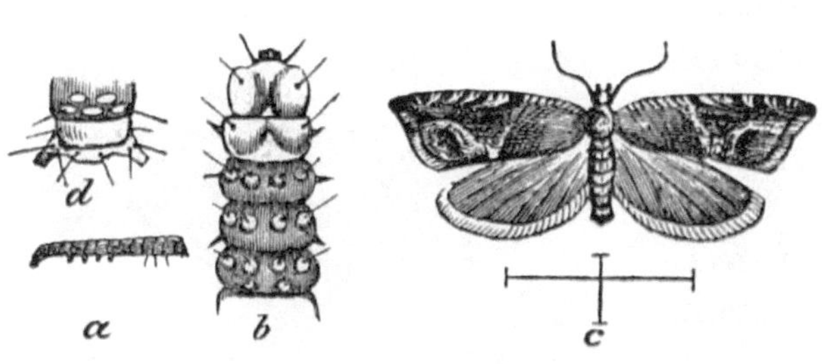

STRAWBERRY LEAF-ROLLER
a, larva, natural size; *b*, head and first three joints of body, enlarged; *c*, moth (cross shows natural size); *d*, anal shield of larva, enlarged.

between 1835 and 1840 in the vineyards of Bourgogne will long be remembered. Over immense tracts of land, when vintage-time came, there was not a single bunch of grapes to go into the basket. The greedy caterpillars ruined the country."

"Didn't the people try to get rid of the creatures?" asked Louis.

"They tried various methods, but with little success until finally one proved effective, and that the simplest and cheapest of all. Let us note by the way, my little friends, what an advantage it is to be acquainted with the habits of an insect that does us harm. If this moth's peculiarities had not been studied, if it had not been known that its larvæ hide themselves in the fissures of the vines and the trellises, there to lie torpid all winter, our vineyards might still be suffering from this terrible enemy. This fact being known, the remedy was not far to seek.

"It is this: in winter the vines and trellises are scalded with boiling water, the water being heated over a fire in the middle of the vineyard. "With a coffee-pot about a liter of hot water is poured on each vine so as to reach all the parts where worms may be lurking. Protected by its tough bark, the vine itself does not suffer from this scalding bath, while the caterpillars are completely destroyed. By this method the vineyards of Bourgogne were so entirely rid of the dreaded moth that no further ravages of any account have been reported."

"Couldn't the moths come back again some time, as many as ever?" asked Jules.

"That is hardly possible if at their first appearance the coffee-pot of hot water is brought into play.

"The other leaf-rolling moths of this family are of less importance. The leaf-roller of the plum-tree lives first on the blossoms of the tree; later it makes a roll of leaves and lines it with silk. The moth has a large white spot at the tip of each fore wing.

"The cherry-tree leaf-roller has about the same

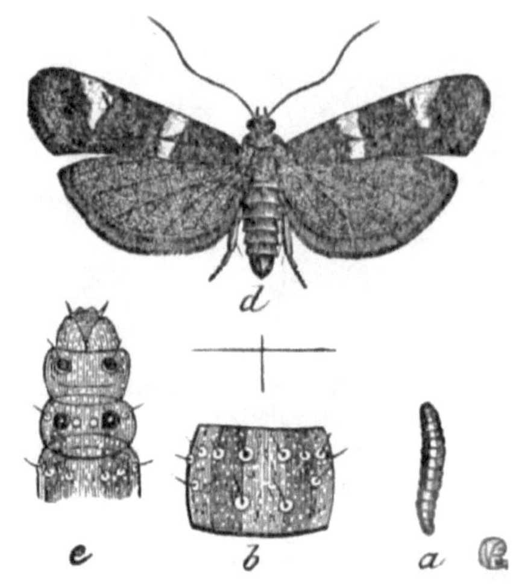

LEAF-TIER

a, larva, natural size; *b*, segment or joint of larva; *c*, head and part of body; *d*, moth (cross shows natural size).

habits. Its moth is recognized by two wide oblique stripes of the color of rust on its fore wings. On the pear-tree lives a leaf-roller with a triangular white spot in the middle of each fore wing."

"I don't remember ever having seen the moths you are telling us about," said Jules.

"They are too small to be noticed by any one who is not on the lookout for them."

"I have often seen the nests of leaf-rolling caterpillars on fruit trees and bushes and all sorts of plants. There are leaves folded lengthwise so that the edges join and make a sort of tunnel; others are in twos or threes or more; and there are some fastened together in a big bunch, all twisted and ragged, with silk threads holding them together. On opening these nests of leaves and silk I have sometimes found a caterpillar and sometimes a spider."

"Various spiders with too little silk to spin a large web for catching flies make an ambush by bringing the edges of two or three adjacent leaves together. Like the leaf-rolling caterpillars they use silk threads to hold the pieces of their abode in place, but their ultimate object is quite different. The rollers bring the leaves together so as to nibble them in peace, safely hidden away in the shelter thus formed; the spiders bring them together to make a simple abode for themselves and an ambush from which they can pounce upon such insects as come within their reach."

"The spiders that make a nest of leaves joined together do not harm trees?"

"I should rather say they are helpful to trees. They are vigilant guardians, always on the watch for flies, gnats, little moths, and other ravagers that would come and infest the trees with their eggs."

CHAPTER LI

THE HOP-MOTH

"WHAT IS that pretty butterfly in your box, next to the pyralis?" Emile asked his uncle when the latter was showing the children some of his specimens of moths and butterflies. "It has silver wings bordered with red."

"That is not a butterfly, my boy," replied Uncle Paul; "it is a moth that infests hop-vines."

"Are hops those things they make beer with?"

"Beer is not made from hops, my boy; it is made from barley. First the barley is slightly moistened, after which it is kept at a mild temperature. The grain begins to sprout just as it would do if sown in the field. For the nourishment of the little plants, which have no roots as yet, a special food already prepared is

HOP PLANT
1, male flowering branch; 2, fruiting branch;
a, male flower; *b*, female flower;
c, single fruit; *d*, embryo.

needed, just as the young kitten, not yet big enough to catch mice, needs its mother's milk. All grain, in beginning to grow, whether it be wheat or oats or rye or any other, requires a special form of nourishment, ready prepared. But where do you suppose it is to be found? You hadn't thought of that. I will tell you. The grain has it in itself. In a kernel of barley or wheat or oats or rye there is a white substance which, when ground to powder, is known as flour."

"Then the sprouting plant feeds on flour?"

"Not exactly; flour is too coarse a food for it. The little plant takes its nourishment much as we do when we are very small. It sucks up water holding in solution the substances needed for its growth. But flour will not dissolve in water, as you very well know; consequently, the little plant would die of hunger right beside its store of provision if the flour were not prepared for it—I might say, cooked for it—in a way suited to its needs."

"That must be a funny arrangement—food cooked for a plant!"

"It is more wonderful than you can imagine. As the sprout pushes upward the flour in the grain is being turned to sugar, real sugar, very sweet and easily dissolved in water; so that the young plant has for its nourishment a sufficient supply of sweetened water or, to express it in another way, a sort of milk."

"Oh, yes!" cried Emile. "Now I understand. Last Christmas Mother Ambroisine put some wheat to sprout in a plate and kept it moist on the mantelpiece. When the little blades began to show, the wheat was all soft and would crush under your fingers; and it gave out a sort of very sweet milk."

"This wonderful transformation of flour into sugar during germination is turned to account by man in making beer. He causes barley to germinate, and when he judges that all the flour substance it contains has turned to sugar he quickly kills the little plants, as otherwise the sweetened liquid would be taken up by them and would undergo another transformation by being turned into plant substance. Accordingly, the grain is promptly dried in an oven, after which it is ground in a mill, and this ground barley is called malt. By adding water and keeping it at a mild temperature we induce a fresh change: the sugar turns to alcohol, which is the essential element of beer and wine."

"The flour of the grain, then," said Jules, "turns to sugar or to plant substance or to alcohol, according to the way it is treated; is that it?"

"Yes, and it can be converted into many other things. Boiled with water it becomes paste. After entering into the composition of beer it can be turned into vinegar by being left exposed to the air and allowed to sour. But we will not now dwell on these various changes. Let us return to the subject of beer. In order to impart to that beverage the bitter taste and the aroma peculiar to it, we use hops. Barley is the fundamental ingredient of the drink, hops are the flavoring.

"The hop-plant is a long, slender vine unable to hold itself up without supporting poles, around which it twines to the height of perhaps ten meters. Its leaves are lobed somewhat like those of the grape, and its fruit takes the shape of cones or catkins similar to those of the pine-tree, but much smaller and composed of thin scales coated with a sort of bitter resin. It is these cones that are used in making beer. Hops are extensively cultivated in Alsace and in Germany. The chief enemies of the hop-vine are two worms, one of which nibbles the roots and the other the inside of the stem or vine.

"The epialidæ are distinguished from all other moths by their very short antennæ. Their larvæ live in the ground and feed on roots. The most important member of this family is the hop-moth, of which the male has white wings touched with silver and edged with a reddish border, and the female has fore wings of bright yellow with tawny edges and two tawny oblique stripes. The grub is whitish, covered with little yellow tubercles overgrown with black hair. It does great damage to hop plantations by gnawing the roots. To destroy it the hop-grower is advised to spray the base of the vine with water in which hog-manure has been left to steep—an application that is said to kill the worms.

"Within the stem of the plant lives the grub of the pyralis that I show you here. The moth has dark-yellow fore wings edged with a scalloped stripe of a lighter shade and marked with a number of red spots. The hind wings are white with purple spots and yellowish edges."

"Alongside of that moth there are two more in your box," Emile pointed out.

"They are the madder-moth and the woad-moth. Madder used to be cultivated for its root, which yields a red dye, the most beautiful and lasting of all red dyes."

"Isn't Mother Ambroisine's Sunday kerchief dyed with madder?"

"Yes; and with the red there are black, pink, garnet, and violet on the kerchief, all obtained from madder. In the methods formerly in use various drugs were first applied to the goods to be dyed, this being done by means of wooden blocks engraved with the desired patterns, after which a bath of boiling water containing powdered madder root brought out all the different colors, at once, their respective tints depending on the drugs previously applied. These colors, of which there were many varieties, had the great advantage of never fading in the sun and of resisting soap; hence madder used to be the most highly prized of dyestuffs and was a source of much profit to Alsace and the department of Vaucluse, the only districts devoted to its culture. Its insect foe was the moth I now show you. At weeding-time it was the custom to destroy the caterpillars, which fed on the leaves of the plant.

"Woad is another plant used in dyeing. Prepared in a certain way, the green matter of its leaves gives a fine blue color. The caterpillar of a leaf-rolling moth eats first the woad leaves and then the stalk."

CHAPTER LII

THE INCHWORM

O NE DAY Uncle Paul was in his garden engaged in an operation on his pear trees that greatly puzzled Emile and Jules. He had a pot of black, sticky stuff with a strong smell, and was smearing it with a brush all around the base of the trees. Oh, how One-eyed John would have laughed if he had peeped through the hedge and seen Uncle Paul daubing the foot of his pear trees with black! But he would have been greatly in the wrong, as is proved by what the boys' uncle said to them that same evening.

"What do you call that stuff you were putting on the trees this morning?" Jules inquired.

"It is called tar, and is a substance derived from coal. To make illuminating gas, coal is put into large cast-iron vessels and heated red-hot, all outside air being excluded meanwhile. The heat decomposes the coal, which cannot burn for want of air. The products of this decomposition are illuminating gas, tar, and coke, this last being a kind of coal of metallic appearance, very porous and light. The gas and the tar are drawn off through a pipe, the coke remaining in the cast-iron vessel. Tar is a very black, sticky substance with a strong odor repugnant to insects."

"Then you put a coating of it around the tree trunks to keep off insects?"

"Certain moths whose caterpillars I fear came through my hedge. The girdle of tar put on at the base of the trunk is to prevent their climbing to the branches to lay their eggs. In that way I protect the fruit trees from the caterpillars that a little later would destroy the foliage."

"But moths can fly well enough, and your tar wouldn't stop

them. If they can't reach the branches by climbing the trunk they will fly up to them."

"For a moth that flies, agreed. If on the contrary it cannot fly, but has to content itself with walking, is it not true that the coating of tar encircling the foot of the tree trunk will prove an impassable obstacle? In the first place, the smell of tar is offensive to the moth, and then if it ventures on the sticky girdle it will infallibly become entangled and die, stuck fast in the tar."

"That is plain," assented Louis. "But are there any moths that can't fly?"

"There are."

"Are the lazy things afraid to use their wings?" asked Emile. "Perhaps they think it's too much trouble."

"How could they use them? They haven't any to use, poor things."

"That accounts for it, then. Moths without wings!"

"Yes, my boy, moths without wings. You shall see some. This one is called by learned men phalæna geometra, which means geometer-moth. You will soon see why it is so named."

"But it has wings, magnificent ones, all dotted with brown spots on a yellowish background."

"Yes, and I will add that the forward ones have dark stripes. Now what do you think of this other moth?"

"That ugly thing isn't a moth."

"You judge by appearances, my dear child, and not by reality. This ungainly creature laboriously dragging along its big, naked, yellowish abdomen, with large black spots, is the female of the other moth."

"I should never have guessed it."

"Neither you nor a great many others. Henceforth you will know that there are numerous species of moths whose females are either wingless or equipped with such mere stumps of wings that they are unable to fly, whereas the males invariably have well-developed wings. Now, the male is not the one to be feared; it is the female with her eggs. The office of the tar girdle at the foot of the tree is to arrest the moth when it tries to climb to the branches where the lay- ing takes place. Repulsed by the odor, it turns back; or if it persists in its endeavors to pass, it sticks to the tar and so perishes."

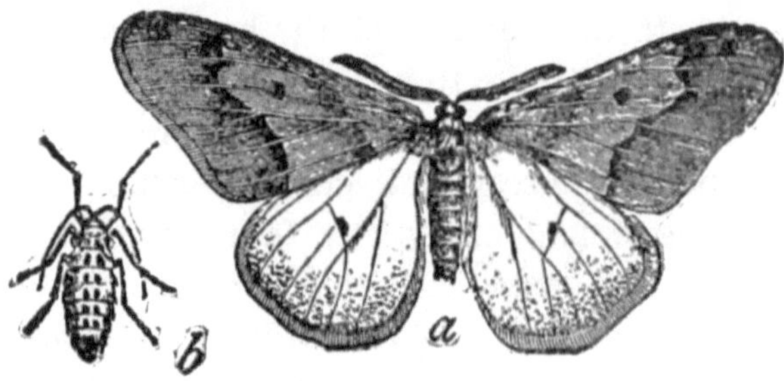

Linden Inchworm
a, male moth; *b*, wingless female;
c, larva, slightly enlarged.

"If the female laid her eggs somewhere else," suggested Jules, "instead of on the branches—for instance, on the ground—wouldn't the caterpillars know enough to climb the trees by themselves?"

"The tar barrier would still be there to stop them. Besides, caterpillars hatched on the ground would hardly think of climb- ing the tree to the place where, in the usual order, the hatching would have taken place. As long as the customary conditions remain unaltered, insects show an astonishing instinct; beyond these conditions they do not know how to act.

"The caterpillar of the geometer-moth is gray with a yellow stripe running lengthwise on each side. It has a curious way of walking common to it and other caterpillars of the same group.

"These caterpillars are long and cylindrical in shape, and they usually have but two pairs of false legs, at some distance from the true front legs. In walking they first rest themselves on the forward legs and then bring up the others by curving the body into a loop or ring. The next movement is to raise the forward legs and advance them in a stride as long as the creature itself, after which the body again bends into a loop by the bringing up of the hind legs as before. These peculiar strides give the worm the appearance of a pair of dividers getting over the ground by alternately opening and closing its two legs. You might say the creature surveys or measures the road it travels, and that is why its moth is known as the geometer-moth. The common name of inchworm applied to the caterpillar is familiar to you as referring to the caterpillar's length.

"Further characteristics are to be noted. Clinging to the branch solely by their hind creepers, these worms remain for hours in the strangest postures, the body stiff and motionless. You will see some stretched out straight, some turned up behind, some arched in a semicircular position. Not one moves, not one shows weariness in these uncomfortable attitudes which demand an incredible amount of strength. You have witnessed the feats of those strong-armed acrobats who, in the side-show at the fair, seize a vertical bar with both hands and without further support sustain themselves in the air, the body horizontal. Inchworms do the same thing, but with this difference: whereas the acrobats are exhausted in a few moments, the caterpillars keep their balance all day if necessary."

"Why do they do all those stunts?" was Emile's question.

"They are not doing stunts, as you call it; they are simply using their natural means of escaping observation on the part of their enemies. By reason of their complete immobility, rigid posture, and grayish hue they are confounded with the small dry twigs which they closely resemble. Unless examined at very short range they deceive all eyes, even those of birds, whose sight is so keen."

"Ah, the crafty rogues! To stiffen themselves and stay perfectly still so as to look like little dry twigs and in that way fool the birds that would come and snap them up, is a very clever trick."

"The name of leaf-stripper, which is also given to this moth, indicates its way of living before it is transformed into the perfect insect. The caterpillar gnaws the leaves of all fruit trees without distinction, and even of other trees, such as oaks, birches, and lindens. For trees that have not been smeared with a tar girdle to stop the moths at laying time there is but one mode of defense left, and that is not nearly so good as the first: it is to shake the infested trees so as to make the caterpillars fall, and then crush them."

"I prefer the tar girdle," said Louis.

"Yes, but it must be applied in time, in the autumn when the moths are about to make their appearance.

"Another moth of this group, sometimes called the winter moth, has fore wings of a grayish wine-color dotted with brown and striped crosswise in a darker shade. The female is a little better favored than that of the one we have just been considering, having wings of a sort, but too rudimentary to admit of flying. It may be seen running over the ground toward the end of autumn, when cold weather is approaching. Its tardy appearance has earned it the name of winter moth. Like the moth of the inchworm it climbs trees to lay its eggs, but can be prevented by the use of tar on the trunk. Its eggs hatch in the spring, and the caterpillars are full-grown by May. They are generally blackish, with white, yellow, or green stripes running lengthwise. On leaving the egg these caterpillars bore the buds of pear, apple, apricot, and other fruit trees. Later they install themselves, one by one, between two leaves, the edges of which they unite with threads of silk."

CHAPTER LIII

SAP-SUCKERS

"WHAT DO plant-lice eat?" asked Jules one day. "I have never seen them feeding on leaves."

"They do not feed on them," his uncle replied; "they drink the sap through a very fine, short, pointed sucker which they carry against the breast when not in use. The insect plunges it into the plant and for whole days without moving drinks the sap at the point pricked. When this place is sucked dry it passes to another, but without much change of position. The plant-louse is a sedentary creature; to move around a stem no bigger than your little finger is for the louse a long journey fraught with perils not lightly to be faced, a few steps forward to make room in the rear for some fifty children as fast as they are brought into the world being about all that the boldest of these creatures dares to undertake. But plant-lice of the last generation of the year have wings and lay eggs which in the spring renew the race annihilated by the cold of winter. These winged lice are no timid stay-at-homes like the others: they gladly quit the natal leaf to see a bit of the world. It is their business to travel hither and yon and lay their eggs in many places so that in the following spring all plants shall have their share of lice, and it is to fulfill this duty that they are expressly provided with wings. Clouds of these traveling plant-lice, dense enough to obscure the light of day, have been observed.

"Many other insects have, like the plant-louse, a straight, pointed sucker which they plunge into the substance they wish to drain of its juice, and which they hold against the breast when not in use. The cicada furnishes us a very good example, as do

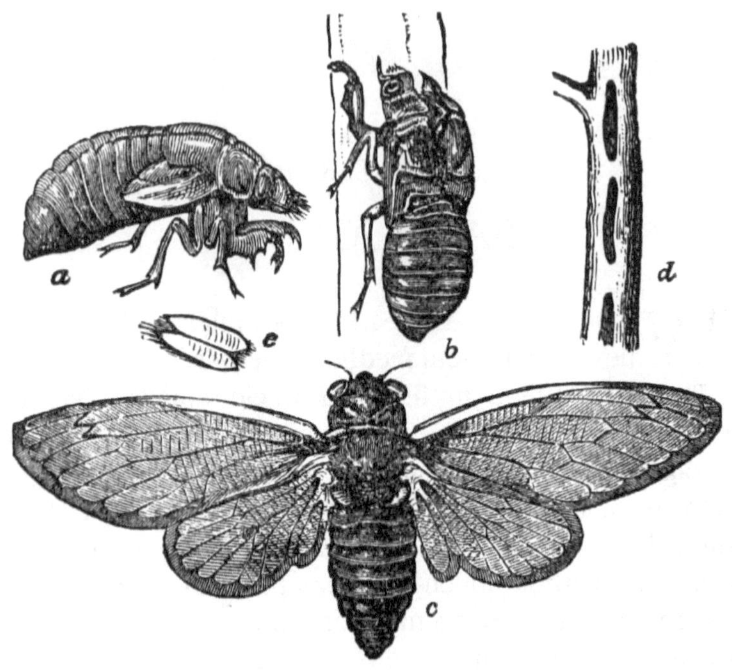

PERIODICAL CICADA
a, pupa; *b*, cast pupa-shell; *c*, fully developed insect;
d, punctured twig; *e*, two eggs. (*a*, *b*, *c*, natural size; *d*, *e*, enlarged.)

also the large bugs found on trees and on many plants. The cabbage feeds two of them: the harlequin cabbage-bug, which is red with numerous black spots, and still another cabbage-bug of a bluish-green color with white or red spots.

"Bugs of this class have four wings, the upper pair covering the other pair when in repose. The forward half of each upper wing is hard like the beetle's wing sheaths, but the other half is membranous and of fine texture. This structure makes them half sheaths for protection and half wings for flying, and it is because of this peculiarity that insects of this sort are called hemiptera, or half-winged creatures. The cicada is a half-winged insect, as is also the plant-louse, although its upper wings (I am speaking of winged plant-lice, of course), instead of being one half hard and the other half of a more delicate texture, have the same fineness and transparency throughout. But the most striking characteristic of these insects, and the one that determines their mode of life, is the beak for sucking. So we will call hemiptera all insects equipped with a pointed sucker which lies against the breast when in repose, and we will not concern ourselves with the question of wings, whether half or entirely membranous."

"Do the hemiptera form an order by themselves?" asked Jules.

"They form an order in the same way that coleoptera, lepidoptera, hymenoptera, diptera, and so on, form each an order. But hemiptera do not undergo so thorough a transformation as other insects, being born with very nearly the form they will always have. The chief change consists in the growing of wings, which the insect does not have at first, but acquires later when it has attained sufficient size. In some species several generations succeed one another before the winged state, which is the perfect one, is reached. Plant-lice belong to this class, the earlier generations of the year having no wings, and only the last being equipped with them.

"A hemipterous insect with habits somewhat like those of the plant louse causes considerable damage to pear trees. It is commonly called the flea-louse of the pear, and is a small reddish insect with diaphanous wings that fold at an angle like the two sides of an acute-angled roof. It is found on pear trees, and more rarely on apple trees, toward the end of April. The eggs are laid one by one in slight gashes made in the leafstem by the female with a little auger situated at the end of the abdomen. The larvæ that come from these eggs

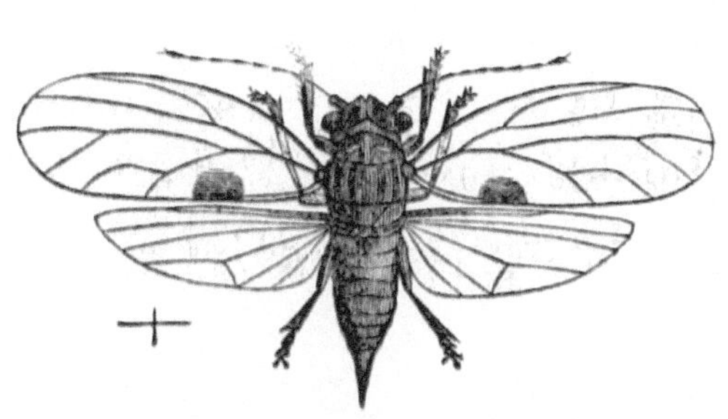

PEAR-TREE FLEA-LOUSE
(Cross shows natural size)

grow rapidly and differ from the perfect insect only in their lack of wings. By sloughing the skin these larvæ become nymphs, short and stubby and already having on each side a rudimentary wing. In its final form the insect acquires perfect wings. In all three of its successive stages the insect plunges its sucker into the tender bark, or into the leaves, and sucks the sap. The best way to destroy these creatures is to use a hard bristle brush on those parts of the bark where they are to be found in multitudes."

CHAPTER LIV

QUEER MUSICAL INSTRUMENTS

UNCLE PAUL had placed in the lettuce bed two large pots half full of water and set into the ground flush with the surface. He said they were a trap for mole-crickets, which, from the withered appearance of some of the plants, he suspected were in the garden. One morning, on going to look into the pots, Emile found three drowned mole-crickets in them. That evening Uncle Paul told the children about these creatures.

"The insects Emile found in the trap," said he, "are called mole-crickets from their habit of burrowing into the ground like moles and from their resembling in certain other ways ordinary crickets. The mole-cricket has the common cricket's long and slender antennæ, its two flexible filaments at the end of the abdomen, and its rough wings which are rubbed against each other so as to make a sort of singing noise. It is a formidable ravager of our gardens."

"Do crickets really chirp with their wings?" asked Emile, in surprise.

"Yes, my boy. In chirping the cricket raises its wings, which are dry and wrinkled,

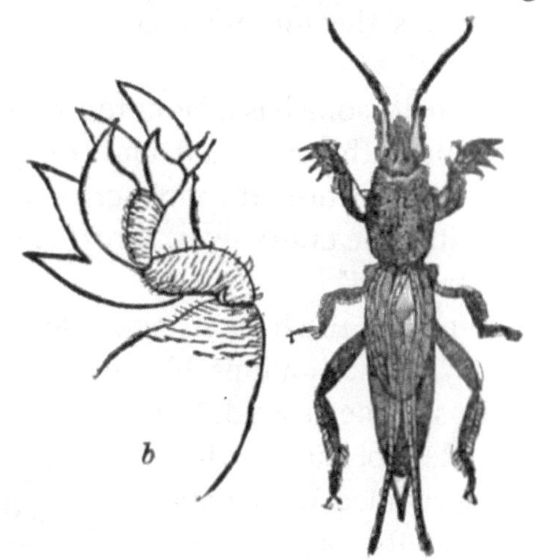

MOLE-CRICKET
a, adult, somewhat enlarged;
b, fore foot, greatly enlarged.

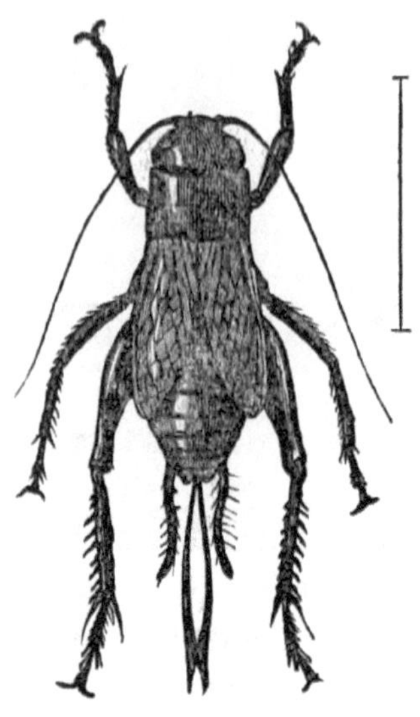

FIELD CRICKET
(Lines show natural size)

and rubs the edges together vigorously. The other chirping insects do about the same. The vineyard grasshopper, the one with the large green and yellow belly, has on its back two round scales which fit together and rub against each other. They constitute its musical instrument. Other grasshoppers play the violin; that is to say, they scrape the rough edges of their wings with their big curved thighs as bows or fiddlesticks. The cicada has under its stomach in a double cavity, protected by covers capable of being raised more or less, two dry and shiny membranes stretched as taut as drumheads. The insect sings by making these vibrate in their cases."

"Does the mole-cricket say *cree-cree* like the ordinary cricket?"

"No; its song has a monotonous sound, being a sort of sharp buzzing, rather subdued, and continuous."

"And why does the mole-cricket sing? What an ugly creature with its little crafty eyes, short wings, big stomach, and frightful fore feet!"

"It sings to cheer its solitude and call its mate. You think it ugly; I find it admirably equipped for the work it has to do. It lives in the ground, just as moles do, and like them it is provided with a special tool for digging in the earth and cutting the roots that bar its way. Have you ever noticed a mole's fore

RED-LEGGED GRASSHOPPER
(FEMALE)

feet? They are broadly shovel-shaped and furnished with strong claws. The mole-cricket's fore feet are very much like them, being short and wide and edged with saw-teeth. With this pair of powerful tools the insect digs its subterranean tunnels."

"Then that," said Jules, "must be the reason for calling it a mole-cricket: it has the mole's wide feet for digging."

"I should like to know," Emile interposed, "what the mole and mole-cricket do under the ground."

"They hunt for worms and all kinds of insects for food. In their subterranean operations both cut with their fore feet the roots that obstruct their progress, but the mole, exclusively carnivorous, does not eat them, whereas the mole-cricket, living on both animal and vegetable matter, nibbles them at its pleasure. Nor does it disdain a tender lettuce leaf when at night it comes up above ground to get a little air and cultivate the acquaintance of its neighbors. Hence the mole-cricket does a great deal of damage in gardens by laying bare the roots of young plants when it is boring its tunnels, or by severing these roots with the saw-like edges of its feet, or by nibbling them when hungry.

"Not far beneath the surface of the ground the female makes her nest, which is in the form of a hollow ball of earth about as large as your fist. In this cavity, after it has been carefully smoothed and prepared, she lays her eggs, to the number of three or four hundred, after which she remains in the neighborhood as if to watch over them. When first hatched the young ones are white all over and look like big ants. When the ground is spaded these nests should always be destroyed.

"The mole-cricket's domain is composed of passages running down to a greater or less distance, with hunting galleries just under the surface. To dislodge the insect from its retreat a little oil is poured into the hole where it is thought to have taken refuge, and then plenty of water from the watering-pot, until all the passages are inundated. Threatened with suffocation by the oil, which interferes with its breathing, the mole-cricket soon comes to the surface. One can also use the trap that I have found serviceable. A wide and deep vessel is set into the ground, level with the surface, and half filled with water. Attracted by the coolness, the mole-crickets fall in and drown in the course of their nocturnal promenades. Sometimes, again, at the approach of cold weather holes are dug here and there and filled with horse manure. The warmth of the manure is agreeable to the mole-crickets, and they come and hide in it for the winter. When cold weather begins, these lurking-places are searched and the foolish occupants destroyed.

"The mole-cricket, the house-cricket, the locust, and the grasshopper belong to a family of insects called orthoptera, so named from their straight wings; that is, the lower wings, those used for flying, are folded lengthwise in a straight line when in repose, like a closed fan. Look at the red or blue wings of the crickets that abound in autumn, in dry grass, and you will see them neatly folded lengthwise, while the upper wings, which are somewhat leathery, are usually brought together in the shape of a roof. Many, but not all, of the orthoptera have thick thighs ending in long and bristly legs that serve for jumping. Finally, some of these insects have at the end of the abdomen a terebra, commonly called a sword, its office being to lay the eggs in the ground.

"One of these orthoptera commits terrible ravages in Africa. It is the migratory locust, so named because it assembles in immense swarms and migrates to another region when food fails. The migrating swarm takes flight as at a given signal and moves through the air like a great cloud, even intercepting the light of the sun. Sooner or later the devastating hordes swoop down like a living storm on the cultivated fields of some province, and in a few hours leaves, grain, pastures, fields, all are browsed bare as if swept by a conflagration, the ground showing not a green blade of any kind surviving."

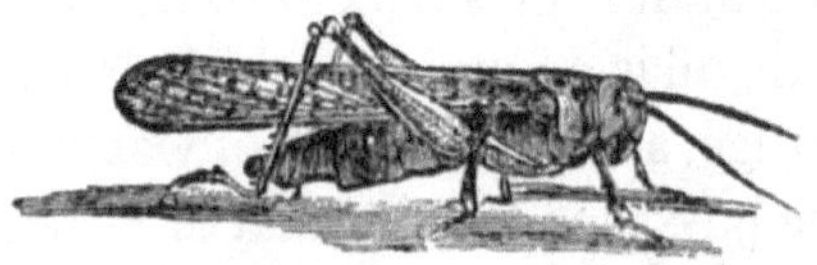

MIGRATORY LOCUST

"If those ravenous locusts travel like that," said Jules, "couldn't they come here?"

"Driven by a favorable wind, clouds of locusts do sometimes cross the Mediterranean and alight in our southern departments. At various times the territory of Arles has suffered this terrible visitation. It should be added that if the country suits them where they chance to alight, the locusts lay their eggs there, and from these there springs a legion of devourers more numerous than the first. To lessen the ravages of this second generation search is made for the eggs, which the locust lays in a cylindrical hole running a few centimeters into the ground. In 1832, in the neighborhood of Arles, nearly four thousand kilograms of eggs were gathered besides bagfuls of the insects themselves. It takes eighty thousand eggs to make a kilogram; hence in that harvest of eggs there were three hundred and twenty million locusts destroyed before they were born. Imagine the ravages of such a swarm of devourers alighting on the vegetation of any given district. Before so terrible a scourge man bows his head and acknowledges his powerlessness, the insect ravager overwhelming him by its very numbers.

"How many other ravagers there are, my children, besides locusts, that by their inconceivable multitude defy our attempts to defend ourselves! You are now in a position to realize somewhat the serious nature of these devastations when you think of all the moths and caterpillars and worms, all the creeping and burrowing and flying insects, of all shapes and sizes and appetites, that attack our gardens and fields. They would certainly gain the upper hand if we had to depend on ourselves in combating them. But fortunately we are most ably assisted in this contest."

www.ingramcontent.com/pod-product-compliance
Lightning Source LLC
Chambersburg PA
CBHW050550190726

48283CB00007B/2083